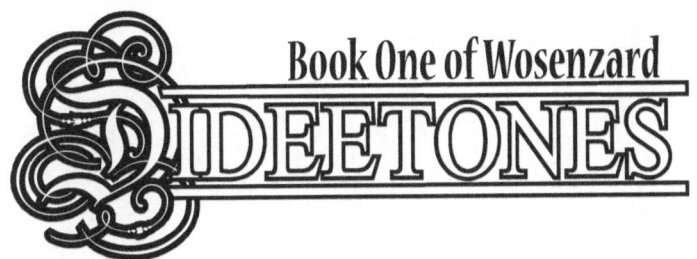

Book One of Wosenzard

IDEETONES

C.S.C. GUIDARRE

Saru Crane

Sarus Crane Books

DIDEETONES

Published by Sarus Crane Books

www.saruscranebooks.com

ISBN: 978-1-60849-001-1

A Mysterious Confrontation . . .

They all turned and were shocked as they saw, on a grassy ridge about twenty feet away, a line of magnificently dressed six-inch dolls. The small figures wore flowing silvery capes, and were eyeing them as well.

"Oh, they're so cute!" Michi exclaimed.

"Silence!" the dolls' leader, standing in the center, ordered.

Michi froze, realizing that the figures she had taken to be dolls were actually alive.

"Doesn't this castle come with normal sized people?" Joseph asked.

"I wouldn't mention anything about size again if I were you," George warned belatedly as the small silvery capes flew up. The garments turned into swords, which came down and fitted into the six-inch soldiers' ready hands. A stunned silence descended on the captives.

"You seem to have defeated those huge but useless trolls, but I warn you, do not be deceived by size. You have challenged the Mighty Guards of Vreeny's Court. Name your champion," the leader spoke once again.

"What is he talking about?" Michi whispered.

"Uhh . . . I think one of us is supposed to volunteer to fight them," George said.

"You've got to be kidding. All tied up like this? Even if they're—" Joseph began.

"Young Master Joseph, don't mention anything about their tiny sizes—"

"Archoy!" Michi and George hushed.

"Oh, me and my big mouth. Me and my big, big mouth—" the housekeeper wailed.

"So be it! Comrades, charge!" the leader shouted, and all the six-inch soldiers bounced off the ground, converging toward the housekeeper with their gleaming blades.

1

OF SIR CHRISTA AND SIR MICHI

MICHI DALLION SLIPPED out the side door and ran down the road from her house toward the Markums' mansion. The early morning sun warmed the ground as she reached the two-story building, and the little girl raced around the side until she came to the back door. Before she had a chance to knock, the door was swung open by Christa Markum.

"Come on in, I saw you from the upstairs window." The golden-haired child held the door open and Michi stepped inside. "Did you ask Jo about going with him in the van?"

Michi nodded. "Yup! He'll have to get Anthony's okay—"

"Did you remember to use the 'poor little me' expression?"

"The double dose."

Christa laughed. "I'm gonna miss you and Jo."

Michi frowned and stuck her hands inside her pockets. Her face brightened suddenly, and she pulled a harmonica out of her pocket. "Look what I've got."

"It's Jo's harmonica!"

"Not anymore—he gave it to me." Michi beamed, then pocketed the instrument.

"Lucky you. But oh, have I got something even better to show you!" Christa grabbed Michi's hand and pulled her down the entryway. The two girls rushed through the mansion, darting around the music room's grand piano and ignoring the somber portraits lining the walls of the gallery. Their light footsteps echoed through the corridors, alerting the two servants in the next room. The servants, clutching their feather dusters in their hands, scurried out of the library just in time to avoid a head-on collision with the two speeding children. The two girls passed row upon row of towering bookcases, and Christa began to slow before finally halting in front of a closed double door. She looked furtively around to make sure there was no one else, then produced a key and unlocked the door.

Michi hurried forward through the double door and into a dimly lit chamber. Weak rays of sunlight seeped from dark stained glass windows high above, casting shadows across the cluttered room. A pile of swords and lances lay strewn against one side of the floor and wall, while several rows of variously sized armor and helmets stood scattered throughout the chamber. Michi took a few steps forward before she stopped in front of a giant suit of armor. "Christa! This could've been the best playroom. Why did you wait until now to—"

"Shh. We're not supposed to be here at all. Remember I promised to show you a new secret? Well, I better do that before you move away."

Michi followed close behind her friend as they made their way through the room, the two looking back over their shoulders repeatedly. At the far end, Michi saw a grandfather clock standing in the corner and went to investigate.

Christa parted a hanging tapestry and pushed against the wall behind it. "You came at a good time, Grandpapa's still sleeping. Help me, will you?"

Michi turned from the clock and joined Christa by pushing against the wall with her whole body. The wall gave way so fast that the two girls fell in a heap onto the floor of a concealed room. A musty smell assailed their nostrils and the girls wrinkled their noses.

"There's a light switch here," Christa said.

The switch gave a soft click when pressed, and the light revealed that they were in a wide hallway. The girls advanced slowly as they turned their heads from side to side. A huge wardrobe, two bookcases, and various sizes of urns stood on the left, while many old chests with heavy locks were on the right. All were covered with thick layers of dust and looked like they had not been touched for quite some time.

Michi whistled. "Wow! Treasure chests! Let's check them out."

"Sorry, I don't have the keys. Oh, don't touch them. You might leave handprints—especially the dusty ones."

Michi frowned in thought. *What good is a secret room if you can't touch anything?* She turned to search for something that wasn't covered with dust. The far end of the hallway was in semi-darkness, and she advanced toward it. Suddenly, a pale purple-blue light glowed from the end of the corridor.

"Ahh...here it is!" Christa grabbed Michi's hand and pulled her toward the far side of the hallway.

When they reached the end, there was a long and curved table against the wall, with a glimmering object placed atop a red velvety cloth in the center.

Michi's eyes widened. "Why, it's a magnificent helmet, and it's squeaky clean!" Her fingers ran over the precious stones that decorated the strange helmet, and the purplish-blue light glowed stronger. "Wow! Look at all the sparkling jewels. Do you think they're real?"

Christa's hands paused close to the impressive helmet while eyeing it with trepidation. "I don't really know."

Michi giggled. "How silly of me—of course they are. That's why it's kept in this secret place. Come on, Christa, you can touch it. It won't bite."

Christa brushed her fingers over the smooth gems. "Do you think it belonged to some king long ago?"

"That's it! I bet this magic helmet turns little kids into brave warriors," Michi declared and lifted the helmet. "Gee...it's even heavier than your grandpa's history books. Here, Sir Christa, your helmet awaits you."

Christa laughed and made a sweeping gesture. "After you, Sir Michi."

"Okay! Help me, will you?"

Aside from being heavy, the helmet was full of hard-to-grip intricate designs. The two girls fumbled for quite some time, but the stubborn helmet seemed to resist. Finally, when they were on the verge of giving up, the helmet relented and suddenly snapped on.

A pair of cerulean eyes stared at Michi. "Hey! There's a mirror inside this helmet. Wait a minute, wrong color." No sooner was the complaint issued than the eyes turned dark brown. "That's better..." The brown eyes started to become black, then slowly turned green. "What's going on here? The colors and lights are all wrong."

Christa raised her voice. "You're not looking through the eye holes, Sir Michi."

"Oh." Michi tried to look out through the helmet's eye-holes, but because her head was so small, the holes were positioned near her forehead. She tilted her head upward and tried to peek through from under. When Michi started to fall backward instead, she gave up on that idea. "Your turn, Sir Christa."

Taking it off was a little bit easier, but some of Michi's hair caught in the helmet as they pulled it off her head.

"Better get the hair off, or Grandpapa might find out," Christa said.

"I'll get them off after you have your turn," Michi said, then she held the helmet over Christa's head. "Here, let me help you." The helmet seemed lighter now, and Michi was able to put it on Christa without much trouble. "There, how do you like it?"

"I can't see anything." Christa tilted her head way back, then fell backward and sat on the floor.

Michi burst out laughing.

"Shh...help me out of it, will you?" Christa urged.

After pulling the helmet off her friend, Michi started to clear her brown hair from it. One particular strand was stuck inside a groove and wouldn't budge. Michi tilted the helmet to have a better look, and saw three strands of golden hair embedded beneath hers. *How did Christa's smooth hair get stuck in there?* She gripped all four strands and pulled just as she heard a loud noise. "What's that?" Michi asked in alarm.

Christa tilted her head to listen. "It's only the grandfather clock."

The girls paused as the clock rang for seven strikes. To their horror, the silence did not return, and the fading rings revealed the sound of footsteps approaching.

"Give me the helmet!" Christa hissed.

Michi shoved the hair into her pocket and passed the helmet to her friend, who immediately returned it to the table. Dashing back down the secret hallway, the two eight-year-olds bumped and pushed their way out from behind the tapestry. The footsteps came into the armor room, and Michi scanned her surroundings. *Drats! No escape.*

"Who's there?" asked a rasping voice.

"It's j-just us, Grandpapa. Oh—Hi, Cedric. Michi's moving away, and she-she wanted to say goodbye to the place."

"Good morning, Mr. Markum. Hello Cedric, I just can't take my eyes off this interesting tapestry—" Michi babbled. One could never go wrong by using the word interesting, as her older sister Rosalyn always said. Michi glanced, for a more convincing show, in the general direction of the ornamental image. Then took a second look. *What are those naked women doing up on the wall?*

Cedric, Christa's older brother, cleared his throat. "I think you two have spent enough time in here. Christa, why don't you show Michi your doll collection?"

The two of them marched, under the watchful eyes of old Mr. Markum, out of the armor room and into the library.

"Do you think they know?" Michi whispered.

Christa shook her head and pointed her finger toward the corner of the library. Michi saw Pauline, the Markums' housekeeper, dusting bookshelves. They hurried past the gallery, the music room, and out into the garden. Michi climbed onto a swing under an old walnut tree while Christa stood motionless, gazing at the back door.

"Am I in trouble! We're not really allowed in that room at all," Christa said.

"You mean you've never been in there before?" Michi asked.

"It's off limits."

"Christa, it's your own home! I can understand that I'm not allowed in there, but you?"

Christa gave Michi a rueful smile. "The armor room is always locked, and I was told never to go in."

"Then how did you find out about the secret room and the helmet?"

Christa hopped on the other swing. "I overheard Pauline talking to someone about it a few days ago. It was in the middle of the night, and I was going to the kitchen to get a glass of water. I stopped by the entrance when I heard Pauline whispering to someone about a glowing helmet."

"You know, she probably was the one that polished the strange helmet till it shone. Why do you suppose she missed all the other stuff?"

Christa tilted her head. "Come to think of it, the other person was probably the new gardener we hired. You see, Pauline repeated that he should leave all the dusty chests, wardrobe, urns and bookcases alone. Something about not leaving any handprints—"

"That's it! It was a trap to catch thieves. I've heard about how police catch people by their fingerprints. Whew! Am I glad you told me not to leave any prints."

"You're right. The dusty furniture must be a trap in case the locked door didn't keep the thieves out."

"Wait a minute! What about the key to the armor room? Where did you get that?"

Christa grinned. "Pauline left it inside a watering can."

"I wonder if she knows it's missing."

"She hasn't said anything about it yet. I suppose Grandpapa'll give me a talking down, then send me to return the key ... the key! I left it in the door! Now I'm really going to get it. Do you think I can move away to Backland Hectares with you?"

"Oh, that'd be wonderful!" Michi shouted as she leaned back on her swing.

"But Pauline said Backland Hectares is full of wild Southland Natives, and they don't speak the way we do. They sleep on bamboo—Oh, and I think there're no toilets."

"Yeah, our new housekeeper, Archoy, said that the Southlanders don't use toilets. They just squat down over an open hole and do their thing. But Rosalyn said our new home'll be the same as here. They built it that way, I think."

Christa slowed down her swing. "But Backland Hectares is millions of miles from here. Why, it's not even on our map."

"Christa, you silly, it's just in a different country—the Kingdom of Lanhur, in Southland somewhere." Michi peeked at Christa's downcast face. "But you're right, it's too far. I'll miss you."

Christa sighed and scuffed her feet on the ground as she swung. "Are you all packed?"

"There wasn't much to pack," Michi said, then grinned. "I stuffed Rosalyn's flowery laced dresses under my bed."

"Super! You can finally get rid of those annoying hand-me-downs." The girls laughed.

A silence then fell, save for the creaking of the two swings. Michi looked over the well-tended garden and swung higher. Outside the fence she saw endless glorious blooms of white, pink, red, and blue disk-shaped asters stretching to and beyond the main road. Their rich colors almost formed a winding dragon, slowly rising over Aster Meadow. Michi looked up at the distant sky. By tomorrow she would be far away from the Kingdom of Anguo. What would Southland be like?

Christa kicked her legs out to speed up the swing. "Why does your family want to move out into the boondocks?"

"Something to do with Dad's new job. Jo said the city's not too far away from our new home, and there're buses."

The slamming of a car door stopped their conversation. Michi saw her mother and Mrs. Emily Markum coming, and she slowed the swing.

"Hello, Christa—Michi." Cheryl Dallion greeted the girls when she reached them.

At her side, Mrs. Markum smiled. "Girls, why don't you two come inside and have some tea and cookies?"

"Good morning, Mrs. Markum. I'm afraid Christa thinks she's in trouble, but it really was my fault. I insisted on seeing the room where the naked women were." Michi spoke quickly, congratulating herself on the smooth handling of the situation. *After all, what are friends for?*

"No, it was I who took Michi there."

Mrs. Emily Markum's eyes widened. "Naked women? Are they still there?"

"Oh, yes." Michi nodded. "I think old Mr. Markum and Cedric are still in there."

"Come along, Michi. Time to go home." Cheryl Dallion used her stern voice.

"Mrs. Markum, can Christa move away with me?"

"Michi!" Cheryl Dallion hushed.

Now what did I do? "No cookies?"

Mrs. Dallion hurried her daughter down from the swing. "I'll see you tonight, Emily. Michi, say goodbye to Christa."

The girls hugged and parted with promises that they wouldn't ever forget each other, then Michi followed her mother to the car.

As soon as they got in, her mother swung around to face her. "I don't want you to say anything about your visit, and what you saw at the Markums' place today, to anyone..." She paused, then emphasized, "Especially about the naked women."

Michi flooded with relief. *Is that all?* "Wild horses wouldn't drag it out of me."

Mrs. Dallion seemed to relax, and she passed a scrapbook to Michi. "Christa asked her mother to buy it for you."

The scrapbook had a colored, picturesque flower garden on the front cover. Michi spent the rest of the trip home thumbing through the book, looking at the occasional flower designs on some of the pages. She would have to put something very special on the first page, preferably a memento that would highlight her friendship with Christa. Then a thought occurred to her—a fancy scrapbook like this must have cost a lot of money. She ought to also give something of value to Christa, but what?

CEDRIC TOOK THE key his little sister had left in the door lock and entered the armor room after his grandfather. While old Mr. Markum walked toward the far end of the chamber, Cedric closed and locked the double door. He then sauntered over to join his grandfather.

Old Mr. Markum stopped in front of the tapestry. "What do you think?"

"Interesting."

His grandfather frowned. "You know what I'm talking about. Sometimes I think you're just as bad as those two little ones."

"I'll take that as a compliment. If you're asking me about the key, I think Christa borrowed it. If you're asking me about whether they discovered the secret room, I'd say absolutely."

Old Mr. Markum shoved the tapestry aside and marched in. "If they touched anything, I'll skin them alive!"

Cedric eyed the half-opened hidden door and the lighted interior. *Well, I guess the girls are in trouble.* He was careful not to mention anything about the light switch as he followed his grandfather into the concealed corridor. *Not that it matters. The whole room is probably full of the two rascals' fingerprints anyway.* But to his surprise, a quick inspection revealed the hidden chamber devoid of any prints. Cedric breathed a sigh of relief, but his grandfather seemed disappointed.

Old Mr. Markum scratched his head. "The wardrobe and the war gear chests are untouched...so are all the parchments on the bookcases. Why, even my beautiful vases have been left alone! What does this mean?"

"That your antiques are out of style."

"Bah! Those two'll dig their hands into anything. Especially Michi."

Cedric walked toward the curved table at the end of the long hallway. "Isn't that helmet of yours supposed to glow purple-blue when someone is within twenty feet of it?"

"Zanquei does not belong to me, Cedric. It was entrusted to the descendants of Lord Chris Markum, the only peace loving lord of the Kingdom of Anguo during the Ang-Lan War—"

"Yes, I know. 'The Peace Lover shall guard Zanquei until the rightful owner, Zansern the Undefeated, reclaims it.' That was Lord Chris Markum's pledge, and in return the lives of the people of Anguo were spared."

"It is good that you remember our history. In the near future you, too, will have to take up your responsibility as a descendant of Lord Chris Markum."

Cedric knew the legend well of Zanquei, the powerful helmet that only Zansern could wear and wield. *But how can we possibly find Zanquei's rightful owner?*

"Should we gather all the mighty warriors of the kingdom and have them try on the helmet?"

"Grandson, this is not Cinderella's glass slipper we're talking about. Aside from possessing uncanny power, Zanquei is full of precious stones. Thieves would kill to own it, and still others would take it in the hopes of discovering its hidden power. We must guard it and keep it from harm."

"But for how long?"

Old Mr. Markum turned on the light above Zanquei and walked to stand in front of it. "I asked your great-grandfather that very same question. 'A thousand years, or until its fire is extinguished' was his reply before he died."

"Until its fire is extinguished..." Cedric repeated the phrase and pondered the words. Zanquei somehow looked different. Cedric couldn't tell exactly what it was, but he sensed something was changed. He moved his hand to touch the helmet.

"Be careful! It burns," old Mr. Markum warned.

This troublesome helmet must have been in our family for close to a thousand years. Maybe today is the day. Cedric picked up Zanquei. "It's cool to the touch and it's light."

"What?!"

"Here, feel for yourself."

Old Mr. Markum hesitated a moment, then took it from Cedric. "Why, it's lighter than all the other helmets in our collection. How could it go from the heaviest to the lightest within a few days?"

Cedric shrugged his shoulders. "Beats me, but it sounds like a great money making scheme. Madams! Lose half of your weight in less than a week."

"Grandson, I wish you would take this matter more seriously. I don't mind your dilly-dally ways with the ladies, but you can't take the same devil-may-care attitude with Zanquei." He placed the helmet back on the table.

"Don't worry, I can assure you that my attitude toward the helmet is entirely different," Cedric said.

Old Mr. Markum shook his head. "Now we've got another problem. I have no idea what happened, but it seems special gloves are no longer required to handle Zanquei. This means our job as guardians has just become harder."

"Or easier. Maybe our obligation is over. Grandpa, has it ever occurred to you that the purple-blue light now missing might have been the fire?"

Old Mr. Markum stroked his chin. "I don't dare assume it. In any case, this secret hall is no longer a safe hiding place for Zanquei. Cedric, we must find another."

"Let's just leave it in plain view with the other helmets. Or better yet, stuff it inside the giant armor—"

"Why, it's so crazy and daring, it just might work!" Old Mr. Markum picked up Zanquei and made his way to the exit.

Cedric turned off the lights, then followed his grandfather out of the hallway. He shut the secret door, the tapestry falling back into place as he strolled over to the giant suit of armor. He took the huge helmet down from the armor, and old Mr. Markum placed Zanquei inside. Oddly enough, it was a perfect fit. After Cedric replaced the large helmet, the two of them stood back and surveyed their handiwork. When they were assured that not a trace of Zanquei showed through the huge suit of armor, they turned and smiled at each other.

PAULINE, THE MARKUMS' housekeeper, was glad she had not entered the armor room when she found the doors ajar. If she had, she most certainly would not have been able to explain her presence in the forbidden armor room when old Mr. Markum and Cedric came moments later. As it was, the housekeeper only had enough time to hide behind some bookshelves before the old man and his grandson came into the library. On seeing them enter the armor room, she had moved out from hiding to hear the conversation between the girls and the two men. From what she heard, the housekeeper was sure that Christa and Michi were hiding something. She didn't like that the girls saw her when they marched out of the armor room. It made it harder for the girls to confide in her.

When Pauline saw Cedric Markum close the double doors, she crept out of the library and made her way to the kitchen. The housekeeper went to look through the window above the kitchen counter, and when she saw the new gardener working nearby, she went out to meet him.

"Good morning Owlut," Pauline greeted. "I think I know who took the key."

Owlut glanced about him. "Is it a good idea to talk about it right now?"

"It's urgent. We must somehow find out what Christa and Michi saw in the armor room."

"So those two were the ones that stole the key. Did they discover the secret room?"

"I wish I knew. I don't even know how long they were in the armor room before the old man found them. You know the Dallions are moving away—"

Owlut held up a staying hand. "They are coming to dinner tonight, aren't they?"

"Why, yes. But—"

"I'll give you a pinch of a special powder during lunch. You can put it in the food tonight. Make sure the girls eat it and leave everything else to me. Now go!"

Pauline hesitated. She wished she had enough courage to ask him if the powder was harmful.

Owlut sighed. "It's harmless and it only lasts a short while. Enough time for me to ask them questions. And they won't remember afterwards."

Stunned that the gardener seemed able to read her mind, Pauline turned and fled.

BY THE TIME Michi and her mother reached home, they found a big moving truck parked in front of their house. Only the large furniture would be going with the moving truck. Mrs. Dallion's fine china, expensive jewelry, Mr. Dallion's violin, music books, and all the other irreplaceable items would be going with the smaller moving van.

A couple of movers almost collided with her, and Michi dodged under a table. The workers continued without pausing. With the bustling of activity, she could've been gone much longer without anyone even noticing it. Suddenly, the table above her was lifted, and Michi frowned. Was she invisible? When three movers with big boxes came her way, she stood up and scurried toward the stairway, but bumped into her own luggage before reaching the stairs.

Michi saw Rosalyn's cello propped up against the wall nearby the bottom of the stairs. *Why not give it to Christa? From the size of it, the wretched thing probably costs a bundle. But Christa dislikes the cello just as much as I do.*

"Sweet, you don't have much stuff, do you?"

Michi spun around to see her beloved second brother, Joseph, lift her suitcase and test its weight.

"I travel light." She'd heard someone crack that joke before, and thought it was worth repeating. Her brother laughed. *Good old Jo, the only one in the family who has any sense of humor.*

Joseph handed a shining new harmonica to Michi. "Isn't it a beauty?"

"Wow! It's also bigger than your old one. Cedric must have spent a fortune on this parting present. I still like your old harmonica better, though."

Joseph ruffled the top of Michi's already-unruly hair, then took the new harmonica from her.

Christa likes Jo's old harmonica. Michi reached into her pocket and took out the instrument. "Jo, can I give your old harmonica to Christa as a keepsake?"

"I gave it to you, Sweet. So you can do whatever you want with it—you might want to clean it first."

"Thanks!" *Eww...what happened to the harmonica?* There were cookie crumbs, sticky candy pieces, and even hair on it. Three strands of golden hair mingled around some brown hair. Now, where did they come from? She put the dirty harmonica on top of the scrapbook and was about to go upstairs when she remembered. She had the perfect thing for the first page! Michi ran up the stairs and almost collided with her sister, Rosalyn, when the latter suddenly huffed out of her room.

Rosalyn gave Michi a disapproving look. "Where have you been? Roaming around the neighborhood like a stray, I shouldn't wonder. Just look at you—you are a sight! Don't you ever comb your hair?"

"Of course not, how can a dog comb hair?" Michi said sarcastically.

Eyes blazing, Rosalyn put her hands on her hips. "You have a serious attitude problem—"

"Yes, and it's very contagious," Michi retorted and purposely brushed past her sister on her way to her room.

Rosalyn jumped back as if afraid of being contaminated. "You are hopeless!"

Michi shrugged her shoulders and walked into her room.

"Archoy! Hurry it up!" she heard Rosalyn shout to their housekeeper. Michi shut her bedroom door.

Having Rosalyn for company on a long journey would be hazardous to anyone's health. She hoped Jo could convince her older brother, Anthony, to switch and let her sit in the van instead.

In her own room, Michi carefully removed the hair from the harmonica, then taped her brown strands along with

Christa's golden ones right in the middle of the first page of her scrapbook. She considered the rest of the empty pages, deciding to gather unusual leaves and flowers from around the neighborhood to press into the book. Michi cleaned the rest of the harmonica, then dashed down the stairs. On her way out, she left the instrument with her mother to give to Christa that night.

An hour later, when Michi thought she had enough leaf and flower samples, she came home and began to press them into the scrapbook. While busy in her room, she heard the noisy moving truck leave. *Well, there goes the furniture.* She guessed "Southland, Here We Come" music was in order.

The small white van was ready half an hour after the big moving truck left. *Better get in the van while the getting's good.* She stuffed her flower collection and scrapbook inside her pack. Then Michi rushed out to hop in the back seat of the van and waited. A while later, Archoy came out with a basket in her right hand and a huge tote bag in her left. It seemed the new housekeeper would be riding with her in the back, and Michi scooted over to make room.

"Thank you, Little Miss," Archoy said with her lilting accent.

Michi sized up the tote bag the housekeeper placed on the floor. "What's in there?"

"I've rescued the lovely name brand dresses you'd forgotten under your bed, Little Miss."

Drat! "What's in the basket?"

"Something I prepared for our long ride," Archoy said, and handed the basket to Michi.

Michi lifted the cover, and the scent of a well-prepared luncheon rose from the basket. *I think we'll keep this new housekeeper of ours.* Michi reached in and took out an apple.

Mrs. Dallion and Joseph came out from the front door, and she was still giving him last minute instructions when her husband drove up with Anthony. Joseph walked over to the car while Anthony exited, and Michi's two brothers started to talk. Michi held her breath, and when she saw Anthony nod his head, she breathed a sigh of relief. It looked like she'd be having a picnic lunch in the van with Jo—oh, and Archoy. Michi smiled, then frowned when the house-keeper took out a comb and started to brush her hair.

Michi's parents, Anthony, and Rosalyn would be hav-ing dinner with the Markums, then driving to her Uncle's place to stay the night. According to her father, the car would make better time than the van, and hence could take a couple of detours.

The hired driver got into the van, and Joseph sat on the passenger side. Michi's parents said goodbye through the open windows, and the van pulled off the curb. She waved to their neighbors as they turned up toward the highway at the end of the street. They went steadily southeast, and the trip was pleasant enough.

After her lunch in the van, Michi began to chat with Archoy. As soon as she found out the housekeeper was from Southland, she pestered her to talk about the people and the place.

"Well, Southland is part of the Kingdom of Lanhur, and the kingdom is ruled by three councils in the north—the Elder Council, the Council of Defense, and the Modern Council."

"Which one is the most powerful?" Michi asked.

"Oh! The Elder Council, of course. It is said that the wise men in it have certain magic powers, and there's a prophecy that says someday the Great Bai King, with the help of his wise council, will return to rule once again."

Michi tilted her head. "What sort of magic?"

"For one thing, the leader of the wise men is at least one hundred and fifty years old, and yet he looks not above forty. All the Southlanders love him, for he forbids the council from interfering with the Natives' ways. Although lately, the Modern Council is pushing for changes."

"What kind of changes?"

"Oh…the latest proclamation was that all children, before the age of nine, must start attending school."

"You mean the Southlanders didn't have to go to school before the change?"

"Most of the Southlanders are Natives, and they are all farming folk. What good is schooling when you already know all about farming just by growing up with your folks?"

Someone ought to fire that lot of Modern Council! "I'll stick with the old man anytime," Michi said.

Archoy gave Michi an intense look. "You would? The old man's against freeing the slaves."

"You mean there are slaves in the Kingdom of Lanhur?"

"Mostly in Southland. For, didn't you know, the Great Bai King had a famous slave named Ilee. And it was largely due to the loyalty and devotion of this slave that the Bai King defeated the cruel warlords during the Ang-Lan War."

"But surely you're talking about the Northwood Sorcerer. It was his witchcraft that turned our victory against the Lanhurians into defeat a thousand years ago, or so I was told."

Archoy laughed. "Is that what you Anguorians called him? I can assure you Ilee the Faithful was no sorcerer."

"Then how did the Bai King get his magical army?" Michi asked.

"After your Anguo Warlords defeated the young king, his soldiers were scattered. The king and his trusted slave, Ilee, escaped to the Northwood Forest. Tired and wounded, the young king fell to sleep under an ancient tree while Ilee stood guard. It was said that the Golden Harp Fairy happened to pass through. She was moved by Ilee's devotion to the young Bai King. The Fairy granted the king an army as powerful as Ilee's loyalty to his master. And with that mighty force, the Bai King swept his enemies wherever he went."

In her bedtime stories, Joseph had, on occasion, read to Michi the tales of the Ang-Lan War. Her brother had always felt that their own country was wrong to invade the Kingdom of Lanhur. Although most of the Anguorians believed that the Bai King's surprise victory was due to witchcraft, Joseph felt it was destined. Michi, however, was fascinated by the mythical version of the story.

"I had no idea a slave helped free your country! Though I'm glad everything has been peaceful between us since. I want to hear more about this Ilee."

Archoy, pleased with the request, settled into a more comfortable position. "The Bai King freed Ilee as a reward for his faithfulness, and discouraged slavery in the north. But when the king died, Ilee and his descendants moved south. It was said that they brought with them a vast fortune, and with it large cities, like Nunjai City, sprung up in Southland. Throughout the years, many mixed marriages occurred between Ilee's heirs and the Natives. Today, those that can claim direct lineage to Ilee the Faithful are much respected by the Southlanders."

"Are you one of them?"

"Now, that would be telling, Little Miss," Archoy said.

"Well, what about in Nunjai City? Is there anything good there?" Michi asked.

Archoy smiled patiently. "It's the biggest city in the south side of Southland. When we get to Firmiana Town, if we were to go down a bit further to Nunjai Village, then take the east route using a water buffalo cart over the undeveloped terrain, we would reach the City of Nunjai."

"Oh! Jo, did you hear that?"

Joseph, who was indeed listening, shook his head. "After we reach Firmiana Town, we are supposed to hire another van which will take us over the paved road to Ilee City."

Although she had no idea which way was really shorter, Michi still tried to persuade Joseph. "But that would be so far out of our way, wouldn't it?"

"Nonetheless, we'll be going the long way," Joseph said firmly.

Michi looked out the window. Too bad Jo was in the front seat, otherwise she could have used a "poor little me" expression on him—it never failed to get what she wanted from her beloved second brother.

"Oh, now, Little Miss. Ilee City's just as grand from what I've heard," Archoy comforted.

Michi frowned. *It's the water buffalo cart ride I'm interested in, you ninny.* And she decided to spend the rest of her time brooding.

2

YOUNG CAPTAIN HUA

MICHI WASN'T THE only one lost in thought. Hundreds of miles from the Dallions' little white van and across the border into the Kingdom of Lanhur, Captain Hua, wearing a weather-stained cloak and sitting under the shade of a large yucca, was pondering. After ten years of intense training by his great-grandfather, Hua had become the youngest immortal to pass the challenges at Mowong Castle and earn his title.

Anxious to avenge his father, Hua was not pleased with his first assignment. He did not want to wander aimlessly looking for Dideetones, tiny doll-like Tensengin Immortals. To him, that was a job for the weak and idle. Instead, he wanted to find that cunning slave woman. The one that had shocked the immortals with her ability to use Zunji skills. Hua ached for the confrontation and a chance to take his revenge.

After wasting two months in the wilderness searching fruitlessly for the Dideetones, Hua had made a decision—forget the pesky Dideetones. He was close to the territory where the slave woman had been sighted and pursued many times by the Senginfan Defenders. By searching this area himself, Hua was hopeful that he would stumble upon her.

The well-rested young captain took a final sip from his water bottle. He bounced up to continue his search, making for the Bayjai Lookout Point. The day was hot and the road was rough and uneven. Yet Hua, on foot, made stunning speed.

When he reached the bottom of the Lookout Point's hill, Captain Hua bounced off of a huge rock and flew up to the top. His sudden appearance startled a flock of resting sparrows, and they scattered wildly in a rush of wings. Hua gave a guilty glance at the now empty tree. *I might look human, but I better be more careful displaying my skills. I don't want to cause a group of humans to have heart attacks next.* Hua was unaware that, if any human was indeed nearby to see, they might have believed him to be a flying angel. Though his cloak was tattered and he had no wings, his flowing blond hair reflected the sunlight, and his graceful features seemed angelic as he leapt and glided through the air.

After he landed on a nearby rock, Hua shaded his eyes and scanned the terrain. A band of merchants, on the south side of the slave route, were traveling slowly north. The captain paid them no mind and continued his search. Movement in the distance caught his eye and, focusing, he gave a start of surprise. A fleeing figure in a cape was being pursued by six riders on the north side of the slave route. Hua blinked, stunned at his good luck, before his eyes gleamed with vengeance.

Hua bounced off the lookout point and glided down the hill. He then dashed away toward the southwest, with the intent to cut off the fleeing figure. Unbeknownst to the captain, a little white minivan had just crossed the border from the Kingdom of Anguo into Bayjai, and was now heading southeast toward the same West Slave Route.

When Captain Hua reached the outskirts of the well-traveled slave route, he slowed. He stopped to listen intently when he came to the lower ground east of the main road. The captain would have to climb, with care, to the top of the hill if he was going to search the Slave Route Junction without being detected. Since there were not many trees or plants for concealment, he advanced cautiously. Hua stopped when he heard voices coming from the other side of the hill. He listened for a while—*these people are speaking in Anguorian. Where have they come from?* One of them, the one with the clear and high-pitched voice, kept insisting about a ladies' room—*whatever that is.* Curious, he started to move up the hill once again, but stopped and ducked behind a bush when he heard footsteps. The dense bush blocked his sight and movement. *Well, this should be safe enough. If I can't see them, they definitely can't see me.* Hua listened intently, and realized the speakers were coming his way.

MICHI WAS UPSET at herself for not taking the chance to go to the restroom before they crossed the border into the Kingdom of Lanhur. And she had no qualms letting her displeasure be known.

"No one had the decency to remind me to head for the ladies' room when the going was good," she said as her brother stood by the overheated engine while the driver added water to the radiator.

"Now, Little Miss, one only goes when one needs to."

"Not when ladies' rooms are scarce. Why didn't you warn me that we would be entering wild country back at the border?"

"That was more than three hours ago. Sooner or later, you'll have to get used to going in the wild," Archoy reasoned.

I'd rather it's later.

Joseph walked over and ruffled her untidy hair. "Sweet, it's still going to be a while before we reach any inns, so I suggest you make do with the outdoor ladies' room."

"Oh, alright. Archoy, will you please bring the jacket and protect me from any peeping Toms?"

Michi and Archoy reached the top of the small hill, and they descended down the other side. "No peeking!" Michi shouted over her shoulder.

"Now, Little Miss, this is far enough, there's no one around."

Michi pointed to a sagebrush ahead. "There's the perfect outdoor ladies' room, complete with potted plants. I'll face the bush while you cover me from the other side, okay?"

"Of course. Now don't get too close to the shrub."

Well, we're moving to live among the Natives, so I'll just have to get used to squatting down and doing my thing. Call it Basic Native Training if you will. She was very proud of herself when a few moments later she saw her handiwork trickling down the hill into the bush. *Why, I'm even watering the plant.*

Pleased, Michi got up. "The ladies' room is all yours, Archoy. Want me to hold the jacket for ..." She froze and eyed the rustling bush.

A peeping Tom!

"Aaack! Come out, you—Thief—Robber—Sneak—" she shrieked. This had never happened to her before, and little Michi had a hard time thinking up the proper name, on the spur of the moment, for the scoundrel. But she was plenty mad all the same as her eyes narrowed and she placed her hands on her hips while waiting.

An intimidated, cuddly, bear-like dog peeked its head out of the sagebrush, and Michi's anger dissolved in an instant. "Ohh! Archoy, it's a cute puppy dog! Come here, you little white furball." The dog shuffled toward her open arms. Michi lifted it up and hugged it to her, then patted the good-natured little puppy.

"Now, Little Miss, put the wild dog down, who knows what it has been eating."

"Oh, Archoy, anyone can tell he's well groomed. He's got the most unusual eyes. They're golden with a hint of sea-blue underneath. His owner must be nearby, though I don't see any dog collar. I've got to show this cute puppy to

Jo!" She ran back up the hill, shouting as she came to the other side. "Jo! Jo! Look what I've found! Can we keep—"

Her brother cut her off with a sharp voice. "Michi! Go back down the hill and don't come back unless—"

But she had already reached his side. She watched the stirred-up dust and the fast approaching riders with awe. Tall and grim, the travelers were all dressed in silver war gear. Michi stared at their metal helmets with protruding spikes and their dark flowing capes. Then, the insignia on their large shields and the center of their breastplates caught her attention. *What sort of animal is that?* The design had a twisting body swirling with its two long and curved horns centered in a diamond. Michi continued to look at the unusual symbol as the riders halted a short distance before the van.

Archoy came to stand between Michi and Joseph. "These are Northlanders, but I've never seen them dress like this before," she whispered.

"Have you seen a runaway slave woman wearing a dark green cape come this way?" the foremost warrior questioned.

"We're travelers from the Kingdom of Anguo. Our car overheated just a little while ago and we have been trying to cool off our engine since," Joseph replied.

The tall warrior gave Joseph a long look. "In that case, you wouldn't mind if we search your van." The other riders were already advancing toward the car as their leader spoke.

Joseph moved to stand before their path. "We are good citizens of the Kingdom of Anguo and are protected by the peace treaties. No one may search our van without my permission."

Jo! What are you doing? These people don't look like they're just going to bow and withdraw. They seem more likely to ride you down and apologize later—if that. Michi stole a nervous glance at the warriors' swords, but still moved to stand beside her beloved brother.

"Stand aside if you do not wish to be harmed," the leader ordered, irritation evident in his voice.

Joseph shook his head. "You back off, or you'll have to face the Elder Council's wrath."

A stunned silence descended on the group. Michi could tell these bullies had not met much resistance before now.

Mom would be so proud at the extent Jo's willing to go through to protect her fine china.

She changed her mind about her brother's wisdom when the Northlanders unsheathed their swords and slowly advanced toward them.

Uhh...Jo... but her train of thought was broken when she felt the little dog wriggle out of her arms and land on the ground. To Michi's horror, the little puppy moved to stand not ten feet in front of the six imposing warriors and started to bark at them.

"No! Come back here little puppy!" Michi shouted while she dashed to the dog's side.

At that moment, something incredible happened. The aggressors backed away, sheathed their swords, then turned and rode off as if the very devil was on their heels. To Michi's dismay, the silly little dog barked and chased after them.

Michi ran after the puppy. "Stop! Come back here—Fifi White Furball—you're not their match, come back before they trample you!"

Joseph caught Michi and scooped her up. "Come on, Sweet, we're leaving."

"Jo! My puppy—"

"The slave woman's in our van, and she's wounded," Joseph pressed.

Why didn't you say so earlier? She stopped struggling and they returned to the van, but a quick inspection of its interior revealed no sign of the wounded woman.

"We'll stay longer just in case she comes back. In the meantime, the car could use a little more cooling off." Joseph glanced around the area. "That slave woman needs help. She's very hurt and couldn't have gone far. Let's look for her."

Michi, Joseph, and Archoy divided to search the surrounding area while the driver stayed with the van. Michi took the area where her lost puppy had gone, in the hope of finding it again.

"Sweet, don't wander too far. Archoy, please stay nearby her. Everyone, we meet back here before sunset," Joseph called out.

Why, that's probably only half an hour from now. Michi ran while looking from side to side. *The slave woman and Fifi White Furball have to be here somewhere.* She had no idea what gender the puppy really was, but had automatically decided on Fifi if female, or White Furball if male.

"Little Miss! Little Miss! Now come along, we've wandered far enough," the housekeeper urged.

"Archoy, don't worry. Can't you see the horse tracks? We can just follow them back to the van," Michi said, pointing at the clear marks.

"But young Master Joseph wants us to get back before dark."

That was when Michi realized that the sun was indeed setting. She stood and watched with fascination the ever-changing multi-colored sky. *My first sunset in the Kingdom of Lanhur, and here I'm looking at the ground.* Suddenly, she heard low growls and the leaves rustling from behind some yuccas.

"My puppy!" Michi dashed away from the horse tracks.

When she reached the yuccas, she slowed and walked to the other side. An animal halfway inside a thorny bush was struggling with something, and every now and then it growled. *My little dog, and the poor thing's stuck inside there.*

"Don't struggle, Fifi—" Michi soothed, but paused when she heard a loud growl.

That doesn't sound like my puppy! She backed off and saw, under the failing light, that this animal had a stubby tail nothing like the dog's. On closer inspection, she found the animal had long and silky orange fur with a tint of gold that reflected in the sunset's glow. *What an unusual color! What's it doing?*

Michi heard a faint whimpering sound issue from somewhere in the center of the shrub. "Come on out of there! You leave my puppy alone!"

The strange animal completely ignored her and continued to advance deeper into the bush. Michi grabbed the hind legs of the animal and pulled.

There was a screech, and the angry animal whipped around. Michi found a ferocious orange-gold wildcat with tufted ears staring at her.

She ignored the fuming cat, but turned her attention to the bush once again. "Don't be afraid, it's just a nasty cat. Are you alright, Fifi—" At this, the wildcat bared its sharp teeth and hissed, just as Michi continued, "White Furball?" This time the animal surprised her. It purred like a kitten and sauntered to her.

"I suppose you expect to be rubbed and patted, but we'll have to hold all that good treatment until we find out what you did to my little puppy."

Michi went back to calling toward the bush. "Fifi White Furball—" she cajoled while the silly wildcat rubbed and purred around her feet affectionately.

"Oh, now, Little Miss. Not another one of those strays, please," Archoy, who had finally caught up to her, chided.

"Archoy, I think my puppy's stuck inside this thorny bush, but I can't see too well."

"Little Miss, that puppy of yours barks so loud it must have scared the riders' horses halfway up Bayjai by now."

"That's true. I can't imagine my brave Fifi White Furball hiding away from this little harmless cat." Michi bent down and rubbed the big cat.

"Come along, Miss Michi, before it's too dark for us to make our way back safely."

She hesitated. *Did I imagine that little whimpering sound?*

Then they heard Joseph calling them, and Michi and Archoy hurried off toward the van, unaware of two pairs of watchful eyes from behind another yucca tree.

THE ENERGETIC PUPPY bounded off, following the galloping horses for a while. It then wheeled away northeast, cutting across the West Slave Route. The dog reached the outskirts of the route on the east side of the hill before it slowed down and sniffed the ground. It picked up a scent and shot off again, going straight north this time.

Soon the puppy could see its quarry bouncing and gliding ahead. The dog sped up, then sprang high above the ground. In midair it turned into a six foot tall cloaked warrior and glided toward the flying green cape.

The slave woman spun suddenly and threw, while still in the air, a snowflake-like projectile straight toward her pursuer. Captain Hua anticipated such a move from his opponent. While flipping his cloak like a net to trap the flying projectile, he shot a hidden weapon straight at his opponent's left shoulder. Taken by surprise, the caped woman reacted a fraction of a second too slow, and the sharp-edged snowflake weapon embedded deep into her shoulder. The slender figure plummeted to the ground. She tried to rise, but the effort was too much for her. So the slave woman sat on the ground and watched the approach of her pursuer instead.

Captain Hua glided to the ground, then advanced toward her. *Bravo! The woman can still sit after receiving that shoulder wound—but not for long.*

Hua was about fifteen feet away from her when the slave woman spoke with an effort. "Where did you get this Flying Snowflake?"

"From my father. Who received it from you seven and a half years ago."

Her eyes flew to his young and handsome face, and on seeing the hatred in his eyes, nodded her head. "Why didn't you aim it at my heart?" she whispered.

"I thought you might like to get a taste of what you have put my father through."

"You knew I was hiding in the van, so why did you stop the riders?" she asked, changing the subject.

"I don't like innocent people getting hurt. Why did you leave the van?"

"I don't like innocent people to get hurt, as well."

At that moment, they heard riders approaching. The slave woman tried to get up once more, but collapsed with the effort.

The Senginfan Defenders soon arrived at the scene. They dismounted from their horses and knelt in front of Hua. "Captain, forgive us for not recognizing you earlier," the leader of the riders said. "We sensed a strong and mysterious power and were following it. Now I realize it must have been you with the Zunji Light. If we have interrupted your mission, please deal with us as we deserve. However, we came as soon as we sensed your call."

My mission? Let's not talk about the part where I was held, patted, and squashed by a little human girl. Oh, skip the part about her calling me Fifi White Furball also. Whatever the Senginfan Defenders thought about the captain's bizarre behavior, they were too well trained to question it. *I'm going to have to watch my step from now on. Dignity, that's what I need.*

He cleared his throat. "It is understandable; you had no clue I was anywhere around. Anyways, no harm done.

Here's the slave woman you've been pursuing." After he saw the shocked expressions on the riders' faces, Hua added, "She's not dead—just unconscious."

"May we search the prisoner, Captain?"

"You can if you wish, but I don't think she is carrying Zanchou, the Zunji Sheath. If she was, she would certainly have tried to use it when we fought just now."

The Senginfan Defenders rose and advanced toward the slender figure lying on the ground. "Do not touch the Flying Snowflake! It is poisonous and there's no antidote," Hua warned.

All six of the riders halted. "The Flying Snowflake!" they exclaimed, focusing on the embedded weapon.

"Have no fear." Hua flipped his cloak. Another snowflake-like weapon flew out of it, and the young captain caught it with his gloved right hand. "Here's the other one."

"Mighty Captain," the Senginfan Defenders saluted.

"Call me Captain Hua."

The riders moved to stand by the caped woman, and were about to bend down and search when they saw a tiny movement inside the cape nearby the prisoner's feet. Instantly all six defenders unsheathed their swords and stood poised, ready to strike, but the movement stopped.

"Stay your hands! Back off and put your weapons away," the young captain ordered.

The riders backed away, and Hua advanced to stand by the now motionless cape. "Come on out, little one. It's alright, I've been looking for you."

After a breathless moment, the action beneath the green cape resumed and, a few seconds later, a tiny six-inch mud-doll emerged. Hua heard a sharp intake of breath from the others. *So this is the doll-like creature I've been spending the past couple of months looking for. Mother always said when you want them, you can't find them, but when you're not looking, there they are. Well, I wasn't looking, and here it is.*

Young Captain Hua suddenly remembered his manners. "My name is Hua, and these are the valiant Senginfan Defenders. Senginfan Defenders, meet our friend the Dideetone, or rather a Dideetonie, I believe."

The tall warriors were in awe as they watched the mud-caked and ill dressed little creature waddle to stand in front of their captain and address him timidly. "I'm Pollyanna, wife of Windune."

"Nice to meet you, Queen Pollyanna. Mowong the Mighty received King Windune's Didee-jewel Summon two months ago. He sent me here to fulfill the obligation." Hua recited the words that his mother had instructed him to say on meeting the ever cheerful, young, and polished Dideetones. Hua wrinkled his nose as an unmistakable stench reached his nostrils, but he stood to attention and waited for the female Dideetone to make her next move. He was speechless when the disheveled and tired little Dideetonie started to weep. *A Tensengin Immortal crying?! This is almost as shocking as finding out what an outdoor ladies' room is for the mortals. Not quite, mind you, but close.*

Poor Queen Pollyanna allowed herself half a minute for grief. Then she wiped, unwisely, her eyes on the already tear-stained and mud smudged sleeve, if one could still call it that. The gallant captain immediately produced his own clean hankie, bent down, and passed it to her. The Dideetonie grabbed the white material, mumbled, "Thank you," and proceeded to blow her nose on it. Then she began to hiccup.

Well, if she doesn't survive this thing, the cloth would at least be the perfect size to cover her body with. What am I thinking of? If she dies, it would mean my mission failed. No! It's not going to happen! "Please, is there anything I can do for you?" Hua invited urgently.

Sensing the wisdom of collecting her personal grief and getting on to more important business, the queen calmed herself. "I was the one that issued the Didee-jewel Summon—and yes, there is something you can do for me. My granddaughter Leianna is in need of help—you see, we were both hanging on to this woman's cape while these Senginfan Defenders were pursuing her. Leianna fell off somewhere on the Slave Route Junction, I don't know exactly where, but I know it's close to where the Outsider's van was parked."

Now that I know what Dideetones smell like, I think I know where Leianna is. "Come on, let's look for her." Captain Hua placed his palm on the ground right in front of the Didee-queen.

While Queen Pollyanna climbed onto his palm, the leader of the defenders stepped forward. "Order us, Captain Hua."

The young captain turned toward the west and frowned on seeing that the sun was setting. "Carry on, you're doing a good job," he replied.

"Yes, Mighty Captain," the riders answered in unison.

Just before he dashed off, Hua heard a stern interrogating voice.

"Tell us, slave woman, where is Zanchou?"

Well, I guess the captive has regained her consciousness, but I can't bother with that now. No matter, she's paralyzed from her neck down anyway. He dashed toward the Slave Route Junction. As they traveled, Hua asked the Dideetonie to fill him in on the details and was stunned to hear what she had to say.

"Ever since the Didee-council refused to aid Mershen, the Golden Harp Fairy, the Tensengin High Council stripped us of our magical powers. In addition to abandoning us, they also let loose the ancient evils. We have been hunted by the ferocious mousasus for almost a thousand years. Without the protection of our lost Didee-tunnel, the line of the Mighty Didee race is now no more."

"Mousasus? What sort of creatures are they? What kinds of weapons do they use?"

"The most terrifying, huge, and cruel beasts of the ancient world. Their knife-like teeth and sharp claws could tear you apart in a mere second, and they are capable of climbing, digging, pouncing, and on occasions even flying—"

"Flying?"

"Yes, didn't you know the mousasus are pets to the dragons? Just like hunting dogs to the humans, the mousasus are dragons' hunting partners."

Captain Hua frowned. "And these gigantic creatures have been flying around hunting you?" *This is hard to believe. Why haven't there been any reports of such sightings?*

"Well, at least they used to, but I think they have not been doing much flying for quite some time. Probably realized we Dideetones are underground dwellers, and there was no need to look for us in the sky. But these fiendish creatures would still have been no threat to us, if only we had not lost the door to our Didee-tunnel! Without its protection, we had no choice but to migrate south, hoping to join our Southern kin. I will not bore you with the gruesome details of our hardships, but a little more than four months ago, our group was trapped in the Bayjai Canyon. The sly mousasus had also divided up, and some blocked our retreat. Others were waiting for us at the canyon's exit. Slowly but surely they picked us off. Finally the brave guards of the Didee-council volunteered to escort my husband, my granddaughter, and me out of the canyon by making a Didee-sacrifice-shield ..." Here she stopped and started to weep once again.

I think I understand things better now. Hua gritted his teeth. *Wait till I get my hands on these creatures.* "So you and your granddaughter escaped?"

She nodded her head and continued. "We were separated from my husband during the terrible struggle. Leianna and I made our way the best we could."

"Why didn't you use the Didee-jewel Summon earlier?" the young captain interrupted.

"We had no idea about the summon. I stumbled upon it by accident."

Odd that King Windune had no knowledge of the summoning power. "Why didn't you stay where you were after issuing the summon?"

"Leianna and I tried to, but one of the mousasus tracked us down. We were forced to run for our lives once again. We eluded him for weeks, but this afternoon the cruel beast finally trapped us between some rocks. We knew it was only a matter of time before the beast pawed the rocks loose and had us. Then suddenly, we heard horses galloping, and our pursuer moved away. We climbed on top of one of the rocks just in time to see a caped woman dashing toward us. I shouted, 'Lei! Grab and hang on to her cape.' It was a tricky business, for the woman bounced off a nearby rock and flew up into the sky. We caught the edge of her cape just in time. She glided, outdistancing her pursuers—and ours of course. Good thing Leianna and I hung on with our dear lives."

Hua stared at the Dideetonie. "You mean you two were dangling from her cape tail for hours?!"

"Dangled, bounced, flew, glided, jolted . . . and poor Lei fell off when the caped woman slowed down suddenly—"

"Shh . . ." Hua urged as they reached a yucca and heard voices. He glanced about himself and found no one had detected them yet. The duo quickly hid behind the tree.

"Fifi White Furball—" a melodic voice called.

Oh, it's that human girl. Hua peeked out. *I wish she wouldn't call me that.*

A gasp rang out when Queen Pollyanna saw the creature around Michi's feet. "Ai! The mousasus—the horrid creature will get my Leianna."

"What horrid creature? Where's the mousasus?" Hua asked.

"Why, that girl's got the ferocious beast purring like a kitten!"

Hmm...The young captain eyed the harmless cat and almost laughed out loud. *Control yourself, get everything into perspective.* He looked at the tiny six-inch queen and did manage to get her perspective, somewhat.

"Odd," Queen Pollyanna said, "we tried to guess the mousasus' proper name—as you know, that's the first step in controlling the ancient beasts. I recall, in desperation, we tried the name Fifi, and this particular one got very violent and upset. Yet, did you see how this girl was able to repeat it without provoking any angry reaction from the beast?"

Oh great! I happen to have the same name as the mousasus. No! She happened to name me after the mousasus. I mean...I better stay away from her.

"Michi! Archoy!" Hua heard someone shouting from the direction of the van.

Hua saw the mousasus leave with the humans. He came out from hiding and approached the thorny bush. *That Michi girl thought I, the puppy, was in there, but...could it be?*

He placed the queen gently on the ground. "Stay where you are. I'll just take a quick look in here."

Hua parted the prickly brush slowly and heard a whimpering sound. "It's okay, Princess Leianna," he soothed.

"Lei! It's Grandmammy! Are you alright?" Queen Pollyanna shouted.

A moment later, the captain had located the six-inch princess, caught between some sharp thorns and branches. Hua rescued Leianna, brought her out of the bush, and placed her next to her grandmother. The young captain crossed his arms and smiled with satisfaction as he watched the two Dideetonies on the ground crying, laughing, and hugging each other. *I never liked sob sister stories, but this one is not so bad.*

3

WHEELING AND DEALING

JOSEPH, FLASHLIGHT IN hand, met Michi and Archoy as they were coming back.

"Sweet, that animal doesn't look anything like the Fifi dog that chased the riders away."

"I lost my little Fifi White Furball. But this one's gentle enough. Jo, I really thought I heard a whimpering sound coming from the bush this wildcat was pawing—"

"Could it be the slave woman?" Joseph interrupted quickly.

"No, the thorny bush's not big enough to hide a person."

"It was probably a mouse or a squirrel, young Master Joseph," the housekeeper added.

He nodded his head. "We've got company."

"Oh no! Not those terrifying Northlanders again," Archoy wailed.

"Calm down, these are traveling merchants going north on business. Some are heading for Bayjai City; others are going all the way to Northwood. Most of them can speak our language, and they're quite interesting folk. Come on, let's help them set up their camps."

Traveling merchants—Ooh! I wonder what they sell? Michi loved to visit bazaars, and she quickened her steps.

At least a dozen big tents, plus numerous small ones, were being set up all around their van. *Looks like we're boxed in. Why, that can only mean . . .* "Jo! We're staying the night?!"

"I thought you might like that."

"Oh, young Master Joseph, is this such a good idea? I mean, there's no proper bedding, and no—" Archoy began.

"It's already night, and we have to stay somewhere," Joseph said. "The cook has agreed to feed us, and she's also willing to share her tent with you and Michi. The driver and I can make do with the seats in the front of the van. I believe her cooking's quite famous—her name is Bayjai Arma. Sweet, the pink tent right next to our car will be your bedroom tonight. See the big cooking fire in front of Arma's tent? That's where you get your chow." He then chuckled when Michi, followed by the enthusiastic cat, dashed off toward the cook and the food.

Michi approached the tent and saw a large awning extending from its front. Beneath the awning lay several tables surrounded by scattered cooking pots, flour tins, and water buckets, as well as a standing rack holding assorted spices. Next to the rack, a crude stove stood above an open fire. The soft glow of the cooking fire mixed with the fading light of the sunset and created a ghostly atmosphere. In the midst of this outdoor kitchen, an old woman was bent over an open flour tin.

Michi watched as the woman straightened. "Are you Bayjai Arma, the greatest cook in the Kingdom of Lanhur?"

Ignoring Michi's excited wildcat sniffing around, a smile played across the wrinkled face. "Ho ho! Just for that, a double serving shall be dealt out to you, my little courteous guest," said the woman cheerfully, her cheeks apple red.

Wow! Mrs. Santa! "Thank you! I'm Michi. My cat and I are here to help you." Michi omitted the word "eat" as she introduced herself. Her cat was now pawing the vegetables on top of the table.

"Why, you must be the little lady who appreciates good cooking, as I was told by a certain generous young man."

"That's my brother, Jo. He's the best!" Michi announced proudly while the eager cat sniffed the entrance to the pink tent.

Bayjai Arma paused and studied Joseph, who was helping a group of old men set up their tent on the other side of the van, then nodded her head. "A true gentleman too. Now, let's see, how about putting the vegetables inside that bucket and washing them for me?"

"Sure! Come on," Michi called out to the cat as she grabbed a handful of carrots and plopped them into the pail. The wildcat moved away from the tent and sauntered to the bucket, then started to drink the water.

"Hey! You're supposed to help. Here, take these," Michi scolded and pointed at the potatoes on the table. The silly cat ignored her and continued to slurp the water. "You don't help, you don't eat!" she threatened.

Amazingly, the wildcat stopped and moved to the table. The cat stood on its hind legs and put its paws on the table's edge. It then carried the vegetables in its mouth, moving to the bucket and dropping them into the water.

"That's better." *Huh, this wildcat can do chores just like the Markums' hunting dogs.* The hunting dogs could stand on their hind legs and open doors, fetch papers, slippers, and of course, wild game. *This is no wild cat. She must have had an owner who taught her this neat trick. I wonder where's the cat's master?* Being a young girl who had seen and even tried on a "magic helmet," then watched a puppy chase away six gigantic warriors, Michi soon dismissed the unusual behavior of the cat.

She instead bent down, humming a tune, and washed the veggies. After a while, she started to pass the washed vegetables to the animal. "Now, put these back. Make sure you stack them in piles that are fit for kings."

Bayjai Arma's deep fried pork chops began to fill the campsite with a delicious aroma, and Michi swallowed hard. She sped up her washing.

"Arma! How much do you want for that clever and fine looking animal?" a voice boomed.

Michi jerked her head up to see that her cat had returned the washed vegetables to the table by stacking them like pyramids—a potato pyramid and a carrot pyramid. *Huh! I wonder how they stay up so high? Come to think of it, how did my cat reach so high to . . .*

"Merchant Benny, the clever cat belongs to this little lady here," Bayjai Arma spoke.

Michi jumped up and dashed over to pull her cat, who was hovering in mid-air putting the finishing touches on the top of the pyramids, down to the ground. *What are you trying to do? Make me look bad?!*

"My dear girl, I am Benny the Merchant of Northwood. You must come to my tent, and choose whatever you wish in lieu of the cat," a bearded and stout man said as he walked into Michi's view.

"The cat is not for sale. However, I would like very much to take a look at your tent and see what treasures you have."

Merchant Benny gave a calculating smile. "Come, I shall give you a private viewing of my best merchandise. How about a purebred Nain horse, the most majestic horse in the world?" he invited.

"Now, now, Benny, let the little girl eat first. Come Michi, I've got fresh crumpets, fried pork chops, and sweet pudding ready for you."

"Gee, thanks. Mmm . . . smells heavenly. Jo! Come and eat."

Joseph, who was walking over to another tent, looked back. "You go ahead, Sweet. I'll wait for Bayjai Arma's famous stew."

Oh, I'll have some of that too, when it's ready. Michi sat by the cook and started to eat while her cat chased and pounced on a loaf of bread. The bread rolled under Michi's feet and she picked it up, then threw it out into the dark wilderness. "Go! Fetch!" she shouted. An echo that sounded like a yelp followed. *The night air here is certainly different. Even the echoes sound strange.* The cat flitted away into the darkness. Michi went back to her food, and as she ate, she realized the cook must have traveled this route many times in the past.

"Arma, have you ever seen or heard of six Northlanders wearing silver war gear riding on gray horses?"

"Aye, you must be talking about the Ghost Chasers on this West Slave Route. Used to be seven of them, and they were after a ten foot tall warrior ghost, as I've been told. But the riders have been chasing a green caped female ghost now."

"Ten feet tall?! Wow! Why were they after him?" Fascinated, Michi stopped eating and turned to get the details from the cook. Unaware that the wildcat had returned, and was now taking pork chops from her plate, she continued to listen intently.

"Can't say for sure. But about eight and a half years ago, they stopped searching for him. These Northland warriors joined the plantation slave hunters, but were more interested in pursuing a particular slave woman traveling with a boy of about five."

"I know there are slaves in Southland, but what are plantation slave hunters?"

"Ah. Little one, you must understand a bit about history. You see, the biggest landowners in Southland are the Nuhohs, the Bonhas, and the Hinowas. Both the Bonhas and the Hinowas have their huge plantations in Bayjai, whereas the Nuhohs are way down southeast at Backland Hectares—"

"Backland Hectares! Why, that's where my new home's going to be. I think the Nuhohs are our new neighbors."

"Is that right? Well, that's news indeed. An Outsider family will be neighbors to the old-fashioned Nuhohs. Interesting."

Uh-oh! Is that good or bad? Michi turned to her food, and frowned when she found there were no pork chops left on her plate. She saw her cat take another loaf of bread and run off into the darkness. *Probably found a secret place to bury the loaf in.* She ate some crumpets, then turned back to watch Arma make more dough with stunning speed. The experienced cook could make bread, fry pork chops, cook beef stew, and talk all at the same time.

Arma tasted the broth from the stew. "Ahh...my beef stew will be ready for veggies soon. Now, where was I? Oh yes, the Nuhohs and the Bonhas were decent slave owners, but not so the Hinowas. And as a result, the Hinowas' slaves tried to escape whenever the opportunity arose. The Hinowas hired many retired law enforcement officers as plantation slave hunters. And these hunters traveled between the Northwood, Bayjai, and Nunjai borders recapturing the runaway slaves."

"Did they ever catch the slave woman with the five year old boy?"

"This woman was no ordinary slave, as she could carry her boy and fly in the sky—I've seen it with my own eyes once. It was eight years ago; a tall and slender caped woman with her little boy joined our traveling band. She was quiet, but she had healing skills you wouldn't believe. This woman earned her keep by becoming the healer in our camp. She was very mysterious, and often went off during the night. My dealings with her were limited to her picking the most unusual herbs and plants for me to use to enhance my food. In return, I would give her all my leftovers—no questions asked. To be honest, my cooking skill improved tremendously during that time, and I received the famous title 'Bayjai Arma.' I found out later she had been helping the runaway slaves and feeding them—"

"Why, she's a heroine! Oh, do tell me she and the boy were not caught."

"Well, one day these Northlanders with strange gear came riding into our camp and started to search from tent to tent. Their leader, the only one not wearing war gear save for a long sword, was at least six feet in height. I remember him well...a very striking figure sitting on a powerful steed, with his cloak flowing behind him. As the other riders got close to my pink tent, this slave woman with the boy in her arms came out of nowhere, and when her pursuers saw her, she dashed out of the camp. Suddenly she bounced up at least thirty, maybe forty feet above the ground, then flew away—"

"You mean she flew like a bird?!"

"Aye! I thought I was seeing things. The leader of the ghost hunters went after her instantly, followed by the other six riders. And then the six foot leader also bounced up, flying in pursuit of the slave woman."

"But did he catch her?" Michi stood up and asked eagerly.

"I didn't see because, to my surprise, a group of slaves rushed out of my tent and headed the other way as soon as the riders left. And a few minutes later, the plantation slave hunters arrived but found nothing. Oh, you needn't worry, as a week later, I heard they were still looking for the green caped woman and the little boy—"

"Green caped woman! Why, could she be the same one..."

Arma shook her head. "You must be talking about the green caped ghost. She travels alone from what I've heard. Can you imagine a compassionate mother leaving her little boy behind without someone to care for him?"

"No, especially not our heroine...so what happened to her and the boy?"

"Rumor has it that they did some real clever disguises and escaped, not to Northland, but either down southwest to the Nain tribes or up northwest to join the Outsiders."

Her exciting tale now finished, Arma picked a large potato from the top of the pyramid and tossed it up in the air. Then, the cook swirled a paring knife in the air for a flash of a second, and the potato skin was peeled in one unbroken string. As the peeled potato came down, the cook sliced it in the air, then sent the pieces into the huge boiling stew pot, whacking the sliced veggies with the back of her hand like a tennis racket.

I've got to learn this trick! Michi jumped up and down. "Let me try! Oh, let me!"

Bayjai Arma, pleased with herself, passed another paring knife to little Michi. "Now, step one, toss the potato up as high as you can—good! Step two, move your right hand real fast in a circular motion before the veggie even reaches the knife—step three, Cut! Cut! Cut! And step four—Whack!"

Michi's whole unpeeled potato came down and hit her with a smack. "Ouch!" she yelled, while the cook's peeled and sliced ones plopped into the pot. Michi thought she heard sniggering, but she spun around and saw nothing. *Even the wind's laughing at me!*

The famous cook was already peeling and cutting another one, and another one... *Well, I'm going to master this thing even if it kills me.* With determination, she picked a big one and threw it way up. But the darn thing was coming down so fast, she only had enough time to wave her knife up in the air a couple of times, then skip step three completely and go straight to step four, which was whacking the veggie into the pot. The potato flew out into the dark wilderness. There was a smack, what sounded almost like a yelp, and a pause. Then, to her surprise, peeled and sliced potato pieces flew back from the darkness and plopped into the stew pot. *Did I do that?* She even thought she heard cheering. She immediately picked up another potato and threw it high in the air, waving her paring knife a couple of times, and whacking the veggie into the darkness. This time, the peeled and cut-up potatoes flew instantly back and landed inside the cooking pot. *I'm getting better!* She took up another one and repeated her two and a half step improved version of the routine.

Another loud thump sounded, and the potato dropped to the floor. "Ouch! Little Miss, please sit down and eat your food properly—and don't play with the potatoes," Archoy, who had come to check on Michi, scolded as she rubbed her forehead.

"Oh! Archoy, you don't understand. I was getting it!"

The housekeeper, looking at the bruise nearby Michi's right eye, shook her head. "Yes, I see. And now I also got it."

Drat! Why does Archoy have to show up just when I'm on a roll? Michi observed the fast diminishing veggies on the table with regret. Then some children, who had apparently finished their chores from another tent, started to play. The children's laughter distracted Michi. She dropped the paring knife and dashed over to join them.

Technically, the Didee-jewel Summon had been fulfilled. But on listening to Princess Leianna's recounting of her adventure to her grandmother, Hua realized that had it not been for little Michi's timely interference, his mission would have been a failure.

"Oh! Lei, your face...the mousasus clawed your beautiful face..." Queen Pollyanna touched the deep scratch marks with sadness.

"Grandmammy, it's just my face. I'm still alive. When the mousasus inched into the bush and heard someone calling 'Fifi,' the beast flew into a rage and swiped its right paw at me. I closed my eyes at the pain in my face, thinking that was the end, and I let out a whimper. When I heard the rustling of twigs, I realized that I was still alive. I could feel the mousasus' hot breath on my face, and its fangs were not two inches away. Just as the beast was about to bite, the human child pulled it out of the bush and saved me from a terrible death. When the child ignored the monstrous beast and soothed, 'Are you alright, Fifi,' I was afraid for her life. But then she continued, 'White Furball,' and the mousasus purred like a kitten. Oh, Grandmammy, 'Fifi White Furball' must be the beast's whole name!"

How do you like that, letting a little girl beat me to it. Captain Hua's pride made him feel he would have to do more in order to even out the score. Besides, he couldn't just leave the two Dideetonies out in the wild without some kind of protection. If something happened to either one of them after he left, it would be all for nothing. Hua had not anticipated problems like this when he left Mowong Castle two months ago.

Babysitting a couple of mud-dolls wasn't quite what he was trained for, and he voiced his concern tactfully. "Your Highness, may I inquire as to what your plans are from here?"

The two Dideetonies came back to reality, and the queen turned to him. "Lei, this is the gallant Captain Hua, who was sent by Mowong the Mighty to fulfill my Didee-jewel Summon. Young Captain Hua, this is my granddaughter Leianna."

Under the soft moonlight, Hua saluted while Princess Leianna executed a graceful curtsy and thanked him.

Just at that moment, the wind brought a tempting aroma to their nostrils, and Queen Pollyanna sniffed. "It would be nice to have some hot food for a change. Where do you suppose the delicious smell is coming from?"

Hua remembered the band of traveling merchants he saw from the Bayjai Lookout Point earlier in the day. "Traveling merchants are camping nearby," he replied. He looked at his pouch and suddenly realized that he was carrying no human money. Hua glanced at the hungry Dideetonies and decided to keep calm. "Come, you shall have some hot food." *That is, if I can manage to steal some.*

Carrying the Dideetonies, Captain Hua made his way cautiously toward the campsite. He arrived near the pink tent and halted in the darkness. Hua could see the cooking fire, a plump woman busy with cooking, little Michi bending down singing and washing, and the mousasus stacking a couple of impressive veggie pyramids. He was also aware of another pair of watchful eyes in the form of a bearded middle-aged man. The stout merchant had his eyes on the mousasus. The animal was completing the pyramids by tiptoeing—*No! By hovering in mid-air!* The queen was right. The ancient beast was capable of flying. The mousasus was now also bigger in size than it had been back at the yucca tree. *The beast can grow larger or smaller…it's a Flexer!*

Captain Hua was not surprised when Merchant Benny offered to buy the mousasus. Though he almost laughed when he saw Michi rush over to pull down the cat. He was glad that the little girl hadn't been greedy. Hua did not relish having to go after the mousasus from the Merchant of Northwood's tent. And when little Michi started to munch on a plate heaped with food, Captain Hua noticed that the Dideetonies sat up straighter on his hand and strained their necks to get a better look at the tempting food.

"Grandmammy, that loaf of bread looks too good to be pounced upon like a toy," Princess Leianna commented, eyeing the bread the mousasus was playing with. Her stomach growled. "Excuse me," she apologized.

"My poor Lei, you must be famished." The grandmother hugged her little princess close to her as the young captain watched the hungry duo with anxiety.

Stealing food was also not part of his training. *What to do?* Hua brooded. Suddenly, a submarine-shaped object issued from the pink tent and hurtled toward him. "Ouch!" Hua, who was engrossed in his thoughts, yelled when the loaf of bread hit his head.

"Oh! Catch it, Lei! Here—here—I've got it!" Queen Pollyanna caught the foot-long loaf of bread, not a very wise idea for someone who was only six inches tall, and she fell flat on Captain Hua's left palm with the slobbery dirty bread on top of her.

"Aaa!" Leianna, who was also fumbling with the falling loaf, stepped off the edge of Hua's hand and began to fall.

He caught her with his other hand and placed the princess on the ground. Hua immediately removed the loaf from the queen and placed his left palm on the ground.

"Are you alright?" he whispered while Leianna rushed over to her grandmother.

"Grandmammy! Grandmammy!" the princess called while Queen Pollyanna cried out, "The bread! What happened to the bread?"

Then they heard a low growling sound, and the Dideetonies froze. Coming toward them was the vicious mousasus, and it seemed the beast was ready to pounce.

"Fifi White Furball, come here!" Captain Hua commanded.

The cat sauntered over while the queen and princess huddled together shivering.

"Smell! No biting! No scratching!" The Flexer Beast came closer. "Do not be afraid. Let her smell you. She will remember your scent, and she will never hunt you again. Princess Leianna, I'm going to order her to lick your face. It's necessary because she is a Flexer, and her claws are poisoned. Without treatment your wounds would begin to rot in two days. It will sting a little, but you'll be fine after she licks you. I'm afraid the scars will remain the rest of your days, though. There's no cure for the marks of the ancient beasts."

"Go ahead, I'm not afraid. Scars on one's face are supposed to mean bravery, and I'll be proud to wear such a mark of courage to the end of my days."

Hua was moved. He knew many worthy knights proudly wore their scars...*but a princess?* On his order, the orange mousasus licked the princess's wounds and the beast seemed to become very attached to Leianna after that.

Captain Hua considered the mousasus while the beast was licking Leianna's wounds—*why not? It's time the animal did something for her long-suffering victims.* "Fifi White Furball...Go! Fetch pork chops," he commanded the moment the mousasus finished.

The cat instantly rushed back to the pink tent, and as Michi turned to Arma for an exciting part of the story, stole the pork chops from her plate.

Captain Hua found a smooth rock, placed his not-so-white hankie on top of it, then invited his guests to sit down. Soon Queen Pollyanna and Princess Leianna were feasting on warm, fried, jumbo-sized pork chops.

Hua crumpled the slobbered bread in his hand and wrinkled his nose. "Fifi White Furball—fetch bread."

When the new loaf of bread was delivered to the "dining table" moments later, the captain took out his dagger and sliced some for his customers. Hua watched the hungry duo eat the stolen food and smiled. *Someone did call me a thief, a robber, and a sneak today.* Then he took out his water bottle and shared it with the Dideetonies.

While he was putting the bottle away, his attention was caught by what Bayjai Arma was retelling to Michi. He advanced closer to the tent. *Why, I do believe the cook's talking about the slave woman and her little boy!*

Captain Hua listened intently. *So the slave woman is a healer. That's news indeed.* When he heard little Michi pronounce the slave woman a heroine, Hua clenched his fists. *Don't get upset, she's just a little girl, what does she know?* He listened with an aching heart when the cook came to the part about the six-foot leader. "...I remember him well...a very striking figure sitting on a powerful steed, with his cloak flowing behind him..." Hua touched his cloak. *Revenge isn't as sweet as what I had thought. I...I would that my parents could be happy as they once were.*

His attention was arrested again when the conversation at the pink tent centered around the fate of the slave woman and the boy. The mortals thought the slave woman and the green caped female ghost were two different people, but Hua knew they were one and the same. His curiosity aroused, Hua wanted to know what happened to the little boy that disappeared on that fateful night seven and a half years ago. *Let's see. He would be thirteen now. Arma was right! The slave mother couldn't have abandoned her child. She must have left her boy with someone...but who?*

He eyed the cook with suspicion, but on seeing Arma do her potato peeling trick, Hua was impressed. The captain had never visited a kitchen in all his seventeen years of brief existence, and he was fascinated by the neat trick. When little Michi jumped up and down shouting, "Let me try! Oh, let me!" Hua thought he wouldn't mind having a go at it himself. He chuckled when he saw the potato smack Michi's face. Hearing his sniggering, the Dideetonies, who had finished their big meal, came over to stand beside him.

"What's so amusing, Captain?" the queen wanted to know.

Hua bent down, placing his left palm on the ground, and his guests climbed on it. He straightened up and was about to enlighten the queen concerning the trick in the outdoor kitchen. Before he could utter a word, however, an unidentified flying object hit him near his left eye. Hua let out a startled yelp. But now being experienced, he caught the falling projectile with his right hand and tossed it up. In one swift motion, he drew out his dagger, swirled and peeled the falling potato, sliced it, then sent the pieces back toward the open kitchen straight into the stew pot.

No sooner had Queen Pollyanna and Princess Leianna started clapping and cheering than another potato flew toward them. This time, Hua leisurely met the veggie with his dagger and sent the pieces back within seconds. *Finally I'm doing something closer to what I was trained for.* Though entertaining six-inch dolls wasn't quite what his master had in mind when Hua's great-grandfather taught him dagger maneuver routines. The Dideetonies giggled when they saw little Michi send the next potato in a totally different direction, hitting Archoy's forehead.

While the queen and the princess were in a merry mood, Captain Hua stared at his dagger and frowned. Instead of putting his weapon away, he brought the blade closer to his nostrils and sniffed. Puzzled, Hua bent down and retrieved the two strings of potato skin, smelling them. *Another Dideetone!* He was very sure that what he had cut up were potatoes, but how did the scent get on the veggie? *That's all I need, a whole population of Dideetones in my charge.*

Hua assessed the situation in the outdoor kitchen. Only the cook was left, and she was facing the other way. *I think I'll have a look in the pink tent.* He dashed over to the tent, followed by the mousasus. On finding the entrance closed, he took out his dagger. Before he could make a move, Leianna started to work on the knots. She was fast at untying them, and soon they slipped into the tent without being detected. The mousasus went straight to the corner, where sacks of potatoes and carrots were stored. It sniffed at them, then growled.

"Fifi White Furball, come," Hua whispered at the same time ten Didee-guards bounced out from between the sacks and landed on top of the tallest bag. All ten guards were dressed in shining war gear, and they stood poised, with drawn swords, ready to do battle.

The leader of the guards spoke with a menacing voice. "Release our fair Northern kin and take this foul beast of yours out of here if you know what's good for you!"

Great. Now I'm challenged by six-inch toy soldiers—this mission stinks. I'm going to have to have a talk with that Arma cook sometime; she ought to have her pink tent fumigated.

"Stay your hands, fair guards of the south. I am Polly, and this is my granddaughter Lei. We were separated from our party four months ago at the Bayjai Canyon. If it weren't for this gallant knight, Lei and I would have met our deaths today. This is the brave Captain Hua, who has tamed the ancient beast—behold the obedient mousasus standing next to him."

The Didee-guards observed, with suspicion, the vicious-looking beast standing by the tall warrior, the dagger in Hua's right hand, and the "ill-dressed" Dideetonies on his left palm. Captain Hua put his dagger away and placed the Dideetonies on the cot to his left, then stood back. To the Didee-guards' astonishment, the orange mousasus moved close to Lei and licked her scarred face while she patted the huge beast.

All ten guards threw their glimmering swords up in the air, and when the blades came down they turned into small cloaks that fitted over the Dideetones' heads.

Impressive!

"Pardon us, we have been on the road searching for news of you and the others for much too long. I'm Xeiyén, and these are my comrades. We are Didee-guards to the Mighty

Vong, the South Council Leader of the Dideetones. Might we find out whom you serve?"

The question surprised Hua, but he was even more surprised by the queen's reply. "Lei and I, we serve King Windune." *Hmm...I wonder why Queeny is withholding their true identities?* Being a young warrior, the captain was clueless when it came to the opposite sex's feelings and pride. While on the run living from danger to danger, Queen Pollyanna had disposed of the fineries befitting a queen, wishing only that her beloved granddaughter might survive the ordeal. But now faced with the grand warriors of the South Didee-council, the queen felt ashamed. Leianna placed a comforting hand on her grandmother, and smiled encouragingly.

"Well, looks like you've found your Southern kin, so I'll just be on my way. It was nice meeting you—uhh...Polly and Lei." Hua, relieved to see that the Mighty Vong's Didee-guards seemed to have retained their magical powers, took the opportunity to say goodbye.

"Dear Captain Hua, my granddaughter and I are greatly indebted to you. Before you go, may I ask that you take the mousasus with you, and dispose of the beast in whatever way you see fit?"

"Grandmammy! Fifi White Furball was only doing what she was told!"

"Lei! Have you forgotten how your own parents died? Not to mention so many others...the beast must be dealt with! Farewell, valiant captain. Till next time."

Captain Hua saluted, then motioned to the Flexer beast. The two moved to the exit, but Leianna stayed them.

"Captain! May I ask what you are going to do to Fifi White Furball?"

Now that his mission was complete, the captain had regained his sense of humor. He stared straight at the mousasus. "Well, I haven't had my dinner yet, so I think I'll just..."

"Oh please, couldn't you just take her back to your home and keep her as a pet?" Lei pleaded as she rushed to the edge of the bed.

"Lei! There's a whole world of difference between eating the thing and making it a pet," Queen Pollyanna scolded.

Captain Hua's lips quirked. "I was going to say, I think I'll just take Fifi here to join Benny the Merchant of Northwood for dinner. Would that be okay with you?"

"You're thinking of selling the mousasus to that dishonest merchant?" Lei pursued.

"Actually, I was thinking of swindling a fine horse from Merchant Benny. But if you think Fifi and I shouldn't dawdle on our way home, I suppose we could skip the social part and go straight to 'borrowing' the horse."

Princess Leianna's bluish-violet eyes sparkled. "I knew you wouldn't harm the poor beast. Thank you again, brave captain. Goodbye, Fifi White Furball."

As Hua stepped out of the tent, he heard Xeiyén's voice behind him. "A splendid fighter Captain Hua seems to be. The warrior that gave him the black eye must be a worthy opponent. Wish we had been there to watch the thrilling struggle between life and death..."

What black eye? What worthy opponent? The young captain was mystified, but had to dash away from the pink tent because a group of people were making their way toward the tempting scent of the famous stew.

He passed the temporary pens where the travelers kept their beasts of burden, and saw only ordinary horses, donkeys, camels, and the common oxen. *Well, if I had a purebred Nain horse, I would keep him in my tent just like Merchant Benny.* Somehow he knew the meddlesome little girl wouldn't be able to resist having a look at the goods in Benny's tent, so Hua followed little Michi's scent. He made his way to the biggest tent on the other side of the camp. On reaching the flap to the entrance, he stood outside and listened.

"Sweet, are you alright? Your eye! What have they done to you? Merchant Benny! If you or any of your men laid a hand on my little sister, you'll rue the day you were born!"

That's the voice of the courageous Outsider who barred the Senginfan Defenders' path earlier. Hua pushed the flap and entered. He stood in semi-darkness near the entrance, and saw Joseph facing both Benny and a muscular man who had his arms over Michi's neck. The air between them was tense, and none noticed the captain's quiet entrance.

"Now, now, calm down young man," the sly merchant said. "We're just showing your little sister around—"

"Jo! Come and see, there's a lot of neat things in here—"

"Michi! What happened to your right eye? Tell me what happened!"

"This merchant wanted to know my cat's name, and when I told him it was 'Wildcat,' he wasn't happy with it. And his friend Buddo volunteered to help me with my memory. When I told them there's nothing wrong with my memory, Buddo here hugged me, then you came."

I wonder when she got the black eye?

Joseph took a menacing step forward. "Let my sister go!"

Just at that moment, two slave hunters jumped from the dark corners of the tent and attacked Joseph from both sides.

Hmm . . . to help, or not to help?

"Watch out Jo!" little Michi shouted, noticing the figures rushing toward her brother.

Joseph leapt back. His attackers whipped past him, slamming into each other. One fell backward onto the floor while the other stumbled. But before Joseph could rush to his sister's side, Buddo lifted Michi up. Her right hand fumbled blindly and grasped onto a wooden shaft lying against the tent.

"Don't move or your little sister gets it!" Buddo threatened.

Hua saw Michi try to lift the mace up and hit her captor with it. *Ooo! She's vicious!* It seemed the shaft's end was too heavy, though, and the captain saw Michi give up halfway through the effort. The mace swung down and smacked the muscle man's behind.

The spiked war club stunned Buddo, and he cried out in pain as he dropped Michi. He then swung around just in time to see the mace hit merchant Benny's foot.

"Ouch! Ouch!" the merchant screamed.

Hua saw Joseph catch Michi and pull her behind him. Joseph grabbed a spear from the assortment of weapons that lined the tent and jabbed Buddo's back with it.

"Move away from the mace—slowly," Joseph warned while Michi looked around her. She snatched up a decorated vase from the floor and stood ready to throw it.

Of all the things, she just had to pick the most valuable item in the room.

It seemed the Merchant of Northwood agreed with Hua. "Don't do anything rash! Let's negotiate. Ask your little sister to put that vase down," the mustachioed man urged.

"First you tell me who's responsible for my sister's black eye?"

"Uhh...how should I know? She came in with it—"

"Let's try it again, and I warn you, I'm running out of patience," Joseph cut in sharply.

Merchant Benny's expression cleared. "Ah, yes. You Outsiders love to sue one another for the smallest injuries, but there's no need for that sort of stuff here. You want compensation for her bruised eye, well let's see what we can do ..."

Joseph frowned, but Michi spoke quickly. "I want you to free Shanui, the fifteen-year-old slave girl, and her twelve-year-old brother Dei."

The Merchant of Northwood rubbed his beard and pondered. "I paid a handsome price for those two. The boy was supposed to take care of my prized horse. As for the girl ... I'll tell you what, I'll free the boy—"

"No! You'll let them both go," Joseph said, backing Michi.

"But your sister has only one black eye ..." the merchant argued.

"And one vase," Joseph reminded.

This is good stuff! I must observe closely.

"Ah yes. Alright, I still have the new slaves' papers here somewhere ... tell your sister to give me the vase now and I'll sign the release forms when I find them."

"Why don't you look for the papers and bring them to Bayjai Arma's tent, say in ten minutes," Joseph suggested as he ushered Michi toward the exit.

Buddo bent down and was about to pick up the mace, but Joseph shot the spear with such remarkable precision that the spearhead went through the wooden shaft and nailed the mace to the ground.

"No, no, Buddo, let them go," Merchant Benny said. "I'll see you two at Arma's in ten minutes—Oh Michi, dear girl, do watch where you're going."

Captain Hua dashed out, followed by the mousasus, and they moved to the side of the tent. A few moments later, Michi and Joseph left Benny's big tent. Hua entered the tent again, in time to see the angry Buddo pull the weapons from the floor. "Why won't you let me deal with him, he's just a boy," Hua heard Buddo argue.

Benny looked up to see Hua and the unusual beast entering his tent. "Why don't you try it with this boy—and don't harm the cat!" the merchant suggested eagerly.

Buddo whirled around, aimed at Hua, and shot his spear. Hua caught the shaft with ease and continued to advance. The two slave hunters moved cautiously this time around the teenage boy and the beast. Buddo lifted the mace above his head and yelled, charging at the intruder. Hua leapt up above the swinging arc of the spiked weapon and landed in front of Benny, leaving the two hunters to fall over themselves while trying to dodge the mace. Captain Hua pointed the spear at Benny's chest.

"And what do you want for your black eye, stranger?" the agreeable merchant asked.

Black eye? "Since you don't have a boy to groom your horse anymore, I'll just take that purebred Nain horse off your hands."

The Merchant of Northwood's eyes narrowed, but he gave a crafty smile. "Come this way, stranger—to my inner tent."

Benny flipped the flap to an inner room and motioned for Hua to proceed. The moment the captain entered, a sack popped over his head.

"I've got him!" a tall slave hunter, who had been hiding on the other side, cried out. The overjoyed hunter waved the sack over his head, but the bag that was supposed to have held Hua's upper body was mysteriously empty. Merchant Benny entered, and his smug face turned to rage. He saw the stranger now standing by the majestic white horse, examining it. Benny cursed and kicked at the flabbergasted hunter, who was looking back and forth between the bare sack in his hand and the young stranger by the horse.

"Well, nice doing business with you, Merchant Benny," Hua voiced, pleased with what he found. He guided his new horse toward the flap. As he exited the inner tent, Hua suggested to the puzzled hunter, "Next time aim for the legs."

Hua reached the outer tent and passed a full-length mirror by some cushions. He stopped to take a closer look at the black eye that was staring back at him. *Huh! I wonder how I . . . oh, never mind.* Also in the reflection was the mousasus, now three times its original size. It sat on top of Buddo while the two hunters circled the beast at a safe distance.

Suddenly, the flap to another inner room opened. Two scantily clad slave girls holding plates of fresh fruit and bread came out. Upon seeing the ferocious ancient beast, the slave girls paled and dropped their golden platters. Screaming, they dashed back to the inner room. Hua saw the glimmering of a dagger before the flap closed again. *Ah, another one of those hidden traps. I wonder what treasure lies beyond?* Being a warrior, the young captain could not resist the challenge and he entered the inner chamber, followed by his white horse.

Hua was confronted by the slashing of a short blade. Although the attacks were quick, they were nothing compared to any of the dangers from Mowong Castle's challenges. Hua smoothly caught the attacker's hand and plucked the weapon from it. The assailant then surprised him by withdrawing to the far corner of the tent, next to a pile of soft pillows, and holding a sharp hairpin strangely. Hua realized the hairpin was pointing at the attacker's own throat.

"Don't come any closer, or I'll kill myself," a feminine voice warned in Native dialect.

The midget was a girl! Amused, Hua studied the frightened dark eyes intently as he extended the short dagger, handle facing out, to the girl. "Here, I didn't know you were trying to kill yourself—you could have fooled me," he said, also in Native dialect.

The large eyes turned a different shade as the girl tilted her head to get a better look at the tall stranger. At that moment, another midget tried to attack Hua from behind. The captain, still looking into the pair of lovely eyes, grabbed the shirtfront of his new assailant with his left hand and lifted the small form up.

"You leave my sister alone!" the kicking and hitting boy shouted.

"Dei! It's not the bad merchant!" the girl cried out, and the little boy stopped fighting. "Who are you?" she asked.

"I'm the knight in dusty armor, and I'm here to pick up a headstrong girl of fifteen and her twelve-year old delinquent brother," Hua replied with a devilish grin. He then hoisted Dei onto the white horse.

"Where are you taking us?" the brother and sister asked in unison.

"To my gingerbread house, Hansel and Gretel," Hua teased, and on seeing their frowns, he smiled wryly. "A meddlesome little girl and her champion of a brother have bargained for your freedom, and I think the papers are being signed as of now."

"Freed?!" the shocked duo cried out. Then the little boy, his voice tinged with suspicion, added, "Oh yeah? With what?"

"I believe Merchant Benny traded you for one black eye," Hua informed him.

"Huh?"

Some humans are just too slow on the uptake. Captain Hua turned back to look at the girl encouragingly, and she advanced slowly toward him.

"You really don't have to point that pin at your throat anymore, you know. I think you've made your point."

The girl's cheeks flooded with color and she put the pearl hairpin away. She then took the short blade from Hua. "And me? What did the bad merchant take for my freedom?"

"A priceless vase," he said softly, then lifted her up and put her behind Dei.

They exited Merchant Benny's tent, the young captain and the mousasus walking on either side of the purebred Nain horse. The wind blew toward them as they made their way leisurely to Bayjai Arma's tent, and they could hear the loud voices before they even reached the outdoor kitchen.

"Mark my words, there's going to be trouble. The Merchant of Northwood has been eyeing Shanui ever since he saw her at the Firmiana Inn a year ago. And here he was, finally able to have her..."

"You're right. It's all my children's fault, they were the ones who told the Outsiders about the slave girl and boy."

"Your children did the right thing, and we must take it up from here. We all know there are shady dealings going on. Merchant Benny and the Hinowas have been bullying too long."

"Now Arma, you must understand, some of us have our families to think of... if only the Council of Defense's regiments would come and patrol between the Northwood, Bayjai, and Nunjai borders, instead of the cutthroat slave hunters."

"Don't think for a moment that all the Council of Defense's armed forces are saints. Many of them have joined the less reputable Modern Council members, and have been using their power for personal gain."

"I would put my money only on the Wise Man Gurleon and the Old General Chium Soonchi and his followers—"

"Hush, I think someone's coming!"

Hua halted in the darkness, helped the children down, then urged them to join the crowd in the open kitchen.

They thanked him, and Shanui hesitated. "Are you not coming?" she asked.

"No, you go ahead—put that knife away."

She complied, and Dei grabbed his sister's hand. "Come on!" he shouted. Dei dragged his sister toward the pink tent while Shanui turned and stared indecisively at Hua.

"Your name, Knight in Dusty Armor, may I know your name?" she cried out.

"Hua."

"What—? Your name, please."

Must be the wind . . . "Hua."

"What?"

Hmm . . . this could go on forever . . .

"Ahh, here are the children," Arma fussed on seeing Shanui and Dei. "Come and have my beef stew, guaranteed to soothe one's tummy and make little ones grow strong." She led the children away from the darkness, toward the warming light of the cooking fire.

"Well, Fifi White Furball, I guess it's just you, me, and the horse." Hua mounted his steed, taking one last look at the open kitchen, and saw Michi guarding the decorated vase like a mother hen. Hua smiled. "Until next time—my worthy opponent," he whispered, then rode off.

4

MANY MEETINGS

BENNY STUDIED THE gathering merchants around him with contempt—he never liked competition. Had things gone the way he wanted, the Merchant of Northwood would have eliminated all his competitors by force. But Benny was a patient man. He would get the better of things in the end. He always had. His eyes strayed to the lovely Shanui, who was eating a bowl of stew. *The foolish girl. She could have had fineries and delicacies, but instead she's wearing servant's clothing and eating stew fit only for rough laborers.* It was a minor setback, having to wait longer for the girl, but Benny enjoyed and thrived on a good chase.

"Come on! Sign the paper already! You don't have to eye Shanui's stew with such greedy eyes, Merchant Benny. Why, you can have a bigger bowl if you wish—after business of course," Michi hustled.

He gave her a dark look. *Just you wait, little girl. You don't know who you're dealing with here.* Benny took out the official documents, signed, and passed them to Joseph.

"Much obliged." Joseph passed the papers to Shanui.

"Keep the papers safe, dear," Bayjai Arma said. "You and your brother are free."

"Thank you for coming to our rescue," Shanui said to the Outsiders while Benny took the vase from Michi.

Archoy grabbed the opportunity to be social. "Merchant Benny, that is really one gorgeous vase. I hear you've got loads of wonderful stuff in your big tent. I would love to have a look."

The merchant eyed the big bruise on the housekeeper's forehead. "The store's closed for the night, Madam." Then he turned to Joseph and Michi. "I'll not say thank you, or nice doing business with you, but I'll say we shall meet again."

"Here, have some stew. Guaranteed to soothe one's temper," Michi said.

Enjoy your triumph while you can, Outsiders. Benny huffed off toward his big tent.

As soon as Benny entered, Buddo informed him that he had visitors. Benny cursed. He wasn't in the mood to be bothered by anyone at the moment.

"I see you have my vase. Very good, Benny old boy!" a voice boomed.

Benny smiled ear to ear. "Councilman Trumbond! What pleasant wind has brought you all the way out here? And who's this handsome young man beside you?"

"This is my son, Brutan. Son, you've met Benny once, when you were five," the robust councilman introduced.

"I remember you, Uncle Benny. You were the one that gave me my first bow and arrow set. A superb gift that was, as I recall."

"My dear boy! It has been eight years, and you have grown up to be a dashing young man. Come! You must join me at my table and we can talk about the good old times."

The trio walked toward an inner tent containing a low table laden with the choicest of tidbits and finest of wines. Benny placed the priceless vase next to Trumbond's seat.

The councilman beamed with pleasure. "Ahh ... this is the real thing!"

"It certainly is, but it has cost me more than I bargained for."

"You shall be well compensated, Merchant of Northwood. Now tell me what's all this fuss about." While Trumbond waited for Benny to start his tale, the councilman took out a small feather duster and pointed it at the gorgeous vase. At a slight movement of his wrist, the decorated pottery turned into an unattractive vase.

"I can never get over your little magic duster's amazing power," Benny said. "No one will ever give this plain vase a second look now, very clever. Wish you had been here when I was having difficulty with some troublesome Outsiders."

While Merchant Benny spilled his woes to the newcomers, his slaves served a ten-course meal complete with matching wine and dessert. When the merchant was done with his account, Trumbond was alarmed.

"Benny! You didn't offend these people—"

"Of course not!" Merchant Benny interrupted with displeasure. "You know me better than that. My motto is to always keep my cool when dealing with strangers. I like to get to know my opponents, or rather customers if you will, then plan my deal around them."

"If you're counting on the slave hunters to raid the camp tonight so you can recover your slave girl, I suggest you forget about it for now."

"How so? I sent runners to fetch them as soon as the meddlesome Outsiders left my tent—"

"Benny! You are not listening to me! I say forget about it for now. If you really want to know, I passed your group of cutthroats on my way here. They informed me that the Ghost Chasers ordered them to stay away from this camp. And as I approached your camp, for a fraction of a second, I sensed a strong and mysterious power. I believe it was the Zunji Light. Do you know what that means?"

"What!" Benny jerked upright, wine spilling from his glass.

"Yes, my friend, it's a good thing you kept your cool tonight. Otherwise the slave girl, the slave boy, and the Nain horse wouldn't be the only things you lost."

The Merchant of Northwood touched his neck with a sweaty palm. *I'm lucky to be alive.* But in the meantime, his keen nose detected the biggest deal ever, and a crafty smile appeared on his face. "The higher the stakes, the bigger the profits. Cheers!"

After dinner, Benny's mood improved further. Two of Councilman Trumbond's servants came in carrying an ancient treasure chest. They placed the chest in front of the merchant and opened it for his inspection.

"All yours, Benny. Oh! Here are the gold and silver serpent keys for the trunk. Worth a fortune themselves." Trumbond passed the keys to Buddo.

Benny's eyes glinted as he picked up a green jade gourd from the chest. *The Echoing Gourd! With this, Shanui shall be mine forever.* He carefully placed the jade gourd back in the trunk. "Buddo! I'm putting you in charge of these treasures—careful with them."

"Yes!" The muscled man snapped his fingers. Two slave hunters rushed over to carry the heavy antique trunk, and a slave girl led them away to a storage tent.

Trumbond flopped down onto a pile of cushions. "Benny old boy! Brutan and I, we've got some urgent business to attend to down south. We'll be leaving before dawn tomorrow. I'm counting on you to deliver my vase. How about you take it to your castle and I'll swing by to pick it up."

Benny beamed. "No problem, Councilman, come anytime. You and Brutan are welcome, always."

XEIYÉN, LEADER OF the Didee-guards, stood atop the Outsiders' van and watched the gathering at the outdoor kitchen. He saw many traveling merchants arguing around Bayjai Arma's food-laden table. Xeiyén and his comrades had joined this particular group of merchants for almost a week, yet this was the first time the Dideetone had seen the humans more interested in arguing than eating. His eyes strayed to Michi, who was hugging a big vase, and the Dideetone froze. *Didee-jiny! Am I seeing things?* The unusual but symmetrical gold design on the pottery looked just like the lost door to the ancient Didee-tunnel. Although he had only seen the entrance to the tunnel once, Xeiyén was positive that the priceless vase was identical in every aspect to the lost door to the Didee-fortune cave.

He closed his eyes and remembered back to when the Mighty Vong led his household and Didee-guards south, after the disagreement in the Didee-council three thousand years ago. The party had traveled from the Didee-palace under the protection of night, through the vast forest, and reached the outskirts of Northwood City before daybreak. That area was far from the protection of trees, bushes, or caves. As a result, Xeiyén had instructed the Didee-guards to surround the Mighty Vong's family. But the Mighty Vong spoke a command and, amid two huge rocks, an opening to a smooth tunnel appeared. While the other Didee-guards escorted the Mighty Vong's family into the ancient tunnel, Xeiyén had stood on top of one of the big rocks and scouted out the land.

Just like I'm doing now, standing high above and scanning the landscape. But on that special occasion three thousand years ago, Xeiyén had observed the entrance to the tunnel. To his surprise, he found that the tunnel was actually a strikingly decorated bell-shaped vase. The rim of the pottery was the opening to the cave, the body formed the beginning of the secret tunnel, and the bottom of the vase was embedded within the rocks. He distinctly remembered the matching gold patterns on the well-polished surface to the tunnel entry.

Xeiyén, coming from generations of Didee-artists, had a feeling that the vase the little girl was holding now and the entrance to the ancient Didee-tunnel were one and the same. The door to the ancient treasure had disappeared, according to the news one thousand two hundred years ago. Communication between their Northern kin and the south Dideetones had come to an end soon after that.

Where did this human girl get the vase? What is she planning to do with it? By the manner the girl was holding the vase, it was evident that she was aware of its worth.

Xeiyén didn't have long to wait for the answer to his second question. The leader of the Didee-guards was speechless when he found that the most treasured possession of the Dideetones was the price of freedom for a couple of young slaves. He knew that the Merchant of Northwood was one of the most ruthless businessmen in the Kingdom of Lanhur, but he had had no idea the merchant could stoop so low as to swindle a child. *Why, that treasured vase is worth more than a hundred times all the slaves in the kingdom.*

Xeiyén watched the Merchant of Northwood carry the vase and leave the outdoor kitchen. It was then that Xeiyén made a quick decision. He would steal the priceless vase from right under Benny's nose. *Why not? After all, the merchant got it for a steal. But I do feel bad for that little girl. She really is okay even by the Tensengin Immortals' standards.*

Xeiyén turned to give Michi an admiring look, but his attention was arrested by a sight above the little girl. A bucket of water, ten feet from the ground and supported by a Didee-hook, floated slowly over Michi's head toward the pink tent entrance. *Didee-jiny!* Just when Xeiyén was about to bounce down and investigate the bizarre situation, Xane, his second in command, landed beside him.

"Hello, Cousin. I see you are relaxing as usual while your underlings are scurrying around doing slave work."

Xeiyén frowned. "What's so hard about keeping an eye on two Dideetonies? And what's that bucket doing parading above the humans?"

"That water bucket, my dear cousin, is the first installment of the two-baths-a-day routine ordered by the Dideetonies."

Xeiyén quirked his brow. "It's as bad as that?"

"Oh, Lei's not so bad. It's Polly. There's no pleasing her."

Ah, the hoity-toity grandmammy. The Captain of the Didee-guards smiled. "Did you try crackers?"

Xane grinned. "Polly doesn't want a cracker! Polly doesn't want a cracker! Polly wants a bath!"

Xeiyén laughed, and Xane studied him with deep affection. "It's nice to see you in a merry mood, Captain of the Guards."

"You didn't come all the way here just to hold my hand—what's in your hands anyways?"

"Do you think these towels are extra soft, perfumed, and cuddly?" Xane held up several bath towels in his right hand, and a garment in his left. "How about this outfit? Is it classy, elegant, and in style?"

Xeiyén recognized the skimpy clothing as belonging to the young slave girls from Benny's tent. "You must be desperate."

"Oh! We all are! According to Grandmammy, this is our last chance to show our Southern hospitality. I'm open to suggestions, Cousin."

The thought of his Didee-guards scurrying around looking for bubbled bath water, scented soft towels, and female undies was priceless. *Too bad this is our last chance. I wouldn't mind seeing what Polly's reaction would be to the scanty outfits.*

Xeiyén swung down from the top of the van. "Come on! Let's take a look at the bag the Outsiders left in the van."

"I think you should know," Xane said as he followed his cousin, "her High and Mighty has already done her kitchen window shopping and refused all the models in the open kitchen. The way she criticized their clothes, you'd think she's the real queen."

Xeiyén held back a smile. "Dear Cousin, when was the last time you saw a female Dideetone?"

"Ages. I see your point. Guess I'm out of practice."

After landing on the back seat of the van, Xeiyén took out his Didee-hook and tossed it toward Archoy's bag. The hook acted like a hand, opening the huge tote bag. Then, the Didee-hook shimmered, splitting into many small coat hangers hovering over the bag. Rosalyn's flowery and laced dresses, in miniature sizes, began to pop out of the bag, and they floated up to the hangers.

"The store is open, take your pick. According to the housekeeper, these are name brands and of the latest fashions."

Xane dropped the items in his hands and rubbed his palms together. "Say—these are most certainly classy, elegant, and in style. Do they come in matching hats, shoes, and purses?"

"'Fraid not. Stop goofing off!"

"Just kidding." Xane took out a small box, bounced up to the hanging outfits, and started to "glamorize" them. "Gold! Silver! Diamond! Sapphire! Ruby! Pearl! Emerald—!"

Rosalyn's flowery dresses now shimmered, covered with extravagant jewels and golden embroidery. Glittering in the moonlight, they had become priceless treasures that any noble would vie to own.

"Oh, don't de-glamorize the rejects when you're done," Xeiyén said. "I'm sure the human girl would appreciate the improvements. And tell the others I'm calling a meeting in half an hour."

"Does that include her High and Mighty?"

Xeiyén gave Xane a severe look. "Especially her." He picked up the towels and the scanty outfit that his cousin had dropped on the back seat. "I'll deliver the towels and return the garment. See you in half an hour."

Xeiyén bounced out of the car window, making his way to the pink tent. He saw one of his guards pacing back and forth behind the tent, and Xeiyén landed next to him.

The Didee-guard dove for the articles Xeiyén was holding. "Oh! Thank goodness," the guard exclaimed.

Must be more desperate than I thought. This madness has got to stop. Why, my guards are acting out of character—even their voices sound strange! Xeiyén backed off, holding the outfits out of reach. "Not these, you idiot!"

"There's no need for name calling, Captain Xeiyén. Grandmammy and I really do appreciate what you and your guards are doing for us."

Xeiyén paused and took a good look at the guard. "Didee-jiny! Lei, what are you doing dressed like one of my guards?"

Princess Leianna gave Xeiyén a rueful smile. "Would you rather I join Grandmammy and turn your Didee-guards into Didee-handmaidens?"

His features softened. "I'm sorry, Lei. I didn't mean to be rude. It's just that there's an urgent matter—"

"And two silly Dideetonies are keeping you away from adventure, fame, and glory," a voice from inside the tent interrupted. Queen Pollyanna, wrapped in a sack, stepped out from a small flap in the back of the pink tent. "Captain, give me the towel and whatever garments you've got, then give me five minutes."

I guess I'm going to get a chance to find out what she thinks of the scanty outfit, after all. Keeping a straight face, Xeiyén passed the clothing to Lei. "We're having a meeting in twenty minutes." Then he turned and made for Benny's tent. *With any luck, I should be able to retrieve the Didee-tunnel door and be back for the meeting with time to spare.*

Xeiyén reached the biggest tent on the far side of the camp, then went around to the back, slipping in a moment later. He found himself in a storage area piled high with trunks, both locked and open. Of the ones that were open, some were filled with gold platters, bowls, and goblets, while others were filled with fine silk, ornamental jewelry, and laces.

Xeiyén bounced on top of one of the locked trunks and peeped through the key hole. *Just gold coins.* He froze when he saw the flap to the storage area open. Two slave hunters, carrying a huge antique trunk, entered. A slave girl followed them, with Buddo close behind.

"Careful! It's fragile! Yes, set it down next to the silk trunk. Okay, you may leave." Buddo took out two keys, one gold, one silver, and bent down to lock the trunk. Straightening, he left the keys in the key holes and stood back. "Any thief trying to open this chest will be in for a niiiice surprise." Buddo snickered before leaving the tent.

After Buddo left, Xeiyén bounced down from the gold coin trunk and landed in front of the chest with the serpent keys. *So, the vase is in this trunk.* He studied the lock for a while, then took out his Didee-rope and gave the serpent keys a sharp crack.

A loud hiss sounded in reply. Two snakes, one gold and one silver, wriggled out of the key holes. The gold snake lunged toward the Dideetone as the silver one turned to attack the Didee-rope.

Xeiyén did a summersault and landed on the silk trunk, narrowly escaping the gold snake's jaws. His Didee-rope fared better, smacking the silver snake's tail once. The enraged snake whipped around to retaliate, but the Didee-rope had already returned to Xeiyén's hand. The snakes hovered by the keyholes and glared with beady eyes at the little thief.

I need my Didee-hook. "I'll be back," Xeiyén shouted.

The snakes let out a frustrated hiss, then returned to the key holes and transformed back into the gold and silver serpent keys.

Xeiyén left the tent and made his way to the outdoor kitchen. He saw that the traveling merchants were finally showing their usual fondness for food.

Xeiyén arrived at the back of the pink tent and entered by the small flap. On seeing their captain, the Didee-guards stood up and saluted, then sat down again. Xeiyén glanced across the bunk bed and saw Polly, wearing one of the Outsiders' "glamorized" garments, eyeing him with disapproval. Xeiyén ignored her completely and turned to smile at Lei. He was arrested by her deep bluish-violet eyes. *Is it humor I see in the depths of those beautiful eyes? One can drown in them if one is not careful.* The Captain of the Didee-guards shook himself to clear away the heady feeling.

He focused his attention on his comrades. "As you all know, about twelve hundred years ago, the door to the Ancient Didee-tunnel disappeared. I don't have to go into detail on how much our Northern kin suffered without the protection of the safe passage—"

A sob broke out and Xeiyén froze. All ten Didee-guards turned to look at the two crying Dideetonies with shock. Xeiyén frowned. *I don't like this. Our Northern kin lost their magical powers. But to show such signs of becoming mortal . . .*

Lei put her arms around Polly, then lifted her tear-filled eyes to face the Didee-guards. "Please excuse us."

Xeiyén tried to remember what the mortals would say in such situations. "You've both had a long day. Why don't you rest here. My comrades and I can continue our meeting in the Outsiders' van—"

Polly took a deep, shuddering breath and controlled her emotions with great effort. "No Captain, please go on. Lei and I are very much a part of this."

"Very well. I have reason to believe that the door to our Didee-tunnel was stolen, and is now locked in an ancient chest in Benny's tent."

Murmurs broke out and Xeiyén held up his hand for silence. "I have seen the vase tonight right in the open kitchen. A little human girl named Michi traded our priceless door for the freedom of two young slaves—"

Shouts of amazement rang out, and everyone seemed to be talking at once. Xeiyén looked at the Dideetonies and found them whispering to each other.

He waited patiently, and was rewarded for his trouble when the Dideetonies stopped talking and Polly turned to him. "Captain, I don't think Michi stole the vase—"

"Of course not. The human child could not be more than seven or eight years old. How she came by the vase is not as important as how much Benny actually knows about the real worth of the vase. Because only a Dideetone . . ." Xeiyén paused and gave Polly and Lei a meaningful look before continuing. " . . . or a Dideetonie can give commands to the Didee-tunnel door."

Polly became indignant. "Captain! You don't have to hint that Lei or I would be so stupid as to be captured and used by this merchant."

"Grandmammy, Xeiyén's only trying to tell us that it is of the utmost importance that we don't put ourselves under the mercy of the bad merchant."

"Thank you, Lei," Xeiyén continued before the hoity-toity grandmammy could think of a retort. "I tried to open the chest the vase was stored in, but was confronted by two guardians. I think we can tame them, but we might alarm Benny and his cutthroats before we have the serpents under our power."

"You are right as usual, Captain," Xane said. "Now all of us must be even more careful than before. The humans must not know about us. So, what do you suggest we do?"

"It's time for us to cross the boundary and venture north."

"But the Mighty Vong forbade us from crossing the north border," one of the Didee-guards voiced.

"With three exceptions. Either by his order, to rescue King Windune and his household, or in pursuit of the Didee-tunnel door. I'm advising that we bide our time and keep an eye on Benny and his men. We know the merchant is on his way back to his lair. Opportunities should present themselves as we travel north with him. Now, the question is should we move to Benny's tent, or stay with the pink tent?"

All the Didee-guards agreed that, although staying with Benny would make it easier to spy on him, the risk of detection far outweighed the convenience. Bayjai Arma's pink tent would remain as the base of the Didee-guards' operations. Xeiyén divided tasks for each of his guards, and they left to fulfill their duties immediately. He held a smile in check when he saw Xane's dismay at being assigned the job of bodyguarding the Dideetonies. *I'll deal with his complaints when the time comes.* Xeiyén moved to the entrance of the pink tent and peeked outside. In the outdoor kitchen, he saw that the humans were near the end of their meal. Then he saw Joseph and Michi get up from the table.

"Everything's so yummy! Jo, Arma really is a great cook," Michi said as she licked her lips.

Joseph grabbed a napkin and wiped Michi's face. "More than made up for missing the Markums' dinner banquet?"

"You bet! But I do miss Christa—I wonder how she's doing? I only hope their guests are as pleased with their food as I'm with mine."

"Well, Sweet, it's going to be a long traveling day tomorrow, so I suggest we get ready for bed early."

"Alright, Jo."

Xeiyén saw Michi come toward the entrance to the tent, and he backed off. "The humans are done with their gathering, so let's disappear." Xeiyén, Xane, Polly, and Lei hid behind the potato sacks before Michi entered the tent.

WHILE MICHI PREPARED for an early night, the Markum mansion, where her journey first began, had visitors. Prince Norlen of Nain and his faithful servant, BoDak, were sizing up the Markums' estate from a safe distance. Their original plan of sneaking in had been abandoned when they found, on reaching the mansion, that it was full of activity. The young prince on his royal steed seemed engrossed in the to-do at the grand entryway.

BoDak's stomach growled, and he stole a glance at the youth. "Your Highness, should we try the back? It might prove a bit easier."

"Bo, explain again to me what you meant this morning when you said that we were being summoned."

BoDak scratched his head. "It's the necklace, Your Highness. I mean your necklace. You know—the one you refuse to wear."

Prince Norlen turned to stare at the jewelry-laden barbarian of a warrior. "Are you sure it's not your earring making you hear things?"

"Oh no, Your Highness. And it's your earring—the one you refuse to wear."

"Ah. Well, we've already come this far. A further delay in our search to recover the stolen Nain horse shouldn't make much of a difference. Would you like to join Lord Markum's guests for a feast?"

BoDak swallowed hard. "I would like that above all things, Your Highness. But of course we're not invited."

Prince Norlen regarded his servant's downcast head. "Bo, do you have my royal seal?"

"Yes, Your Highness. Safely tucked away right here in my pouch." He retrieved an ornate ring and held it daintily up to the youth.

Prince Norlen vaulted down from his purebred Nain horse. "Get on the horse and put the ring on." The prince bent and scooped a handful of dirt, then smudged his face.

"Begging your pardon, Your—"

"Bo! Stop calling me 'Your Highness,' and do as I say."

The bewildered servant got on the horse. "Which finger should the ring go on, Your High-I mean Prince Norlen ... "

The young prince guided his horse toward the well lighted and crowded entryway of the Markum estate. "Which one doesn't have any rings yet?"

BoDak lifted his hands and examined them. "Uhh ... they all have your rings—you know, the ones you refuse to wear. Oh, wait, my right thumb."

"Put it there, then." They entered the open iron gates. The young prince smiled and nodded to the gawking footmen and pageboys as they walked up the paved driveway.

BoDak struggled with the ring. "I can't. It's too small— Your Highness! Where are we going?"

"Shh ... Let me do the talking. Oh Bo, you are now Prince Norlen, so act like it."

"What? I—"

"That's an order!"

Before the confused and frightened warrior could ask any more questions, they heard voices from two beautifully dressed girls coming their way.

"Oh Rosalyn, look, we've got more guests. Have you ever seen a more gorgeous horse?" the girl with the golden blond curls exclaimed.

"And a more exotic rider?" the brunette called Rosalyn teased. The girls giggled.

Prince Norlen stepped in front of the girls, bowed, and executed a Nain greeting sign while BoDak sat frozen atop the noble white horse. "My master Prince Norlen of Nain greets the ladies of Lord Markum's court."

Both girls stopped giggling as their eyes filled with wonder. The brunette recovered first and made a curtsy to the jewelry-laden "prince." The blond haired girl followed suit.

At that moment, a maid approached them. "Miss Natalie, Miss Rosalyn, come, dinner is served."

Natalie smiled at the warrior on top of the horse. "Pauline, His Royal Highness Prince Norlen of Nain has come to call on Grandpapa."

"Very good, Miss Natalie. I'll see to the accommodations for His Highness." Pauline bobbed to the new guests then dashed away.

A smile twitched at the corner of the dirt-smudged young Prince's mouth. *It's working! Looks like the Markums will be having more guests than they were expecting. Now, to get Bo established in the lion's den.* "His Royal Highness Prince Norlen of Nain requests the honor of escorting Lady Natalie and Lady Rosalyn to the dining hall," he said. On seeing the girls' faces become animated, the Prince gave BoDak's foot a dig, and the giant warrior vaulted down from the horse so fast that the girls' jaws dropped in admiration.

Looking straight at his dear servant who looked like he was about to faint, the young prince bowed and motioned for BoDak to proceed. "Your Highness, your dinner awaits you." With satisfaction, he watched as his frightened servant suddenly transformed into a gallant prince.

BoDak walked toward the girls with dignity, and the little ladies offered their hands. The warrior took each hand in his, then lifted Natalie's to his lips, kissed it, turned, and did the same with Rosalyn's. The girls sighed and seemed ready to swoon. But of course BoDak would suffer none of it. Not before he had his meal anyway. He ushered the girls firmly toward the entrance.

While all eyes were on the trio, the young prince guided his horse toward the back of the mansion. He passed bustling servants carrying trays of drinks and hors d'œuvres. The well dressed nobles were strolling by a lighted marble fountain on the side of the building, sampling from the lavish trays. Prince Norlen kept to a path that was under the dark shadows of the trees, and continued to edge his way to the back. He stopped when he saw two figures, engrossed in a hushed conversation, beneath a walnut tree next to several swings. Prince Norlen recognized one of them to be Pauline.

"How was I to know that Michi would suddenly change her mind and leave with her other brother," Pauline whispered.

"What about Christa? Why can't you get her to take the stuff."

Pauline shrugged her shoulders. "She's not even coming down for the feast. I can't get the little girl to eat if she doesn't want to. Look, Michi is the food monster, and with her gone—"

"It is imperative that I find out what the girls saw in the armor room this morning."

"Have a heart, Owlut, I'm running off my feet with the extra guests—" Pauline stopped when the balcony door, on the second floor above the tree, opened and light streamed out.

Prince Norlen saw Pauline rush to the back door near the walnut tree, open it, and disappear within. Of Owlut, he saw no sign.

OLD MR. MARKUM and his grandson Cedric stood by the study room table, their heads bent over a thick volume.

The old man turned to his grandson. "What do you think?"

Cedric straightened. "I think his ring is real alright." He flipped the book to the next page and pointed to a drawing of a jewelry-laden barbarian warrior on a Nain horse. "Recognize the earring?"

"Yes," old Mr. Markum said. "Two pieces of jewelry match perfectly." He stroked his bearded chin. "To protect the secret of Zanquei, we have not used our title since Lord Chris Markum, yet this Prince Norlen uses it as if it was the most natural thing to do."

Cedric frowned slightly. "Did he?"

"Didn't you hear Natalie and Rosalyn telling everyone—" Old Mr. Markum stopped and frowned also. "I see what you mean. Come to think of it, this Prince Norlen hardly said a word."

"Except to conveniently drop his royal seal, say 'Whoops,' then allow you to pick it up and examine it at close range."

"By Jove, he did it on purpose. And to think I was congratulating myself for checking up on him so artfully."

"Hardly. That ring was never on his finger before tonight."

"How do you know that, Cedric?"

"Two things. The exposed part of his hand was perfectly tanned, and the royal seal is too small for his fingers."

The old man slowly nodded his head. "What do you suppose is his purpose for this visit?"

"If it wasn't for the authenticity of the royal seal, I'd say he was here to con us out of a meal."

"No," his grandfather said. "He cannot be here for that."

Cedric shrugged his shoulders. "Might I suggest that you go down and continue to receive your guests—"

"Goodness, you are right." Old Mr. Markum moved to the door of his study room. "See what you can do about Christa. She can't just stay in her room and sulk," he said before leaving.

Something happened in the secret Armor Room. I'm not quite sure what, but I better keep an eye on Christa until I know just how serious it is. Cedric knocked on his little sister's bedroom door.

"Come in," Christa invited.

He opened the door and saw his sister sitting on the edge of her bed. "Hello, not coming down to receive our guests?"

"Not interested." Christa rose and walked out to the balcony.

Like that, huh. I guess I'll have to use a little persuasion. He went to join her. "What's wrong?"

Christa leaned over the railing. "I miss Michi and Jo already."

"Ah. Well, Anthony and Rosalyn are here."

Christa shrugged her shoulders and gazed moodily down at the empty swings.

Cedric put his arm around his little sister's shoulders. "By the way, we're getting the royal treatment. Let's see. We have Lord Hegan of the Anguo Council, who has been asking for you. Prince Norlen of Nain, a very intriguing fellow—looks and eats more like a barbarian than a prince. You'd be interested in his story. The poor fellow is on a quest to retrieve his stolen Nain horse. There's also Bill and Rachael Jones, Ambassadors to the Kingdom of Lanhur—"

Christa turned to look at her brother. "The Joneses are going to Lanhur?"

"They are the newly appointed ambassadors, and yes they'll be going to their new post within a few days. Come Christa, you must go say goodbye to Rachael. She has been asking for you, also."

"Will they be stationed nearby Southland where Michi's new home is?"

Cedric shook his head. "The Ruling Councils of the Kingdom of Lanhur are in Northland. Besides, Mom would never agree to your staying with the Joneses, no matter how fond Rachael is of you." On seeing Christa's crestfallen face, he reached into his pocket and took out Joseph's old harmonica. "Michi left this for you."

"Jo's harmonica!" Christa grabbed it from him. "Michi said nothing about this—Oh! She's the best of friends.

Now I'll be able to play it when I miss her and Jo. You must teach me to play better, though."

"Sure thing, Christa," Cedric said. "Come on, let's join the others." He offered his hand, and she took it. Together they walked away from the balcony and out of the bedroom, unaware of the motionless shadow beneath the walnut tree.

Before they even reached the formal dining area, Cedric and Christa could hear Lord Hegan's voice boom above the others'. They smiled at each other, then Cedric encouraged his little sister to join Lord Hegan.

"I'm sure you will be more than pleased with your new home, Cheryl. I've been told by the highest authority of the Anguo Council that my request was sent to the Kingdom of Lanhur along with all those other important documents. And even more, it was granted by the leader of the Elder Council himself. Imagine that. The most powerful man in the Kingdom of Lanhur overseeing your family's needs! And I should say nothing is too good for Rosalyn and my little Michi—which reminds me I'm going to miss that little rascal. Say, where is my Dumpling Christa?"

"Here I am, Uncle Hegan." Christa materialized behind him.

"Oh! My little Christa-in-the-box, where have you popped out from?" Lord Hegan reached out, and Christa went into his arms. The burly old man crushed Christa's small form, then held her out at arm's length to study her features. "Do I detect sadness in those beautiful blue eyes of yours, little one?"

Christa gave a good imitation of Michi's "poor little me" expression, and Lord Hegan melted on the spot. "Emily! Get the bedroom next to Christa's ready—I'm sending my men out for Michi. Which route did you say Jo was taking, Cheryl?"

Christa's eyes lit up and she seemed ready to shout for joy, but visibly checked herself when her Grandpapa gave her a severe look. The little girl was in the bad book on account of her early morning armor room incident. She turned to Cedric, who was now sitting between Rosalyn and another dainty young maiden, for help. But Christa's pleas were lost, as both girls were engaged in a competition for Cedric's attention. The two girls were giggling, batting their eyelashes, and leaning heavily on him. For his part, Cedric discouraged neither's advances, taking the opportunity to stroke both ladies' backs. The sight of the barbarian prince reaching out for another helping of the pot roast plus trimmings further distracted Cedric. Amused, he quirked a brow at his grandfather. Catching his grandson's expression, the old man turned to BoDak and frowned.

Rachel Jones, sitting across from Cedric, smiled and waved to Christa. The little girl waved back, but looked at Rachael pleadingly. The kind old lady immediately leaned forward, amidst dishes of pot roast and trimmings. "I think Christa could use a little helping also," she whispered.

Cedric took the hint and came to his little sister's rescue. "Hegan old buddy, it's too late. You've gone and made the most powerful man in the Kingdom of Lanhur oversee the installation of the Dallion's toilet at Backland Hectares. I'm afraid with such comfort, they'll just settle in and won't be back anytime soon."

"Cedric!" Emily Markum scolded.

BoDak reached out for still more of the pot roast.

Lord Hegan patted Christa's hand. "True, too true. Cedric's right. The toilet is in—the Dallions'll have to stay."

Emily Markum lifted the huge platter of fresh fruits. "Fruit salad, anyone?"

Cedric smiled. *There's nothing more effective than mentioning the unmentionables when it comes to a diversion.* Then he caught his grandfather's eye and winked at the old man when BoDak volunteered to take the fruit platter from his mother.

Old Mr. Markum scratched his head and gave the prince a queer look. He then stood and faced Mr. and Mrs. Dallion, Anthony, and Rosalyn. The old man lifted his goblet. "As much as I'll miss you all—I'll drink to your health and to our friendship, may it endure forever."

"Hear! Hear!" and "Cheer! Cheer!" rang out as all the guests lifted their drinks for the toast.

Pauline, holding a tray with a bottle of wine and a small wine glass, rushed from the kitchen to the formal dining area. She refilled old Mr. Markum's goblet, moved to Lord Hegan's side and refilled his, then filled the small wine glass and handed it to Christa.

Christa gaped at the filled glass before looking eagerly to her grandpapa. Old Mr. Markum scowled, but Lord Hegan gave a jolly laugh. "A little wine never hurt anyone. The girl'll have to learn to drink the stuff sometime."

Seeing old Mr. Markum relent, Natalie and Rosalyn insisted their glasses be filled with wine, also. Pauline cheerfully went about filling for them and the other guests, and when she saw Christa down the wine for the next toast, she grinned.

YOUNG PRINCE NORLEN stood rooted to the spot. *I'm going to solve this mystery if it's the last thing I do.* He strained his eyes and scanned the area surrounding the walnut tree. There was nothing suspicious. So, where did Owlut go? Then he heard voices coming from the balcony above the tree, and his attention was caught by the sight of the fair haired little girl and the handsome youth leaning over the railing. Prince Norlen listened to the conversation up on the balcony with interest. Suddenly, the prince realized that he was no longer alone. Owlut had somehow appeared under the walnut tree once again and was listening as well. Norlen mentally cursed, upset at himself for breaking his watch to look up at the balcony. But the scene between the girl and the youth had been too eye-catching.

The mysterious man under the walnut tree was obviously interested in the little girl. The prince stood patiently and fixed his eyes on Owlut. Time passed, and he thought of BoDak sitting at the food-laden table, and smiled. The silence and the stillness of the air was suffocating, and the Nain horse flicked its tail. Prince Norlen immediately reached out and patted his horse, but the motionless figure under the tree moved. *Oh well, so much for detective work. It was a good try anyway.*

At that moment, a strange voice issued from the figure, who was now facing the back door. "Christa under my spell, come to the swings."

Prince Norlen held his breath, and was amazed when he saw the little girl come out from the back door and move to stand, rigid, by the swings.

"Christa under my spell, tell me what you saw inside the armor room this morning."

"Naked women."

Owlut's jaw dropped and the young prince covered his mouth with his hand to smother a titter.

Then he saw Owlut lean toward Christa and sniff. The little girl hiccuped, and Owlut stood back. "You are drunk!"

The back door opened, and out stumbled BoDak. "I say—this is nice—and—cozy—" The clumsy warrior staggered toward the swings.

BoDak! He's drunk, too. What kind of wine do they serve in there?

BoDak grabbed one of the swings and leaned on it. "Begging your pardon—Miss—These are the—swings— aren't they?"

Prince Norlen turned to see Owlut's reaction, and found that the mysterious man had once again eluded him, disappearing into the darkness. Norlen guided his horse, making his way to the walnut tree. The prince took a good look at Christa, and found her glazed and unflinching eyes most puzzling. He waved his hand in front of her. No reaction. He snapped his fingers at her face. No reaction. He turned to BoDak and saw his servant had settled on a swing.

"Your Highness. Your Highness—" Prince Norlen whispered.

BoDak fought to reopen his eyes. When he succeeded, he muttered, "Oh yes," and fumbled around in his pockets. With a smile, the jewelry-laden warrior pulled out a string of grapes from the inner pocket of his vest and handed them to Prince Norlen. Then a couple of apples and pears from his pants pocket followed. Suddenly, BoDak turned to Christa. "You're freed—after you take—a—nap."

Prince Norlen also turned to look at Christa. He saw the little girl yawn and begin to fall. The prince rushed over and was just in time to scoop her up into his arms. *What a pickle I'm in. It would be most embarrassing if I'm caught right now.*

"So, the food from Lord Markum's generous table is not enough to quench your thirst, sir knight. You are now resorting to abducting the fairest lady of Lord Markum's court," Cedric Markum said, arms folded across his chest and leaning against the wall by the back door.

Oh, great! Do I drop the fruit, or do I drop the girl? Or both? Prince Norlen did nothing but stand, holding the incriminating evidence.

"What—did she—see in the—armor room?" BoDak slurred.

Cedric Markum came toward them. "Is that why you are after my little sister?"

Quick, think of something. "Ahh . . . actually, we're trying to save your sister from this unholy place."

Cedric stopped. "What are you talking about?"

That's it, get him on the defensive. "I don't know the particulars, but your little sister obviously saw someone in the armor room dilly-dallying with some naked women. Some blackmailers are trying to squeeze the details out of her by getting her drunk."

Cedric's eyes narrowed. "And just how does getting my sister drunk help?"

That's a good one, let me think... The sudden silence was broken only by the unmistakable snoring coming from Christa. "Well, you know what they say. Many times when people are drunk, they're more apt to tell the truth—you know, uninhibited subconsciousness." The prince turned to look at the snoring damsel in distress. "In her case, she konks out instead."

"And you truly believe in all this mumble jumble you just said?"

"Well, it's logical—"

"Relax, you've convinced me. Who are you, anyways?"

"I'm the pageboy to His Royal Highness Prince Norlen of Nain."

"Nice to meet you, pageboy. I'm Cedric. Let me have Christa, and you can help your master to his room."

Prince Norlen breathed a sigh of relief, handed Christa to her brother, then went and helped BoDak to his feet. Together, they followed Cedric to the back door and entered the house. The moment the door closed, Cedric dashed away toward the music room.

He placed Christa gently on top of the grand piano, then moved to the harp that was hanging on the wall, swinging it to one side. Cedric motioned to Prince Norlen. "Come on!"

The prince dropped BoDak and rushed to Cedric's side. He saw that there were two spy holes, and Cedric was already looking through one of them. Prince Norlen helped himself to the other.

Through the hole, the prince saw that he was looking back at the walnut tree and swings from a different angle. Then he saw a most amazing sight. From the tree above, there was a flutter of wings. A bird descended, then transformed into a human. *So, that's how Owlut eluded me.* "It's Owlut," the prince said.

"Yes, he's an owl."

Prince Norlen stood to attention. "You are saying he's a Superior Demon?"

Cedric turned to the prince. "I don't know about superior, but he certainly is a demon." Then he turned back to look through the hole again. "Well, he's talking to himself. Wish we could hear what he's saying."

The prince dashed to BoDak's side and leaned his ear close to the earring. " . . . sleep, then you are all released from my spell," he heard Owlut's strange voice saying. *Now I'm beginning to understand.*

Prince Norlen stood up. "Aside from your sister and my master, who else drank this potent wine?"

"Practically everyone except me—oh, and the servants, of course."

The prince smacked his forehead. "Pauline! I wonder what mischief she's up to?"

Cedric grinned. "Oh, her. I gave her my potent wine when everyone wished the Joneses well at their new post as ambassadors to the Kingdom of Lanhur. It was the third toast, I do believe." On seeing the pageboy's puzzled expression, he elaborated. "Pauline used to work for Bill and Rachael Jones. They were the ones that introduced her to come and work for us."

"I see," Prince Norlen said. "What would be more natural than having a former servant wish her ex-boss well by drinking a toast—"

"Exactly! Which reminds me, I'm famished. Let's put these two to bed, then we'll go hunt up some chow. I'm sure we can find something more substantial than apples, pears, and grapes, Your Highness." Cedric paused when he heard a sharp intake of breath from the prince, then winked. "Although I'm afraid there's not much hope of finding pot roast with all the trimmings, there are ribs."

BoDak stirred and the prince eyed him with affection. "Cedric, meet BoDak, my faithful servant."

"Oh, yes. The pot roast monster. We've met."

Prince Norlen smiled. "I thank you for your generosity." He then made a Nain greeting sign, and Cedric returned likewise.

"Well met, Lord Cedric Markum," the prince said at the same moment Cedric said, "Well met, Prince Norlen of Nain." Then the two youths clasped their hands and laughed, much the same way Lord Chris Markum and the King of Nain did more than a thousand years ago.

5

GENTLE PERSUASION

IN THE EARLY hours of the night, all was dark and quiet around the campsite except for the snap of the cooking fire and the whispering in Bayjai Arma's outdoor kitchen. Xeiyén, Captain of the Didee-guards, perched himself atop one of the warm rolls that the cook had set on the rack to cool. "Now Arma, let me get this straight. You're saying that Michi helped herself to the vase in Benny's tent, then turned around and traded it for the freedom of those two slaves?"

"I know it sounds far fetched, but that's what Jo told me. Although Michi insisted that her black eye was essential in the bargain as well—"

"That's another thing. Who gave her the bruise?" Xeiyén interrupted.

Bayjai Arma stopped kneading the dough and chuckled. "She did. And she's responsible for the huge bruise on Archoy's forehead as well. Oh, and she probably wounded whoever was out there in the dark while she practiced her potato peeling tricks last night. A fitting punishment for the nosy fellow."

"Didee-jiny!" Xeiyén bounced off the bread roll forcefully and landed on the kitchen table, scattering the flour. "Arma, are you saying that Michi gave Captain Hua the black eye?"

The cook gave an amused laugh as she went to take out a batch of bread from the crude stove. "So that's who was

lurking out there. I don't recall anyone by that name joining our camp. This Captain Hua must be a wanderer."

"He's a whole lot more than that! He's the Senginfan
Defenders' new captain."

The cook spun around to face the Dideetone. Her hand
holding the fresh bread made contact with the hot stove,
and she let go with a yelp. The Didee-rope instantly left
Xeiyén's side and snatched the falling bread from the air.
Bayjai Arma ignored her burnt hand or the Didee-rope's
impressive bread rescuing routine. "Xeiyén! How did you
know?" she exclaimed with horror.

"Polly introduced us." Xeiyén shook his head at the
incredulous look that appeared on the cook's face. "Calm
down, Arma, no harm done so far. This Captain Hua is
nothing like the others—he's very young, though strength's
in him, and he's got a sense of humor."

Arma quirked a dubious brow. "Really?"

Xeiyén nodded. "Highly skilled, and yet not quick to
anger. An unlikely combination for a Senginfan. It was Lei
who mentioned the potato projectiles Michi flung at the
captain. They alerted him to our hiding place in your tent.
You really are taking a great chance by allowing us to stay
with you; my comrades and I thank you for your kindness."

"You know I love the company, and since I'm now a
mortal, there's no danger of detection by the Senginfans."
Lifting her hurt and wrinkled hand for show, Arma smiled
ruefully. "I doubt anyone who knew me before could recognize me now. Aging is a fascinating process. You ought
to try it sometime."

"No thanks."

Realizing that Arma had failed to grasp the significance
of Hua's bruise...a mere mortal could not possibly have
bruised any Senginfan Defender without the use of special
gear, much less their captain...Xeiyén decided to spare her
further distress. *I've never heard of potatoes as deadly weapons*

before, but there's always a first. Remembering that "misery loves company" was one of the humans' sayings, he decided to comfort her instead. "In a way, Polly and Lei are much like you. They've lost most of their magical power. However, they were stripped of it, while you gave it up voluntarily."

Bayjai Arma tilted her head and frowned. "And is that supposed to cheer me up?" She lifted her chin with pride. "Xeiyén, Captain of the Didee-guards," she declared, "I'll have you know that I might have a human body, but I'm still a Tensengin Immortal in essence. And any mortal suffering is only going to give me chills."

Xeiyén slapped Arma's pinky finger. "That's the spirit!" Arma gave him a scolding look, and he bowed. "Areama, the most sympathetic handmaiden of the Golden Woods, I stand corrected."

On hearing her ancient name, Arma's feature softened. But perhaps the remembrance was too much for her, as she quickly changed the subject. "So the queen and the princess are traveling incognito. I wonder why."

"You know, Arma, I suspected she was the queen, but how come you're so sure of it? Have you seen her before?"

"You forget that I was often present at the Tensengin High Council meetings. I was there during the Golden Harp Fairy's request for aid. At that time, the Didee-king and queen were there, and Vreeny persuaded them to deny her request."

"Vreeny! That evil one deserves no mention." Xeiyén kicked a bread roll. "I for one would have rather aided the Golden Harp Fairy—even if it meant risking the Senginfans' wrath. If only the Mighty Vong had not left the council, he could have stopped that serpent Vreeny from poisoning the Didee-king's mind. I wouldn't put it past that evil one to have had something to do with the missing Didee-tunnel door. And Merchant Benny's just the sort to do shady dealings with him to obtain it."

Arma rescued the kicked bread roll from falling off the table. "I don't know how the bad merchant got the vase, but you can always enlist Michi's help once again. If anyone could swindle a deal from him, she's it."

"Talk about the fearless young generation of the human race." He paused and studied Arma intently, then chose his next words carefully. "Did you know she's got a scrapbook inside her pack that emits Zunji Light for all immortals within miles to sense?"

"No! Really? How could that be?"

Xeiyén shrugged his shoulders. "I was hoping you could enlighten me, seeing as it was more in your line of work."

"My dealing was only with Zanchou, the Zunji Sheath, and a perilous business that turned out to be. In the end, I had to give up my magical power to protect it. However, I can't help but feel uneasy about this glowing scrapbook you say Michi is carrying—her being a mere mortal, and a young one at that. Wait a minute! How did it escape Captain Hua's attention?"

Xeiyén cleared his throat. "I broke one of the Didee-rules and placed a temporary protection over the scrapbook as soon as we came upon the van."

"Oh, Xeiyén, thank you. I dread to think what would have happened if you didn't."

"Now hold your horses, Arma. The shield only lasts a short while. The sooner Michi leaves, the safer she'll be. I wouldn't be surprised if Captain Hua came here to investigate that unknown Zunji Light—" Xeiyén paused and chuckled. "I'm afraid I've set a difficult riddle for the young captain, and will probably receive a fitting punishment from the queen one of these days. I've never seen Her Royal Highness taken in so completely by anyone as she was with Captain Hua."

Bayjai Arma was all attention. "So she's still siding with the Senginfans. Did she tell you everything that happened after she met the young captain?"

"The queen has played very close to her chest since joining us. I have had better luck with Princess Leianna, but I'm afraid her grandmother didn't open up completely even with her. You might find out more about the young captain by questioning Shanui or Dei, seeing as it was Captain Hua who brought the pair out of Benny's tent."

"So it was this young captain that Dei was babbling about. I must find out more during my trip north with Shanui and Dei—but you're right, this matter with Michi and Jo is more pressing."

Xeiyén murmured in agreement, then looked toward the eastern sky and realized dawn was near. "If only we could somehow persuade Joseph and Michi to leave soon—" He broke off and bounced down from the pastry loaded table.

Xane, Xeiyén's cousin, flipped open the bottom of the tent and held it. A moment later, Polly exited while Xeiyén strolled over to meet her. "Good morning, Captain. Will you tell your cousin that Lei and I don't need a babysitter," the queen huffed.

Xane rolled his eyes while Xeiyén noticed that the queen's hair was still damp from a wash. *I guess Queeny wasn't kidding when she demanded baths twice a day.* However, he restrained from criticizing.

"This is hardly the place to discuss such matters," Xeiyén cautioned. He gave Polly a meaningful look by glancing toward the direction of the cooking fire where Bayjai Arma was humming a song while bending over the stove. He turned back to Polly just in time to see Xane lasso the queen and bounce out of the way. An instant later, a foot stuck out from the bottom of the tent and landed at the very spot Polly had been standing a moment before. Xeiyén cursed and moved under the shadow of a bucket as the first knot closing the tent was undone, and a pair of sleepy brown eyes peeped through. On seeing Polly suspended from a rope, the drowsy eyes came to life and grew huge.

"Hello, Dolly. What are you doing all tied up?" Michi asked, undoing the last knot of the tent flap. As Michi stepped out of the tent, Xeiyén released his Didee-hook. It stuck to the top of the awning, and the loose end of Xane's Didee-rope extended to attach to the Didee-hook.

Michi lifted her head to see a pitiable six-inch doll hanging midway from a rope, tied to a hook on the awning. "Oh! This is low! Arma, did you see? Some nasty child has been cruel to her doll."

Bayjai Arma straightened and turned, then gasped. "Didee-jiny!"

"So that's the poor doll's name. Who's the mean owner?"

"Uhh..."

"Come on, Arma, out with it."

"Couldn't we have a proper sit down breakfast?" A loud voice approaching from the side caught everyone's attention.

Bayjai Arma spun around the same time Polly started to struggle. Xeiyén cursed again. He blew a quick puff of air which turned into a gust of wind, tousling Polly and covering her movements. The strong wind whipped Michi's hair and the hanging rope about. Michi put a hand out to steady the swinging rope, then patted the still damp dolly's hair reassuringly as she scrutinized the approaching customers.

Out of the semi-darkness emerged a tall and athletic middle-aged man with a fair looking teenager. "No son," the older man said, "we need to get to the Firmiana Inn before noon, so we only have time for a breakfast to-go. However, Bayjai Arma is just as good a cook as Benny's—if not better."

They reached the pastry-laden table. "Hello Councilman Trumbond," Arma greeted. "I had no idea you'd joined our camp."

"It was a last minute decision, Bayjai Arma," Trumbond replied. He looked toward Michi, but his attention was arrested by the tied up Polly instead. "Brutan! What's your doll doing hanging in the middle of the awning?"

The teenager stared blankly at the horror-stricken Polly. "Uhh . . ."

Michi put her hands on her hips. "Yes, Brutan, tell us why your doll is so cruelly tied and hung to dry?"

"It's not—" Brutan began.

"Son," Trumbond interrupted, "I know you didn't think it was cruel to hang the doll up to dry after you washed the flour out of it. However, it's still not a pleasant sight, so I suggest that you cut it down."

Eyeing the large flour tin near the kitchen table, Michi sucked in her breath. "Your son smothered this poor doll with flour, too? Why, Councilman Trumbond, you ought to be ashamed of yourself for bringing up such a blood-thirsty boy."

Brutan shook his head vehemently. "I did no such thing, and it's not my—"

"That's enough! Now go get your doll," Trumbond ordered.

Xeiyén saw Lei appear from within the tent, rushing toward Polly, and he cursed for the third time. Grabbing his own Didee-rope, he quickly lassoed Lei, pulling the princess to him as Brutan came to Michi's side. Lei started to protest, but Xeiyén hushed her. "Be quiet, Lei!" After he saw the hurt in her eyes, his expression softened. "Are you okay?" Lei nodded her head, and they turned to witness Brutan take out a pocket knife.

Bayjai Arma moved to join Michi and Brutan. "Just a minute, Brutan," she said. "The rope is of no use to me if it's too short, so let me untie it."

The moment the doll was untied, Michi grabbed it from the cook and examined it closely while Arma wrapped the rope around the palm of her hand. "Hey! This can't be your doll. Rosalyn has a dress exactly like this one, and I know sometimes her clothes come with a matching dress doll as a bonus."

"I'm pretty sure this was the doll that Merchant Benny gave to my son on his fifth birthday," Trumbond insisted, as Brutan gave him a startled look.

"Oh yeah? Okay, Brutan, describe your doll's outfit." When the young boy's eyes strayed to the doll, Michi squashed Polly to her bosom while turning sideways to hide it from Brutan's view.

"Uhh ... It's a fancy dress with lots of beads," Brutan said.

"There!" Trumbond said triumphantly.

Michi ignored him and turned to Brutan. "What about her shoes?"

"Uhh ... I don't remember."

"Hah! Likely story. If I had a doll with a pair of glass slippers, I would never have forgotten it—"

"That's it, glass slippers. I just remembered," Brutan corrected belatedly.

"Well, this can't be your doll then." Michi pulled up the dolly's long skirt to reveal a pair of boot-clad feet, then she showed it to Brutan.

The teenager shrugged his shoulders. "So Cinderella lost her glass slippers last night, big deal!"

"And that's not the doll's name, either!" Michi argued.

"If you fancy the doll's expensive clothing, we'll let you keep it," Trumbond said. "But the doll was a special gift to my son and I must insist that you return it to him."

On hearing the councilman's suggestion, everyone's eyes widened, including the doll's. Michi recovered first. "How did Merchant Benny get a hold of an exclusive design years before it was out in the market?" she asked.

"Well, you know Benny. He's the sharpest businessman around," Trumbond said.

"All the same," Arma said, "I think it would be best that you have the merchant come to confirm your story."

"That's an excellent idea! Son, you stay here and I'll go fetch Benny," Trumbond said. Without giving anyone a chance to protest, he left in the direction of the biggest tent.

Bayjai Arma started to whistle as she picked up a small ball of dough and fashioned a person out of it.

"Arma, are you going to make a gingerbread man?" Michi asked while she moved to the table, followed by Brutan.

"No, I'm making a little magic man," the cook said, then placed her hands above the dough man. "Come to life, little dough man." Arma cast her spell, clapping her hands together. A flashing spark and a wisp of smoke appeared. She then placed the dough man on the ground and waved her hand in the air. "Stand up!" Immediately the cute dough man stood up, and Michi and Brutan gasped. "Sit down," Arma directed, and the dough man obeyed instantly, to the delight of its audience. "Dance!" Arma commanded, and the dough man danced while the cook hummed a tune. Both Michi and Brutan laughed. Arma gave the dough man a final order. "Stop! Go to sleep!" The dough man stopped dancing and lay down upon the ground.

"Arma! How did you do it?" Michi asked excitedly while Brutan shouted, "Let me—Stand up!"

The dough doll did as Brutan commanded, and the youth turned to Arma. "How much do you want for your dough man?"

"Actually I was going to give it to Michi, seeing as she doesn't have a doll of her own—"

Brutan swung around to face Michi. "I'll trade you!"

Michi considered the soulful looking Polly, then looked down at the fascinating dough man. "Ohoo…" She stamped her feet with indecision.

"Hurry up, make up your mind!" Brutan hustled.

"Don't rush me!" she scolded, then her eyes rested on Rosalyn's distasteful outfit and she shoved Polly into Brutan's hand. "Here."

Brutan looked at the overdressed doll with distaste the same time Polly started to sing. But it sounded more like croaking, and Michi wrinkled her nose while Brutan shook the doll to stop the unpleasant sound.

"Stop it! Leave the poor doll alone. It's not her fault that her battery's running down—that's why her singing's terrible," Michi explained.

"It's my doll and I'll do anything I want with it," Brutan said, his eyes glinting as he carried Polly toward the cooking fire.

"Wh–what are you going to do?" Michi asked.

A devilish smile broke out on Brutan's face. "None of your business!" he shot back.

When he reached the burning stove and moved Polly toward the fire, Michi waved her hands frantically. "Okay! Okay! You can have the magic dough man—" Before she even finished, Brutan was already back by her side, and Michi found herself holding Polly once again.

"You made a wise choice. See you," Brutan told Michi. He turned to the dough man. "March!" Brutan ordered, and together they left the open kitchen.

Michi watched the obedient dough man march at a neck breaking pace to keep up with Brutan. "Will your dough man be alright?" she asked Arma.

"Of course. What could Brutan possibly do to it?"

"Cook and eat it."

"But that's what a gingerbread man's for," Arma reasoned. She then pointed at Polly. "She, on the other hand, is still not out of the woods yet."

Michi hugged Polly to her. "What do you mean, Arma?"

"I think Councilman Trumbond's going to make his son return my dough man for your doll. And I'm loath to think what Brutan'll do to this poor dolly when he finds he's stuck with it."

Michi tilted her head and thought for a moment. "Jo! Jo!" she shouted, running toward the van.

As soon as Michi left the open kitchen, Xeiyén bounced up to the table carrying his Didee-rope, which still had one end wrapped around Lei's waist. The Didee-rope set the princess down next to Xeiyén.

"Captain, I'm not a cow!" Lei said hotly. "And what are you doing exposing us to a human?"

He let go of the Didee-rope, and Lei tied a bow around her waist with the dangling rope while Arma came over to stand in front of them. "Lei, may I introduce you to Areama, the most sympathetic handmaiden of the Golden Woods," Xeiyén said.

Lei let out a tiny gasp while Arma smiled at her tenderly. "Hello, Lei. Don't mind him, just call me Arma." The cook turned to Xeiyén and her expression became serious. "I'm afraid Trumbond knows the secret of the Didee-tunnel, and I think Benny got the vase for him. Not knowing its true worth, of course."

"Yes," Xeiyén said. "It's obvious that Trumbond is hiding his excitement at seeing Polly suspended from Xane's Didee-rope. If she's captured, he'll force her to command the Didee-tunnel door. It was an ingenious move to create the dough man, Arma."

"Nothing compared to your magic touch on it. Will it last until Brutan reaches Benny's tent?"

"Xane's following Brutan, so I imagine—"

At that moment, Xane landed on the table. "Not any more. They're all coming—Joseph, Michi, Trumbond, Brutan, and Benny."

"Oh goody, customers," Arma teased while she unwrapped the Didee-rope from her hand and handed it back to Xane. "This is yours, I believe."

"Thank you for rescuing it."

"You're welcome, Xane."

"Come Lei, let's move to those spice jars, and Xane, do something about the dough man," Xeiyén said.

Xane nodded and moved away before Trumbond, Benny, and Brutan arrived in front of the outdoor kitchen. Brutan turned to the approaching dough man and gave an order. "Stop—go to sleep." The dough man stopped marching and lay down on the ground immediately. Brutan turned back to face Arma just as Joseph and Michi reached the cook's side.

"Some magic dough man you got there," Joseph said.

"Yes, isn't it," Brutan agreed.

"Oh, Jo! He can do more than march and sleep," Michi said just as a rumbling cart came toward the outdoor kitchen.

"Bayjai Arma! Give me a couple of your breakfast specials, and please make it snappy. We're in a hurry," the passenger of the cart bellowed.

Everyone looked at the approaching cart, and Michi gave a sudden gasp. "Stop!" she screamed.

The driver of the cart began to rein in, shouting, "Whoa!" The horses, however, were not quick enough to stop.

"My dough man!" Brutan yelled while Michi shouted, "Dough man, get out of the way! I mean 'dance'—No! I mean—" They rushed from the open kitchen as the wheels of the cart steamrolled over the poor dough man before stopping.

Michi and Brutan reached the side of the cart at the same time. They eyed the pitiable dough, stuck to the wheel like a flattened piece of chewing gum. "Oh, no!" Michi exclaimed, while Brutan muttered, "Oh, look at your dough man."

Michi's eyes narrowed. "What do you mean, 'your' dough man?"

Brutan shrugged. "I think you should talk to the driver about running over your dough man."

"What did I run over?" the driver asked, hopping down to take a look. "What's that? Bird poop?"

"No," Michi said. "I wish it was."

Brutan stuck his hand out. "Give me back my fifth birthday present from Uncle Benny," he demanded.

Michi held Polly tighter while Joseph stepped out of the open kitchen. "How old are you, Brutan?" Joseph asked as he came to stand between Michi and Brutan.

Brutan glared defiantly at Joseph. "I'm thirteen years old, and don't tell me I'm too old to play with a doll. It's not a toy so much as it has sentimental value, and I like it."

"Yeah right! You like it so much that you strangled it, hung it, and were going to burn it," Michi scolded.

Joseph spared a glance at the sorry doll. "Brutan, without delving into your strange hobbies, right now it seems there's the question of this doll's ownership. Here's where I can help. Michi, give the doll to Bayjai Arma."

"Alright Jo," Michi said, moving back to Arma's side and passing Polly to Arma.

"This doll was made the same time the exclusive dress was designed. Arma, will you please look for the outfit's tag and compare it with the mark under the right foot of the doll?"

Arma complied, taking off the little boot from the doll. "The marking under the doll's foot is exactly the same as the one on the tag of this dress."

Michi leaned over to take a look. "Oh! There're numbers inside the center of the mark—4855."

Her brother smiled. "Councilman Trumbond and Merchant Benny, I'm pretty sure you will both verify with me that this is Anguorian year 4855."

"Yes, I deal with the Outsiders from time to time, and this is their year 4855," the driver of the cart chipped in, intrigued by the happenings.

"Jo! This means it can't be the doll Merchant Benny gave to Brutan."

"That's right, Sweet. This doll didn't exist eight years ago. If Merchant Benny gave Brutan a doll for his fifth birthday, it must be a different one."

"Jo! You're the greatest!" Michi cheered and her brother winked at her.

"Would you like to see for yourself, Councilman Trumbond?" Arma, holding Polly's exposed foot, offered.

"I don't think it's necessary, Arma," Merchant Benny intervened. "There was never any need. One glance and I knew it wasn't the same one at all. Trumbond, on the other hand, wouldn't know one end of a doll from the other, so you must forgive him for his confusion."

Arma beamed. "Perfectly understandable. Now, Councilman, what would you like?"

"How about two of your delicious breakfast specials—"

Trumbond's words were interrupted when a wailing Archoy rushed out of the pink tent. "Oh! Young Master Joseph! Who would have thought I could sleep like a log in a tent."

"Don't worry about it, Archoy, and good morning. The driver is also up, so we might as well have some of Arma's pastries for breakfast, before our early start."

"Yes," Archoy said. "Very good, young Master Joseph. Good morning Little Miss. Why Arma, you've got quite a few customers already."

"Yes, I must hurry and get four breakfast specials ready," Arma said as she moved to where the spice jars were stored. She gently placed Polly on the shelf and picked up some bags, then moved to the pastry table.

Lei saw that Polly was only a short distance from them. "Grandmammy," she urged.

"Not now!" Xeiyén hushed her.

Polly ignored Xeiyén's warning and opened her mouth. "Lei, is it—" she began, but was silenced when one of the gold buttons from Xeiyén's shoulder strips flew to stick on her mouth.

Trumbond shifted his position to get a better look at Polly, and Lei gasped. "Don't move, Grandmammy," she whispered.

Then, Michi moved in front of Trumbond to reach for a pastry, and the councilman moved back to allow her room to pick up a jelly roll.

"Jo, Archoy, come and eat," Michi invited, taking a bite.

"Sweet, I'll eat in the car. We have to leave soon."

"But what about the bazaar? I didn't get to see much last night," Michi complained while Arma paused.

"We're a bit behind schedule—" Joseph began, then stopped on seeing Michi's "poor little me" expression.

"Michi, how do you like my jelly rolls?" Arma asked.

"They're yummy. You must be the best pastry maker in the Kingdom of Lanhur."

"There's one place that can compete with my pastries—"

"Really! Where?"

"The Firmiana Inn and their famous Nine-layer Southland Native Cake," Arma said.

"Nine-layer cake! It sounds delicious. Does it really have nine layers?"

"Yup!" Arma said. "They make that for their lunch customers, and you'll pass the inn on your way, too."

"Jo! Did you hear that?"

"Uh-huh. I suppose we'll have to stop by and get you some on the way," Joseph said.

"Thanks, Jo!"

"I'm afraid the inn opens for lunch at eleven, and usually by eleven-thirty their delicious nine-layer cakes will be all sold out." Arma shook her head with a resigned expression.

"How long does it take to get there, Arma?" Michi asked eagerly.

"At least four hours by car—" Arma began.

"Jo, will we make it if we leave now?" Michi interrupted.

Her brother chuckled. "Still a food monster, eh? Go ahead and have a light breakfast here, Sweet. You too, Archoy. We're leaving in twenty minutes, which should give us plenty of time to get to the Firmiana Inn by eleven. Arma, how about you pack a few more of your breakfast specials for us?"

"Don't you worry about it, Jo," Arma said. "I'll have a basket full of goodies ready for you."

"Thanks. Now I really must go and get ready." Joseph ruffled his sister's hair, then left.

Archoy, who was moving toward Michi, stopped and inspected the doll. "I see a button came off when you dressed this doll with your clothes, Little Miss," she said. "You never can trust these so-called name brand clothing companies. Just look at how much it's shrunk."

Lei waited until Archoy went and joined Michi for breakfast. "Now can Grandmammy come to us, Captain?" she asked.

"Not until Trumbond and his gang leave," Xeiyén answered.

Lei waited anxiously while Arma served her customers, and when Trumbond glanced toward the spice jars, the princess shivered. She leaned toward Xeiyén.

"It's okay, he's not looking at us," Xeiyén soothed.

"He's looking at Grandmammy."

"Yes, but don't worry. Now that Trumbond knows Michi and her brother are going to the same place he is, he'll be leaving soon."

Lei nodded, then rested her head on Xeiyén's shoulder and he frowned—what a strange un-Didee-like behavior. It disturbed his peace of mind, and Xeiyén schooled himself to concentrate on the doings in the open kitchen. He saw that Trumbond was finally leaving with Brutan and Benny.

Xeiyén commanded the gold button on Polly's mouth to return. "I think the coast is clear, Lei—Lei?"

"Huh?" Lei moved away from Xeiyén with a start.

Did she fall to sleep? "I said it's time for Polly to join us."

"Oh. Right..." Lei's face flooded with color and Xeiyén's frown deepened. She turned quickly and moved to her grandmother's side. "Grandmammy, are you alright?" she whispered.

"Lei! I feel stiff. I think that cousin of the captain's has gone and turned me into a real doll."

"Grandmammy, Xane wouldn't do that."

"Yes, he would! He's been hoping something awful and humiliating like this would happen to me," Polly insisted while she struggled to sit up.

"You're just a little stiff from holding yourself still for so long. Here, let me help you." Lei put her grandmother's boot back on, then helped her to stand up, and together they made their way to Xeiyén. They stood watching Xeiyén's blade come down from the top of the tent and turn back to a cloak, which fit over his head.

"What was it doing up there?" Polly asked suspiciously.

"Grandmammy, it was Xeiyén's blade that reflected the dress tag onto your underfoot. Wasn't it clever?"

"Hmm...as long as it wasn't aimed at me, I suppose it's—"

"Grandmammy! You wouldn't think..."

Polly gave Xeiyén a dark look. "He wasn't adverse to silencing me by buttoning my mouth. What would he do if I was not able to hold back a sneeze? Order his sword for a swift execution, I shouldn't wonder."

Xeiyén shook his head in disbelief, but Lei gazed at him so pleadingly that he checked his rising temper. "Xane'll be here soon," he said. "Have him take you both back to the pink tent and wait for me there."

"Where are you going?" Lei asked.

Is she nagging? "To follow Trumbond and see if he's the one that has the Didee-tunnel door now, instead."

"Be careful!"

She is nagging! "If I don't come home in time for breakfast, just start without me," Xeiyén shot back as he bounced off.

"Your rope! Don't forget your rope," Lei prodded.

Xeiyén paid her no mind. *She's definitely nagging.* He caught up with Trumbond and the others before they reached the big tent. Xeiyén listened to the conversation between Merchant Benny and the councilman with interest.

" ...I'm merely taking your advice and staying out of the Outsiders' ways. Now, if you fancy Anguorian dolls, I most certainly can get you some much prettier than Michi's, and for a very reasonable price," Benny said.

"You just guard my vase with your life until I return, Benny. And don't get too greedy," Trumbond warned.

"Have I ever failed you before, Councilman ... " Benny started to protest, but Xeiyén heard no more, for he was already on his way back to Arma's tent.

He landed on an egg sesame pocket, and Arma turned sharply toward him. "Xeiyén! Have respect for the customers' food."

"You know it'll taste even better now that I've stepped on it. Anyway, where's everybody?" Xeiyén said while he hopped down from the egg pocket.

Bayjai Arma picked up the food that Xeiyén had just stepped on, placing it in the bottom of the basket she was preparing for Joseph. "Michi and Archoy are getting ready to leave. Shanui and Dei are keeping them company, eating inside the van. The poor kids. You know they refused to eat in my kitchen once they found out Benny had been here earlier?"

"It is your intention, then, to deliver them to their aunt at the Bonhas personally?"

"Yes. I've been trying to find a way to stay and search the Bonhas' estate without creating too much suspicion, anyways. I'm on a special quest, searching for a lost diary, and my latest discovery points to the Bonhas. Wouldn't you know it, last night Shanui mentioned that they would like to go live with their aunt, who works at the Bonhas' estate. I grabbed the opportunity, and with a little artful suggestion from me, Jo actually paid me not only to escort Shanui and Dei to Aunt Shalin, but also to stay for a while and make sure they settled in."

"A perfect cover for your spy work! Well, Arma, whatever fate has in store for you, it seems that right at this moment good fortune is smiling upon you," Xeiyén teased.

"Aren't I sneaky? Though I must admit that Jo's a real gentleman. He even gave Shanui his new address and extracted a promise from her that she'd contact him if she or Dei ever needed any help."

Xeiyén smiled. "With a mischievous sister like Michi, Joseph has certainly had to become as steady as a rock. I hope they won't have too much trouble with an irate Trumbond when he finds out later that Polly is no longer with them. How long do you think before Michi comes back to search for her doll?"

"There was a close call while you were gone, but Shanui and Dei's timely arrival distracted her. And I've got an emergency pack all prepared." Arma waved the basket filled with the best of her pastries at Xeiyén.

He laughed. "That ought to get her mind off more than just a doll."

Arma covered the picnic basket with a violet cloth. "Jo didn't call her a food monster for nothing. Well, I'm off to send her on her way, although I must say I'm going to miss her dreadfully."

6

BOND FIRE

OWLUT MECHANICALLY TRIMMED the hedges near the side entrance to the Markums' kitchen, listening to the conversation between the lead chef and the butcher from town.

"Here's the steaks and sausages Pauline ordered." The butcher passed the packages to the chef. "Where is she? It's not like her to not come and pass the day with me."

The chef leaned forward. "She's lying in the kitchen corner all drunk, if you can believe it," he whispered.

Owlut stopped working and moved closer to them.

The butcher's eyes widened. "No! You mean our prim and proper Pauline—drunk?"

The chef nodded with a smirk. "Must have helped herself to the expensive wine during the feast," he said. "The bartender told me she practically wrestled the wine tray from him."

"Goodness, Cook. Who would have thought. Pauline, an alcoholic!" the bewildered butcher exclaimed.

Of all the idiotic things. There must have been a hundred varieties of food served last night, and she just had to choose an old vintage wine to put the powder in. Then, to drink the stuff herself! Owlut started to trim the bush viciously, as if it was Pauline's head.

"The nobles're a bit tipsy as well. If you've noticed, none are about—and here it is, mid-morning already." The lead chef backed off and waved his hands in the general vicinity of the surrounding area.

"Aye, they've the right to lay in if they've a mind to. I've heard there was quite a bit of traffic here last evening."

"That's right," the chef said. "I was nearly run off my feet preparing the extra food. Though, I must say I outdid myself with the pot roast. It was superb!" He kissed his fingertips. "His Royal Highness Prince Norlen of Nain ate at least seven helpings."

"You don't say, a prince!" The butcher wiped his sweaty palms against his pants as if he was ready to slice more of the choice cuts from his shop for the royalty. "My customers'll not mind a bit of this news—"

Just at that moment, Pauline popped her head out and greeted the butcher cheerfully. The lead chef mumbled something about marinating steaks and went into the kitchen with the meat packages. The butcher took in the housekeeper's disheveled appearance with unease, and when Pauline seemed to have some business with the gardener, he was glad to take his leave immediately.

Owlut stood behind the now much shorter hedges watching Pauline's approach with much displeasure. He knew the housekeeper could have no recollection of what had happened after she downed the powdered wine, but it still irritated him to see her blissfully unaware of the blunder she had caused. *I'm normally not a violent sort. How come I feel like strangling her?*

"Yoo-hoo, Owlut. It's a beautiful morning, isn't it?" Pauline bent down and picked up some of the scattered branches, throwing them into a pile nearby the bush. She went about repeating the chore closer to the gardener, and whispered to him as she drew near. "Christa took her medicine with a glass of wine last night." Pleased with her little joke, she laughed and snorted. "How did it go?"

Owlut gave her a disgusted look. "Good grief, woman, did you sleep in your uniform last night? Go and make yourself more presentable."

A clueless Pauline checked for creases on her long skirt, and was mortified to find it was wrinkled beyond recognition. "I...I don't understand..." She moved her hands over her pleated skirt in an effort to smooth it out.

Pauline had always prided herself on the neatness of her appearance, and Owlut had never seen her in this light. Eyeing the bewildered and disheveled housekeeper's face, Owlut was suddenly reminded of his Lucielle. He frowned.

Seeing the gardener looking at her face with an odd expression, Pauline tried to tug in the loosened tendrils from her forehead, and wailed when she found out she had somehow lost her hairpins. Then she realized that the top buttons of her prim and proper high necked shirt had come undone by some unknown misfortune. She covered her exposed chest with her hands and screamed as she ran back to the house.

Owlut cursed. While Pauline was all efficiency and business-like, it was easier to deal with her. But this...with a downcast head, he moved to a concealed spot and slumped down. *What am I doing here?* Putting his head between his hands, Owlut groaned.

Looking at his pitiable form, no one would have guessed that he was once one of the most respected advisors of the Tensengin High Council. Being one of the wisest, Owlut had been sent to live among the mortals and to learn what had caused the breaking of the once peaceful Tensengin Immortal Realm. However, he had ended up falling in love with Lucielle, a mortal. He married her and spent eighty of his most wonderful years with her. But when Lucielle had passed away, Owlut, an immortal, tasted the bitter fruit of human sorrow.

The sudden crunching of leaves nearby brought Owlut back to his present predicament. He peeped through the dense bush and saw the barbarian warrior riding on the Nain horse. *Now, where would Prince Norlen be going?*

Watching the muscled man glance over his shoulder from time to time as he made his way cautiously, Owlut decided to follow him. The barbarian had interrupted his interrogation of Christa last night, and that alone warranted a closer inspection.

CEDRIC MARKUM WATCHED from the corner window as BoDak left the Markum mansion on Norlen's Nain horse. The barbarian had decided to continue on ahead to find and retrieve his own stolen horse. *I would feel better if I knew where Owlut was at this moment.* "Norlen, did you sleep well?" Cedric inquired while he leaned on the window sill.

Prince Norlen came over to stand beside him. "Nothing disturbed my rest. I thank you for giving me one of the best rooms—"

Still keeping an eye on BoDak, Cedric put up his hand to halt Norlen's polite speech. "I'd have offered a tent for you out in the woods, which would have been more to your liking. However, because we've got a night owl on the loose, I felt it best that we play it safe and stay indoors after dark."

"I exercised my horse this morning, and I must inform you that Owlut is definitely not nocturnal. He was up and about when I arrived at the stable. He was very curious about Bo—asking me some rather interesting questions."

"It was good that you kept up the pretense last night."

"Yes, I'd say he even recognized the jewelry Bo wore."

Cedric straightened abruptly. "You're kidding! He must only have had a glimpse last night, and yet he was able to tell?"

"Uh-huh," Prince Norlen said while he pulled out the braided necklace hanging inside his shirt. "His knowledge included this necklace that was hidden inside Bo's tunic yesterday. Bo insisted on leaving it behind before he went after his Nain horse this morning."

Strange, I've seen that necklace before also. Cedric whistled. "How? I wonder."

"It was the unusual braided chain that tipped Owlut off. He asked me if it came from the sire of that particular Nain horse I was about to take out for a ride."

"And?"

"I told him yes," the prince said. "No point in trying to deny it. I got the feeling he knew, and was trying to test me. I think my frank answer put him at ease, which was my objective." He pointed his finger at an object in the distance. "Oh-oh! Bo's wearing a tail."

Cedric's eyes followed the direction of Norlen's pointing finger. When he saw Owlut following Bo, he tensed. "Sure BoDak will be okay?"

"Bo's a worthy opponent. You just haven't seen him at his best. There isn't a man that can stand against him when it comes to combat," the prince assured.

"I was thinking more along the lines of strategy," Cedric said.

"Bo will never rest until he gets his Nain horse back. I doubt Owlut fancies horse flesh, so he probably won't give him trouble." Prince Norlen paused and fingered the braided necklace in his hand. "Besides, once Owlut realizes Bo's no longer wearing this necklace, he'll probably turn back."

"So that's why you had Bo wear that high necked shirt—to buy us some time. Well, hopefully this will be the last we see of that demon for a while," Cedric said when he saw both Bo and Owlut disappear from view. *Time to find out what brought him here all the way from Nain.* Cedric sauntered across the richly decorated room and perched himself on the edge of the antique desk. "I'd like to think that you stopped by our estate just to get acquainted with me, but somehow I believe there's more to it than that."

Prince Norlen paused a moment before replying. "You're right; although now that I've met you, I'm glad of it." He gave Cedric a smile. "As you know, for a fortnight, Bo and I were tracking a certain disreputable scoundrel who had cheated Bo out of his Nain horse. When we came upon the border before sundown, Bo inquired around and the innkeeper from town confirmed seeing the bearded man named Benny with a kingly horse a couple of days earlier. Yesterday morning, as we were leaving the inn to follow Benny's tracks into Lanhur, Bo suddenly insisted on changing course to come here, babbling something about being summoned—"

"The time!" Cedric interrupted. "Norlen, tell me the exact time when this happened?"

"Well, we of the Nain tribes don't abide to any time table. We're more of a free roaming and come-what-may sort of people. However, I do recall looking up at the sky, and judging from what I remember of the sun, I'd say it was somewhere around seven in the morning."

"Seven…that's about the time that Michi and Christa were in the secret room. We've got to get Christa to tell us exactly what happened yesterday morning."

Prince Norlen grinned. "Think we'll have better luck than Owlut? I mean getting your younger sister to tell us about more than just naked women."

"There's only one way to find out. Come on, let's go find her," Cedric invited. They walked down the corridor to Christa's room. "I assume there was something in last night's wine that put the victims under Owlut's spell."

"Yes," Prince Norlen said. "Pauline was the one that put the powder in the wine. It usually lasts only a few hours and leaves its victims with no recollection of what happened. But in this case, the vintage wine made the effect more potent—hence the victims' drunken states. The earring BoDak wore also enabled him to hear Owlut's commands. That was why, even though Owlut's order to go to the swing was issued to Christa alone, Bo made his way there as well.

I might add, in his normal alert state, Bo should have been there through cleverness, trying to spy on Owlut."

Cedric snickered. "Oh, I don't know. The way he showed up suddenly still managed to throw Owlut off well enough, and possibly rattled our night owl so badly that he won't be able to think straight."

"I get the feeling that under normal circumstances, Owlut wouldn't have been fooled so easily," Prince Norlen said. "I still think the truth will dawn on him soon enough."

"Let's hope it's much later. I fear our fate may hinge on us being able to take advantage of the slight edge we have," Cedric said as they reached Christa's bedroom.

"Maybe we should wait until—" Norlen began, but Cedric knocked on the door.

"Relax, it's Christa and she's usually the first one up in the morning."

"I'm feeling rotten right now, so stay out if you're faint-hearted," Christa said from inside her room.

Cedric opened the door and walked in. "Hello, Christa. It's just us chickens."

"Oh it's you. Cedric, did I konk out after drinking that tiny glass of wine last night?" Christa, sitting up from her bed, asked.

Cedric studied Christa with a frown. "Did you just wake up?"

"I've been awake for a while, but my head felt strange and I can't remember much of what happened last night, or even coming to bed."

"Your head, does it hurt?" Prince Norlen asked with concern.

Christa was suddenly aware of the stranger. "Who are you?"

"Oh, allow me to introduce Prince—" Cedric began.

"I'm Norlen, Lady Christa," the prince cut in, "and I apologize for my untimely intrusion."

On seeing Norlen's serious expression and hearing his severe words, Christa threw her head back and laughed. "I'm just Christa and you don't need to apologize. If you're a friend of Cedric, then you're a friend of mine. To answer your question, no, my head doesn't hurt. It's just that I've never felt like this before. You know, out of sorts."

"Well, it might be serious. So why don't we test your memory by having you describe what you can remember, say early yesterday morning," Cedric prompted.

Christa gave Cedric a knowing look. "I'm not that dense, brother. You and this new friend of yours are here for a reason. Now, out with it, and I warn you, I want to be included—"

"Okay, deal, Christa." Cedric raised his hands in surrender. "If there's any action, you'll be a part of it."

Christa flipped her hair back with a toss of her hand. "That's more like it. Now, what do you want to know?"

"I can see I'm going to have to undo Michi's bad influence on you, but for now, let's have all the details of your misadventure in the armor room."

"You mean inside that musty and dusty room behind the naked women, I suppose."

Norlen turned to Cedric and quirked his brow.

"They're on a tapestry. You know, the women," Cedric explained.

"Ah, interesting."

"That's what Michi thought also," Christa said. "Now, are you still interested in what we did in the secret room?"

Both Cedric and Norlen nodded, then they sat down on the bed while Christa retold the events of the previous morning. Cedric refrained from interrupting his sister until she came to the part where Michi tried on the helmet. "You mean Michi actually put the helmet on!" he exclaimed.

"Uh-huh."

"Did it fit?"

"Well, she did look funny. You would too, if your head was too small."

"Christa, you said it was the purplish-blue glowing light that led you to the helmet. Now, this is very important. How long did the light stay on?"

"It was on all the time."

"Are you sure?"

"Oh yes. It was on even when I put it on—"

"You mean the helmet also fit you?" Cedric burst out in amazement. *The darn helmet probably fits everyone!*

"It was a poor fit, because I couldn't see too well—Cedric! I remember now! The light, it did stop glowing."

"When?"

"I know it was still glowing when the grandfather clock struck. I remember seeing clearly Michi's alarmed face at the noise. After the clock stopped chiming and we heard footsteps—that's it! It went dark when Michi passed the helmet to me, because I remember I tried to put the helmet back at the same place, but it was pretty dark. I'm afraid I was more worried about being caught inside the secret room than putting the helmet back in the same spot, so I just dumped it on the table and got out."

"That's why I thought the helmet looked different," Cedric said. "Not only because it stopped glowing, but it was tilted at an angle."

Prince Norlen cleared his throat. "Christa, excuse me for interrupting, but could you tell me what time it was when the grandfather clock struck?"

Christa shrugged her shoulders.

"Seven," Cedric said meaningfully.

Norlen smacked his forehead. "The same time Bo babbled about being summoned!"

"Who's Bo?" Christa asked.

"A pot roast monster," Cedric enlightened.

"Oh! You mean the barbarian prince."

Cedric and Norlen laughed. "Bo's really alright once you get to know him—" Norlen started to say when he was interrupted by a knock on the door.

"Come in," Cedric invited.

The door opened and the Markums' lead chef popped his head in. "Pardon me, Lord Cedric, but there's a visitor with some urgent business for His Royal Highness Prince Norlen of Nain. No one knows where His Highness can be found, however."

"Where's Pauline?" Cedric asked.

The lead chef moved into the room and closed the door. "She's not feeling quite herself this morning, Lord Cedric."

Cedric's jaw tightened, and the chef rested his weight on one foot nervously. "Cook, this visitor, did you ask for his name?" Cedric asked.

"He only said he's the tribe adviser for Prince Norlen and that he would wait for His Highness in the library." The lead chef shifted his weight to the other foot. "I think there are other horsemen with him . . ."

"How many?"

"I-I couldn't tell. You see, they stayed outside the gate and under the shade of the trees."

Cedric cursed, but Norlen placed a reassuring hand on his friend's shoulder. "I'm sure it wasn't due to any lack of hospitality from your court."

On hearing what Norlen implied, dismay entered the lead chef's eyes. "These others, they never rode up to the house, Lord Cedric. That I swear. Why, I only thought they were with this tribe adviser because their horses were all white like his. Though they were all dusty."

Cedric stood. "And that would only mean they had a long and hard ride, my dear Cook. Which means they are badly in need of refreshment, so I'm counting on you to see that the riders and their horses get plenty of food and rest."

"Yes, Lord Cedric, right away!" The lead chef's chest puffed up with importance as he reached for the door handle.

"Tell them it's Guiffren's wish that they take their horses to Lord Markum's stable, and that they should then wait for him under the walnut tree," Prince Norlen said.

The lead chef gave the boy a queer look, but nodded his head and opened the door before rushing off.

Prince Norlen stood. "It probably looked mighty strange to him that a mere pageboy was sitting on Lady Christa's bed while his lord was standing. Not to mention giving orders. Well, Cedric, let's go see what Guiffren has to say."

"You're not shaking me off that easily," Christa said, jumping out of her bed. "I'm coming with you!"

Cedric looked back over his shoulder. "Come on, then."

They entered the library together, and all eyes went to the tall and lean figure facing the fireplace. "Guiffren, what news?" Prince Norlen asked.

The rugged man spun around and made a Nain greeting sign, then immediately leapt into speech. "Your Highness, the fat's in the fire. The Nain Oath Cauldron came to life yesterday morning. I assembled the riders and came looking for you instantly, but I fear it might still be too late..." He stopped when he realized that the prince wasn't alone.

"Cedric, Christa, this is Guiffren, my adviser. Guiffren, meet Lord Cedric Markum and his sister, Lady Christa," Prince Norlen introduced.

If it was possible to swoon with delight, Guiffren would have done so at that moment. "The descendants of Lord Chris Markum! This is good tidings indeed. My Lord Cedric, you must don your gear and assemble your men to ride with us this instant. Zansern's helmet must be delivered, and its protection is of utmost importance."

"I'm coming with you also, Guiffren," Christa insisted.

Guiffren gave a startled exclamation. "Are the young ladies of Lord Markum's Court trained in combat as well? This is most heartening! I'll not hide the fact that we'll need every able swordsman we can gather—" He paused when a muscled man, wearing a tall white hat and sharpening a strange weapon on a white cloth, appeared in the library.

"Lord Cedric, the horses are attended to and all is ready at the walnut tree. Will there be anything else?" the lead chef inquired.

Cedric cleared his throat. "Yes, see to my gear."

"You-your girl?" the confused cook uttered.

"Go to my grandfather's study and get the key to the armor room, then come and open the double door."

"Yes, Lord Cedric."

Guiffren watched the chef's departing back with approval. "What's his specialty?"

"He's most skilled with a carving knife," Cedric replied.

"Ah. A regular killer—excellent!" Guiffren nodded with satisfaction.

"How many riders, Guiffren?" Prince Norlen asked.

"Seventy, Your Highness, all the best."

I guess all seventy of them are devouring our other guests' food at this moment. A disconcerting image of seventy pot roast monsters feasting under the walnut tree flashed through Cedric's mind. *I better offer some to Guiffren here before it runs out.* "You must be in need of the rest of the food—I mean rest and food after such a long ride, Guiffren."

"You are kind, Lord Cedric Markum, but I must counsel that speed is needed. The rightful owner of the helmet Zanquei has summoned, and time will be consumed searching for his whereabouts. Might I inquire as to how many of your men will join us, and how soon?"

Bemused, Cedric mentally counted all the Markum estate workers, throwing out the occasional toothless and kiddy ones, and came up with fifty including Pauline. *I'm pretty sure we can sober her up somehow.* "Fifty—" he uttered.

"—and they're all ready," old Mr. Markum cut in as he strolled into the library followed by the cook.

"My Lord." Guiffren bowed and executed the Nain greeting sign.

Old Mr. Markum waved him on. "Come Cedric, you must don your gear and ride with them soon."

Maybe I did drink some of Owlut's potent wine last night, and this really isn't happening.

"Guiffren, Cedric's right. You must take your meal with the others while he prepares his gear and fetches Zanquei," Prince Norlen commanded.

"Yes, Your Highness. The good tidings I bear shall lighten their hearts as our riders partake of their hasty meal," Guiffren declared and bowed, then followed the lead chef out of the library.

Old Mr. Markum unlocked and entered the armor room, followed by Cedric, Christa, and Norlen. "Cedric, there's got to be a suit of armor in here that'll fit you," old Mr. Markum said.

"No kidding. Do you have any idea how heavy they are?" Cedric asked.

"Those fifty knights that your father sent from the Anguo Council will not take orders from just anyone."

And suddenly I'm in charge of a group of knights. Isn't this going a bit too fast? "When did they arrive?"

"Last night with your Uncle Hegan. Didn't you know?"

"I don't recall seeing them at the feast last night."

"They're traveling under the guise of Lord Hegan's servants and stayed at the guard house last night. Remember, Cedric, these men swore to serve only Lord Chris Markum's descendants, and they were trained by your father. He's staying at the Anguo Council where he's most needed, and he's counting on you to aid Nain as Lord Chris Markum did. Which reminds me, where's that confounded Prince Norlen?"

Norlen stepped forward, then made the Nain greeting sign. When his hand rested on his headband, he retrieved a blue stone from within. He held the stone on the palm of his hand and showed it to old Mr. Markum.

The old man gasped, but recovered instantly and nodded his head. Then he stepped aside and motioned for Cedric to come forward.

So, we are doing the stone trick today. Now, where did I put mine? If I end up having to rummage through my underwear drawers to find it, I hope Norlen'll understand. Cedric executed the Nain Greeting sign in reverse order, and when his hand rested on his left shoulder, he felt a hard spot in the folds of his draped neckline. *Huh, how did it get in there?* He retrieved the purple stone, then held it in the palm of his hand to show Norlen.

The two stones began to glow. "Cedric! Norlen!" Christa exclaimed. "You've got the same kind of jewels as the helmet in the secret room!"

Norlen smiled while he slowly brought his stone closer to the purple one, and when his hand touched Cedric's, the whole armor room glowed purplish-blue.

Christa clapped her hands. "Oh, it's beautiful!"

Then the grandfather clock started to strike the hour of twelve. "Cedric! Norlen!" old Mr. Markum bellowed. "Keep the fire glowing. Christa! Be quick! Come help me take off the giant armor's helmet."

Grandfather and granddaughter rushed to the giant armor, and the old man picked Christa up. She plucked the huge helmet off, and her grandfather put her down on the floor. He immediately took the helmet from her and put his hand in to retrieve Zanquei. "Oh—No! Where is it?"

Cedric whirled to look, and Norlen moved with him. "Cedric, don't break the contact!"

"But without Zanquei—" Cedric began.

"We must keep the Bond Fire going," Norlen explained.

"What did you just say?"

"I said let's make sure the Bond Fire, a fire made from bonds of friendship, stays on."

"The Bond Fire...bonds of friendship—Christa! Come quick!" Cedric urged, and his sister dashed to him. "Put your right palm up and make sure it touches ours."

Christa did as she was told just as the clock struck the twelfth time. But the purplish-blue flame started to die.

"It's fading. What are we missing?" Norlen asked.

"Michi! We're missing Michi," Cedric answered in dismay.

Christa fished Joseph's harmonica from her pocket with her left hand, placing it on top of her right palm. Instantly the purplish-blue flame burst into new glow and everyone laughed with the purest of joy.

"Christa, you did it!" Norlen praised.

"How did you know what to do?" Cedric asked.

"I saw you both had something in your hands and I didn't—" Christa began, but Cedric and Norlen broke out in new laughter.

"We're too dense for her, Norlen."

"Definitely! Though I don't know about you, but I don't think I can keep holding the rock in this position indefinitely," Norlen said.

"Me neither. Will you hurry up and look for Zanquei, Grandfather?"

"Cedric, what's Zanquei?" Christa asked.

"The helmet you and Michi tried on in the secret room."

"They put on Zanquei!" old Mr. Markum exclaimed.

This is no time to be modest. "Uh-huh, and before you fly off the handle, Grandfather, I think you should know that one or the other is probably Zansern, the Undefeated. As soon as they tried the helmet on, Prince Norlen was summoned. It probably even triggered the Nain Oath Cauldron."

"Wait, you mean Zanquei fits both of them?"

"Well, one at a time, but yes."

"By Jove! Then how will we fulfill our oath? Which of them should we protect?" Old Mr. Markum shook the helmet in his hands violently.

"My Lord, allow me." Guiffren, who had just entered the armor room, rushed forward. Then, he knelt and bowed in front of old Mr. Markum, his hands extended.

The old man handed the giant helmet to him, and the Nain tribe adviser stood. Carrying it in front and above his head, Guiffren walked to Cedric.

I'll look pretty funny in that big thing, but at least I'll be able to breathe. Guiffren held the helmet above Cedric's head and it acted like a funnel, sucking the purplish-blue light into it while the armor room dimmed. When the rest of the room was in darkness, the light from the helmet streamed out through its eye holes, then leapt to the giant suit of armor. Purplish-blue flames filled the suit, and it burst into a blinding light. Cedric closed his eyes. He felt a tremendous force whipping all around him, and he yelled when his hand broke off contact with Christa and Norlen. "Christa! Norlen! Christa . . ."

"Cedric! Cedric!"

Christa's calling me. "Yes?"

"I want a suit of armor too," Christa demanded.

Armor? Cedric opened his eyes. "Christa, where are you?"

He felt something pounding at him, and he lowered his head to look. "Christa! What are you doing way down there?"

A smaller Guiffren appeared next to Christa. "Lord Cedric, might I suggest that you only show your wrath when our enemies are about."

Enemies? Yeah, right, what enemies? He looked around and caught a movement just outside the double door. *Wrath*—"Pauline! Get in here!" The armor and weapons rattled while the walls shook. *Earthquake!* Cedric grabbed Christa and his grandfather. "Come on Norlen, Guiffren, let's get out of here!" he shouted. He then noticed Pauline cowering on the library floor. "Get a hold of yourself!" Cedric barked. The bookcases rattled and books spilled from the shelves, crashing to the floor. Cedric placed his sister on his shoulder. "Christa, hang on to my neck."

"I'll try."

Cedric grabbed the housekeeper just in time as a book-case behind her collapsed. Then, they were in the gallery, the music room, and out of the house. The sight under the walnut tree and beyond took Cedric's breath away. Row upon row of armor-clad knights and dark cloaked Nain riders stood to attention before him. They gasped on seeing him rush out the back door, but recovered instantly and knelt with bowed heads. He stood looking at the rows of kneeling figures in amazement. *No earthquake is going to rattle these well trained combatants.*

"Cedric, put me down! What'll the Knights of the Anguo Council think of you?" his grandfather scolded.

He put his grandfather and Pauline down, but the latter crumpled to the ground at his feet.

Christa stayed where she was. "I like it here, Cedric. You do get a better view up high."

Norlen moved to stand beside Cedric. "One of us should give a speech. Though keep your voice down if you're going to do it."

Cedric stared at the unfamiliar blue hair and the braid with a purple jewel dangling on Norlen's right side. "I think you should, since you've had time to pretty yourself up."

"Pretty myself?"

"When did you get the time to dye and braid your hair?"

"Y-you mean I've got purple hair and a braid like yours?" Norlen asked in horror.

"Lord Cedric, Prince Norlen, this is hardly the time or place to discuss attire," Guiffren advised. "Someone's got to give a rallying talk."

They both turned to him. "You talk to them," Cedric and Norlen said in unison. They rushed back into the house.

"Mirror! We need a mirror," Norlen suggested.

"Yes, a full length one."

"I don't think we've got mirrors tall enough for you both," Christa said.

"No!" Cedric and Norlen exclaimed, and the whole house shook.

They saw the lead chef come toward them. "Cook, do we have a tall mirror?" Cedric asked.

"I've got just the thing, Lord Cedric. Please follow me." He took them to the kitchen, and when they reached the giant freezer, the cook motioned for them to look into the glossy freezer door.

Cedric's eyes were at the same level as the top of the freezer, and he bent to take in his whole appearance. "Why, I've got the giant suit of armor on! Oh great, I've got purple hair and a braid with a blue jeweled hair tie. How embarrassing."

"You shouldn't complain. At least you can hide it when you put the helmet on. What about me?" Norlen asked.

"You could always wear your cloak and put the hood up."

"I think you both look very distinguished and dashing," Christa complimented.

"Really?" they asked dubiously.

"Yup!" Christa said. "And tall, too."

Oh, I almost forgot. "Cook, how tall is the freezer door?"

"Eight feet, Lord Cedric."

"Eight feet!" The utensils in the kitchen rattled.

"If you two are through admiring yourselves, maybe you could get on your horses and get going," old Mr. Markum suggested, standing in the kitchen entrance. "Since Zanquei has disappeared, and all these strange happenings have been triggered, either Christa or Michi must be the key. Christa is here, but we must quickly find Michi."

"First things first. Are there horses big enough for us to ride?" Cedric asked doubtfully.

"Not while you're all excited. Calm down and you'll return to your normal size."

"Easier said than done," Cedric said.

"Here are some old parchments from the secret room that might be useful to you," the old man said. "I'll find someone to serve as your squire."

Suddenly, the lead chef knelt in front of Cedric. "Take me with you, Lord Cedric. Allow me to serve you."

"Well Cook," Cedric said, "perhaps it's destiny. I guess we'll go on this journey together. Go take the parchments from Grandfather and tell Pauline she's to accompany Christa as her personal maid."

"Yes, Lord Cedric!" Cook said and took the papers before leaving.

"Christa is too young to travel so far—" old Mr. Markum began.

"I promised her that she could join me, Grandfather. Would you have me go back on my word? Don't worry, she'll probably be safer with us and the knights, anyways."

The old man sighed. "All is ready then. I'll say my farewell here." He moved forward and Cedric rushed to hug his grandfather.

Christa released one of her arms from Cedric's neck and circled it around her grandfather's. "Grandpapa, come with us."

The old man took Christa from Cedric and held her tightly for a second. "My little Christa, your Grandpapa's too old. But never fear, I shall be here when you return."

"Hey, Cedric! You're back to your normal size," Norlen said.

Cedric turned to look at his friend. "So are you, but I'm afraid your looks haven't improved."

"Neither have yours."

"Grandfather, if any of my girlfriends should come to call, just tell them I'm out. Don't say anything about my latest hairdo or my unstable condition, will you?"

Old Mr. Markum shook his head. "I've warned you about your dilly-dallying ways with the ladies. One of these days, Cedric, it's going to catch up with you."

"Lord Cedric, Prince Norlen, your royal steeds are ready. What should I do about Pauline? She claims she can't ride a horse," Cook announced, standing at the kitchen doorway.

"Just tie her to one," Cedric suggested with annoyance. "Christa'll ride with me. Tell Guiffren we'll be there shortly."

"Yes, Lord Cedric."

"Grandson, about Pauline—"

"I know. It was an excuse to tie her up. She can't do much harm to anyone that way. Keep well until we return, grandfather. Norlen, let's go."

"Cedric, where're we going?" Christa asked while they made their way to the back door.

"To catch up with your rascally friend, where else?"

"You mean Michi! Oh, Cedric, what are we waiting for? Come on!"

7

WATER BUFFALO CART RIDE

MICHI'S ANXIETY GREW as the van once again stopped alongside the dirt road to help some stranded stranger. It seemed everyone on the West Slave Route that morning had one problem or another, and their moving van had now become the roadside emergency rescuer. *We might as well put a siren on top of our van to make it official.* This time it was a bicyclist with a flat that couldn't be patched any longer, due to the sheer amount of old patches on the poor wheel already. Joseph tied the bike to the top of their van and they made a detour to take the bicyclist home. Every mile they traveled away from the slave route took them further away from the Nine-layer Southland Native Cake.

"Archoy, what time is it?"

"It's just a little after twelve, Little Miss."

No! My nine-layer cake! "How do these people survive when we're not here to save them?" Michi asked crossly.

"From what I've heard from the Natives, it's usually the other way around," Archoy said.

"What do you mean?"

"Oh, they say the Natives are usually the ones that have to rescue the Outsiders on the road. Something about how your modern gadgets don't work too well in the Kingdom of Lanhur. They joke about the Outsiders' cars being more trouble than helpful."

Michi's back stiffened and she crossed her arms. "Well! I didn't know that's what those Natives we rescued were laughing about. If I did, I certainly would have insisted that

Jo leave them where they were," Michi huffed, then nodded her head toward the dusty and shabbily dressed teenager sitting between the driver and her brother in the front. "How about this bicyclist? I haven't seen him laugh yet."

"No, he won't be laughing. His mother woke in the middle of the night with severe aches and pains. He's ridden his bike half the night to get to town and bring a doctor to come and see her."

"Half the night! Doesn't his own village have a doctor?"

"There's an old man in his village that helps with minor injuries and such, but he wasn't able to ease her pain."

"Well, where's the doctor?"

"The doctor was already out seeing another patient, but his wife said she'd send him out as soon as he gets back."

"I hope this doctor has something faster and more reliable than a bike."

"Oh, of course!" Archoy said. "The doctor has his own personal pedicab and driver." Forestalling Michi's next question, Archoy continued, " ...that's a three-wheel carriage, with a driver peddling in the front and passengers sitting comfortably in the back."

"And I suppose the extra passenger weight makes the tricycle go faster than a bike," she said sarcastically.

Joseph turned to look at Michi. "Sweet, are you hungry?"

Michi gave Joseph a "poor little me" expression. "I've been saving room for the nine-layer cake, but if we're not going to make it, then maybe I better eat something else."

"Have some pastries, but don't give up on the nine-layer cake yet."

"Alright, Jo." Michi looked out the window and sighed.

Archoy passed the basket to her. "Here you are, Little Miss."

"Thanks," Michi said half-heartedly, then she removed the violet cloth from the basket. One lonely bread roll and two egg sesame pockets stared up at her. *Bad news does travel together. How did our supplies get so low?* Remembering that her brother had been offering Arma's breakfast specials to the people they stopped to help along the road, a lump formed in Michi's throat. She lifted her head to look at her brother, and found the dirt smudged face of the Native youth peeking at her basket. A picture of the teenage boy holding his bike over his head and running, as he had been when they came upon him, flashed through Michi's mind and she tried to swallow the lump in her throat. *He must be hungry and tired, yet he couldn't abandon his useless bike.*

Michi picked up the roll and one of the sesame pockets, then offered them to him. "Here."

Eyes filled with wonder, the shy Native turned to Archoy, and the housekeeper beamed while speaking to him in Native dialect. When Archoy was done talking, the teenager said something back, then smiled timidly at Michi and took the food from her.

"I told him you have the Firmiana Inn's nine-layer cake in mind, and he's welcome to the pastries. He said thank you and he'll eat the egg pocket now, but if you don't mind he would like to save the bread roll for his mother. He thinks it might be easy enough for her stomach."

"Of course I don't mind, and I hope his mother feels better soon," Michi said. She tapped her brother's head. "Jo, want an egg sesame pocket? It's really good!"

"I have my mind set on the nine-layer cake also, Sweet. And I'm going to wake their cook up from his afternoon nap to make it for us if that's what it takes," Joseph promised.

Michi laughed happily. "I'll wait for him to make it, then."

"In the meantime, why don't you take a nap, Little Miss," Archoy suggested.

"That's a good idea. Sweet, it'll make the waiting go faster."

Michi rested her head on her pack. "Okay, but just a short one." She fell to sleep and in her dream, Michi was jostling with faceless competitors for the last piece of the Firmiana Inn's nine-layer cake.

MANY MILES TO the south and at the end of the West Slave Route, the Firmiana Inn's dining area was already packed to capacity. George Gurleon, guiding his buffalo around the traffic jam, stopped when he saw the innkeeper approach him.

"George, I'm so glad you're here. We're almost out of fresh poultry. Can you swing to the courtyard and unload the crates there?"

"No problem. Looks like you have quite an assortment of travelers eating at your inn."

"Yes, it's one of those days. We have Councilman Trumbond and his son here, and we've even got a couple of Nain Riders. You know how rare that is," the innkeeper informed.

"No kidding! The riders, they're just passing through?"

"They avoid us whenever possible. If they come, it's information they seek."

"So what do they want to know?"

Enjoying the attention he was getting, the innkeeper moved closer. "They wanted to know if a certain Anguorian teenager and his little sister, traveling in a van, have arrived yet."

"You mean they're interested in a couple of Outsiders?"

"Uh-huh. And what's more, our esteemed councilman is also interested in these two Anguorians. He wanted to be informed the minute they arrive."

George whistled. "Sounds like something's brewing. Did you say the two'll be arriving in a van?"

The innkeeper grinned. "So you know about the troubles the Outsiders' contraptions develop the minute they enter our land? Anyhow, they'll probably get here late tonight, or more likely tomorrow. In any case, I've got a million and one things to see to. I'll meet you in the back later."

He rushed off with a wave, and George steered his buffalo cart toward the courtyard behind the Firmiana Inn's kitchen. George halted near the back door and unloaded several crates of chickens. *I wonder why Dei's not here to chat with me.* He peeked in the kitchen from time to time, wishing to exchange news with his young friend. Everyone was bustling and no one seemed to have time to stop even for a small chat. George was a little disappointed, but he understood that Councilman Trumbond was a tough customer to please. *I'll go look for Dei before I leave.*

The innkeeper came out of the kitchen's back door. "George, thanks for delivering these so quickly," he said as the youth unloaded the last crate.

George patted his buffalo. "Big Thunder's the one that did it."

"He's the strongest and fastest buffalo I've ever seen. Anytime you want to sell him, I'll pay top dollar, George."

"Sorry, no go," George said, then changed the subject. "You've got more than the usual number of guests today."

"Yes, but I'm short handed," the innkeeper complained.

"How come?"

The innkeeper moved closer to George. "Shanui and Dei were sold by their uncle to Merchant Benny yesterday," he whispered.

"No! I knew he'd threatened to sell them a few times in the past, but I never believed he'd actually do it. It must have been a great deal of money."

"Oh yes," the innkeeper said. "Their uncle has gambling debts up to his neck, and Merchant Benny made him an offer he couldn't refuse. I've never seen Benny pay for anything that generously before."

"They're both excellent workers, especially Shanui."

"I never knew how much she did until she left. But even I would not have paid the amount Benny did."

"Of course not, because you're too nice to own any slaves. You can bet they're going to be put to work until Benny gets every cent back plus more," George said with disgust.

The innkeeper smirked. "I don't think Benny had work in mind when it came to the beautiful Shanui. I think she's—" The innkeeper stopped as a rumbling cart entered the courtyard and halted next to him. "Hello, Cousin. I thought you were going to Bayjai City. Did you forget something?"

The passenger of the cart vaulted down from the seat. "We forgot the contracts, isn't it stupid?"

"Well, they must still be in the safe," the innkeeper said before he turned to the driver of the cart. "If you want any lunch you'll just have to help yourself in the kitchen. You know I'm shorthanded right now. I certainly miss Shanui and Dei."

"You aren't the only one. I'm sure Merchant Benny's losing sleep over the Firmiana beauty right at this moment. Did you know they'd both been freed?" the driver of the cart said with pleasure.

The innkeeper blinked. "Really? Well, who would have guessed. Even the bad merchant can't escape love."

"Who said anything about love?" the driver started to say, but his horses moved suddenly. "Whoa!" he shouted. "These two have been given me trouble since early this morning."

George walked to the pair of restless animals and patted their heads. He then started to examine them. "Did something happen to frighten your horses?"

"Not that I know of," the driver began, then paused in thought. "Well, they did run over something that an Anguorian little girl called a dough man. She was pretty upset about it. But, really, it was just some animal droppings."

George frowned as he walked around the cart and gave it a once over. "You mean this?"

"What?" The driver hopped down from the cart and came to stand next to George. "Well! Now this is really something." He gaped at the blob that had clung to his wheel through hours of rough road. "The little girl was right. It wasn't bird poop after all."

George tilted his head and examined the blob intently. "You know, if you take a closer look, it really does have the shape of a man," George commented. He attempted to peel it off, but felt the blob resist. *It must be my imagination.* He tried again with a little more force, and he let go when he felt the strange blob pushing his hand away. "Oh, come—!" he started to say, and to his surprise, the blob hopped onto his hand.

"Good! You got it off," the driver said.

George squinted at the strange flattened blob on his palm. "I can't imagine your horses being frightened just because they ran over him."

"Are you sure my horses were frightened?"

"If George says your horses were frightened then that's what they were," the innkeeper interrupted.

The driver shrugged his shoulders as George moved to his own cart. George raised a warning hand to Big Thunder. "Stay," he commanded and pressed the blob onto one of his wheels. The buffalo attached to his cart jerked its head suddenly and started to move. "Whoa, I said stay, Big Thunder! Calm down." But the buffalo continued moving forward until the cart's wheel rolled over the blob. Then it slowed, stopping a moment after that. George scratched his head. "This is most curious."

"Yes, I've never seen Big Thunder behave like that before," the innkeeper agreed.

"My horses have been doing strange things like that all morning, but I'm not complaining. After all, I traveled from the Slave Route Junction to here in only a little over five hours."

"Then you must let your horses rest before you go on," George insisted.

"Yes," the innkeeper agreed, "lead them to my barn and come join us for a bite to eat."

After the other cart left the courtyard, George patted Big Thunder. "Well, Big Thunder and I have some deliveries to the H and S Village, so we'd better be off."

"H and S?" the innkeeper said. "Oh, you mean the Hide and Seek Village. George, that's a long way. You're not going to make it home tonight. What'll Sara say?"

"My mother says that it's okay for me to stay overnight elsewhere now that I'm a teenager. But since I'm taking the shortcut, I should still make it home tonight."

"The shortcut! Why, that's hard to find and easy to get lost in, even during the day. Are you sure you ought to try it at night?"

"I'm pretty sure I'll be back to your inn before dark, and Big Thunder knows the way from here to home blindfolded."

"All the same, George," the innkeeper said, "you'll not get home till the wee hours of the morning. I can't think Sara'll be happy about that."

"Tell you what. I'll stay at H and S for the night if I can't start back at a decent hour."

"Do that and I'll throw in a super sized Firmiana Luncheon pack for you," the innkeeper offered.

"Deal!" Before he followed the innkeeper into the kitchen, George went back to the wheel where the blob was stuck to the cart. He put his hand under it. "Come!" he commanded, and to the youth's delight, the blob returned to his hand.

MICHI WAS AWAKENED by strange noises. She tried to decipher what they were, but a gruff voice interrupted her thoughts.

"Sorry, no vans—plenty of buffalo carts for hire—can get you a good price..."

Michi's eyes flew open. *Angel from heaven*—did she just hear no vans, plenty of buffalo? Then her eyes met the most wrinkled face she'd ever seen, and she cringed. *No angel, this.* The weather-worn face broke out into a smile, with heavily stained teeth, as the old prune turned and surveyed the rest of the contents in the van. It was then that Michi realized her head was lying on Archoy's lap. She rubbed her eyes and sat up.

The housekeeper smiled. "Nice nap you had, Little Miss."

Their van was parked across from a partly flooded field, and Michi soon discovered the source of the strange noises. Water buffalo were wallowing in the mud of the nearby field, and were snorting loudly. Michi had never seen a real buffalo before, but she had seen them in picture books. These buffalo were huge; some of them were taller than the farmers, and had large curved horns. *What splendid animals!* Somehow the bulls reminded Michi of the insignia on the shields and breastplates of the Ghost Chasers.

Then she saw the craggy old man back off and face Joseph. "Two carts. One for passengers, one for packages," the harsh voice announced with a heavy accent.

Archoy shook her head and exited the van. The housekeeper greeted the old man, speaking in Native tongue.

Was it my imagination or did the old man just lose a lot of his wrinkles? The not-so-old man suddenly seemed animated as he chatted with Archoy. It looked as if the housekeeper had the situation under control; the middle-aged man was nodding his head and smiling a lot. The man turned abruptly to Joseph. "All is well," he pronounced. "One large buffalo cart—meal included." *Wow! Archoy is finally pulling her weight. Maybe if she bargained some more, the young man might throw in some snacks.* Michi's stomach growled.

She found out later that, while she was sleeping, they had dropped off the bicyclist and continued to Hide and Seek Village. It was then decided that traveling by buffalo cart to the Firmiana Inn would allow them to take a shortcut. And so, the hired hands were busy moving the boxes from the van to their newly hired buffalo cart. Michi walked over to have a look at the buffalo that would be towing them. The powerful bull must have been at least six and a half feet tall, and its huge horns were three-sided. She could see the buffalo's bluish black hide through its thin hair, while its tail swished to flick away the annoying flies that landed on it. She was about to walk closer to get a better look when a teenage boy moved in front of her.

"Don't approach him from behind. Come with me," the lad said.

Michi followed him and they made a wide arc around the bull, coming to the front. The youth gave a handful of hay to the buffalo, and patted its head while the bull ate.

"Oh! Let me," Michi said excitedly.

She grabbed some straw and joined the young lad. When the bull's tongue slurred over her hand to grab at the straw, Michi dropped it. *The buffalo's tongue is rough!* Then she giggled because the silly bull bent his head and tried to retrieve the dropped fodder lodged in the front of her shirt, tickling her.

"I'm glad to see you're enjoying yourself. I'm George," the lad said.

"Hi, George. My name's Michi. What's his name?"

"Big Thunder. Is that your older brother there?" George pointed to Joseph, who was carrying, with extra care, a box of Mrs. Dallion's fine china.

"That's Jo—he's the greatest," Michi announced.

"What's wrong with his leg?"

"There's nothing wrong with his leg," Michi replied without thinking.

"Then how come he's walking with a limp?"

Strange, I've never thought about it before. Jo has always walked with a limp. Is there something wrong with that? "That's the way he walks," she said defensively.

George backed away a little. "Okay. Just wondering."

I bet the nosy boy is also dying to ask me about my black eye. Unaware that the discoloring around her right eye wasn't as pronounced anymore, Michi lost interest in feeding the bull and walked back to the van.

The cart was ready to go and Joseph beckoned to Michi. "Would you like to ride with your new friend up in the front?"

"No, I'll ride in the back with Archoy."

Michi sat facing the back, with her legs dangling over the open cart. When they started to move, Michi almost fell off. She grabbed the side of the cart to steady herself. She looked around the interior of the cart—good thing they tied down the packages. Otherwise, there would be no way she could prevent them from tumbling over her and out toward freedom.

Now that the excitement was over, Michi found she was very hungry. *Well, we've got one large buffalo cart, where's the meal?* Then a horrid thought occurred to her. Maybe the "meal included" meant the buffalo's fodder. She should've eaten the straw instead of feeding it to the bull. Michi stood and looked over the plains, searching for fruit trees, berries, or . . . but there was nothing.

"Archoy, what time is it?"

"Just a little after two, Little Miss."

"Ohoo . . . there goes my nine-layer cake."

George immediately produced a box and passed it to Archoy. "Customer satisfaction is of the utmost importance. And what I have here is the Firmiana Inn's Luncheon, if you don't mind sharing it." As he spoke, he studied Michi's reaction from the corner of his eye.

The housekeeper opened it. "Why, Little Miss, you're in luck!" she exclaimed. "There's a big piece of their Nine-layer Southland Native cake."

"Really? Let me see." Michi grabbed the box. "Oh, it smells delicious and it bounces like jelly. Let me see—one, two, three . . . Jo! It's got nine layers." She passed the lunch box to the housekeeper. "Archoy, can you cut it into four pieces, please?"

"But of course."

Joseph chuckled. "Leave it to you to have us eating our meals in the reverse order, Sweet."

George stretched, deliberately casual, and turned to face Michi. "You can have my piece, if you like. I've had it quite often."

He really is alright. "Gee . . . thanks, George. Excellent customer service."

George beamed.

At that moment, Michi grabbed the side of the cart. "George! Ahead—look out!" she shouted.

George gave an airy wave of his hand. "No worries, Big Thunder and I are in control of the situation." The cart pushed through a mass of overgrowth, somehow slipping through its entwined branches. Michi ducked, a branch narrowly missing the top of her head. Big Thunder continued to descend through a tight path that threaded its way among numerous intimidating brambles.

Joseph looked back at the dense growth. "How did you even know there's a road here, George?"

George seemed pleased with the question. "This thrill is only the beginning of the Hide and Seek Village's Water Buffalo Cart Ride. As my customers, you must now decide on the level of excitement you think you can handle. And I must warn you, once you've decided, there's no turning back. So what's it to be?"

Joseph laughed. "Well, Sweet, are you game?"

Michi waved the brown cake that Archoy just passed to her in the air. "I've got my nine-layer weapon here, so let's go for it." Then she took a big bite. "Mmm . . ."

"George, go ahead and hit us on all sides," Joseph said, chewing on his own piece of cake.

"Okay, here we go! Hang on—" George started to say, when a blinding light encompassed them.

Everyone, including George, closed their eyes and screamed as their cart hurtled downward at a neck break-ing speed. When it finally stopped descending, the cart whipped to the left, zooming like a bullet, toward a castle. Michi opened her eyes just in time to see the drawbridge start to lower. "It's not lowering fast enough. We're going to fall into the moat!"

"It's okay, we'll make it," Joseph insisted while George, twitching nervously, said, "No, we won't."

"George, can we change our tour to kindergarten level," Michi pleaded. The sudden stopping of the cart lurched her forward, and the nine-layer cake that was held tightly in her hand smacked right in her face. "No!"

"Sweet! Are you alright?"

"It's my cake. I've ruined it."

'Well, never mind, you can have mine later. Now, what do you think, should we turn back or enter the castle?"

"Young Master Joseph, Little Miss, look! What's that?" Archoy, voice shaking, pointed to the darkness behind them.

Michi wiped the cake away from her eyes before turning, then squinted. "Little lights, I think—"

"Those are eyes," Joseph corrected. "George, get us into the castle quick," he urged when it became obvious that the approaching eyes also came with big red jaws and sharp fangs.

"Come on, Big Thunder." George guided the buffalo onto the drawbridge, and they sped toward the foreboding castle with its closed gates. "Now what?" George eyed the shut gates with dismay.

"You must have come on this ride before, George. Do something about the beasts," Michi insisted, staring at the drooling animals.

George cleared his throat. "Actually, I've never taken this route before."

"That's not funny, George," Michi said, then yelped when there came a howl.

"I hope they're not too hungry," Joseph said, while everyone focused on the fast approaching beasts. Lean and menacing, with mangy fur, the animals advanced toward them like half starved wolves. However, unlike wolves, these beasts' eyes glowed fiery red.

"Young Master Joseph, maybe there's a doorbell," Archoy suggested.

"Good idea, Archoy. Come on, George, let's investigate." Joseph passed his half-eaten cake to Michi, then hopped down from the cart. "Sweet, you stay—"

"No, Jo, I'm coming with you." She gave the cake to the housekeeper, then jumped down to join her brother and George.

"Little Miss, what should I do with the nine-layer cake?"

"Throw it at the leader of the fangs if he comes too close. Maybe you can blind him," Michi said, removing more of the sticky cake from her eyes.

"No door knocker, but what's this?" Joseph moved to the left, where there was a huge wheel with four gigantic beasts chained to it.

"Oh, I've seen something similar to this in a book. They should be the slaves of the gate. Only a command from the gatekeeper causes the beasts to move and turn the wheel to open the gates," George explained.

"So where's the gatekeeper?" Michi asked.

"They're watching us from the castle wall above," George said.

Michi looked up just as a troll stuck his head out from above. "Jo," she whispered, "we're being watched by a huge demon."

"I think there're three of them—" George began, but was interrupted.

"Hurry and speak the password," a voice boomed, "before the guardians of the Inmee Dungeon are set upon you."

"Open the gates and we'll tell you the password," Joseph said.

A thunderous laugh broke out from above. "Now, that's a new one. If you don't give the password, how's the gate supposed to open?" a loud and raspy voice asked.

"Now, wait a minute, we've all sensed the Zunji Light, and I say that's good enough for me," a different, high pitched voice said.

"How many times have I told you that Mowong the Mighty gave this part of the Inmee Dungeon to Vreeny. The Senginfan Captains, with their Zunji lights, no longer get special treatment. Unless it's on Vreeny's say so," the raspy voice insisted.

"Let's set the guardians loose and have some sport," the booming voice said.

Michi jumped when howls broke out all around them. "They're coming fast!"

"The leader's already on the drawbridge," Joseph noted.

"Well, here goes nothing," George said and brought a flattened blob from his pocket. He touched it to the big wheel connected to the gate. "Stay!" he commanded, and the blob stuck fast.

"What is that?" Joseph asked while Michi exclaimed, "Dough Man!"

The slaves of the gates started to move, and the big wheel creaked and turned. "It's working, let's go!" George shouted.

They rushed back to the cart. "What's going to happen to poor Dough Man?" Michi asked while the gate slowly opened.

"Let's worry about us first," Joseph said. He glanced at the beasts coming toward them. "George, get Big Thunder ready. Let's go as soon as there's enough room to squeeze through."

"Hang on, everyone! This is going to be close," George shouted as he spurred Big Thunder on, guiding the rushing cart through the gate.

I can't leave the poor dough man stuck on that wheel. "Dough Man, come!" Michi commanded at the same moment the leader of the beasts leapt into the air, coming straight for her. As the blob of dough flew toward Michi, it seemed like a mad race between the Dough Man or the beast to reach her first. The snarling jaw opened wide at the same instant Archoy threw Joseph's leftover piece of the nine-layer cake at it. The brown jelly cake plopped into the blood red mouth as the Dough Man passed the sharp fangs and landed on Michi's shoulder. Then, they were through the gates and rumbling wildly across a courtyard, pursued by not three, but hundreds of hideous looking trolls.

"George, faster!" Michi pressed when she saw the tallest of the trolls gaining on them. But the cart began to slow instead. "Don't stop, George," Michi cried as she glanced back, then froze.

Big Thunder was struggling with hundreds of tiny ropes that had been lassoed to his neck and legs, hindering his progress.

"Where're the cowboys?" Michi asked.

"There aren't any," George replied as he passed the reins to Joseph. "Take charge, I'm going to help Big Thunder."

"Little Miss! We're doomed," Archoy wailed. The tallest troll grabbed the back of their cart with one hand, successfully stopping them. "Goodbye, young Master Joseph, Little Miss," the housekeeper bade when the troll's other hand came for her.

"Oh, no you don't!" Michi shouted, grabbing her backpack and smacking it at the troll's huge hairy hand.

A cry of agony issued from the tallest troll. He let go of his hold on the cart and lurched backward, crashing into two trolls behind him. The other trolls dodged the tangled trio and rushed toward Michi with determination.

Michi saw the housekeeper lunge for the carton that held her mother's finest china, beginning to untie the ropes securing it. "Archoy, Mom's going to kill you."

"Better her than these wretched trolls, Little Miss," Archoy declared.

But there was no time for more discussion as the trolls reached the cart. Michi used her backpack like a baseball bat and began to hit at any troll that dared to come near her or Archoy. Soon, ear piercing cries split the sky, and trolls were hurtling away from the cart like baseballs sailing for home runs. The trolls quickly grew afraid of the little creature with the nine-layer-cake-face and her deadly weapon, and the ones that were still standing stopped attacking. They stood, hunched back while swaying from side to side, peering at Michi with awe.

"You know, Archoy, these trolls are all fierce looking, but wimps underneath," Michi said with surprise. "I don't think you should use Mom's china on them. You might kill the poor creatures."

"Get off the cart and run for your lives," Joseph shouted. Behind them, he had been standing in the buffalo cart's front seat, struggling desperately against countless tiny ropes that finally overcame him. The tough little ropes lassoed him down, binding him.

Michi spun around. "Jo!" She released her pack and climbed to the front to get to her brother. A fine rope whipped around her waist, and she paused. Instantly, several other ropes lassoed her. Michi fought to get free, but her efforts were soon over. She found herself tied up like a package, then tossed on the ground next to George. Soon Joseph and Archoy joined them.

"Hello, everyone," George greeted sheepishly.

"George, this Water Buffalo Cart Ride Adventure Tour . . . doesn't it have a wimp button?" Michi asked.

"Now, Sweet," Joseph said. "He did warn us there was no turning back. And we did ask him to hit us from all sides."

"Well, that was when I thought I had a nine-layer weapon, not nine layers of ropes," Michi complained, scowling at her tightly bound body.

"Young Master Joseph, do trolls really eat humans?"

"Well Archoy, I've never associated with them before, so I wouldn't know. However, according to all the books I've read, the heroes are supposed to outwit the dumb trolls and live to tell the glorious tale."

"The trolls aren't the ones that captured us," George said, and everyone turned to him.

"What do you mean?" Joseph asked.

"Look."

They all turned and were shocked as they saw, on a grassy ridge about twenty feet away, a line of magnificently dressed six-inch dolls. The small figures wore flowing silvery capes, and were eyeing them as well.

"Oh, they're so cute!" Michi exclaimed.

"Silence!" the dolls' leader, standing in the center, ordered.

Michi froze, realizing that the figures she had taken to be dolls were actually alive.

"Doesn't this castle come with normal sized people?" Joseph asked.

"I wouldn't mention anything about size again if I were you," George warned belatedly as the small silvery capes flew up. The garments turned into swords, which came down and fitted into the six-inch soldiers' ready hands. A stunned silence descended on the captives.

"You seem to have defeated those huge but useless trolls, but I warn you, do not be deceived by size. You have challenged the Mighty Guards of Vreeny's Court. Name your champion," the leader spoke once again.

"What is he talking about?" Michi whispered.

"Uhh... I think one of us is supposed to volunteer to fight them," George said.

"You've got to be kidding. All tied up like this? Even if they're—" Joseph began.

"Young Master Joseph, don't mention anything about their tiny sizes—"

"Archoy!" Michi and George hushed.

"Oh, me and my big mouth. Me and my big, big mouth—" the housekeeper wailed.

"So be it! Comrades, charge!" the leader shouted, and all the six-inch soldiers bounced off the ground, converging toward the housekeeper with their gleaming blades.

"Young Master Joseph!" Archoy, eyes filled with terror, shrieked while Joseph, Michi, and George tried to struggle to their feet.

I wonder how many small stings I can take before I go down—wait a minute! I'm not going down without a fight! "Fight!" Michi shouted. She gave a final push, managing to stand up. At that same instant, the dough man bounced off Michi's shoulder and flew to intercept the charging six-inch soldiers. *Oh, what have I done?* Michi watched with horror as the poor dough man was sliced into hundreds of pieces by the blades meant for Archoy.

"Dough Man!" Michi cried with grief. The housekeeper turned her head and shut her eyes, as if to avoid the blood that would have splattered onto her face had it been a real man. Rage filled Michi and, uncaring of her bound state, she hopped toward her small enemies. "Charge!" she shouted.

Joseph and George were doing the same thing, and the sight of the three cocoon-like bundles hopping up and down while yelling "Charge!" toward them seemed to have filled their opponents with dread. Michi saw them withdraw, bouncing backward some twenty feet. They landed on the ground, holding their sharp blades ready. She stopped to catch her breath while Joseph hopped to her right, George joining them at Michi's left.

"Any last wishes?" George asked, face grim.

"I wish we had weapons other than our mouths," Michi said.

"Maybe we can talk them to death," Joseph suggested.

"That's Archoy's department. She's the big mouth, remember?" George said, and they laughed. He then gave Joseph a sidelong glance. "I must say that I'm impressed. Nothing seems to phase you both."

"My motto has always been to take things as they come. Worrying gets you no free cookies, as Sweet here would say," Joseph replied.

Michi saw the six-inch soldiers split to form three groups. "Well, I'll take the center dolls. Too bad, they really do look cute."

"Don't let their violet eyes bewitch you, Sweet. Let them have it," Joseph said.

"I'll let the left group have it if you'll do the same with the right, Jo," George offered.

"Right on, George."

When they saw their opponents bounce up and attack once again, all three of them yelled, "Charge!" But before they could even hop, they were knocked down by Archoy, who had tried to join them by rolling herself toward them.

Michi landed on her stomach, and she lifted her head just in time to see hundreds of dough men fly past her toward the six-inch soldiers. *No good! They'll just be cut up again.* "Dodge!" Michi shouted, and all the center group of dough men ducked, escaping the cruel blades. "Attack!" she commanded, and all her dough men kicked and chopped at their opponents. When she saw her dough soldiers in danger of being sliced, Michi would once again order them to duck, then command them to attack. On either side of her, Joseph and George began to follow her lead, yelling commands to the dough soldiers on their side. Michi noticed that there were about ten dough men to each six-inch soldier, odds much to her liking.

"Little Miss, what's happening?" Archoy, who had landed on her back, asked.

"Oh, Archoy, you've got to see this. Here, can you turn?"

Archoy struggled to turn, while Michi used her head to steady the housekeeper. Archoy's hair tickled Michi's neck, and she giggled. Then mischief entered Michi's smile. "Tickle!" she commanded. The change in her dough men's tactics completely threw her opponents off, and to Michi's surprise, her little dough soldiers seemed to know where their victims' ticklish spots were. The fighting had now turned into a playful game instead. She whooped whenever one of her dough men succeeded in making a six-inch soldier giggle. Archoy joined the cheering squad when she was finally able to lift her head to see what was happening.

When all of Michi's dough soldiers simultaneously went after the leader, he bounced out of reach and frowned. "I know you ... but it can't be ... can it? Xane! It's you! Stop, Mighty Guards of Vreeny's Court." Instantly all the six-inch soldiers, save one, bounced out of the battlefield and landed a distance away. Then they threw their swords up into the air, their blades turning back into cloaks.

Oh, so we're having a time-out. "Stop! Come back!" Michi commanded her dough men. Joseph and George did likewise. Michi's eyes widened when she saw ten dough men dragging a struggling six-inch soldier toward them, as well. *We've got a prisoner of war!*

"You've captured one. Very impressive, Jo," George praised.

Joseph grinned. "Not as impressive as you."

George shook his head. "If it wasn't for the untimely suspension, I could have gotten a complete set of war gear for our brave Dough Man Leader."

Michi saw four dough men come forward and drop a hook, a rope, a cloak, and a pair of boots in front of them. *My, we've even got spoils from the war.* "Jo, does this mean we won?"

Joseph and George laughed. "Yes, Sweet. I'm pretty sure they'll sign the peace treaty before you tickle them to death."

"Here he comes." George struggled against the ropes binding him once again, attempting unsuccessfully to rise. "Want to bet he's never fought a war where his opponents' commanders were all tied up?" George asked.

As soon as their little prisoner of war saw the leader approaching, he hissed. "Kill them, Xorro."

"Silence! Vernott, you disobeyed my orders and put your comrades in danger. Not to mention you getting yourself captured. Now, be quiet and let me negotiate for your release," the one called Xorro said. He gave Vernott another hard look before facing Michi and the others. "Freedom for Vernott in exchange for physical freedom for you all."

"Done!" Joseph agreed.

Xorro raised both hands, and the ropes binding them unwound, flying to his palms where they slipped through his cuffs and disappeared. *Wow! I wish I could do that.* Michi sat up and stretched her limbs.

"Release!" Joseph commanded his dough men, and instantly the prisoner was freed. Vernott rubbed his wrists while giving Joseph a dark look.

Xorro pointed to the captured war gear. "Return your spoils of war in exchange for safe passage out of Vreeny's Castle—"

"No! Keep them here, Xorro. My Granduncle will know how to deal with them," Vernott interrupted, eyes glinting.

"You should be worrying about how he'll deal with your insubordination, Vernott," Xorro said with disgust, then he turned to George. "Well?"

Michi cut in before George could speak. "George, ask...Zero—"

"It's Xorro, young one," Xorro corrected.

Sudden understanding dawned on Michi's face. "Oh, Zorro!" She gazed at the tiny leader in awe, nodding her head slowly. She then turned to George. "George, ask Zorro here to throw in some snacks, will you?" Michi grabbed the opportunity to amend Archoy's oversight concerning their water buffalo cart ride.

"Uhh...our food supply is sort of low—" George began.

"Yes! We must give the victors a feast," Vernott suggested with eagerness.

Xorro frowned. "We're not accustomed to entertaining strangers. I'll see what I can do. Will that be agreeable?"

George looked at Michi, and she beamed. "Deal, Zorro," George agreed.

"Vernott, take the gear and return to the others," Xorro ordered. He waited until Vernott was gone before he addressed them again. "My compliments on your impressive battle tactics."

"You weren't so bad yourself, Zorro," Joseph returned.

"Listen to me. Vreeny hates the very ground Vong stands upon. I've got orders to kill or imprison anyone who has had anything to do with Vong or his followers. I don't know what Xane was thinking of, sending you here with his dough soldiers. Though he certainly reminded some of us of the happier times we used to have thousands of years ago. Tickle me, indeed!" He paused and chuckled.

Thousands of years and happier times...no wonder. Michi wagged a finger at the little soldier. "Look here, Zorro. You're a heroic legend, and your ancestors used to fight bad guys and rescue poor innocent people from jail. Now, you're telling us that you work under some bad guy, Vreeny, and are putting innocent people like us in jail instead? Wake up, Zorro. You must rebel. If you're afraid you'll be recognized, why, you know what to do," Michi encouraged.

"You puzzle me, young one. However, I've sworn to serve the king and his council, and am honor bound. Xane understood that. It is good that my Center Guards you just faced were all Xane's playmates back in the old days before the separation. None of them will betray what they have guessed already. But I cannot say the same about the others—especially Vernott. Fortunately, they are of a younger generation and do not know many of the olders' secrets. However, we have already tarried longer than is wise. Come, let me replenish your so-called snacks, and you can be on your way."

George whistled and Big Thunder came to him. He examined the bull while Michi patted it.

One of Xorro's comrades approached them. "Ah. Here comes my Right Commander," the six-inch soldiers' leader noted.

The newcomer smiled at Michi before he turned to Xorro. "Tina is back, and her orders outrank yours. You know her fondness for punishing trespassers. I've got four Xane Packs here in case our visitors are in a hurry." He produced a hook with four bundles tied to it, and threw it toward the cart. The hook hovered above the front, and the packages dropped down onto the front seat.

Michi considered the falling rations with dissatisfaction. *A whole lot of good these tiny Zane Packs are going to be when hunger strikes.* But she was wise enough not to mention anything about size.

The hook returned to its owner, and Xorro's Right Commander pocketed it before facing Joseph and George. He saluted them, then winked at Michi. "Tell Xane it's not fair that his eleventh sense doesn't have a ticklish spot."

Huh? But Michi had no chance to respond, as the Right Commander was already leaving.

Before he bounced away, the Right Commander looked over his shoulder. "Xorro, if you pretend you don't know Tina has returned, then you can deal with the Outsiders as you wish. Until she arrives, anyways."

His parting words seemed to spur Xorro into action. "Hurry!" he shouted. "Get in the cart and let's get out of here." Then he bounced and landed on top of Big Thunder's head. Xorro held onto the bull's right horn and leaned down to speak to the beast.

"Come on, Sweet, let's go," Joseph urged, dashing toward the passenger's seat.

Michi rushed to get in the cart, and before George even took the reins, Big Thunder was off. Michi and Archoy grabbed the rails tightly to prevent themselves from tumbling out and being left behind. *Left behind—Dough Man!* "Jo, we forgot Dough Man's kids," Michi shouted as they passed under an arch and sped through a great hall.

"Good thing you remembered, Sweet. Let's call them."

"Come!" Michi, Joseph, and George commanded together, but nothing happened.

"Maybe we're too far," Michi reasoned. "Jo, we've got to go back for them."

"Well, George, I'm afraid we'll have to."

George stared at them in silence, then shook his head. "I can't. I'm not the one that's driving Big Thunder." He dropped the reins and waved his hands in the air. "Look, no hands!" Sure enough, the cart still sped on without his guidance.

"Can you get Big Thunder to turn?" Joseph asked.

"If I try to turn at this speed, it'll be over for us," George said.

"But if we don't try, it'll be over for Dough Man's children," Michi argued.

They seemed to have reached a large stable, the cart rushing past endless stalls. "It's too narrow here," Joseph said. "Try it after we get out, and before we reach the forest."

"If we reach the forest—look!" George said as he tried to push Big Thunder to even greater speed.

Ahead, they could plainly see that the gated exit to the stable was now closing. *Why do we always have to cut it so close?* But there was no contest this time, as the exit closed well before they reached the gate, and Big Thunder whirled to the side in order to avoid crashing with the heavy barrier.

8

KING XODUNE

THE CART STOPPED, and they saw Xorro bounce from Big Thunder's head to land on top of Michi's backpack. "Stay away," he said while he untied his cape. He held it in his right hand and spun it like a fan's blade, faster and faster. Michi grew dizzy just looking at it. Xorro began to rise like a dragonfly, hovering above the backpack, before he suddenly let go of his cloak and bounced away. His cloak seemed to have increased in size as it floated down, covering Michi's backpack, and then there was nothing.

"Hey! Give me back my pack," Michi demanded, inspecting the spot where it vanished.

Xorro landed on top of the carton that held Mrs. Dallion's fine china. "It's not lost, young one. It's just invisible. Listen to me, all of you. I promised safe passage from Vreeny's Castle for you, and that's what you're going to have. Tina shall be very cross with me if she finds I'm helping any of you, and it will be beyond my power to aid you if she discovers what you're carrying inside that pack . . . " He stopped when two of his comrades landed beside him.

Michi noticed that one of them was Xorro's Right Commander. The six-inch soldiers flew into speech that was unintelligible to Michi, and she instead appraised Xorro with a critical eye. *He needs a new cape. And also a mask.* "Archoy, how are you at sewing doll's clothing?"

"Why, I'm one of the best."

"Good! Sew a mask and cape for Zorro here. And make it fast."

"What should I use for material?"

"How about one of Rosalyn's flowery dresses?" Michi suggested.

"Sweet, don't you think it'll be too flashy?"

"Well, as long as this Tina doesn't recognize Zorro, it shouldn't matter."

"I think the reason Zorro wore black in the legends is so he'd be harder to detect at night," Joseph said. "Also, black is more dignified. You know, to make his enemies fear and respect him."

"Like ninjas," George added.

"Oh. Black—black—" Michi searched around.

"Little Miss, how about the cloth Arma covered her breakfast specials with?"

"Archoy, it's violet," Michi scolded.

"It'll match Zorro's violet eyes," the housekeeper said as she took out a sewing kit from her pocket.

Michi gave the cloth a critical look, then nodded. "Alright, let's do it."

The housekeeper took the violet cloth from the basket.

"An egg sesame pocket! Yum!" Michi exclaimed. She grabbed it from the bottom of the basket and was about to eat, but stopped herself. "Jo, you've only had one bite of the nine-layer cake all morning. Here, eat something."

"Sweet, you go ahead, I'm saving my stomach for one of the Zane Packs."

"Jo, that's not even a mouthful—" Michi began when Xorro suddenly hopped down to the pieces of violet cloth.

"Areama! Areama!" Xorro exclaimed.

I bet that's thank you in his language. "You're welcome, Zorro. Now, try it on for size." She dropped the sesame pocket back in the basket and picked up a little violet strip, with two eyeholes, holding it up for him.

Xorro looked through the holes. "Why did you cut Areama's treasure?" he asked.

"Why, it's for you, Zorro, and you already thanked me. Now, you must stand up for what is right, as is your family's tradition and honor," Michi pronounced. She was about to continue, but the approach of a horse carriage interrupted her.

"Xorro, Tina's here. I'll go talk to her," Xorro's Right Commander said, then turned to his other comrade. "You go and do what's necessary." They both saluted Xorro, then bounced off and out of the cart.

Michi looked at Archoy's busy hands. "Archoy," she whispered, "what are you making?"

"It's a vest. He needs something to cover up those gold tassels on his shoulders. Why don't you help Zorro put on his mask and cape?"

"Good idea. Zorro, hold your mask up and turn around," Michi said. Xorro frowned, but did as he was told. Michi tied the back. "Can you see, Zorro? Is it too tight? Do you like it?" Xorro shook his head, and Michi frowned. "Does that mean you can't see, or it's not too tight, or that you don't like it?"

"Here she comes," George warned, and Michi moved to the side rail to take a look.

She saw a gorgeous enclosed carriage drawn by six black horses, rolling at a dignified pace toward them.

"Finally we'll be dealing with a regular person," Joseph commented with relief.

"Are the shimmering jewels and gold on that carriage real?" Michi asked.

Joseph studied the approaching carriage more closely, then sighed. "Probably." The six black horses came to a halt, and a brief silence followed.

"Why are these humans running loose in Vreeny's Castle," a stern but feminine voice from inside the carriage asked.

"The gatekeepers let them in without our permission," Xorro's Right Commander answered, standing on the vacant coachman's seat.

"Indeed! Why, I wonder. Those trolls are all a witless nuisance. I'll have to speak to my grandfather about them. Put these humans in the low dungeon."

"We already challenged them. They fought with honor and even took Vernott prisoner. Xorro bargained for their freedom in exchange for Vernott's life," Xorro's Right Commander reported.

"Where's Xorro?"

"Out checking the rumor about Vong's spies in the woods."

"I want every spy captured and brought to me personally. Now, take these humans to the dungeon."

"Tina, the Guards of Vreeny's Court have already given their word that these victors shall pass Vreeny's Castle unharmed."

"What did you just call me? Guards, take him down!"

Michi saw a group of six-inch guards pop out from the top of the carriage and make for the coachman's seat. Xorro's Right Commander bounced away and landed on top of one of the black horses. "I called you Tina, which is your name."

"I am Princess Tianna, and anyone who questions my royal heritage or my authority shall be silenced forever."

"Tina, you seem to forget you do not have authority over King Windune's Didee-guards."

"King Windune is dead! You're a guard of Vreeny's Court and you are under arrest."

At her words, Tina's guards attacked the Right Commander once again.

Oh no! Another fight. "Do you think your friend can handle all these guards?" Michi turned to ask Xorro, but found he was gone.

Michi spun, searching for Xorro's whereabouts. She found her answer a distance ahead. Xorro, wearing a violet mask, cloak, vest, and makeshift turban, was fighting sword to sword with the guards while defending his comrade. A second look revealed his Right Commander to be wounded. A flurry of strikes came at the wounded guard, and Xorro shoved him to the side before he slipped like magic between the sharp blades.

Just like a magician. "Archoy, we need to get him a hat," Michi said.

"Yes, Little Miss. I wonder if we'll have enough material to make him a pair of pants, also." Archoy lifted what was left of the violet cloth, measuring it. "It'll be close."

There was a sharp ringing of blades, and a sword thrust brushed past Xorro's neck. Another blade slashed toward the wounded Right Commander. Xorro swept his sword upward, and in mid-strike the blade transformed back into a cape. The whooshing cloth distracted his assailant, allowing Xorro to take down his opponent with a surprise kick. Xorro then flung himself backwards, his cloak again transforming into a blade and blocking the blow for his comrade. His arms struggled against the force, and it was with desperation that he managed to redirect his opponent's weapon to the side.

Xorro stumbled to his feet. Guarding his companion was slowly wearing him down, and despite his victory over one of the soldiers, his opponents became increasingly confident.

George winced as he watched the desperate struggle continue. "You know, Jo, with his comrade wounded, Zorro can't hold the guards for much longer."

"I agree. It's time for us to get close and give Zorro a hand. Let's move."

George steered Big Thunder toward the horse carriage. Xorro hoisted his friend and bounced off the black horse, landing on the front seat between George and Joseph.

"Steer for the exit and I'll open the gate," Xorro said.

"I'll do that, Xorro. You take care of Tina's guards," his comrade urged.

There was no time for argument, as hundreds of little guards rushed at their cart. Xorro lifted his Right Commander and bounced up thirty feet, flying toward the gate. The attackers turned and pursued the pair, charging at them in one giant swarm. Xorro glanced at his friend before abruptly spinning. He flung the wounded soldier toward the gate, and the force caused the Right Commander to hurtle toward the closed exit in a blur of speed. The Right Commander frantically threw his hook into the gateway. He smashed into the wooden door and began to fall, but the attached rope tightened and narrowly prevented him from splattering to the ground below. The Right Commander gave Xorro a long stare, but Xorro was currently preoccupied with the fast closing soldiers.

"Use your Didee-rope to open the gate!" Xorro yelled. He lifted his sword and began to spin the blade. Xorro kept the spinning sword three feet before the closed gate, which enabled him to hover above the ground and formed a barrier which protected both him and his comrade. The respite given by the barrier allowed them a chance to work on the exit.

By the time Tina's guards came to the opening gate, they found that, in place of the door, they were facing a huge spinning blade. All of them dropped to the ground. Before they could gather new energy to bounce up again, the buffalo cart tore down the stone pathway, forcing the guards to scatter or be ridden down. Xorro, for his part, had ceased spinning his sword the moment his attackers dropped to the ground. He and his wounded comrade rejoined Joseph and George in the front of the cart as they sped through the half opened gate.

"If we can reach the forest—" Xorro began.

"Sorry," George interrupted, "but there's a super fast carriage just past the gate, and it's riding us down like a winged buffalo."

Everyone looked back, and hope left them when they saw that the horses were literally galloping inches above the ground. "Are they flying horses?" Joseph asked.

"They're the Inmee Dungeon's Blacks, and yes, they're so fast that it looks like they're flying. No other horse can out-run them, except perhaps a purebred Nain horse. George, you make your way to the forest no matter what happens to me—"

"It's no good, Zorro. We're staying," Joseph spoke while Tina's blacks drew up next to them. A huge net popped out from her carriage, shooting to the side and closing in over their cart. The net stopped Big Thunder in his tracks, entrapping the group, and bringing their ride to a screech-ing halt. Everyone pushed at the strange net, their fingers slipping futilely across the strands, as the ropes seemed to tighten and shrink.

Xorro cursed. "Caught like flies! Don't struggle, it'll only close in on us faster."

"Archoy, quick, use your scissors," Michi pressed.

The housekeeper immediately went to work. "Little Miss, it won't cut."

"The net is made from sea witches' hair, and even my previous sword could not cut it. But let us see what my new blade, made from Areama's violet cloth, can do. Stand back," Xorro said, slicing at the net, and it cut through with ease.

Xorro cast the broken net to the ground next to Tina's car-riage, while George hopped down to check on Big Thunder.

"How dare you destroy Princess Tianna's treasure," Vernott accused, exiting the carriage.

Xorro laughed. "Tina is no princess, and you are not fit to carry my boots."

"You hide your face, but your voice sounds familiar. Who are you?" the feminine voice asked as the carriage's curtains parted. A six-inch doll, with shining dark hair, stepped out.

"Didee-jiny!" Michi exclaimed.

"Didee-jiny? The only one I know who says that . . ." The delicate doll jerked her head up and looked with shock at the masked Xorro. "Xeiyén! Is it you?"

Now that she had a better look, Michi saw that, what she had thought was the doll she left at Bayjai Arma's kitchen, was in reality a living creature. *Of course it's not Didee-jiny. This is Tina, the trouble maker.*

"Don't tell me the high and mighty Tina still remembers her old friend," Xorro scoffed.

"You know you have always been more than a friend to me, Xeiyén," Tina said, her eyes bright.

"Enough! Friends do not betray each other. Fight me or let my friends go. Choose swiftly, Tina," Xorro said.

Tina's eyes narrowed, and she scanned the occupants inside the cart. When her eyes rested on Michi, Tina sniffed. "Too bad the child's face is disfigured. Otherwise, I'd say she could grow up to be quite beautiful."

She can't be talking about me.

"Your judgement of all things has always been only skin deep, Tina," Xorro scoffed.

Tina shrugged her shoulders. "You call these mortals your friends, and you're even willing to fight me to protect them. You haven't changed. You're still as stubborn as ever."

"You, on the other hand, have changed. But not for the better. Now, get out of my way and go back to playing princess." Xorro dismissed Tina and turned to George, who had returned after making sure Big Thunder was none the worse for wear. "Let's go, George."

George pushed Big Thunder on, and they started to move. Tina's carriage kept pace beside the buffalo cart.

"Xeiyén!" Tina shouted. "Have I given you leave?" She uncoiled her whip from her waist and cracked it at Xorro.

"George, make for the forest," Xorro instructed while he caught the end of Tina's whip and yanked. Still holding the whip handle, Tina flew toward him. From under her sleeve, a sharp dagger fell into her hand. Tina slashed the dagger at Xorro when she landed. He bounced back and let go of the whip.

Xorro landed on the handle of Bayjai Arma's breakfast basket, and Tina's whip came cracking at the handle. Xorro sprang up, the strong force causing the basket to bounce. The egg sesame pocket came flying out. Xorro flicked his cloak at the sesame pocket, sending it flying toward the Dideetonie. "Tina, here's something for you. Catch!" The unexpected and unfamiliar object hurtling toward her caused Tina to hesitate. She stood rooted to the spot. The food hit her, and she grabbed at it as she started to fall off the rail. Xorro let loose his Didee-rope at the same moment he landed on the side rail. The Didee-rope wrapped Tina and the sesame pocket together, bringing them back up and placing them next to Xorro.

Tina hugged the egg sesame pocket, inhaled deeply, and then rested her head on it. "It is you! I recognize your scent. Oh, Xeiyén beloved, you do care about me! You even brought me a present."

They were near the forest by now, and the Didee-rope sent Tina and the food back to her carriage. Tina's carriage stopped at the edge of the forest. "Xeiyén!" she shouted, "I'll be waiting for you." Her words echoed as Big Thunder entered the uneven road into the woods.

Xorro bounced from the rail and landed next to his comrade. "How are you feeling?"

"Nothing that won't mend."

Xorro inspected the wound and shook his head. "It's poisoned. Tina's guards are using weapons made in the same way as the deadly torture instruments of the Inmee Dungeon. Only Tina and Vreeny have the antidote. That's why she was so sure I'd have to go to her." He turned to George. "When you come to the fork, take the left."

Xorro took one of the Xane packs and opened it. "I hope you don't mind if I make use of one of your snacks."

"Be our guest," Joseph said.

Michi leaned over and saw Xorro take out a flask, open it, and wash the wound. "This'll make you feel better," Xorro said, "and later—we shall see."

Ouch, that looks painful. "I hope you feel better soon, Berna," Michi comforted.

Xorro looked up at Michi in confusion. "Berna?"

This Zorro really is clueless. "That's short for Bernardo. Your pal, Zorro," Michi explained.

"Sweet, you can't just go around and insist that all of Zorro's descendants have a sidekick named Bernardo. I'm sure Zorro's comrade here already has a name."

Xorro's comrade sat up excitedly. "Xorro! Remember the Lady of the Crystal's prediction?"

Xorro studied Michi. "You puzzle me exceedingly, young one."

They came to the fork, and George guided Big Thunder to the left. He paused, focusing on the little soldiers. "What was the Lady of the Crystal's prediction?" he asked.

Xorro's Right Commander had a faraway look in his eyes, and Archoy repeated George's question. "So what did the Crystal Lady predict, Berna?"

Xorro's Right Commander began to recite, as if in a trance. "From this day on you shall be nameless. But do not despair. As Right Commander, the day will come when the chosen one shall give you your name. Then the true—"

"What's there to predict? Anyone knows Zorro's right hand man is Bernardo," Michi interrupted.

"No one makes light of the Lady of the Crystal's predictions," Xorro's comrade huffed.

"How long ago did she tell you that?" Joseph asked.

"Three thousand years ago."

"Three thousand years!" Michi and Archoy exclaimed in unison. Archoy leaned toward the Dideetone. "Berna, how do you manage to look so young; what's your secret?"

"Whoa, Big Thunder!" George halted the cart, then pointed at the sky. "Zorro, I think Tina sent you a present as well."

Everyone looked up. A Didee-rope, with a bundle attached to it, was circling above Big Thunder.

"The Didee-royal Summon!" Xorro said. "George, turn around and follow it." He started to untie his mask and take off his turban.

George immediately complied. As soon as they turned, the Didee-rope shot off, Big Thunder chasing after it at top speed. They reached the fork once again, but this time they took the other path. "We're going into the Didee-folk dwellings. George, watch out for pedestrians or crossing carts," Xorro warned.

"But I thought you Dideetones were underground dwellers, at least according to the Frontland Hectares' legend," George said.

"And so we are. At least according to you mortals. According to our perspective, you humans are the ones living in the sky. Didn't you know that the world we're currently in is far below the human world?" Xorro replied.

At his words, the group scanned their surroundings with renewed interest. Despite the superficial resemblance to their own world, they now found that there were indeed differences. The stars seemed brighter and closer, and though their surroundings were dark, the air itself was filled with a fine haze of glimmering dust, lighting the path ahead of them. The forest contained numerous towering trees, whose bark and branches were perfectly smooth, giving them a glassy look. And there was a stillness about them that bespoke of a lack of familiar forest life.

Xorro noticed their interest. "Our sky, the stars, the moon," he continued, "everything was originally formed from magic. Including us Dideetones."

"Dideetones! You mean you are the tiny folk . . . I mean the . . . Dideetones that gave Peten the poor farmer his fortune?" Archoy asked.

"Yes, I do believe Peten the Farmer met the Mighty Vong three thousand years ago. It was a chance meeting, and Peten was the only human to be much involved with us Dideetones. At least until now."

"So the children's fairy tale was true all along? That's amazing!" George exclaimed.

At this point, the Didee-rope they had been following entered a dense region to their left. "I think we had better park our cart and go on foot," Joseph said.

"Come Berna, lean on me and let's go," Xorro said, using the new name that Michi had given to his Right Commander.

As they made their way into the thick growth, Joseph and George walked in front to open a path for Xorro and Berna, while Michi and Archoy brought up the rear.

"Little Miss, look, Zorro got his old cloak back," Archoy commented.

Michi saw that Xorro's cloak was indeed no longer violet, but grey. "I hope he didn't lose his new outfit so quickly."

"Actually, just like a magician, he turned the violet cloak to grey. Didn't you see it?" Joseph said.

"Jo! You mean I could have gotten rid of . . . I mean used one of Rosalyn's dresses instead?"

"My disguise was made with Lady Areama's favor, and is a gift fit for kings. Thank you, young one. You are very generous," Xorro said.

"Oh, Zorro, you're very welcome. And you've already thanked me twice before."

They came to a small clearing, and Michi looked around. At first, she saw only a vast forest with numerous tall trees and dense shrubbery around. Then, a piece of bark from the bottom of a tree trunk near them suddenly popped open, and Michi gasped. A six-inch baker, wearing an apron and holding a rolling pin, stepped out from the hollow of the tree.

The tiny baker moved to stand in front of Xorro. "I was told to look out for Xorro. Would that be you?"

"Yes. Tell me where they are."

"At Didee-doc's, in his open patio, two dwellings down. Come, I'll take you."

They followed the baker as he set off, but Archoy stopped and sniffed the air. "Watch where you step, Little Miss."

"Oh, Archoy, it's probably just some doggy poo."

When they came to an old willow tree, Michi noticed that the Didee-rope was hovering above the tree's roots. She saw three mini-sized cots, all with occupants, under the shade of the tree.

"Now, where did Didee-doc go?" The baker looked around him, but froze when he saw shocked expressions from Xorro and Berna.

The two Didee-guards rushed to the center cot and knelt. "Sire!"

The baker gasped as he dropped his rolling pin. "Wh-what did you just call him?"

Xorro lifted his head, giving the cook a stern look. "Kneel before your king."

The poor baker's knees buckled, and he collapsed onto the ground. "Ohh ... Your Majestic-Your Highness ..."

"Hush! What are you doing disturbing my patients?" A small Dideetone, his head popping up from a hole in the ground, scolded the noisy cook.

"Didee-doc! These Mighty Guards of Vreeny's Court claim that this dying traveler is the king," the baker said, his voice shaking.

"The king—you mean King Windune?" the doctor asked, climbing out of the hole.

"What other king do you serve? Speak up," Xorro demanded, his fists clenching.

The doctor, seeing Xorro's dark expression, knelt immediately. "Please do not misunderstand. We were told that King Windune was already dead, and that Princess Tianna would choose her mate to become the new king."

"Well, as you can see, the king lives. And there's still Princess Leianna. So there'll be no more of this nonsense. Now, tell me, how is the king's condition?" At this question, the bundle on the center cot stirred.

A weak voice issued from under the covers. "Xorro . . ."

"Yes, Your Majesty."

"Must find . . . Leianna . . . she must . . ."

"I understand, Sire. We shall search for the princess. Are you very hurt—" Xorro paused when the covered bundle turned, and the bed cloth exposed a rotted little hand.

Archoy screamed. The stench Michi had thought came from animal droppings was actually coming from the wounded patients.

Xorro stood. "I'll be right back with the Xane Packs."

"Stay . . . no time. Xorro . . . you must be . . . new king . . ."

"No, Sire. These wounds obviously are poisoned, but the antidotes from the Inmee Dungeon—"

"No antidote . . . Mousasus . . ."

"Mousasus!" Xorro exclaimed. "Didee-doc, how long since they sustained these wounds?"

"My apprentice, the one that tied the bundle to your Didee-rope, found them near these woods four days ago. They were nearly overcome back then. At their request, we've been trying to contact you since."

The rotted hand lifted a fraction. "Xorro . . ."

"Yes, Sire."

"I command you to . . . end our . . . misery . . ."

Horrified, Xorro sank to his knees. "Sire, do not ask that of me."

"My last command . . . obey . . ." The weak hand dropped back down onto the cot.

Xorro, with bowed head, began to tremble. "Sire—Sire—"

"It would be more merciful to do as the king commands," Didee-doc said gently.

Xorro shook his head. "I can't. I can't—"

Silence fell, and Michi thought Xorro had turned into a statue. He stayed, kneeling on the ground without moving a muscle, for a long stretch of time.

Finally, the silence was broken by Didee-doc when he spoke once again. "The new Didee-king must be brave."

At the doctor's words, Xorro seemed to make up his mind. "Please take Berna and go back to the cart," he said to Michi and the others.

George picked up the slumped form of Berna, and they made their way back to the cart. Michi, who did not quite understand all that had been said, followed the others at a sedate pace. Joseph put a comforting arm around her shoulders. "Come, Sweet."

"Jo, is the king going to be alright?"

"From what they said, I gather that the king's wound is even more poisonous than Berna's. I'm afraid that Tina's antidote won't do much good," Joseph said.

"What's mousasus?"

"I don't know, Sweet," Joseph said. "Sounds like a kind of deadly poison."

Their discussion was interrupted by the sudden appearance of a huge head, peeping out from a tree trunk some distance in front of them. Michi grabbed her brother's arm. "Jo! A troll."

"Stay close," Joseph urged, bending down to pick up a stick.

"Friend—please, friend," the troll uttered from behind the tree.

"Come on out and let us see you," Joseph demanded.

The big form slowly moved from its hiding place. "Me, Didee-troll, Didee-doc's apprentice." The troll that stepped out from behind the tree was huge, towering over them. His overwhelming appearance stood in direct contrast to the 'Didee' prefix in his name—he couldn't possibly have been more unlike the miniature Dideetones.

"Hello, Didee-troll. I'm Michi, and this is my brother Jo."

"Didee-troll catch Didee-rope and sent for you. Your magic can help."

"You need help?" Joseph asked.

"Master's dying patients, they got same thing you got." The troll pointed his big and hairy hand at Michi's face.

Is he trying to tell me I'm ugly? Watch it, Didee-troll!

Joseph peeled a layer of the dried nine-layer cake from Michi's cheek. "Look, it's not the same."

Michi's eyes widened, and she clapped her palms over her cheeks while the troll applauded.

"You must make same magic and show me how!" the troll enthused.

"Archoy! Mirror! I need a mirror," Michi shouted as she rushed in the direction of the cart. When she reached it, she hopped up into the back.

"Little Miss, are you hungry?"

"Mirror! Give me a mirror," Michi demanded.

"You can't eat that! Now I've checked into the—"

"Archoy! How do I look?"

The housekeeper took a good look at Michi's face. "Huh, the nine-layer cake's all dried up and lumpy—here," the housekeeper said, then took out a small mirror from her pocket and passed it to Michi.

Michi took one look at her face and shuddered. "If this is what the nine-layer cake does to my face, think what it'll do in my stomach. I'm laying off the stuff."

"Okay, Little Miss, that leaves the roasted chicken sandwich and pickled vegetables from the Firmiana Inn's luncheon box."

Michi licked her lips. "Roasted chicken! Yummy."

Archoy handed Michi's canteen to her. "Now go down and wash your hands and face first, Little Miss."

Michi jumped down from the cart and walked to a shrub, pouring water from her canteen and splashing her face and hands with it.

"Aaa…" Berna, who was lying on the other side of the bush, exclaimed when a cascade of water and lumpy cake fell on him.

Michi stopped and wiped the water from her eyes, then took a good look. "Berna! What are you doing in the bush?"

George rushed over on hearing the shout. "Sorry, I shouldn't have left Berna there. But Big Thunder needed a rest, and I thought I should attend to him in case we needed to dash off again."

"It's my wound. It made me weak, and the Xane syrup made me sleepy," a drenched Berna said while he flexed his hurt arm, then frowned. "Did Xorro get the antidote from Tina and apply it on me?"

"Sorry, not yet. But I'm pretty sure he can charm her into giving it up," George teased, trying to raise Berna's spirits.

"That's strange. I feel fine," Berna said.

"Then the wound must not have been poisoned after all," George said.

"What's not poisoned?" Joseph asked, walking to join the group. Didee-troll was following him close behind.

"Jo! Behind you!" George screamed.

"Ah, allow me to introduce. This is Didee-troll, Didee-doc's apprentice—" Joseph went no further as a piece of nine-layer cake, issued from the cart, hit Didee-troll in the face.

"Little Miss, they're back! Ohh . . ." Archoy wailed while bending down and picking up the last piece of nine-layer cake, ready to throw again.

"Archoy, calm down, this one's friendly," Joseph assured. The troll wiped the nine-layer cake from his face and studied the brown cake on his palm.

There was a sudden movement, and all eyes turned to Berna. "The king!" he exclaimed. "Did I dream I'd seen King Windune?"

"No, it wasn't a dream. I think you fainted from your wound while kneeling in front of King Windune. I'm sorry, Berna, but your king ordered Zorro to end the misery for—"

"Sire! No!" Berna bounced off and flew toward Didee-doc's open patio.

"Jo! What are you saying?" Michi asked.

Joseph cleared his throat. "Sweet, you know how sometimes a horse is wounded beyond help and the rancher—"

"You mean mercy killing! But this is . . . No!" Michi dashed off also.

"Little Miss! Little Miss!"

Michi ignored Archoy, rushing into the woods. She reached the small clearing where the willow tree stood, and was shocked to see thousands of Didee-folk all kneeling around the tree.

She saw Xorro, head bowed, leaning on his sword while Berna kneeled in front of him. "Berna swears his undying loyalty to his new king. Hail King Xodune," Berna declared, and all the Didee-folk followed, "Hail King Xodune!"

The Didee-rope, with the little bundle tied to it, moved from above the middle cot to hover over Xorro. "Hail King Xodune!" Berna declared the second time, and the Didee-folk followed, "Hail King Xodune!" The bundle held by the Didee-rope popped open, and a silver crown with shimmering violet jewels descended to rest on Xorro's head.

Wow! Looks expensive. Why, Zorro is now king! "Hail King Zodune," Michi shouted with everyone else.

"Well, who would have guessed that Zorro here would become the king of the little-I mean the Dideetones," Archoy said when she caught up with Michi. "Hail King Zodune!" she also shouted.

"I guess the worst is over, and they're hailing their new king," George said, refreshing Michi's memory.

"Jo, you mean Zorro already killed King Windune?" Michi asked.

"There's no blood on his blade, so I would guess the king—" Joseph began.

"Jo! King Windune just moved," Michi interrupted. Heedless of everyone else, Michi rushed to the middle cot and flipped open the bed cloth. The sudden rush of stench almost knocked Michi out. "Archoy, do you have a wash-cloth?" she asked.

Delving into her pocket, Archoy produced a piece of Arma's violet cloth. "Will this do, Little Miss?'

Michi took it, soaking it with water from her canteen, then bent and cleaned King Windune's rotted face. All the Didee-folk gasped at the audacity of the human child who dared to disturb their old king's rest. Joseph and George made their way carefully toward Michi.

"Don't expect miracles, Sweet," Joseph whispered.

The old king stirred, and shifted to face Michi. "Areama...Areama..."

Dideetones are very polite folk. Michi smiled. "You're welcome, Windune."

A hint of a smile appeared on the rotted face. "Areama, the most sympathetic handmaiden of the Golden Woods." The uttering of these words seemed to bring relief to the sufferer, as the old king fell into a peaceful rest.

Xorro watched Michi's strange actions. "Didee-doc," he called, "come quickly and tell me how the king is doing."

After checking, the doctor's face brightened. "Your Majesty, the old king seems to be getting better."

At these words, Xorro sank to his knees. "Areama—Areama—"

Not again! "You're welcome, Zorro-I mean King Zodune," Michi said as she moved to her next patient.

9

MOONLIGHT SERENADE

MICHI SAT CROSS-LEGGED on the grass, eating ribs and sautéed vegetables from the Xane Pack. "George, I had no idea a small package like this could fit so many goodies inside."

Joseph took out a tiny cookie from the Xane Pack and it instantly enlarged to jumbo size. He waved the giant cookie at George. "Yes, this Water Buffalo Cart Ride Tour is certainly filled with a lot of surprises, George. Are you sure you're making any money on this?"

George grinned sheepishly. "Actually, my usual tour consists of just a little dip into a muddy pool and a few mild splashes onto my customers' faces, followed by a regular meal. But you three are far from regular, that's for sure. As for the money, I feel I'm the one that's getting a better deal. I've made three human friends, two Dideetone friends, and one troll friend."

"And if that is not enough riches, I can always fill your cart with precious jewels and gold. Much like Vong did for Peten the Farmer," Xorro, or King Xodune as the Dideetones were now calling him, said as he arrived with Berna.

"Hello King, hi Berna. The gold and jewels were useful to Peten because he was a slave, and the fortune gave him his freedom. We, on the other hand, have you to fall back on if we ever need anything, so why should we burden ourselves carting such a nuisance around?" George teased.

King Xodune laughed, then sat between Michi and Joseph, Berna standing behind him.

"Berna, don't stand breathing down on me. Come, join us," the king said.

"Sire—"

"Sit down, Berna."

"Yes, my L—"

"Don't say it, Berna," King Xodune ordered with exasperation.

"But I must set a good example for the Didee-folk, concerning the proper attitude toward their new king," Berna said.

"I think I'm the one that must prove to them I'm worthy of their respect. Now, sit down."

"Yes, Your..." Berna began, then stopped on seeing the king's stern look. He sat down instead.

"How's Windune and his guards doing?" Michi asked.

"Sleeping soundly for the first time since Didee-troll found them four days ago," King Xodune said. "A good rest is the road to recovery. You truly puzzle me, young one. How did you manage to obtain a canteen of water with mousasus saliva in it, and how did you know that that was the way to save its victims?"

"You mean my water had a deadly poison in it?" Michi asked in alarm.

"The mousasus' claws are deadly, but their saliva is the antidote. You need not worry about drinking it. A canteen of such a mixture is priceless, since it can cure all known poisons. You are generous indeed," King Xodune explained.

"Oh! Little Miss, I shouldn't have told you to waste your priceless water on washing your dirty hands and face," Archoy apologized.

"Drenching Berna with it was a bit of an overkill, but he's not complaining," King Xodune said, and everyone laughed.

"A king that has a sense of humor is a blessing to his subjects. King Xodune, I am honored to serve you," Berna said.

"You are a good friend, Berna. We will rebuild what was lost to the Northern Didee-folk bit by bit, and I will always treasure your advice."

"Then start by reconsidering what I've counseled, Sire."

"Berna, we've already gone through that before. I can't let you take the risk of going back to Vreeny's Castle. They'll arrest you on sight. But I, on the other hand, they still don't suspect. If I play it right, I could go back and get all our comrades to join us without Vreeny being the wiser. It's the only way, Berna."

With desperation, Berna turned to the others. "What do the commanders of Xane's Dough Soldiers think of King Xodune risking his royal neck?"

"I see your dilemma. Under normal circumstances, the king shouldn't be risking his life. But Berna is a fugitive. Isn't there anyone else to send?" Joseph asked.

"Yes, King Zodune, I'm pretty sure young Master Joseph, young Master George, our Little Miss, or even I could go to the castle and pass the message along," Archoy volunteered.

"Haven't you forgotten something, Archoy? A fine target we'll all be as soon as we get out of this forest," George reminded.

Berna winked at the king. "Yes, there's a disadvantage in being too big."

King Xodune and Berna studied Archoy for a moment, then roared with laughter. "You should have seen yourself, Archoy," King Xodune said. "When you were wailing 'me and my big mouth'—it was almost impossible for my comrades and me to keep a straight face when we charged."

"You mean you had no intention of skewering Archoy?" Michi asked in amazement.

"Vernott and the others did, but not us," King Xodune said. "When I tied you up, I purposely left the Dough Soldier out. I didn't know it was Xane's eleventh sense at the time, but I knew you would be ordering it to rescue Archoy."

Gee, I didn't even know it myself. "You did?" Michi asked in surprise.

"You cut it pretty close, though," Berna said. "I was beginning to worry when my blade got too close to her."

"Oh, Little Miss, you had me scared," Archoy scolded.

"Actually, it worked out perfectly," the king said. "I don't think we could have convinced Vernott any other way, which brings us back to who to send to contact our old friends."

"Tina and her guards are expecting me to still be poisoned. I think I can take advantage of that," Berna volunteered once again.

"I still don't like it," King Xodune said.

Michi looked at the darkening sky. "Isn't this a job for Zorro?" she asked.

"That makes it two against one, Berna," the king said.

Berna fixed his gaze on Joseph and George. "What do you think?"

George grinned. "That's true, Zorro. You do have an open invitation under the moonlight with Tina. Why don't you take her up on it for a daring midnight rendezvous?"

"Sweet," Joseph said, "get Archoy to make a mask for Berna, and he can play the violin while Zorro does his thing."

"Rose, don't forget one budding rose, Zorro," Michi added.

"Oh! Little Miss, how romantic!" Archoy said and clasped her hands together. "Berna, come with me."

Dazed, Berna slowly stood. "Will it work?"

"I guarantee it," George assured.

King Xodune watched Archoy and Berna leave. "Is the violin necessary? Berna can't play at all."

"Haven't you ever been in love before, Zorro?" Joseph asked. "Don't you know that when you're in love, everything's beautiful?"

George gave a thoughtful nod. "Yes, that includes screeching violins."

"And when Tina dismisses the hopeless violinist so that she can be alone with you, Berna can roam freely in the castle recruiting for your army," Joseph explained.

"And just what am I supposed to be doing with Tina while Berna is going around having fun?"

"I'll prepare a fun bag for you also, Zorro," Michi said. "Whenever you and Tina run out of things to do, you can always do one of the activities inside the bag."

King Xodune sighed. "Oh, alright. I just hope Berna doesn't take too long."

"Who knows, maybe you'll find this new experience enchanting," Joseph encouraged, and Michi tried desperately to stifle her giggles.

King Xodune cleared his throat. "I told Didee-doc I'd be stopping by before going back to Vreeny's Castle, so I'll see you all later."

"Good luck and good hunting," George said, and they laughed as the king, trying to look dignified, walked away.

"I wish we could be there to see it," Michi said, giving Joseph a "poor little me" expression.

Joseph ruffled her already unruly hair. "Why not? I think we should all go and make sure there are no last minute glitches. George, it's time to romanticize Zorro's carriage. After all, the king has a heavy date tonight."

"So what do you suggest? Spray perfume on Big Thunder and put a bow on his tail?"

"I was more thinking about disguising your cart to look like a honeymoon carriage. You know, all decked out in exotic flowers."

"Oh, Jo! Let me help," Michi shouted, jumping up and down.

"Sure thing Sweet, you do the decorating. George and I'll tend to the details of smuggling us into the castle."

"Woo…that sounds like fun. Couldn't I do both?"

"That's a good idea. We'll decorate the cart in such a way that it'll camouflage our hideout."

"Oh goody! What's camouflage?"

"It means make us blend in with the surroundings—" Joseph started to explain.

Michi scanned the trees around them. "I want to be a palm tree," she said. "I've always wanted to drop one of those huge coconuts onto unsuspecting travelers resting under the shade."

Joseph patted Michi's shoulder, chuckling indulgently. "Don't drop the bomb too soon, and make sure you aim it at Tina. Now go cover the cart with flowers and make yourself into a palm. A couple of stiff tree stumps'll do for George and me. Come on, George, let's move the boxes out of the cart."

"Jo, you don't want to be just a stupid block of wood," Michi said. "After all, we have thousands of talented Didee-folk around here, who probably have nothing better to do. You leave everything to me." She turned in the direction of Didee-doc's dwelling, running while she shouted, "Didee-troll, Didee-troll, where are you?"

I MUST BE insane to let Michi, Joseph, and George talk me into doing this. King Xodune stood, eyeing the preposterous looking cart with dread. "What is this thing called again, Berna?"

"A honeymoon carriage, Sire."

The king looked up at the silvery moon in the sky and frowned. "I see the moon, but where is the honey?"

"Well, there're bees, flowers, and trees in the carriage. Together they make honey," Berna reasoned.

"Ah. The humans like to do things in such a roundabout way. A pot of honey would have done it. Come on then, and let's get it over with."

"Don't forget your disguise, Sire," Berna reminded, putting his own blue mask on.

"Berna, watch what you call me in front of Tina. On second thought, your voice is too distinct. It's better you play mute," King Xodune, or Xorro, suggested while he also donned his mask.

"Good idea, otherwise Tina'll see through us," Berna said, hopping onto the driver's seat.

Xorro settled beside Berna. "I have always thought Tina was silly to be going around in a huge carriage. I never thought I would be doing the same thing myself one day."

Berna took hold of the reins and guided Big Thunder out of the Didee-folk's dwellings. "Many things are like that. You do not know what's it like until you're in the other's boots."

"You think I'm too harsh on Tina about her wanting to be a princess?"

Berna shrugged his shoulders. "I think she's basically a regular Dideetonie. You know, a bit vain. She was better off without Vreeny's influence, though."

"She could hardly do that. After all, Vreeny is her grandfather."

"I've often wondered about that. I don't recall Vreeny ever finding himself a mate, do you?"

"Not that I can remember," Xorro said. "But Vreeny has always kept his personal life private. I was very surprised when I found out Queen Pollyanna was actually Vreeny's sister."

"Really? How come you never mentioned it?"

"Because I didn't know it until Windune told me when we talked just now. He said he never suspected Vreeny's treachery because, after all, he's his brother-in-law."

Berna whistled. "That explains a lot. You realize, according to the Didee-royal rules, Vreeny should have resigned as King Windune's advisor the day his sister married the king?"

Is that why Windune apologized about deceiving me?
"Berna, if what you said is true, then it was not Vong who should have left the Didee-council, but Vreeny."

"Yes. And now much is explained about the second part of the Lady of the Crystal's prediction. Remember, she said that on the day I was given a new name, the true Didee-king would be revealed. At the time I thought it odd that she did not say the new Didee-king, but the true Didee-king instead. According to the Didee-royal rules, King Windune ceased to be king once he deceived the Didee-council. Obviously, the Lady of the Crystal knew even then."

"No one could pull wool over her eyes."

Their talk stopped when they arrived at the edge of the forest, and Xorro studied the distant castle. "Looks quiet enough. What do you think?"

"Can't tell until we get a bit closer," Berna said.

"Let's do it."

They stayed silent as they left the protection of the forest, making their way toward Vreeny's Castle. When they came to the stable's entrance, the gate opened. Vernott emerged, looking ridiculous as he sat on his tiny saddle atop one of the large Inmee blacks. Behind him, a group of Tina's guards followed, bouncing on their giant mounts.

"Halt! What is this?" Vernott challenged, sizing up the strangely decorated cart.

Berna stopped the cart.

"Get out of my way!" Xorro said. "Tina knows I'm coming."

"Ah. Coming for the antidote, are you? It'll serve you better if you learn how to address her. You can ride with us, but you must leave your masked coachman and this—uhh ... flower cart behind," Vernott said.

Xorro shook his head. "I will ride in this honeymoon carriage with my coachman into Vreeny's Castle, or Tina can—"

"Did you say honeymoon carriage?" Vernott exclaimed with bewilderment. He scanned the contents of the cart with interest. "I get it! Bees, flowers, and trees. 'Honey'moon carriage, with a capital H. I see you've been keeping up with the newest trends, good for you. Those giant bees and flowers sure look real, though. What did you do? Enlist the help of not only Didee-artists, but also trolls to make them? Well—Okay, come on. I'll escort you to Princess Tianna."

One of Tina's guards turned his mount and galloped off, presumably to announce Xorro's arrival to Tina. The rest of the guards split into two groups. One rode ahead of the cart, while the other group fell behind to take up the rear.

Why do I get the feeling that I'm trapped?

They started to move again, and Vernott rode next to them. "So you're the spy that Xorro went into the forest to investigate. Are there more of you, or did you sneak out of Vong's hideout to woo Princess Tianna in the hopes of becoming the future Didee-king?"

Woo? "You dress as a guard of King Windune's Court, yet you talk as if you serve a different king," Xorro said.

Vernott laughed. "Come, let's not pretend you know nothing about Princes Tianna's intention to find a mate and the next king. How clever of you to play it cool this afternoon and allow the princess to stew over whether you're interested at all. You even had me fooled. And the added thrill of a disguise…why, you had her pacing back and forth in her chamber with impatience. Poor Xorro would never have thought up such a mysterious and romantic way of wooing her in a million years."

At this, Vernott paused and shot the disguised Xorro a wink. "Listen, Xeiyén—don't look so shocked. I made it my business to find out all about you as soon as Princess Tianna showed her preference. Since the old king kicked the bucket, there're only three of you in contention for the throne. You, Xorro, and Xane. I must warn you that

Vreeny is dead set against you or Xane as the next king, because of your association with Vong." Vernott leaned toward the masked Xorro. "Xorro's going to be a hard opponent to beat," he whispered. "But if you team up with me, Xeiyén, I'm sure we can wrench the crown from Xorro and send him to join Windune."

Plotting my downfall, are you? Just let me get my hands on that pale neck of yours, Vernott. With murderous intention, Xorro crooked his finger at Vernott, who eagerly moved his steed even closer, leaning his head down to Xorro. Berna coughed loudly when Xorro moved his hands to encircle Vernott's neck. Xorro caught himself, and moved his hands above Vernott's head instead. "And what can the new king expect from you, Vernott?"

"Undying loyalty," Vernott declared.

Xorro gritted his teeth while he patted the top of Vernott's head. "Good, very good. I shall remember your declaration when the time comes."

Vernott lapped up the favor like a puppy. "When that time comes, please remember the small service that your humble subject has performed on your behalf." He saluted Xorro before moving back to the front of the procession and leading them through the stable gate.

They rumbled toward Tina's palace garden, and Xorro checked from side to side. *Odd, why aren't there any of my Center Guards around?* He looked to Berna, and from his expression, Xorro knew his friend was wondering the same thing.

Vernott led their cart to beneath Tina's balcony and stopped, then winked at Xorro. "Go for it," he said before leading Tina's guards away.

Now what? Xorro and Berna sat looking at the well-tended garden, and listened to the crickets chirping. Suddenly, from somewhere in the back of the cart, a voice whispered. "Berna, play your violin."

Both Xorro and Berna jumped. "Is that you, Michi?" Xorro whispered while he turned to look back.

"Don't turn around. Stand and look up at the balcony while Berna plays his violin," Michi whispered. Berna took out the violin and positioned himself. "Don't forget the fun bag. It's on the front seat," Michi added.

Xorro reached inside the bag and pulled out a red rose with a small piece of paper attached to it. He silently read the note while Berna played the violin.

"What's that pig squeaking racket? Who dares to invade my private sanctuary?" An irritated feminine voice issued from the chamber above.

I think Tina's in a bad mood.

Berna stopped playing.

"Now what?" Xorro whispered.

"The poem, read her the poem," Michi urged.

Tina came to the balcony. "Xane! What's the matter with you? Have you forgotten how to play the violin?"

"What makes you think he's Xane, Tina?" Xorro asked.

"Who else would be crazy enough to embark on this outrageous charade with you, Xeiyén? Besides, Grandfather recognized all those dough soldiers as Xane's. You're very nutty to play a trick like that on Vernott and the others. But that's what I like about you two. You're so much fun to be with. Not like Xorro, so boring."

Xorro cleared his throat. "You think Xorro is a bore?"

"You know he is. He's always so serious and stuck up. Don't you remember that time you dared me to dress up as one of King Windune's new Didee-guards to be trained under him?"

"What!"

Tina laughed. "You're still sore about losing that bet, Xeiyén? Well, I've never been so proud of myself in my life. I not only enlisted under him, but became one of his best Didee-guards. Why, I even shared his tent—don't look so indignant, Xeiyén. I didn't say anything to you about that because nothing happened. Although I did scratch his back for him when he was bathing—Xeiyén! Are you alright?"

Scar Face! She's Scar Face! Xorro paled and staggered. He leaned on the dividing rail, trying unsuccessfully to collect his scattered wits. *The absurdity! The humiliation! Did my other comrades know?* Xorro stole a look at Berna and found him doubled over and shaking with mirth. *I'll kill him later. Right now I've got more pressing business.* "The way you suddenly disappeared back then was very impressive, Scar Face. I blamed myself for sending you out alone to do that bit of dangerous work—" Xorro stopped and mentally kicked himself. *Concentrate!*

"Oh, it wasn't all that dangerous . . . wait a minute. It was you who sent me out? I thought it was Xorro. But of course, it all make sense now. You knew I was wracking my brain trying to think of a way to disappear before Grandfather found out about my charade. Remember how we laughed when I 'arrived' with Grandfather and found everyone looking for me . . . I mean Scar Face."

Xorro gritted his teeth. "Yes, Xorro, the idiot, sent everyone out searching for you."

"Oh, I wouldn't say he was an idiot," Tina said. "I was kind of moved actually. Although I didn't count on Xorro becoming so fond of me, and I heard he never gave up looking for Scar Face. But let's talk about us. Oh, Xeiyén, I just had an argument with Grandfather about you, and I'm feeling blue."

Concentrate . . . Blue, blue—yes! Xorro offered the budding rose to Tina. "I've got a blue rose for a red lady—"

Titters rang out in the back of the cart while Tina leaned out from the balcony. "What!"

Xorro looked at the fiery violet eyes from above. "I've got a red rose for a violet beauty," he said.

Tina's features softened. "Oh, Xeiyén, how sweet." She let go of her Didee-rope, and it retrieved the rose from Xorro's hand. She took the budding rose from her rope and inhaled deeply. "Mmm…Xane, play something romantic for us. And stop trying to fool me with that awful plucking."

Well, Tina's certainly not in love.

Berna moved the bow, and beautiful string music leapt out. Xorro's eyes popped wide open while Tina sighed. She started to hum along as she smiled dreamily down at Xorro. He studied her soft features with fascination. When the enchanting music ended, Xorro cleared his throat discreetly. "Xane, take a hike."

"Thank you for the music, Xane. You play even better than I remembered. See you later," Tina said.

Berna hopped down from the front seat and disappeared.

This is working! Xorro delved into the fun bag and pulled out a bell. *What am I supposed to do with this? I'll let Tina figure this one out.* "Tina, look what I have," Xorro said while he jingled the bell at her.

At the tinkling sound, Didee-baker appeared out of nowhere to stand in front of him. "You rang?"

"Uhh…Yes."

"Very good, Sire-sir," the baker corrected, then set up a small table with two chairs. Next, he flicked a peach tablecloth on top of the table and placed a lighted candle in the center. Finally, the baker produced a bottle of wine, wrapped in a bucket of ice, and two champagne glasses from his large apron pocket, and began to fill the glasses with wine.

Tina bounced from the balcony and landed beside Xorro. "Candlelight and champagne on ice! Xeiyén, what next?" Xorro passed one of the glasses to her and she took a sip. "So bubbly," Tina said as she lifted her rose red lips and leaned toward Xorro.

He backed off nervously while Tina moved forward to close the gap between them once again. *Quick! Think of something else to do.* Xorro made for Michi's fun bag, then delved into it. He pulled out a strange looking material and frowned. *What is it?*

"Xeiyén! Shame on you," Tina scolded, but she took it from Xorro anyway. "Anything for you, my beloved," she said and blew a kiss at Xorro, then bounced back up to her balcony. "I'll be right back," she assured before disappearing into her chamber.

Don't think about the past. Don't think about Scar Face . . . concentrate . . . Vreeny's back, and we don't have much time. "Is Berna back yet?" Xorro asked desperately.

"Not yet, Sire-sir," the baker said.

Xorro picked up Michi's fun bag and shook it. *It's empty!* "He better hurry up. I'm running out of things to keep Tina busy."

"Maybe you can scratch her back," George's voice suggested from the back of the cart, followed by laughter.

Xorro turned to find the giant bees, flower, and tree decorations detaching themselves from the cart. He blinked in amazement. *Surely this is the work of a high order magic.* "George?"

"Hi, Zorro. How do you like Jo and my bee disguises?"

"Incredible! Just like real bees. But what are you two doing here?"

Joseph and George flapped their bee wings. "Making honey," George said, and Michi roared with laughter.

"Shh . . . not so loud. Calm down, Zorro. You're doing fine," Archoy, disguised as a sunflower, encouraged.

"Archoy, that's the most real and enchanting sunflower disguise I've ever seen. How did you manage it?"

"It's a joint invention of Didee-baker and Didee-troll."

"Joint invention?" Xorro asked.

"It's a combination of Didee-magic and Troll Illusion. Except it's ten times more powerful. At least, that's what they said," George explained in more detail.

"No wonder you fooled everybody. I'm afraid Berna's blue mask isn't as magical as yours. I hope he's alright," Xorro said.

"Stop worrying," Archoy said. "Why don't you sit down and drink some wine. It might help."

Xorro slowly sank into his seat. "What's that thing Tina took from me?" he asked before taking a sip of his wine.

"I don't really know. I found it in the tote bag, and it looked interesting—" Michi started to say, but was interrupted when Tina landed right across the table from Xorro.

"Hello, Xeiyén, darling," Tina cooed.

Xorro lifted his head to look at her and choked on his wine. Tina had changed into a scanty outfit that had belonged to one of Merchant Benny's slave girls. "Tina! You-you…"

Tina batted her eyelashes at Xorro as she struck a seductive pose. "Go ahead and say it. You think I'm sexy."

"Uhh…" Unable to stare at the too-revealing figure without making a fool of himself, Xorro glanced nervously to the side. He saw the giant bees leaning over the dividing rail, gawking at Tina. *I'll never hear the end of this.* Then the palm tree moved over to join the bees. The palm was leaning dangerously over the rail, and one of its coconuts fell from it. Instantly, Xorro drew his sword and threw it at the falling coconut. Like magic, his sword extended in length and skewered the coconut onto the rail just above Tina's head. When another coconut came crashing down, Xorro leapt from his chair and swept a startled Tina off her feet, bouncing out of harm's way. *This so-called wooing is a dangerous game.* But Xorro found it had its compensations when a moment later, Tina's soft and inviting lips covered his. *I shouldn't be doing this with her. After all, as the new king, I am now obligated to another. I must marry Princess Leianna.* He felt Tina's hands caressing the back of his neck, and Xorro abandoned thought while he tightened his hold on her.

"Guards! Take him down!" A harsh voice issued from above the balcony.

Xorro and Tina broke off from their kiss, and he put her down on her feet. Tina clung to Xorro. "It's Grandfather. He doesn't want me to marry you."

Xorro caressed her cheek with his hand. "We're not meant for each other, Tina."

Sadness entered her beautiful violet eyes as she nodded her head, then she dipped her hand into the valley between her breasts and took out a small bottle. She offered it to Xorro. "Here's the antidote."

Xorro closed his hands over Tina's and shook his head. "I didn't come here for that."

She smiled sweetly. "I'm glad, but I want you to have it."

Xorro kissed the tip of her uplifted nose. "Keep it for me. Before you go, Tina, tell me where Xorro's Center Guards are?"

"In the dungeon—" Tina started to say, but stopped when they heard footsteps.

"Tina, come up here if you don't want to get hurt."

Xorro lifted his head to see Vreeny standing on the edge of the balcony. The arrogant tilt of Vreeny's hawk-like nose and overall commanding air gave him the look of someone expecting instant obedience.

"Grandfather, Xeiyén's here on my invitation."

"That's enough! Now come up here this instant."

Tina lifted her chin defiantly. "If you must arrest Xeiyén, then I'll go to the dungeon with him."

Still as stubborn as ever. Xorro lifted Tina and threw her up to her grandfather. "Catch her, Vreeny." While Vreeny flailed, trying desperately to catch Tina, Xorro saw one of the bees hop from the back of the cart to the front to join him.

"Okay, Zorro, tell us where to go," George said, picking up the reins.

"Turn left, go over the bridge, then follow along the side of the lake."

George guided Big Thunder away from Tina's balcony.

"Here they come!" Joseph shouted from the back.

Rows of six-inch guards in black charged into Tina's garden. They paused on seeing the strange honeymoon carriage and the giant bees.

"Kill the insects, but I want the masked intruder alive," Vreeny ordered from the top of the balcony. Immediately the black guards drew their swords and advanced toward the moving cart.

"You were right. A couple of stumps would have been a safer disguise for you and George. Sorry, Jo," the palm tree, or rather Michi, said.

"No sweat, Sweet. You couldn't have known that Vreeny wasn't an insect lover."

Michi glanced at the rage-filled Vreeny, now clutching at Tina's arm, one last time. "If there's a mean looking Dideetone, Vreeny's it."

"Watch out for his Triple Pyramid Strategy," Xorro warned, as one-third of the pursuers formed a triangle formation, the tip charging at them with increasing speed. "We've got to get them before they bounce up," Xorro instructed.

Big Thunder raced across the long bridge, the cart bouncing and rumbling as it made its way. Michi dropped the last of the coconuts from her fake palm. It rolled down the bridge with increasing speed and crashed into the left side of the triangle formation, bowling over a group of the six-inch soldiers. The remaining soldiers continued their pursuit.

"That was a little off. Here, try again," Joseph said. He picked up the coconut that had almost struck Tina earlier and handed it to Michi.

She aimed it more carefully this time, successfully breaking up the triangle. "There!"

"A spare, not bad, Sweet," Joseph encouraged.

However, the second set of pyramid soldiers came up from behind. They bounced ten feet above the ground and charged at them.

"My turn," Xorro offered while he retrieved both his sword and the coconut from the rail. He bounced up ten feet as well, then flew toward the oncoming castle guards. The terrific force of the coconut charging straight at them was too much for the pyramid soldiers. Their leader was thrown back and his followers scattered, dropping to the ground. Xorro beamed when he heard Joseph shout, "A strike!" and Michi's cheer.

The third set of pyramid soldiers now appeared above him, and Xorro threw himself to the side as they descended. Their spear-like formation allowed them to hurtle downwards faster than the eye could follow, and it was only by inches that their charge missed smashing straight down upon him. Instead, the group of soldiers crashed into the bridge directly behind the buffalo cart and its screaming occupants. The bridge quaked violently and pieces of wooden debris rained down.

The assailants trampolined back into the air, scattering briefly across the sky before regrouping. Xorro swung his sword with the coconut over his head and bounced into the air, heading straight for the leader. Before the soldiers had a chance to complete their maneuver, Xorro flung the coconut into their midst. The hard fruit scattered the falling soldiers, and as he rushed upward past them, he laid about him with his sword. Whoops and cheers sounded from the cart below at his victory, and Xorro continued to ascend, just for the sheer joy of being in combat.

Suddenly, Xorro noticed that the shouts from his friends on the ground weren't cheers. He looked down just in time to see a dark passage open at the end of the bridge. Xorro noticed that everyone in the cart was looking up at him, pointing their hands toward the sky while shouting something. *Drats! Don't they know they're going into the Inmee Dungeon?*

He started his descent immediately. "George! Stop Big Thunder!" he shouted. It was then that he heard Michi's loud voice.

"Vreeny's above you with a net!"

The last Xorro saw of his friends, before he was caught by the sticky net, was Michi and the others screaming as their cart hurtled downward and was swallowed by the dark passage.

10

The Pursuit

Two cloaked Nain Riders sped north on the West Slave Route toward one of the hills by the Slave Route Junction. Their tired but proud Nain horses labored uphill until they reached four figures standing at the summit. The riders halted and saluted, then one of the riders inched his horse forward. "Your Highness, they never arrived at the Firmiana Inn, and there's no sign of them on the slave route from here to the inn."

"Where could they be?" Christa Markum, who had been hoping to camp out under the stars with Michi, asked with exasperation.

Her brother, Cedric, put a comforting arm around her shoulders while Prince Norlen looked at the bright moon with a frown. "We could see you clearly out there, so it can't be that we're missing them in the dark. Guiffren, is there possibly a shortcut which took them away from the slave route?" Norlen asked his advisor.

"Not if their destination is the Firmiana Inn, Your Highness. The West Slave Route is the most direct way to the inn," Guiffren replied.

"Yes," Cedric said. "Jo mentioned his plans to me, and he meant to get there last night."

"A cart driver confirmed to me that the Outsiders were making for the inn this morning, Your Highness," the other rider said, inching his horse forward. "They wanted to be there by eleven. Something about obtaining the famous nine-layer cake."

Cedric rolled his eyes. "Yes, that's definitely them."

"So, where are they?" Prince Norlen asked.

"Every other cart going to the Firmiana Inn got there by noon. This bodes ill . . . " Guiffren said, beginning to pace. "The key to Zanquei's disappearance may lie with Michi. But this could bring danger to her, as well. We must hurry."

Christa turned pale and looked up at her brother. Cedric patted her shoulder, then raised his hand to halt Guiffren's ominous thoughts. "Now, let's not jump the gun. Knowing Jo, there are two things that would make him change his plans. Either it was for Michi's sake, or it was to help someone. We can discard the first possibility because they were already going to the inn to get her some cake. That leaves us with the second possibility."

"They left the slave route to help someone," Prince Norlen said.

"Your Highness, since the trackers are here, I'll send them out immediately. If indeed the van has taken a detour, they'll find it," Guiffren assured. He turned to the riders. "Before you go and tend to your horses, tell the trackers that I want them saddled and ready."

The two riders nodded and rode off.

"These Nain Trackers just had a long and hard ride with us. Will they be able to go on again so soon?" Cedric asked with concern.

"They are trained to ride in a state of semi-sleep, so they'll be ready. By tomorrow morning, we should have some news of your friends, Lord Cedric, Lady Christa," Guiffren said.

"Good. I think Cook has already assigned some of the knights for the first watch, so I suggest that we get our rest," Cedric said.

"I'll see that the riders are settled for the night—" Guiffren began, but was interrupted by a commotion from the foot of the hill.

"Halt! Advance no further," they heard one of the knights on watch challenge.

Everyone turned and saw a small figure stumbling toward the sentries.

"Help me," a feminine voice begged as the faint sound of horse hooves rose from behind her.

Christa started to run downhill. "She needs help!"

"Lady Christa, please wait!" Guiffren cried, flinging his arms out in a futile attempt to catch her. Cedric and Norlen also dashed down the hill toward the lonely figure.

By the time they arrived at the bottom of the hill, the knight that halted the intruder had drawn his sword and was pointing it at the frightened girl. "Who are you?"

"My name is Shanui," the girl began, then she cast a fearful glance backward at the approaching horsemen. "Please don't let them take me . . ."

The other two knights placed their hands on the hilts of their swords and faced the oncoming horsemen.

The band of riders slowed, stopping some twenty feet away, before their leader spoke. "We are runaway slave hunters. Thank you for capturing this troublesome slave girl for us."

"Slave girl?" Christa asked, puzzled.

"Yes. The Merchant of Northwood paid a handsome price for her two days ago, but she escaped—" the leader of the hunters began to explain.

"Do you have proof?" Guiffren interrupted.

"Absolutely! I have here a sales contract between Benny the Merchant and this girl's uncle." The leader reached into his top pocket to produce a document. He vaulted from the horse and came forward, handing the paper to Guiffren.

The Nain's tribe adviser scanned the contract with care. "Well, it looks authentic enough. Here, Shanui, what have you to say for yourself?"

"It is true that Merchant Benny bought me two days ago, but last night a kind Anguorian and his sister bargained for my freedom," the slave girl explained.

The slave hunters laughed, but Cedric took a step forward. "Describe the Anguorian and his sister to me, Shanui." The slave girl turned to look straight at him, and Cedric was taken aback. He had never seen a more alluring pair of dark eyes in his life.

"The Anguorian was a tall teenager with a limp," Shanui replied, "and his sister was a very cute brunette who loved food."

"Jo and Michi!" Christa gasped.

Before she could say more, the leader of the hunters cut in. "What could the Outsiders have to bargain with, that the richest merchant in the Kingdom of Lanhur would covet?"

Horror entered Christa's eyes as she raised her hands to her cheeks. "Mrs. Dallion's finest china...oh, they're in trouble."

"Yes!" The slave girl nodded her head eagerly. "It was a priceless vase."

Cedric looked startled. "A vase? I don't think..." he started, but paused on seeing the pleading dark eyes. "Describe the vase to me, Shanui."

"It had matching gold patterns all around the rim."

Christa shook her head. "You must have remembered wrong, Shanui. I don't think they had a vase like that."

"Oh, but they must have," the slave girl said.

"Runaway slaves are always inventing stories like this. If what she said was true, then why would they leave her all alone upon this deserted route, after paying such a handsome price for her?" the leader of the hunters argued.

Knowing that Joseph would never have left Shanui to fend for herself after helping to gain her freedom, Cedric had no choice but to believe that the slave girl was lying.

But, loathe to leave a helpless girl in the company of such cutthroats, he turned to Guiffren. "What do you think?"

"The document of purchase is authentic," Guiffren said. "If someone bought her freedom, then the Merchant of Northwood must have signed the release paper. But that part of the contract is still attached to the end of this sales agreement, without any signature." Guiffren waved the document in his hand at Shanui.

"Last night, Merchant Benny signed the release paper and handed it to the Anguorian teenager named Joseph, who then gave it to me," the slave girl insisted.

"Where is it?" Guiffren asked.

Excited, the girl dipped her hands into her pockets. A frown marred her perfect features as her fingers poked through the holes of her pockets. "Oh, no!"

All the hunters gave the slave girl a skeptical look. "As you can see," the leader said, "she's just trying to get your sympathy. You must not mind her and turn her over to us. We know how to deal with the likes of her."

Guiffren inclined his head and, as he handed the document back to the leader, the slave girl stepped toward Cedric with her hand outstretched. "Please, you must believe me."

Even with the shabby clothes and the dirt-smudged face, she's the most beautiful girl I've ever seen. Cedric mentally shook himself. "Think carefully, Shanui. Did Jo give you anything else that might prove he indeed gained your freedom for you?"

The frown deepened on her lovely face, and Cedric had a hard time resisting the temptation to rush over and smooth out her troubled forehead. Suddenly the frown disappeared. "Yes!" she exclaimed. "He wrote his new address on a piece of paper. He told me to just contact him if I ever needed help."

"That sounds like what Jo would do. Show me the paper, Shanui," Cedric encouraged.

"I put it in my pocket . . . " She trailed off with dismay.

The leader of the hunters smirked. "There she goes again. I've been recovering runaway slaves for more years than she's been alive, and I know all their tricks." The leader stalked over to the slave girl's side, dragging her to a spare horse. Christa, Cedric, and Norlen moved to stop him, but Guiffren stayed them. With sympathetic eyes, they watched the leader hoist the slave girl onto the saddle. "Thanks again for your help. Enjoy your visit," the leader said before mounting his own steed and setting off.

"Is she really a slave? Is it even legal, Cedric?" Christa asked, watching the departing riders.

"I'm afraid so. Grandfather warned me about getting involved with slavery in the Kingdom of Lanhur. You were right to stop us from interfering, Guiffren," Cedric said, though he still shot a longing look toward the shapely figure of the departing Shanui.

"I happen to know Merchant Benny's reputation regarding his slave girls," Guiffren said. "He has never released any so far, and with one look at this one, I knew she wouldn't be freed at any price. Although I don't blame her for trying, I do feel we ought to leave this alone."

"Good advice, Guiffren. Now, let's get our sleeping bags and hit the sack," Prince Norlen suggested, receiving murmurs of agreement from the others.

After Guiffren left them to attend to other business, Christa, Cedric, and Norlen stretched out in their sleeping bags and looked up at the bright moon lighting the sky.

"Mmm . . . the air is so clean and the sky's so clear. Despite the bumpy and deserted roads, this really is a beautiful country," Cedric said.

"If you think this is nice, wait until we reach the eastern shore, Cedric. But how about you, Christa? Sure you want to sleep out here in the wild? We do have a comfortable tent set up for you and Pauline—Christa?"

There was no reply. Cedric glanced at the sleeping bundle next to him and smiled. "She's already asleep, Norlen. You know, I could get used to long rides and camping out in the wild. It's really not so bad."

"How's Christa holding up?" Norlen asked.

"Like a little trooper. You know, she claimed my armor was the most comfortable seat in the Kingdom of Anguo."

"Really?"

Cedric chuckled. "We've been on the road for more than ten hours, with only two brief stops. Yet both times she complained, saying we shouldn't stop because Michi would get further away from us."

"I hope we catch up with Michi and Jo tomorrow, otherwise Christa's going to be disappointed. Besides, Guiffren seemed very anxious. I've never seen him this worried before."

"From the way he talks, I gather we're riding to a war. If you can believe it."

"It may come to that—" Norlen stopped when he saw Cook coming toward them.

On seeing Christa asleep, Cook approached quietly. "Lord Cedric, Prince Norlen," he whispered. "I'm sorry to disturb you, but Guiffren wanted me to pass this to you. He said it might be important."

Cedric took the paper from him and read it, then sat up immediately. "I knew it! The slave girl was telling the truth. Where did you find it?"

"One of the Nain Trackers found it near the spot he believed the Dallions' van parked last night," Cook said.

"They're fast workers, these trackers," Cedric praised, passing the paper to Norlen. "That's Jo's new address, and it's his handwriting. Know what this means, Norlen?"

Prince Norlen bolted upright as well. "Saddle our horses, Cook. We've got a date with a bunch of cutthroats. And a damsel in distress."

Cedric stood, scowling at Norlen. "I do believe that was supposed to be my line. Just be sure that when we're done crushing them, you leave the lady to me."

Norlen rose to his feet. "Now why should I leave the field wide open for you? This Shanui may prefer me to you."

Cedric's eyes narrowed to a mere slit. "Have you looked in the mirror lately, Norlen?"

With a challenging stance, Norlen faced Cedric. "Have you?"

"Lord Cedric, Prince Norlen, please, Christa's resting," Cook reminded.

Both Cedric's and Norlen's features softened. "Cook, tell Pauline to stay with Christa until we return with Shanui. Now go get my gear and saddle our horses."

"Yes, Lord Cedric," Cook said before leaving.

"I don't think those slave hunters are going to just hand Shanui over to us, so I guess Guiffren's fears were not ill founded after all," Cedric said while he picked up Christa's sleeping form and carried her toward the tent.

Norlen walked beside him. "We'll avoid a fight if possible, but we might not have a choice. I watched them as they rode off. They're making their way north toward Bayjai."

"Or more likely Northwood, but we'll catch up with them before then thanks to your Nain horses, Norlen."

They arrived at the tent, and Pauline flipped open the flap. Cedric and Norlen entered. "I'm holding you responsible for Christa's safety, Pauline. If she's missing even one thread of golden hair when I return, you'll have me to answer to. Do I make myself clear?"

Color left the housekeeper's face. "I will guard her with my life, Lord Cedric."

Cedric gently placed his sister on one of the cots, then turned to face Pauline.

The housekeeper cowered under his stern stare, and she lowered her eyes. "I will not fail you, Lord Cedric."

At that moment, Cook came in with Cedric's armor and a parchment under his arm. "The night can get chilly, so go fetch a couple more blankets, Pauline."

After she left, Cook closed the flaps and placed the gear on an unoccupied cot. Then he unfolded the parchment. "I think you might find this bit of information concerning your suit of armor to be of interest, Lord Cedric," he said.

Both Cedric and Norlen bent over and studied the chart with fascination. "No wonder I felt so refreshed and energized after such a long ride," Cedric said. "Even Christa felt the power of the armor just by sitting on it."

Norlen pointed at a series of drawings. "Are you thinking what I'm thinking?" he asked.

"Let's try them out," Cedric replied.

A few minutes later, after Pauline came back with the extra blankets, Cedric, Norlen, and Cook were grinning as they exited the tent.

"Too bad the tent is too low and small to try out the last two figures' instructions," Norlen said with disappointment.

"Maybe we can give it a try while we're fetching Shanui," Cedric said.

Their conversation was broken, however, by a peculiar sight. Word had spread to the Nain Riders and Knights of the Anguo Council that their lords were preparing to fight the slave hunters, and all were itching for some real action. And now everyone, except those unlucky few on guard duty, was packed before the tent in the hopes of being chosen for the fun.

"What's going on here?" Cedric asked.

"Word must have spread that Shanui's a jewel of the first water, Cedric. I'm afraid we've got competition," Norlen joked.

"And might I ask why you two are all geared up in the middle of the night?" Guiffren inquired, appearing suddenly behind them.

"You should know, Guiffren. You're the one that insisted we see the paper Jo had left for Shanui, knowing we'd have to rectify our blunder," Cedric said.

Guiffren twitched. "And how did you come to the conclusion that a piece of paper with your friend's new address on it meant Shanui was freed?"

"Let's face it, Guiffren," Cedric said. "Had Shanui produced this paper as evidence before, we would have confronted the hunters with it. Besides, this must have been for Shanui . . . Jo has no reason to write his address down just to practice his penmanship. And again, it makes no sense to give Shanui his new address if she was to be a slave all the rest of her life. So we can only conclude that somehow she was freed. And Jo is just the type that would give Shanui his new address in case she needed help in the future."

Guiffren pursed his lips and thought for a moment. "You seem to understand your friend quite well. In this case, I'm inclined to go along with you. Take some of your blood thirsty knights with you, but our Nain Riders have been on the road three days without much sleep, and I insist that they stay behind to catch up with their needed rest."

"They can all stay behind—" Cedric began.

"No," Guiffren interrupted. "I'll feel better if you take some others with you. And I suppose it would be useless to try and dissuade you from this madness, Prince Norlen?"

"You suppose rightly, Guiffren. I think we have wasted enough time talking, so let's go," Norlen replied.

In the end, seven knights were selected to accompany Cedric, Norlen, and Cook in their pursuit of the slave hunters. There was no trouble following the trail, because their quarry had made no attempt to cover their tracks.

As they rode, Prince Norlen made an effort to learn more about Joseph. "So you think your friend threw away a fortune to buy this girl her freedom, then just let her go with some other guy?"

"With Shanui's looks? No way! It's more likely that Jo found some motherly figure who was willing to take the beauty under her wing. Jo is like that, you know, always helping everyone else. I, on the other hand, would have helped myself and taken her to my castle instead. To be honest with you, I was thinking about sneaking out, after you had fallen asleep, and going after her myself."

Prince Norlen laughed. "I was thinking the same thing."

"It's good to know great minds think alike. I'll tell you what, Norlen. We'll both go after her, and when she makes up her mind, the loser will withdraw with good grace."

"But before then, all is fair in love and war," Norlen insisted.

"Deal!" Cedric said.

Unaware of the exasperation on Cook's face, Cedric and Norlen laughed as they urged their mounts to greater speed. They continued on for an hour before the knights halted. Their scout, the youngest of the seven knights, returned to report that the hunters were only a fifteen minute ride from them. However, their quarry seemed to have met up with another band of slave hunters, and there was an argument among the hunters concerning the slave girl.

"What about?" Cedric asked.

"The second set of hunters insist that all slave hunters had been ordered to stay away from the Slave Route Junction until further notice," the scout reported. "They claim the first set of hunters broke this rule, and the slave girl was therefore recovered under unfair advantage. The idea is that the reward should be split. My lord, with the second set of hunters, their numbers are now more than doubled."

Norlen leaned forward. "Did you say there's an order for slave hunters to stay away from the Slave Route Junction?"

"Yes, Prince Norlen."

The prince frowned. "By who?"

"They didn't say, Your Highness."

"I don't understand this business about the Slave Route Junction, Cedric. Why order the hunters to stay away? And now all our men are camped there. I can't help feeling uneasy about this."

Cedric looked back toward the direction they had come, and thought for a moment. "Maybe we should go back."

Cook stroked his chin. "Lord Cedric, might I suggest that this is the perfect opportunity to try out the techniques from the last two drawings in the parchment?"

"Cook, you're a genius!" Cedric exclaimed.

"Unfortunately, the distance was too small inside the tent…and now the distance is too great," Norlen said.

Cedric and Norlen thought for a moment, then slowly turned to size up the unsuspecting knights. "Has your knightly training included tree climbing?" Cedric asked with a wicked smile.

"Yes, my Lord. We have ropes and hooks that enable us to climb as high as need be, within reason," the scout replied.

"Within reason?" Cedric asked.

The same knight looked at the scattered trees surrounding them. "If we're to climb these trees, then we could only go up to a height which would hold our weight," he explained.

"Ah. Well, here's the plan," Cedric said. "Let's split up. Norlen and I'll go on to rescue Shanui while you knights start back now at top speed. As you ride back, set up a long, makeshift rope pulley through the tree tops back to the camp, using my braid as a rope."

"Your braid?" the scout questioned.

Cedric nodded solemnly. "It grows."

The knight blinked and appeared no less confused.

"Lord Cedric, since I'll have the longest ride, let me start now," Cook suggested.

"Okay, Cook, just remember that you stay on the ground," Cedric said.

Cook nodded, turned his horse back to the Slave Route Junction, and was off.

"There goes the heaviest of us. Now, who's the lightest here?" Cedric asked, and the young scout inched his horse forward.

"Okay. Norlen, you explain to the others and send them on their way. I'll get Light Foot here up into the tallest tree," Cedric said. He detached his blue-jeweled braid and passed it to the young knight.

After taking the braid from Cedric, the scout started to shed his armor and Cedric grinned. "You're getting the idea, Light Foot. The higher you climb, the easier it is for the subsequent posts down the road. Don't forget to send your horse and—uhh . . . your gear with the others when they ride off."

The rest of the knights were not slow at catching on to the scheme after Norlen explained it to them. Before Light Foot reached the top of the tallest tree, they were off with not only his horse, but Cedric's and Norlen's as well.

"Well, I've lost my braid, so it's up to yours to send us to where Shanui is, and also to bring us back here within an hour," Cedric said to Norlen.

"Piece of cake," Norlen assured while Cedric grabbed his friend's purple-jeweled braid and tested it out. Like magic, the braid extended in length.

Cedric lifted his head. "Light Foot, can you see us?" he bellowed.

"Yes, Lord Cedric. Even your armor is now glowing purple."

"Good. Next time you see this lighted armor, be ready to grab us. And whatever you do, don't lose my blue jewel."

"I won't, my Lord."

"Ready, Norlen?"

"Just don't yank too hard. I might get a headache."

Cedric feigned a hurt look at the suggestion, before giving Norlen's braid a hard yank.

"Ouch!"

Cedric chuckled. "That ought to teach you to try and steal my girl."

Prince Norlen grabbed his own braid and, lifting it, gave a quick snap of his arm. This sent the end, along with Cedric, cracking toward the north with a tremendous force. Cedric shot down the road, almost lost his hold on the braid, and cursed. "Norlen! You brat!" he shouted while Prince Norlen snickered. Cedric quickly did the same with his end of the braid and sent Norlen flying ahead with a howl.

So it went on, with them taking turns yanking, whipping, and cursing at each other as they shot wildly along toward the north at a speed even Nain horses could not match. Suddenly, while in the air, Cedric saw movement from the ground ahead. "Norlen, a rider." This time, Cedric stopped yanking when he landed on the ground.

"That was fast," Norlen said while Cedric let go of his braid, which began to retract.

"Too bad, I was getting the hang of throwing you about," Cedric said with regret.

"You wish. Now, let's go find Shanui."

They walked cautiously toward the area where Cedric had seen the hunter. Midway there, Norlen's foot caught, and he stumbled. Cedric quickly steadied him.

"What was that?" Norlen asked.

"Shh. I think it's a sentry. Luckily for us, he's asleep."

"My, he must be tired," Norlen whispered.

They reached the spot where the horses were kept, but there were no guards posted. *Strange. The hunters should know how important their horses are along a deserted stretch of road like this.*

"Cedric, look." Norlen pointed to three slumped forms beneath a tree ahead. "Think they're asleep as well?"

"It would be pretty strange, considering one of them has a knife stuck in his back," Cedric whispered.

"Really!" Norlen leaned forward and took a good look. "What do you suppose happened?"

"Beats me. Let's stay under cover and circle around," Cedric suggested. They cautiously made their way in a roundabout fashion. This time, it was Cedric who tripped over a body on the ground. They made a point of examining it, and realized that it was a corpse rather than a sleeping sentry.

"Cedric, this guy is from the second group of hunters."

Cedric eyed the slit throat and the trickling blood with distaste. "Yes, we didn't see him with the first group at the Slave Route Junction earlier. When you said we had a date with a bunch of cutthroats, that's literally what they were. I don't like the idea of helpless Shanui being with them. Let's hurry and find her."

They hurried to the three bodies under the tree. "They're all dead, and again, they're all from the second group of hunters," Cedric said.

"Come to think of it, remember the horses we just passed? I think they were all grey, not black. The first group of hunters must have killed the second and rode on with their own blacks."

"You're probably right. Still, it's hard to believe that they killed the others just to keep the reward for themselves. Anyway, let's free the horses and be on our way."

They returned to where the horses were kept and started to loosen the ties for the greys. Norlen approached one of the last horses and was surprised to find that it still had a rider slumped over its back. "Cedric, look."

"Is he dead?"

Norlen felt the weak pulse. "No, but he's unconscious and he's lost a lot of blood."

"If he's the rider I saw when we got here, then he must have passed out not too long ago," Cedric said. "We can't leave him here to die. Let's get him off the horse and see what we can do for him." He moved to Norlen's side to help with the wounded, but tripped over something on his way.

"Cedric! Are you alright?"

"Yes, I'm getting used to tripping over bodies."

"Another one! The way we keep tripping over dead bodies, you'd think we were in a graveyard."

Cedric checked the body on the ground. "Yeah. Except this body's from the first group of hunters."

"Really?" Norlen said. "I wonder who killed him. Cedric, this horse is actually black. I thought it was grey at first glance because the rider's wearing grey, and he's slumped over the horse. I'm going to apply some Nain Desert Fern on his wound to stop the bleeding." He pulled the back of the hunter's collar down. "Cedric! Take a look at his wound."

Cedric went to Norlen's side, taking a look at the deep bite on the back of the hunter's neck. "This is most curious! We didn't see any hunting animals with the slave hunters we saw earlier."

"And it's illogical to think the second group of hunters' animals, if they had any, attacked their own owners," Norlen reasoned while he took out what appeared to be a piece of golden-brown colored fur from his pocket. He pressed the fur over the bite, and the bleeding stopped. "This should clean his wound and help him heal."

"What is it?"

"A very rare Nain desert plant that has many healing powers—especially for animal bites."

"I think he's going to live through this, thanks to you. How about you lead the black away from these restless greys, and I'll finish freeing them."

Norlen judged the massive form of the wounded man. "Okay, but hurry up. To prevent his wound from opening again, I'm going to need your help getting him down from the horse."

Cedric quickly untied the rest of the horses. He returned to Norlen, who had guided the black horse away from the trees. Norlen placed his cloak on the ground, and together they carefully lifted the wounded man from the saddle, setting him on Norlen's cloak.

By then, the wounded man had regained consciousness. He grabbed Norlen's arm, then lifted his head. "They ... are not ... slave hunters ..."

"Take it easy," Prince Norlen said. He put his other hand under the hunter's head, helping him to lie back down. "You don't want to reopen your wound. There must have been at least twenty in your group, yet we found only five others. What happened to the rest of you?"

"Dead ..." the hunter uttered. He let go of his hold on Norlen's arm.

"Who killed them? Where are their bodies?" Norlen asked.

"And how did you get that deep bite on the back of your neck?" Cedric added.

"It seemed ... a beautiful fox ... but it wasn't. Its bite killed. It attacked so fast ... the others, they'd start convulsing from a bite ..." At this, the hunter broke off to catch his breath. Fortunately, the Nain desert plant was doing its work well, and with every passing moment color and strength seemed to return to him.

"I ate my antidote pill before it bit me ... but still fainted from the poison. When I awoke, a cutthroat had thrown me on his horse. The others also had the dead slung over their saddles, and they were off ... I was lucky, my rider was the last to leave. I killed him without raising the alarm."

Norlen considered the fallen rider on the ground. "From the knife wound to his side, I'd say you have had very special military training. Who are you?" Norlen asked.

"My name is Jack … I'm not one of the slave hunters. I was a personal guard to General Chium Soonchi. I'd just retired and was on my way home. I came upon the slave hunters … they seemed friendly, so I rode south with them. Then, we met those cutthroats that were riding north on black horses … to think I've been through countless conflicts without a scratch, then on the day I retire from military service … " Jack, with a wry smile, paused again to catch his breath.

"You said the others took the dead with them. Why burden themselves with the dead?" Cedric pondered.

Jack shrugged. "It seems for some reason they didn't want to leave the ones that were killed by the fox."

"Was Shanui with them?" Norlen asked.

"Yes … wait a minute, you both look so young that it didn't occur to me, but are you the ones they were trying to lure away from the Slave Route Junction?"

Alarmed, Norlen and Cedric looked at each other. "What do you mean?" Norlen asked.

"No time to explain! Your camp's going to be attacked, or maybe it's already under attack. These cutthroats were only a diversion, and the main group of soldiers were sent to raid your camp. And from what I've heard, what happened here is nothing compared to what they have planned for your companions."

"Christa!" Cedric cried out with alarm.

"Yes, they're going to capture her and make someone called Lord Cedric Markum surrender."

"The despicable blackmailers! Let me get my hands on them," Cedric cursed, unaware that he had now grown in size.

Jack took a long look. "I can see why they wouldn't want to confront you, Lord Cedric. Unfortunately, it looks like their plan worked. To return to the Slave Route Junction from here will take more than an hour, even with the fastest of horses. I'm afraid it's too late for you to get back and help your people. Furthermore, the cutthroats seemed to think they could make you fight Prince Norlen of Nain—"

"What!" both Cedric and Norlen exclaimed.

Jack studied the two giants. "I see. Nice to meet you, Prince Norlen. I assume you applied Nain's Desert Fern on my wound. Thank you for saving my life. Let me think, I just might be able to repay you both. Lord Cedric, you can't surrender because they'll force you to fight Prince Norlen in exchange for Christa's life. It's pointless to go back to your camp now, without taking something to bargain with for Christa's freedom. Hurry! Take the black. Instead of returning directly to your camp, ride on to catch the group of cutthroats that led you here. Capture the girl named Shanui and they'll have to exchange her for Christa. But please, whatever you do, don't let on that there was a survivor from their attack here."

"Don't worry, we're not about to confide in those blackmailers," Cedric said while he checked his watch. "Norlen, Cook'll reach the Slave Route Junction in ten minutes. Let's show these cutthroats what speed really means. Jack, rest here and we'll be back for you in a few minutes."

Not allowing Jack any time to ask questions, Cedric and Norlen were off. It was a somber affair as they once again used Norlen's braid to make their way north. Their progress became smoother this time, since they weren't at each other's throats, and it began to resemble the "Leaping Frog" technique from the parchment. As a result, not only were they now able to take turns scouting what was ahead, their speed also doubled.

Soon they saw their quarry. They were amazed that the black horses, each bearing a rider plus the dead, were galloping so fast they seemed to fly.

Even Nain horses would be hard put to chase them. Good thing we're able to cheat. Despite the gentle glow of Cedric's armor, none of the riders seemed to be aware that they were being pursued. Then Cedric saw Shanui, and he signaled to Norlen.

The Prince flicked his braid and sent Cedric over Shanui's horse. Cedric swooped down on her like a bird of prey, plucking Shanui off the horse with his left arm, and carrying her back up into the air at another flick of the braid. While Cedric and Shanui were still in the air flying toward the north, Norlen dug his heels in. This time, he sent his braid toward the opposite direction. Instantly, Cedric and Shanui were jerked from their progress and hurled toward the other direction. They shot over Norlen, and the "Leaping Frog" was now on its way south.

The leader of the cutthroats was the first to realize what was going on. But by then it was too late for the cutthroats to do anything. Their horses were no match in speed.

Not knowing what giant creature had torn her from the horse, Shanui struggled futilely in Cedric's strong hold.

"Shanui, remember me?" Cedric asked.

The beautiful girl seemed to recognize his voice, and she paused in her struggle. Their eyes met, and Cedric winced at her frightened look. *Well, of all the girls I've met, she just had to be the one to see me at my worst.*

There was no time to improve their relationship, however. They quickly came to the spot where Jack, who had wrapped himself in Norlen's cloak, was awaiting them. Cedric sent Norlen toward Jack, and Norlen let go of his own braid to scoop up the wounded man with both arms. Knowing his friend would have to rely now on his head movement to guide the braid, Cedric eased his right hand to accommodate the change.

They continued in this way through the forest, flying past the surrounding trees. In no time at all, they again reached the point where they had separated from the knights.

They flew toward the tallest tree, where the beginning of the makeshift pulley awaited. It seemed Light Foot was looking out for them. The brave young knight stretched himself out from the top of the tree, still holding the other braid Cedric had given him earlier. Using Cedric's detached braid as a rope and the blue jewel as a hook, he swung the makeshift grapple toward Norlen's purple jewel. As soon as the two jewels met, the whole area glowed purplish-blue. Cedric and Norlen were drawn toward the tree top, no longer needing to use the Leaping Frog technique to continue forward.

When they landed upon the tree branch, Light Foot yanked the end of Cedric's braid he was holding. It extended instantly away from them, at a slight downward angle. Hanging on to Cedric's long, rope-like braid, Light Foot became the first to go down the new aerial ropeslide, followed quickly by Norlen holding Jack, and Cedric with Shanui bringing up the rear.

They slid down the magically extending braid and soon came to the next post. Here the second knight, on top of a lower tree, caught the falling rope. He also yanked at the end of the braid, and it once again extended toward the south at a downward angle. This time, the second knight became the first in line to slide down the extended ropeslide, followed by the others.

And so it went, with Cedric's braid retracting from the north while extending to the south. The subsequent knights were collected and slid along from their trees until they at last came to Cook, who had just reached the outskirts of the Slave Route Junction. *This is fantastic! We're all here just as quickly as if we had ridden back an hour ago with Cook.*

Cook, on the other hand, did not seem to realize that above him, the makeshift ropeslide had arrived early. He continued to ride toward their camp, desperately focused on the hints of fire and smoke rising from it. It soon became obvious that their camp at the Slave Route Junction was under attack from all sides. Rising from the center came the cries of battle and the ringing of swords. Tents burned, wounded were strewn across the field, and horses galloped riderless.

Cedric and the others approached the camp quickly, sliding down from above and causing the northern sky to slowly glow a purplish-blue. On the ground, no one seemed to notice the new light, and the fighting continued.

Cedric could see that the attackers had tried to isolate the camp, maneuvering to surround them and cut off all access to help. Despite this, the Anguo Knights and Nain Riders had been able to keep a small route to the north open. A very good thing, considering that the makeshift ropeslide would need a safe landing strip. It was toward this narrow opening that Cook had been urging his horse. As Cook approached the ruined tents, their enemies suddenly became aware of him. The archers prepared to take down the fast approaching horseman.

"Cook!" Cedric shouted in warning, and the whole sky rumbled. A shocked silence fell upon the battlefield. Every fighter jerked his head up to look, and finally noticed the glowing, purple-blue light rushing toward them. Then all jaws dropped as the figures within the glow became clear: a beauty clinging to a giant armored knight, another giant holding a lumpy bundle, and seven knights in various states of undress, all dangling from a magically extending rope.

Cook had also turned at Cedric's shout, and upon seeing them, reined in his horse and vaulted down quickly. He started to run, turning halfway to judge the position of the falling rope. As the group approached him, he smoothly caught the rope with one of his hands. He continued to sprint down the path, one hand holding the extended rope.

It looked as though Cook was flying a kite, but in reality he was trying desperately to bring the group down with grace.

Unfortunately, none of the knights had any prior experience with this particular maneuver. The anxious knights started their descent too early. They smashed onto Cook in succession, piling into a crooked heap in the middle of the battlefield.

Well, at least Light Foot is on top of the pile, rather than on the bottom. Everyone watched as seven half-clothed knights tried to untangle themselves from the mess with as much dignity as they could muster. Although the knights had shed most of their gear, they at least had kept their swords. As soon as they succeeded in untangling themselves, the knights stood and drew their swords, ready to join the fight.

Cedric and Norlen, in contrast, had been looking for an opportunity to impress Shanui. Both their descents were executed with grace and style. On landing, Cedric let go of Norlen's braid and it returned to its normal length while the two jewels separated. Then Cedric reattached his braid behind his left temple once again.

"Cedric! Norlen! Am I glad to see you," Christa called, handing a shield to Pauline. Then, as she ran toward the two giants, she gave a cheerful shout. "You saved Shanui—that's wonderful!"

Cedric gently slid Shanui down his armor and released her as her feet touched the ground. He turned and picked up his sister. "Christa, are you alright?"

"Oh, I'm fine. Pauline said you wouldn't be back in time to save us, but I never doubted you," his sister declared.

Cedric smiled. "Thanks for the confidence, Christa."

Guiffren came to join them. "Might I remind you we're in the middle of a fight? Let us postpone the social events until later."

At his words, Cedric put Christa down and scanned the battlefield, finding that the fighting had resumed. But their appearance seemed to have filled the Nain Riders and Anguo Knights with confidence, and their soldiers began to gain ground. The seven half-clothed knights formed a protective circle around Lord Cedric, Lady Christa, and Prince Norlen as they drove back the nearby intruders.

"Okay, Guiffren," Cedric said. "You can tell us how glad you are to see us later. Christa, I need you to do something for me. Will you look after Shanui until I return?"

"Of course. Shanui, come and stay with me and Guiffren. He's an excellent archer, so we'll be safe with him," Christa invited, then took the shield from Pauline. "Pretend this is an umbrella and the arrows that come our way are just rain drops. Let's keep dry."

Shanui moved toward Christa, but Pauline was loath to give up the protection Christa's shield provided.

"Pauline!" Cedric barked. "Take the wounded man from Norlen and attend to him. If he dies, I'll bury you with him."

The housekeeper jumped, then dashed quickly to help Jack. Shanui moved to stand next to Christa, sharing the protection of the shield together.

"Okay, Cedric, I've spotted their leader." Norlen pointed to the top of the hill opposite their camp. "He's got archers all around him."

"Cook, my helmet," Cedric ordered.

"Yes, Lord Cedric." Cook retrieved the giant helmet and shield from his saddle, then advanced to stand in front of Cedric. "Lord Cedric, I don't think your shield is going to deflect all the arrows—"

"Not for both Norlen and myself. Leave it. But don't worry, I know what to do," Cedric said as he again detached his blue-jeweled braid. Cook helped his master put on the helmet. Cedric turned to look at Shanui and caught her watching him. "Stay under the protection of the shield," he cautioned. Shanui's cheeks flooded with color and she nodded shyly. *She likes me!* Cedric smiled at the lovely girl and waited until she ducked under the shield before he lowered the visor on his helmet. He grabbed Norlen's braid. "Come on, Norlen, send me to the other hill." At that, Cedric was sent flying toward the opposite hill by Prince Norlen's braid.

The enemy archers shouted and lifted their bows to shoot poisoned arrows at him in the sky, but Cedric spun his detached braid in front of him, creating a vast shield. The arrows were deflected and fell to the ground. After another round of arrows, the front archers split to stand on both sides of their grim-faced leader. Cedric landed lightly near the top of the hill and yanked Norlen's braid. The move sent his friend flying toward the hill—however, the enemy's leader seemed to have anticipated such a move. He suddenly sprang up and flew fast into the air toward Norlen.

Cedric realized too late that his spinning shield was just a tad low, and his opponent sailed past it. Even worse, with their leader safely hidden behind Cedric's shield, the archers resumed shooting their arrows. Cedric had no choice but to continue spinning his braid to protect Norlen and himself and, unfortunately, also his opponent.

Norlen saw the enemy closing in and drew his bow. He shot three arrows in fast succession. The leader deflected the arrows with a flick of his gleaming sword, sending them back toward Prince Norlen.

"Norlen, watch out!" Cedric shouted. Desperate to save his friend, Cedric jerked Norlen's braid once again. The enemy's leader calmly watched the twisting braid's sudden movement, and landed easily upon it as the braid whipped toward him. Cedric had successfully sent Norlen out of harm's way from the arrows, but their opponent had now gained momentum from the braid's force. The leader bounced off Norlen's braid with tremendous power.

Too late once again, Cedric realized his mistake. The leader wasn't interested in fighting him or Norlen, but was aiming for Christa and Shanui. Borrowing strength from the whirling braid, the leader now shot toward the opposite camp with stunning speed. Cedric gritted his teeth, knowing he had just helped the enemy reach his sister and Shanui.

"Cedric! Leaping Frog," Norlen urged.

Their only hope to get back to the camp in time was to rely on their new Leaping Frog technique. But the enemy archers were prepared to shoot them down if they were to attempt it. With his armor, Cedric had a chance of protection. Not so with Norlen. "No, it'll leave you an open target for the archers," Cedric said.

"Then the Sideways Dragonfly will have to do—hurry."

Cedric swept Norlen's braid to the side and they both rose, weaving their way into the air. Continuing to spin his own braid, the force propelled them back toward their own camp and protected them from the archers. *This is too slow.*

Cedric and Norlen watched helplessly as the leader redirected every arrow Guiffren shot at him with thoughtless ease. Cook leapt forward and deflected the returning arrows as Guiffren continued to aim, trying to bring the fast moving enemy down. Soon, though, Guiffren ran out of arrows and instead drew his sword to wait alongside Cook for their opponent to land.

Cedric noticed that none of the Anguo Knights or Nain Riders were close to Christa or Shanui. He realized that their enemies had lured the knights and riders away, knowing their leader was coming for Christa. No sooner had the thought occurred to Cedric than the leader surprised him once again. The leader threw his sword up into the sky, drew his own bow, then shot a rain of arrows with incredible speed. The arrows went in multiple directions, three of them aimed straight at Christa's shield. The first arrow knocked the shield out of her hands, and the other two followed the first close behind.

"Christa!" Cedric and Norlen both roared.

Quickly taking care of the arrows that came for him, Cook dove to deflect the two arrows aimed at Christa. He was only able to reach one in time. Cedric saw Shanui dive in front of Christa and shield the little girl with her own body. The arrow made its mark, and Shanui fell to the ground with a poison arrow piercing her neck. Christa cried out and sank to the ground. She bent over Shanui. Cedric's hand tightened on Norlen's braid, and his grip cut into his palm. Every movement below seemed to pass in a blur.

The leader caught his falling sword while still in the air. He landed on the ground and continued to advance toward the girls. Guiffren and Cook rushed to bar his way, clashing their swords with the enemy's. Their blades were no match and shattered instantly, throwing their owners backward with a terrific force.

At that point, Cedric and Norlen finally moved out of the archers' range, and Norlen immediately sent Cedric flying over him. Cedric raised his spinning braid above his head and flung it outward to capture the advancing leader. Before the noose even settled over his opponent's head, Cedric saw him disappear, then reappear a few feet ahead. *Is this guy even human?!* The leader continued his quest without a backward glance.

While Cedric was dealing with the leader, Norlen finally reached the campsite and landed next to Christa. On the other side of the leader, Cedric landed a distance some forty feet away. To avoid making the same mistake, this time Cedric let go of Norlen's braid at once, and it retracted instantly. Sandwiching their opponent, the two giants closed in on him. *Now we have you.* Cedric drew his sword and smiled grimly. He saw the seven half-dressed knights, who had made their way back to Lady Christa as soon as they saw her plight, also advance toward the leader.

"Cedric! Shanui needs a doctor!" Christa cried out.

"She's not dead?" Cedric exclaimed, stunned. Norlen spun around and rushed back toward the girls. *Norlen, you fool! Never turn your back on your opponent.*

The enemy's leader raised his sword and charged after Norlen. Light Foot, the closest knight, leapt forward and swung his sword at the leader. The enemy's blade shot back in an arc. The impact brought the young knight to his knees and shattered his sword. The leader lifted his glimmering sword and brought it down to finish Light Foot. Cedric flung his blade to deflect the sword. This time, the unexpected force from Cedric's flying blade caused the leader to stumble. In an instant, Light Foot drove the remains of his broken sword into the leader's stomach.

Before the young knight had a chance to draw his sword out, three enemy riders had reached their leader in a cloud of dust. Without stopping, one of them bent down and scooped their wounded leader up, and they galloped off.

In the distance, a blast of horns resounded in the early morning sky, and Cedric saw their enemies start to retreat. The remaining Anguo Knights and Nain Riders looked to their leaders for a command to pursue. Guiffren gave no signal, and they watched their enemies depart, picking up their own dead or wounded as they rode east. Cedric took off his helmet and passed it to Cook, leaving everything else to Guiffren. He made his way quickly to Shanui, and saw that Norlen had already removed the poison arrow from her lower neck. Cedric sucked in his breath when he saw the ugly black wound on the otherwise flawless skin. "How is she?"

Norlen shook his head. "While the arrow itself missed anything vital, I don't know what kind of poison they feed to the tips. She's already running a fever."

"Couldn't your Nain Desert Fern help?" Cedric asked in desperation.

"Don't knock it. It's due to that special plant that I was able to draw the arrow out without letting her bleed to death. But I'm afraid I don't have the antidote to cure her."

Christa started to cry, and Cedric realized with a start that he had forgotten about her. "Christa, are you alright?"

"S-She saved my life..." Christa stuttered, wiping the tears away with her sleeve.

"Yes, I know. And somehow I know she didn't save you just to see you cry."

Christa gave a trembling smile. "We're going to make her well again, aren't we, Cedric?"

"You bet. Now go get Pauline and tell her to prepare a bed for Shanui. I'll carry her there shortly."

"Okay, Cedric," Christa said before running off.

Cedric moved over, ready to pick up Shanui.

"I'm letting you carry her only because your armor has some healing power. So don't think I'm leaving the field to you," Norlen said with grim humor.

Cedric grinned at his friend's attempt to cheer him up. "You've touched her neck, so it's only fair I get the rest." He bent and gently picked up Shanui.

"Hey, Cedric, thanks for keeping an eye on my back."

"Thank Light Foot for that, Norlen. It would be poetic justice if he got the girl in the end."

Norlen snorted. "You've got a point there. After all, he's got a head start—he's already half naked."

"Did you hear what the others called those seven knights?" Cedric asked.

"Yeah, the Magnificent Naked Seven."

They both gave a short laugh, hiding their heavy hearts as they walked toward the tent prepared for Shanui.

11

Black Eye and Bo-peep

Cheerfully unaware of his master's troubles, BoDak rode north toward a small village. The jewelry-laden barbarian was also completely oblivious to the fact that he now had two tails.

Young Captain Hua followed behind BoDak, studying both him and the strange owl perched casually upon the rump of BoDak's majestic horse. Hua knew it was only a matter of time before Owlut became aware of his presence. But this second purebred Nain horse, ridden by the barbarian, had caught the young captain's fancy. As Hua had never been denied anything he coveted, the young captain tagged along. Approaching the village, Hua saw it was alive with activity. Groups of children scurried about, gathering firewood and piling them into the middle of a huge courtyard. The adults were unloading heavy sacks, slung across black horses tied near a large hut. *Those black horses are beauties. How did the villagers acquire them?*

Bo rode into the yard, and Owlut flew to a tree nearby the large hut. Hua halted his horse just outside the dimly lit courtyard and sat watching. The barbarian's arrival didn't seem to attract much attention, as the villagers continued their chores. Bo reined in his horse. "Here, child. Tell me, have you seen Benny the Merchant of Northwood?"

A little boy, holding a stack of twigs, stopped and looked up at the giant of a man. "W-we did not look in the sacks, honest," the boy uttered in Native dialect, legs beginning to tremble.

"Sorry, I forgot." Bo switched to Native language and smiled down at the boy. "Do not be afraid. I just want to know if Merchant Benny is here."

"He was at the market earlier, but I think he left with the traveling merchants."

"Which way did he go?"

"Back to—" the boy started, but was cut short by the sound of a struggle. A dark-faced slave hunter was dragging a pretty woman from the large hut.

"Hey! Get to work, boy," the slave hunter snapped.

The little boy rushed off while BoDak urged his horse toward the two figures in the doorway.

"Well, well…What have we here? A barbarian!" the hunter said.

"The name is BoDak," Bo said to the hunter before addressing the woman. "If you don't mind, ma'am, I would like to replenish my water supply and—"

"Now, little Bo-peep, you're not suggesting that I let the wench go so she can serve you and your…Say! That's a mighty fine looking animal you got there. What will you take for it?"

"How about a duel. And after I kick your ass, you can apologize to the young woman for your rude treatment of her."

Hua sat straighter on his horse and leaned forward. *I'd like to see the barbarian fight.*

The dark-faced hunter roared with laughter as the woman in his arms cringed. "Fight for this wench? Hardly worth it. But that white horse, now, that's something else."

Hearing his laughter, three other hunters exited the hut to investigate. "Cut it out before Ciron returns," one of them warned.

"Come on, we all know why he sent us ahead while he and his friends went back. If they're going to have a good time with Fiona, I don't see why we can't have a little fun ourselves," the dark-faced hunter said. He tried to kiss the woman, who turned her face away.

BoDak cracked his knuckles. "Let her go."

"Make me," the hunter challenged.

BoDak vaulted from his horse, and the hunter shoved the woman away from him. The hunter drew a dagger and slashed at Bo while his friends shouted encouragement. Other hunters rushed from their huts, and when they found what the fight was about, they cheered and placed bets on the outcome. But there was no contest. Before a minute had passed, BoDak had already wrenched the weapon from his opponent. He kicked the dark-faced hunter in the rump, and the poor fellow sprawled to the dirt in front of the woman's feet.

"Apologize!" Bo roared before three other hunters jumped him.

This is more like it. At least the fight is more evenly matched. Hua sat and enjoyed the fight until he heard horses approaching. The others, including the Natives in the courtyard, seemed unaware of the new arrivals.

Four riders entered the village, then changed course and rode around the courtyard until reaching Hua. They reined in their horses and saluted.

"Captain! What a surprise to see you here. Do you wish me to stop the fight?" the leader asked.

"No, Ciron. Let's see how good the barbarian is."

They all turned just in time to see BoDak make short work of his three opponents. The rest of the hunters now saw how good the barbarian was, and decided to join forces. From then on, BoDak got as much punch as he gave, and the fight became bloody. In the end, three of them succeeded in holding Bo while the rest of them took turns knocking him about.

When it came to the dark-faced hunter's turn, he took a hunting knife from his friend and waved the weapon in front of BoDak. "What was it you said about wanting me to apologize?"

"I . . . changed . . . my mind . . ." Bo spat out as he struggled against his captors.

"Oh?"

"I'm . . . going to . . . make you . . . bleed . . . like a . . . pig . . ."

The others laughed as the dark-faced hunter turned red. He aimed the knife at BoDak. "You shouldn't have said that, little Bo-peep. Now, I'm going to kill you."

Ciron drew his bow and arrow, ready to intercept, but Hua stayed him. Just as the dark-faced hunter threw his knife at BoDak, twelve tiny star-shaped projectiles flew from a secret slot in BoDak's headband. One projectile deflected the coming knife, and the weapon hit the fighter who was strangling Bo instead. He howled and let go of his hold. The other small weapons hit eleven different spots on the dark-faced hunter's body, who screamed suddenly in agony. With one of his captors down, BoDak soon freed himself from the other two holds. Once again, he faced his opponents, ready for fun.

"He's just toying with them, isn't he?" Ciron commented.

"So it seems. He's getting his early morning exercise. It'll be a while before he gets tired of them. Tell me, Ciron, did you really think you could conceal the dead from all these villagers just by stuffing the bodies into sacks?"

"I left instructions for the hunters to start a bonfire, away from the humans, and burn the dead without creating any commotion."

"Instead, they decided to just stuff the bodies in sacks and order the villagers to do the dirty work. Not to mention take advantage of the women. By the way, who ordered the killings anyway? When my father ruled here, nothing of this sort ever occurred. What sort of a leader are you, Ciron?"

Ciron sucked in his breath. "Permission to speak freely, Captain," he requested after a moment of silence.

"You're an old friend of my father's and like an uncle to me, Ciron. You do not need my permission to speak the truth."

"Since the time your father sustained that wound and retired, the Western Region has become leaderless and lawless."

"How so? Are you not in charge?"

"My dear Captain, how can a demon command the Senginfans? Not to mention dealing with the Senginfan Defenders. To tell you the truth, I'd have retired also if I hadn't promised your father that I would keep an eye on things until he got better. I might add that when I made that promise, none of us had any idea of how serious his injury was. I'm sorry to bring it up, I know it's most painful."

"No, Ciron, I should be the one to apologize. I see it now. You're doing your best, while the likes of Fiona and Yewza flit about, killing needlessly. I assume all the dead here have the Vixen's mark on them, and as usual you have to clean up after her mess. You must have used up all your fortune by now, compensating the families of the dead."

"Oh, I got Benny the Merchant to donate for that."

"Really? I got this Nain horse for a bargain from Benny, also. I've been traveling for two months now, and all I hear is how ruthless the Merchant of Northwood is. But the way I see it, the guy is really a Santa Claus."

Ciron and his three friends laughed. "That's the first time I've heard the greedy merchant being likened to Santa. Young Captain Hua, you've got a lot to learn."

"How about you teach me," Hua suggested. A snap from the branches above alerted him suddenly that Owlut was now close, and listening.

"Are you saying what I think you're saying?"

"Yes, with a little twist. Instead of becoming my advisor, as you were to my father, be a real uncle to me. How about it?"

Ciron was speechless as his three demon friends slapped his back to congratulate him. "Alright!" one of them shouted. "Now that one of us is the uncle of Captain Hua, we demons can walk proudly, even in front of the Senginfans."

"Hua, do you realize what you're saying?" Ciron asked.

"Yes. From now on no one will dare defy you. Any who do will be brought in front of the Mowong Council," the young captain said. He unclasped the brooch from his weather-stained cloak and handed it to Ciron.

"Did you hear that, Ciron? Not the Demon Council or the Senginfan Council, but straight to the Mowong Council!" another of Ciron's friends exclaimed, then he took a good look at the brooch now pinned on Ciron's vest. "Why, that's a Mowgen Symbol! With that brooch, you could command the Senginfan Defenders to carry out any of your wishes! Ciron, let's start by arresting Yewza—"

"Now, now, this is not a license to kill. Let's not get too carried away here," Ciron scolded, holding a smile in check. Then he moved his black horse close to Hua's white one, and they clasped hands as the other three demons cheered.

Since the time BoDak had broken free, the fight in the courtyard had turned into a disaster for the hunters.

Now, other than moans from the injured, the courtyard had become quiet. The Natives, much as they would have loved to cheer for Bo, were smart enough to watch without making a sound. As a result, everyone in the courtyard was suddenly aware of the cheering issuing from Ciron's friends.

"Lesson one, Hua, watch how I deal with this," Ciron said with relish. He guided his horse toward the center of the yard, followed by his friends.

Hua smiled. *Father's right. Uncle Ciron can't resist a chance to be a teacher.*

Ciron eyed his wounded underlings sprawled across the yard. "What's going on here?" he questioned, his voice stern.

"It's just a friendly fight, Ciron," one of the hunters said.

"I see. And you, stranger, what have you to say about using my hunters as punching clowns, and one in particular as your pin cushion?"

BoDak snorted. "Your men gave as good as they got—I ain't exactly a vision of loveliness."

"Ah. And what was the prize?"

"I already kicked the pin cushion's butt and made him bleed like a pig, but he still hasn't apologized to the lady for his rudeness."

"I ain't apologizing to no lady," the dark-faced hunter said as he scowled.

Ciron looked at the eleven bleeding wounds, the two on the hips close to the hunter's manhood in particular. He rubbed his chin slowly. "I wonder. If the twelfth 'pin' hadn't been deflected, where was it supposed to hit?"

Bo grinned from ear to ear. "Want me to finish the job?"

"No!" The hunter turned white and stumbled to the woman who was leaning in the doorway. "I'm sorry if I made you uncomfortable, but you are beautiful—I wouldn't have gone any further without your consent, though."

The woman nodded her head shyly, stole a look at his wounds, and sucked in her breath. She produced a hankie from her pocket and held it out to the hunter. He moved to accept the cloth, stumbled, and she rushed to his side to steady him. She guided him to sit with her beneath the shade of a tall tree nearby, and began to tend to his wounds, resting her head occasionally upon his shoulder.

BoDak was left speechless. "Life is not fair," he muttered bitterly.

Is this a lesson of some kind? Say … lesson number one point five?

Ciron turned to where Hua was watching and winked before addressing the villagers. "I'm sorry if my men didn't explain clearly about these dead bodies. They were Merchant Benny's slave hunters who unfortunately met a poisonous animal that bit them. Their bodies carry the poison still, so please help us burn them."

At his words, the villagers gasped and immediately resumed piling the bundles on top of the wood, though a bit more carefully this time. When finished, the village headman brought a torch and set fire to the dead. Hua saw the little boy who had talked to BoDak before fetch water for the barbarian and his horse. Ciron had a few more words with the headman, giving further instruction to his three friends, before riding back to Hua.

"I've helped some of these villagers out of tight spots before, including the headman and his family, so we're okay here."

"Ah. Lesson number two, always choose a friendly neighborhood to dispose of bodies."

"Don't make me feel worse than I already do, Hua. The death of Benny's slave hunters was not planned. Things just didn't quite work out. Our part in the scheme of things was to disguise as slave hunters and show up at the Slave Route Junction to recover a runaway slave. Then we were to take her away as fast and as far north as possible. Lord Cedric Markum and Prince Norlen of Nain, the new wielders of the loathsome Bond Fire, would come after her, then Yewza and his troops could overrun their camp. But everything went wrong when Benny's slave hunters met up with us."

Hua nodded his head. "Fiona's not famous for her patience. Is it true that when she turns on her charm, no living creature, mortal or immortal, can resist her?"

"I know of no human who could. After five thousand years, the Vixen still has what it takes. You should have seen Lord Cedric and Prince Norlen, her latest conquests. And those two just teenagers! As for us immortals, only Zansern was never under her spell."

"You forget my father."

"Ah, yes. But he has the fairest maiden of the Golden Woods for his wife, which I might add, is Fiona's sore spot. You know, being reminded that she's not the most beautiful." Ciron paused and studied Hua for a moment. "You're the spitting image of your mother, so I must warn you, Fiona's not going to like your looks when you meet up with her."

Hua feigned a girly voice. "I'll be sure not to take apples from strangers, Uncle Ciron."

Ciron laughed while shaking his head. "You have always been wicked even when you were little. Which reminds me, what are you doing in this neck of the woods?"

"I was looking for some Belna."

"Your mother's favorite! I must warn you, they're very rare. Your father always tried to bring her some, but he wasn't always able to find them."

"Yeah, I know. But I've gotten a pet that's very good at playing fetch, and I sent her out to find some. In the meantime, I would like to take a better look at the barbarian's Nain horse."

"Just look, eh? Well, he's planing to stay here for whatever is left of the night, so you'll have plenty of opportunity to look. The headman has invited me and my friends to stay with him. He's got quite a few slave girls, and a couple of them are gorgeous. Are you interested?"

"No thanks, I'm not interested in becoming a pin cushion like Dark-Face there. I'll have a look at the horse, though."

"The barbarian is staying with the little boy and his mother," Ciron said. "Their hut is the small one next to the pigsty. There's a little awning in the front of the hut, and that's where he and his Nain horse'll be. Well, I'll say goodnight now."

Hua inched his horse forward, and they clasped hands once again. "Goodnight, Uncle Ciron." Hua waited until Ciron rode off with his friends and the courtyard became deserted. "You can come down now, Owlut."

The owl above fluttered its wings and flew down from the tree. A moment later, Owlut stood in front of Hua. "How long have you known I was about?"

"Long enough to find out you're interested in the barbarian's neck," Hua said. "He doesn't have the necklace, you know."

"Yes, I found that out as soon as his tunic was torn during the fight. Then I spotted you. You don't seem to be too concerned that the descendant of Lord Chris Markum is joining forces with Nain. Could it be you do not realize the seriousness of the situation?"

"Could be. As you can see, I'm what the humans call a green kid. What I need is someone wise to keep me out of trouble."

"I knew you were up to something when you took Ciron in as your uncle instead of your advisor—"

"And you, Owlut, are as wise as I was led to believe."

"Cut the flattery and cut to the chase."

"Yes, I left the position open in case you're interested. But do not misunderstand me, I truly think of Ciron as my uncle. I always have. So how about it, Owlut? We can bring peace and harmony to all living things, mortal and immortal."

Owlut snorted before eyeing Hua. "To do that, you would have to have the Wosenzard's trust and cooperation. And somehow I don't see your archenemy playing footsie with you."

Hua shrugged. "There hasn't been any report of those meddlesome female wizards for at least two thousand years."

"Don't let that lure you into a false sense of security. It is good that you have more of your mother in you than your—"

"Let's get one thing straight, Owlut. I adore my mother and I admire my father, and anyone criticizing either of them is going to find me very ungrateful."

Owlut chuckled. "Fiercely loyal just like your mother. Like I said, you've got more of your mother in you than your great-grandfather would have liked. You are absolutely right, someone ought to keep you out of trouble. We're going to get along just fine, young Hua. I can teach you things many have forgotten, while you may help me change my outdated ways."

"Does that mean you'll take the job?"

"Depends. What kind of benefits does this position entail?"

"How about a prime seat on a purebred Nain horse for a starter? It beats sitting on the rump."

"If you mean the barbarian's horse, then I must inform you I'm not interested in becoming a pin cushion, either."

"That leaves only one option; you sit on Black Eye's rump—"

"Black Eye? That's a strange name for a white horse."

"It's a long story. I'll tell you about it sometime. Right now I think we have visitors," Hua said.

"Do you want me to disappear?"

"No, these are Senginfan Defenders, and they seem to be in a hurry. I wonder what's wrong?" Hua vaulted down from Black Eye to stand next to Owlut as they waited for the riders.

"Don't mind me if I make myself look older and wiser," Owlut said, and he morphed suddenly into an old man with white bushy eyebrows and hair.

Hua looked at the wrinkled face. "Just how old are you, Owlut?"

"You don't want to know."

"That old, eh?"

Owlut chuckled, but said nothing. A minute later, fifteen Senginfan Defenders rode into the village and made straight toward Hua and Owlut. All dismounted immediately on reaching the two, and saluted Hua.

"Captain Hua, we were hurrying to Yewza's camp, but sensed your Zunji light," one of the defenders said.

"What seems to be the trouble?" Hua asked.

"A messenger from Yewza reports that the Bond Fire has been rekindled," the defender answered. "The plan to break up their friendship suffered a minor setback, and Fiona has ended up inside the enemy's camp. She risks being discovered at any time. Yewza had to fake injury to avoid a direct confrontation with Lord Cedric and Prince Norlen. He has withdrawn his troops from the Slave Route Junction for the time being. However, he's requesting aid from the Senginfan Defenders so that he can rescue Fiona and break the Bond Fire as soon as possible."

"Negative. Yewza will leave the Bond Fire intact and withdraw his troops completely," Owlut instructed.

The Senginfan Defenders all started at this unexpected intrusion from Owlut, and looked to their captain for confirmation.

"Allow me to introduce you to my advisor, Owlut. However, you will not mention that name to anyone. From now on he will be known as . . . as Captain Hua's Advisor. Or CHA for short. And yes, I agree with his advice. I want one of you to be my messenger. Carry my Mowzui Arrow to Yewza and order his troops to withdraw to—" Hua broke off and waited for Owlut.

Owlut continued where Hua left off. "To the Bayjai Lookout Point. Set up camp on the bottom of the hill facing south, but be sure to post sentries at the top of the hill. Now, this is very important. Yewza's troops must be ready to move south at a moment's notice. I will prepare two different instructions and seal them each in a green and a red pouch. The messenger is to keep the pouches and stay with Yewza's troops. I must stress that no one, and I mean no one, is to open the pouches except for Hua's Messenger."

"When and how do I know which pouch to open?" the tallest of the Senginfan Defenders asked.

"Open the green pouch and follow my instructions when Yewza's troops receive the sign to go south. Open the red pouch only in dire need. The rest of you will split into pairs and take different routes to gather all the Senginfan Defenders in the Western Region. Then make for the Firmiana Inn. We'll meet there. Is this understood?"

"Yes, Cha!" the Senginfan Defenders chorused.

The messenger with Hua's Mowzui Arrow left, and the rest of the defenders split, riding off in different directions to summon all the Senginfan Defenders in the Western Region.

Owlut turned to Hua. "Cha? Couldn't you think of a better name?"

"What's wrong with Cha, Cha? Cha, don't you like the way your name rhymes with mine?"

"I am now getting the feeling I might come to regret accepting this job."

Hua quirked his brow. "So you decided to become a fortune teller? What's the deal with the green and red pouches?"

"Well, for our next step, I figured we'd try to get you a real steed, worthy of the challenges we'll face."

Hua shoved Bo-peep's head to the side and leaned closer to Owlut. "And what steed would that be?"

"I don't want to get your hopes up, so we'll just leave it at that."

"Ooh, mysterious..." There was a moment of silence. "Better than the barbarian's horse?"

"Absolutely," Cha replied. "But for now, let's go find the barbarian and take a look at that horse."

"Hadn't you gotten a good look already?" Hua asked playfully as they made their way to the pigsty.

"You're just dying for me to admit that all I had was a close up rear view, aren't you, kid?"

"Rear views, Owlut," Hua corrected before he broke out into laughter.

Owlut's beard twitched, and he shook his head. "Ciron's right, you are wicked. However, I must inform you that I already had a close inspection of this particular horse at Lord Markum's stable."

"You were there!"

"Keep your voice down, Hua, we don't want to wake everyone."

They arrived at the pigsty next to the small hut and, on seeing BoDak siting against the wall beneath the awning of the hut, Hua and Owlut halted. "His eyelids are lowered, but they're not completely shut. Is he sleeping?" Hua asked.

"Dark-face called the barbarian little Bo-peep most appropriately. He's keeping an eye on the Nain horse even in his sleep. It's not going to be easy for you to get close and take a look at it."

"If we can't go to the horse, then we must get the horse to come to us," Hua said as he patted Black Eye. "Now be a good horsey and go fetch your pal."

Black Eye moved to stand just outside the awning and neighed. The barbarian's horse recognized its own kin and tried to join Black Eye, but was hindered by two reins tied as tethers to a post. The struggling horse snorted, and BoDak stirred. The barbarian settled more comfortably by slumping lower before falling back to sleep. Hua took out a Mowzui Arrow and aimed it at the post where the reins were tied. The small gold weapon flew silently to the awning and sliced the reins from the post, freeing the horse. It then returned to Hua noiselessly while the barbarian's horse now joined Black Eye. The two horses nudged each other affectionately.

"Good horsey." Hua patted Black Eye before shifting his attention to the barbarian's horse. "She's a direct descendant of Noreia Nain!"

"You have a good eye for horse flesh, Hua."

"How is it possible that Prince Norlen was willing to part with it?"

"The prince had the barbarian impersonate him."

"Why?"

"To fool me."

"Don't tell me he succeeded."

"It's a long story. I'll tell you about it sometime. But it looks like this horse has taken to you. How about you?"

"I'm in love with her." Hua rubbed the horse's neck while it snuggled him. "You know you're a beauty, don't you?"

"Yes, and you ought to be a little more careful during your secret rendezvous with your love, Hua. Lesson number three, always keep an eye on the jealous and suspicious owner," Ciron instructed, joining Hua and Owlut.

Hua turned to notice that the slumped form of BoDak was now sprawled on the ground beneath the awning of the small hut. "Hello, Uncle Ciron. You didn't leave those gorgeous slave girls just to come here and spray Demon's Breath on little Bo-peep, did you?"

"No, that was only an unavoidable accident. But he'll come around eventually. I came to update you on the situation. The reason I returned to the area where Fiona attacked the other hunters was because, at the time when Lord Cedric grabbed what he thought was Shanui, he—"

"Shanui?" Hua asked.

"Yes, the beautiful slave girl Fiona is impersonating," Ciron explained.

"And where's the real Shanui?"

"Oh, probably in Benny's arms warming his bed at this moment."

Hua cursed.

"Watch your language!" Ciron scolded. "What'll your mother say?"

"My sentiments exactly," Owlut chipped in.

"Hello, old friend, long time no see," Ciron said. He stared at Owlut's white bushy hair and the deep wrinkles. "I thought it was you up in that tree. You're getting careless. Old age, eh?"

"Good to see you again, Ciron," Owlut said. "You're still as blunt as ever, but let's get back to what you were saying."

"Well, after Lord Cedric made away with Shanui, or Fiona in this case, I found that one of my hunters was missing. So I sent the rest of them this way while I rode back to check out what happened to him. I returned to the spot where Fiona had attacked Benny's men, and found that this hunter of ours had been killed by a well trained solider. From the tracks on the ground, I think the solider is still alive and is now with Lord Cedric and Prince Norlen."

"So there was a survivor. Now Fiona's really in for it. Ciron, how far are Benny and Shanui from here?" Owlut asked.

"The traveling merchants left the market here three hours before sundown, and they probably traveled five or six hours before they made camp. So I would say no more than a two hour ride with Hua's horse."

"Hua, let's go fetch the real Shanui and make a switch before Fiona blows her cover," Owlut suggested.

Hua swung up onto the barbarian's horse. "Okay, old owl, get on Black Eye and try not to lag too far behind. See you soon, Uncle Ciron." Hua leaned forward, patted his steed, and whispered in the horse's ear. "Let's see how good you really are, Bo-peep. Show me." The true descendant of Noreia Nain sprang off instantly.

After a few minutes of sprinting, Hua encouraged the horse. "Come on Bo-peep, queen of horses, you can do better than this." With a toss of her head, Bo-peep doubled her effort, and the wind whistled past while a sensation of his steed slowly rising above the ground hit Hua. "You're getting the idea. Isn't this better?"

As if in agreement, Bo-peep's speed increased and the horse literally flew inches above the ground. "That's it—Noreia in ancient tongue meant flying. Now you truly are a descendant of Noreia Nain!"

After several more minutes of riding Bo-peep north, Hua shifted to look back and found Black Eye galloping at a distance behind. But of Owlut, he saw no sign. Hua frowned. *Now, where is he?* Suddenly, a voice over his head startled him.

"Your way of naming things isn't very flattering at all, Hua," Owlut commented, flying above.

"What's wrong with the way I name things?"

"Bo-peep for the queen of horses?"

"It's the least I can do for using the barbarian's horse," Hua explained.

"If you think you can soften him up by naming the horse after him, you're going to be in for a big surprise. Besides, Bo-peep belongs to Prince Norlen, remember?"

"Don't worry, I just wanted to test her out. I'll return Bo-peep to the barbarian on my way back. Where were you and why aren't you riding Black Eye?"

"I had Ciron bring me up to date concerning certain affairs. As for not riding Black Eye, he's already hard put to keep up with you. Hua, slow down, it'll only take a few hours to fetch the slave girl and bring her to the Slave Route Junction, you know."

Hua eased off just a fraction. "Shanui's not a slave, Owlut. She was freed two nights ago."

"Are you sure?"

Hua briefly retold the events of that night, and how Michi and Joseph freed Shanui and Dei. Owlut listened intently, and when Hua came to the part where he brought the two ex-slaves out of Benny's tent, he noticed that they were fast approaching the traveling merchant's camp. Hua slowed. "There doesn't seem to be any activity. Looks like the whole camp's bedded down."

"That makes it easier to instill Dream Illusion in her."

"I don't like that idea."

"Hua, it's either her, or hundreds of people getting Forgetful Potion. Take your pick."

They arrived at Benny's big tent, and Hua dismounted from Bo-peep. "There's got to be a better way—" Hua started to say, but stopped when he heard hushed voices coming from inside.

"It was a pearl hairpin, Master Benny. She must have hidden it inside her clothing."

"What a stubborn girl! Well doctor, is she dead?"

On hearing Benny's words, Hua guided his horse to the tent's entrance, flipped the flaps, and entered. He stopped advancing when he saw three figures bent over a still form lying on a rug at the far end of the tent. None of them seemed to be aware of Hua's intrusion as they concentrated on the girl.

"The puncture's very deep and she's still bleeding, but I don't think she's dead."

"What kind of a doctor are you? Stop the bleeding!" Benny shouted.

Buddo, Benny's right-hand man, comforted the merchant. "Do not overtax yourself, Master Benny. Shanui's not worthy of your love. Now, there's another woman inside the gourd, and from what I can see, she's mighty pretty—"

"Forget it! She's probably just a reject. If you're interested, go ahead and keep her, Buddo."

"Thank you, Master. I've always wanted a redheaded wench with such shining hair to warm my bed."

"Buddo, the lighting inside the Echoing Gourd can play tricks on you. Her hair is probably oily, and I bet she wears dentures," Benny warned.

Ignoring the warning, Buddo picked up the green gourd from the rug. He closed one eye while he peeped through the opening of the gourd with the other. "Hello, my pretty. Master Benny has given you to me. If you're nice to me, I just might make you my wife. Would you like that?"

"I'll turn you into a toad, you insolent fool!" A sharp voice hissed from inside the gourd.

That's Queen Pollyanna! What's she doing in there?

Buddo chuckled. "I love a woman who fights back. Come, tell me your name, so I can release you from the spell."

"Go away!"

"It's very cramped and damp in there. Besides, you don't want to be only six inches tall for the rest of your life, do you?" Buddo cajoled.

"I like it just fine, thank you," Queen Pollyanna replied. At that moment, two slave girls appeared from a side entrance.

"Buddo! The doctor has stopped the bleeding, so come and carry Shanui to her chamber," Benny shouted. Buddo put the green gourd back down on the rug. "You two are to take care of her around the clock," Benny added.

"Yes, Master Benny," the slave girls answered as the muscled man rushed over, bent, and picked up Shanui.

"Gently, Buddo," Benny cautioned, and they all moved to an inner chamber of the tent.

The flaps to the inner chamber closed, and Hua saw Princess Leianna run out from behind a jug. She stopped in front of the gourd. "Grandmammy, are you in there?"

"Yes."

"I've got to go and get Xeiyén to come and rescue you."

"No! I'm sick and tired of his 'I told you so' looks. There's got to be a way out without him—I have it! Lei?"

Queen Pollyanna's words echoed within the gourd, and Lei's name sounded repeatedly.

"Yes—" Lei began. No sooner was her reply uttered than Princess Leianna was sucked into the gourd.

"Those two have got to be the dumbest Tensengin Immortals I've ever seen," Owlut, now perched on Hua's left shoulder, commented.

"We'll talk about that later. Right now let's get them out."

"Are you sure we ought to rescue those two morons?"

"Cha!"

"Okay. Just wondering. I can get Lei out easy enough, but I can't get Grandmammy out if she doesn't want to give me her real name."

"It's Polly," Hua supplied.

"Ah. An acquaintance of yours?"

"Owlut, the Grandmammy is Queen Pollyanna. Now can you guess who Lei is?"

"Princess Leianna! What happened to her face?"

"Mousasus."

"The mousasus were left behind when the Tensengin Dome was shut? This is the best news I've heard in years."

"If that is the best news, I dread what bad news is like. Come on." Hua let go of Bo-peep's reins and strolled to the green gourd. He bent down and peeped in. "Polly, Lei, it's me."

"Captain Hua?" Polly asked excitedly while Lei warned, "Grandmammy, don't call his name!"

"It's alright, Lei. We'll get you both out now," Hua said and backed off from the gourd.

Owlut turned himself into an old man again and stood over the Echoing Gourd. He cast one counter spell after another—all spoken in ancient tongue. On his fourth try, Polly and Lei were freed.

"Captain Hua, we're in your debt once again," Polly said.

"Think nothing of it, Queen Pollyanna. Let's get out of here before Buddo comes looking for his wife-I mean you," Hua suggested, fighting a smile.

"I wish this friend of yours had a spell for turning that imbecile into a frog," Queen Pollyanna grumbled as Hua placed her on top of Bo-peep.

Owlut peered at the indignant queen from beneath his bushy eyebrows. "I stopped doing that ever since a fool of a queen went and kissed the frog, turning him into a prince—or was it a princess who did the kissing?"

Queen Pollyanna placed her hands on her hips and huffed. "Are you calling us royalty fools?"

Owlut crinkled his nose. "Hmm . . . can't quite make up my mind. A queen that sets traps for her would-be rescuer and a princess that happily walks into one . . . "

Princess Leianna's face turned scarlet. "It was very stupid of me, wasn't it? Instead of helping Grandmammy out, I ended up joining her inside the gourd."

"Perfectly understandable mistake, given the circumstances," Hua comforted while he picked up Lei and deposited her next to Polly. He strolled between Bo-peep and Owlut, and they exited the big tent. Black Eye was grazing under a tree next to Benny's tent, and Bo-peep went to join him. "Tell me, why is it that Dei wasn't with his sister?"

"He's staying with a merchant who offered him a job," Lei replied. "No one knows Shanui's missing because one of Benny's slave girls is impersonating her."

"How?" Hua asked.

"Fiona turned both herself and the slave girl to look just like Shanui," Lei said.

"What about the necessary documents? After all, the original slave release form was signed," Hua pursued.

"Fiona got Merchant Benny to help her with that," Polly said. "In return, he gets to keep the real Shanui inside the Echoing Gourd."

"I don't like that nasty merchant," Lei voiced, "keeping Shanui imprisoned like that and forcing unwanted attention upon her. Did you know she tried to kill herself to protect her virtue? I wish we could do something for poor Shanui."

"I was only in the gourd for a while and I was nearly out of my mind. Captain Hua, couldn't you do something for the poor girl?" Polly asked.

I think it's wise not to ask the queen how she got inside the gourd in the first place. "Well, what do you suggest I do?" Hua returned.

"Maybe take her with you and deliver her safely to her aunt?" Polly suggested.

"Grandmammy, that's an excellent idea! Oh! Think of the fun we'll have watching Benny puzzle over what happened to the real Shanui. He can't accuse anyone of stealing her, either, because Shanui is supposed to be freed. In the meantime, no one needs to worry needlessly about Shanui, because Merchant Benny's slave girl is impersonating her. By the time the magic wears off, the traveling merchants would have reached Aunt Shalin. Imagine Benny's wrath at finding Shanui safely at the Bonhas' estate already."

"We'll frame Buddo to take the rap, and make him squirm like a worm." Queen Pollyanna plotted with glee.

Owlut studied Polly with a frown, while Hua coughed discreetly. "Just keep a safe distance from the Echoing Gourd. Now, tell me, are you still staying in the pink tent?"

"Yes, we are—" Lei started to say when she was interrupted by Xeiyén, bouncing atop Black Eye, followed a moment later by Xane.

"Captain Hua, how nice to see you again," Xeiyén greeted.

"Hello. Cha and I met Polly and Lei here quite by accident."

"Ah." Xeiyén glanced at the queen and the princess to make sure that they were none the worse for wear, before he continued. "Any reason why you chose this location for a social event?"

"Lei and I were taking some fresh air when we came upon Captain Hua and his friend here," Polly said with a challenging look.

"I'm so glad you found us, Xeiyén and Xane, because I think I'm a little tired now. Captain Hua, it was so nice to meet you again," Lei said.

"Yes, now that you mention it, Lei, I find that it's time we should go back to Bayjai Arma's tent," Polly said. "Captain Hua, you have no idea how glad I am that we met again. I'll look forward to our next meeting."

"Until then, Polly and Lei." Hua saluted.

After the Dideetones and the Dideetonies had left, Owlut turned to study Hua. "I won't ask how you met those two, but tell me, why did you rush into the tent when you first heard Benny ask the doctor if Shanui was dead?"

"I wanted to revive her if the humans weren't able to do so."

"I see. Where was her injury, and how serious was it?"

"Between her lower neck and her right shoulder blade, and it's not serious. I'll have no trouble helping her."

"Good! It is a stroke of luck that she happened to be injured now, and at the right spot."

"What! What are you trying to say?"

"If I read Yewza's message correctly, then Fiona is in the enemy's camp. She faked an injury to let Yewza know she wanted his troops to withdraw for now. The wound is most likely from a poison arrow piercing her right neck, and the person attending her is probably Pauline, who's friendly. Hua, it's perfect! All you have to do is to leave Shanui's wound unattended, and Fiona'll take care of the rest. She's an expert when it comes to wriggling herself out of a spot."

"You seem to know how Fiona and Yewza operate. However, I don't like leaving Shanui in that vixen's claws."

"Shanui'll suffer through a mild poison wound with a fever, which will cause her to be delirious," Owlut said. "It's just as well. That way she won't know how much of what went on was her imagination and how much was real. When her fever breaks, she'll lose her voice for a few days. Again, no one will bother her, and by the time she's on the mend, we'll have her installed at her aunt's place."

"Well," Hua said, "it's better than instilling Dream Illusion in her, causing possible memory damage ... or giving hundreds of people the Forgetful Potion and risk the chance of missing one. I'll go fetch her, and we'll be on our way."

"I don't suppose you need any help, so I'll stay with the horses," Owlut said, before there came a shout from within the big tent. "I think Buddo just found that his fiancée is missing."

"Maybe I can steal Benny's future wife as well during the confusion, eh?" Hua teased before moving to the entrance of the big tent. He peeped inside just in time to see two slave girls and a couple of slave hunters disappear into an inner tent next to Shanui's. Hua entered the big tent, making his way quickly to Shanui's chamber, and entered. He saw there was no one inside besides Shanui, who was tossing and turning on a pile of cushions. Hua walked over to stand looking down at the restless form.

"Please ... No ... Don't touch me ..." Shanui uttered in her troubled dreams.

He bent and placed the back of his left hand on her forehead. The cooling touch awakened her, and she opened her fevered eyes. For a moment, Shanui didn't seem to recognize him. But as her head tossed from side to side, his hand's gentle touch soothed her troubled forehead.

She calmed down, and when her eyes were more focused, she gave out a little sigh. "It is you, Knight in Dusty Armor," she whispered, a dreamy smile appearing on her pale face. "Death isn't so bad after all."

Hua frowned. "Hush. You're not dead. Shanui, will you trust me?"

She snuggled her cheek against the back of his hand. "Yes."

Hua's features softened. "Do not tax yourself." He gently picked her up, and a moment later, was out of Benny's tent.

"That was fast. How is she?" Owlut asked in ancient tongue, indicating that they were now to converse in that language.

"She walked in dark dreams before. But aside from a small fever, she is better now," Hua answered in the ancient language, understanding that his tutoring with Owlut was now to begin.

Owlut nodded with satisfaction. "Let's get going." He mounted Black Eye while Hua bounced up onto Bo-peep, not causing any discomfort to the soft bundle in his arms, and they rode off toward the south.

12

THE COLISEUM

MICHI STIRRED UNEASILY from a troubled slumber. In her dream, a fabulous feast was spread before her. Yet each time she tried to eat, a knocking sound would reappear to disturb her. Then she thought she heard Xorro calling. *That's not possible! He's caught in Vreeny's net. Caught! What am I doing at a feast when he needs help?* Michi schooled herself to open her eyes. When she finally did, she found she could see nothing. *Where am I?*

Michi searched her memory and recalled shouting to warn Xorro about Vreeny. Then suddenly their cart had plunged into darkness. She remembered screaming until their cart abruptly stopped plunging, as if they had reached a particular floor in an elevator. Before she could even ask if the others were alright, there had come a stuffy and suffocating smell, which must have put her out. *How long have I been sleeping? Where's everybody?* "Jo! George! Archoy! Didee-baker!" she shouted and grabbed blindly around.

Her hand came into contact with a huge sunflower, and she sighed with relief. "Archoy, I can't see. Do you have a flashlight?" There was no reply, and she shook the housekeeper. "Wake up, Archoy!" Her only response was a loud snore. *Oh, great! What is this place? Dream Land?* She sniffed the air and realized that the suffocating smell was still very strong. *I must have gotten used to it.*

Michi pondered what to do next, and she noticed that the surroundings weren't as dark as before. At first, she thought her eyes might be getting used to the darkness.

But when an unmistakable beam of light appeared some-where ahead, she stood up to take a look. That was when she realized that their cart was actually moving slowly and smoothly forward through a narrow tunnel. The alarming part was that Big Thunder was asleep as well.

Who's pulling the cart? Where are we going? The tunnel brightened as they continued to move. Soon it became clear that the light was emanating from a glistening object between some rocks ahead, and it was also moving. The buffalo cart reached the end of the tunnel at the same time the lighted object finally made its way out of the crack between the rocks. Michi's eyes widened when she realized that their cart had moved out of the tunnel and, instead of falling into a bottomless pit below them, was hovering in mid-air as if waiting for the lighted object. She watched with fascination while the strange fan-like object advanced slowly toward her. The moment it floated above her, she grabbed it with her palm-leaf-disguised hand. But before she could examine it, their cart began to slowly descend into the pit.

To the side, Michi saw that there were holes going across the right of the shaft. She lifted the lighted fan to get a better look at them, and to her surprise, the cart stopped descending. Michi positioned herself over one of the round holes and peeped in. She found herself overlooking what appeared to be a prison cell. The only furniture inside the jail was a cot, and on it was a tiny skeleton. She saw Xorro's Center Guards kneeling with bowed heads around the cot. *Now, I wonder who died?*

As if in answer, one of the guards began to speak. "We must collect our grief and consider what our next course should be. King Windune died without naming the new Didee-king, just as Vreeny claimed. If Princess Leianna has indeed lost her magic powers, then we must swear to serve Tina's mate as our new king. After all, the line of the

Mighty Didee race must be upheld. But I don't think we should declare our loyalty to Tina and her chosen mate until we first discuss with Xorro."

The other Didee-guards started to agree when Berna suddenly appeared by the prison door. "Grieve no more, my friends. King Windune lives."

Xorro's Center guards jumped to their feet. "But who is it that lies on this lonely bed and wears our king's ring?" one of the Didee-guards asked.

"King Windune's faithful guard," Berna answered as he unlocked the prison door, then entered. He walked to the cot and removed the ring from the skeleton's hand. "He was a brave Didee-guard, and his sacrifice was not in vain. Come, it took me hours to find out where you were imprisoned, and getting the key to this dungeon was no easy task. Vreeny is treacherous, so we must leave quickly."

At that moment, Michi saw Vreeny appear by the prison door, about to lock Berna in with the others. She waved her hands frantically. "Berna, the door! Watch out!"

A strong gust of wind was created by her waving of the fan-like object. Michi saw everyone by the cell, including the skeleton, the cot, and Vreeny, lift off the ground and twirl helplessly while the buffalo cart shook. Realizing the lighted fan was the cause, she stopped waving and lowered it. In doing so, the wind stopped, but their cart began a fast descent. *No! We're going to crash.* She lifted the fan-like object a fraction at a time and, to her relief, their fall slowed.

Eager to find out what happened to Berna and the others, she lifted the fan a tad higher and they stopped descending. She lifted it further, and the cart started to ascend. In the meantime, Michi turned her head from side to side, searching for the peep holes. She found an oddly shaped opening on the left side of the shaft instead. Curious, she maneuvered the fan to stop the cart, then looked in. To her amazement, she found herself looking down from above into a giant lighted cavern. In the distance on the ground, row upon row of armor-clad soldiers on horseback entered the cavern from a huge stone gate opposite her. The two tall leaders at the front of the procession especially caught her eye. One of them wore the same silver war gear as the Ghost Chasers who had demanded to search their van a few days ago. As for the other grim-faced leader, aside from not wearing a helmet, he had armor similar to the rest of the soldiers, save for the precious stones on his insignia.

The moment all the soldiers entered, the stone gate began to close. Michi saw the thick cord running along the right side of the huge gate retract upward. When the stone gate finally shut, only a small section of the cord remained dangling over another oddly shaped opening above the opposite gate. The round stone ceiling of the cavern echoed every sound within, and Michi found she could clearly hear the conversation of the distant soldiers.

"Now what?" the grim-faced leader said, giving the enclosed cave a once over. "Sneaking in like this is pathetic. We're given orders to creep around, trying to be their secret trump card, while they're all cozy in their seats of honor. If I was in charge—"

"Yewza, I know you never liked following orders. But unless you're ready to defy Captain Hua's Mowzui Arrow, I suggest you stop sneering at me," the Ghost Chaser said.

"Captain Hua? Hah! I'll deal with him the same way I dealt with his father."

"What do you mean by that?"

"You just wait and see—" Yewza began, but was cut off by a loud rumble that shook the walls. Black and gooey liquid began gushing out from the oddly shaped openings surrounding the top of the cave.

The foul smelling liquid filled the cave rapidly. However, the well-trained soldiers stayed fixed upon their horses, waiting for their leaders to give a command. The Ghost Chaser scanned the openings above the large cave until he spotted the one where Michi was peeping in. He bounced off his horse and flew toward it. Michi's jaw dropped. *Bayjai Arma was right, the Ghost Chasers can fly. Gee ... Is he coming after me? Oh, wait a minute, silly me. I'm just a palm tree.* As soon as the Ghost Chaser landed on the ledge of the opening, he began to search the surroundings. *I wonder what he's looking for?*

"Thinking of hiding up here while everyone else below dies of a slow poisoning or drowns?" Yewza accused, following the Ghost Chaser to the ledge.

"Don't be stupid! I'm looking for the control to open the other gate."

"There must be hundreds of these openings up here. How do you know the control is in this one?"

"Because only two openings are not spouting the foul poison. This one and the one above the gate we just entered. Since we can't go back where we came, our only choice is the other exit."

"Well, you better be quick about it. The soldiers and horses can't take much more."

At Yewza's words, Michi peeped down and found the murky liquid had already reached knee depth, and many of the horses had collapsed. Even some of the riders were doubling over as if in pain. *I better help out.* She started to look as well, and when she saw a thick cord protruding from the top of the opening above, she realized that the Ghost Chaser was right. *This opening must contain the mechanism to open the second gate.* She continued to search the ledges on her side of the opening, mindful not to upset the fanlike object, but stopped when she saw the Ghost Chaser take out a red pouch and open it.

From the pouch he produced a small flask and passed it to Yewza. "Pour this elixir into the poisoned pool. That should take care of the death by poison part. Now I'll deal with the death by drowning." After Yewza left, the Ghost Chaser continued to search for the gate control.

Michi saw the black goo surrounding the horses and soldiers turn clear the moment Yewza emptied the flask. Many horses started to revive and struggled to their feet again. Yewza mounted his steed, then bellowed an order. Michi couldn't quite make out the words over the roar of liquid spilling into the cave. She instead turned back to check the Ghost Chaser's progress, and found him with the red pouch upside down, shaking it.

"Well, Cha, even you couldn't have predicted that the control would be ripped from the wall. The creature that did this must be strong indeed," the Ghost Chaser said to no one in particular as he tossed the pouch.

Uh-oh! If the control is broken, then... The possibility of the poisonous liquid filling the cave and overflowing to the shaft spurred her into action. *I've got to save our cart first...Up, I think.* Michi raised the fan a fraction, and their cart started to ascend. She was unaware that one of her palm leaves had brushed against the red pouch lying on the ledge. A loose thread from the pouch clung to the leaf, and it began to unravel as the cart went up.

Michi stopped their rise to take one last look at the situation inside the cave, and she swallowed hard. *I can't leave them in there to die.* She saw the Ghost Chaser pick up the discarded red pouch to study it, and she waited. *Perhaps he realizes he overlooked something before.* The Ghost Chaser instead gave a hard tug at the red thread dangling from Michi's palm leaf.

"Aargh!" Michi screamed as the cart started to rock. To keep her balance, she grabbed at the protruding thick cord above the opening with her free, palm-like hand. The Ghost Chaser stopped tugging and Michi, still clinging to the cord for support, maneuvered the fan and lowered the buffalo cart to face him. "Don't do that!"

No sooner were her words uttered than an amazing thing happened. The gushing liquid subsided, and there came a loud creaking sound from below. "So you are Cha's lucky charm, here to open the gate," the Ghost Chaser said with relief.

"Correction, Lucky Palm," Michi said. Eyeing the length of thick cord in her palm-like hand, and the dwindling goo trickling from the openings above the cave, she guessed at what the creaking noise signified. "Now tell me, is the gate opened?"

The Ghost Chaser looked down for a moment, then turned back. "Only a crack, but it stopped."

Michi let go of the thick cord. "Here, it's simple, just pull this cord for the butler and the gate will open."

"Butler?"

"It's a joke, you know . . . Never mind, just pull the cord."

The Ghost Chaser immediately complied, but the rigid cord wouldn't budge. He dug his heels in and doubled his effort, but still nothing happened. "No butler," he said, and Michi laughed. The Ghost Chaser was taken aback by her outburst. "Something wrong?"

"Didn't you know you just made a joke? When someone makes a good joke, you're supposed to laugh."

"Laugh?"

"Err . . . You're right. This is no laughing matter. Any more delay and all of us'll be going swimming. Give me the cord. I'm going to continue pulling it downward and finish opening the gate, okay?"

"Alright, but you must let go the moment the gate is opened. Otherwise it will cause this side of the wall to cave in."

"How am I supposed to know when?"

"I'll drop the red pouch when the gate is completely opened. When you see the pouch joining the loose thread on your lucky palm leaf, let the cord go."

"Okay." Michi lowered her fan-like object, and the cord lengthened as the buffalo cart descended. The loud creaking noise started again, and she knew the gate must be opening wider as she went down. She also noticed that the stuffy smell was clearing fast as they descended.

"Hi, Michi, getting used to the eat and rush routine?" George, lying on the dividing rail and facing the back, said as he opened his sleepy eyes.

"Hello, George. Did you have a nice nap?"

"Was that what I was doing? I thought I fainted from a foul smell."

Joseph woke up as well. "Sweet, are you alright?"

"Oh, I'm fine, Jo. Look, I helped myself with this." Michi waved the fan-like object, and their cart started to rock.

"Whoa! Sweet, take it easy with that thing," Joseph warned while George turned green and urged, "Please don't rock the cart."

"Sorry, I forgot." Michi stopped waving the fan, and their cart steadied.

George eased his death-grip of the cart's railing. "What is that thing?"

"It's a magic fan. Oh! Jo, I saw Berna and Zorro's Center Guards."

"Where?"

"Up there, in a jail."

"Jail! Are you sure?"

"Yes, but Vreeny showed up. I tried to warn them, but it didn't quite work out."

Joseph frowned as he looked up. "Where did you say they were? Up there?"

"Uh-huh."

"Sweet, can your fan take us back there?"

"It can, but we can't," Michi said. She showed the thick cord she was holding to her brother. "I have to be the butler and open the heavy gate so all those soldiers up there in the cave won't drown."

"Butler?...Soldiers...cave...drown?" Joseph's frown deepened as he studied Michi. "The foul smell knocked you out pretty good, didn't it?"

"Yeah! When I woke up, I didn't even know where everyone was," Michi replied.

Joseph nodded his head slowly. "Don't worry about it, Sweet," he comforted, then he looked at his watch. "This can't be right! According to my watch, we've been descending for at least fifteen hours!"

This means I've skipped quite a few meals. No wonder I dreamt about food. "Jo, don't you remember our cart stopped plunging after a while?" Michi asked.

"Now, wait a minute," George said. "What's keeping our cart from plunging down right now? Don't tell me it's that cord you're holding, or the red thread dangling from your palm leaf."

"I don't really know, but before the awful smell overcame me, I noticed that our cart stopped. When I came to, everything was dark until this lighted fan came to my rescue."

"Sounds like that fan you're holding is the key to our present condition," George said. "Not that I'm complaining, seeing as our ride is much smoother, but I hate relying on a fan for our lives."

"Yeah, too fragile and feminine for my taste," Dideebaker, hanging on to George's bee wings, agreed.

"Oh, you're up. Maybe you can tell us where we are," Joseph said.

"I think we're descending to the lower levels of the Inmee Dungeon," Didee-baker replied.

"Oh, great, now we're going to the maximum security prison without even a fair trial," George said.

"I'm afraid that's what they do with spies, even in the Kingdom of Anguo," Joseph explained while he helped Didee-baker down from George's wings.

"Spies! Is that what we are, young Master Joseph?" Archoy, the last to wake from slumber, asked with alarm.

"Well, we certainly aren't wildlife, and we aren't Dideetones, either," Joseph said.

"What happens to the prisoners in this dungeon, Didee-baker?" George asked.

"No one knows, because they are never heard from again."

"Uh-oh, this is not good," George said.

"I wonder which is worse. Being down here, or caught in a net by Vreeny," Joseph mused.

"Don't you worry about King Xodune," Didee-baker said. "Once Vreeny finds out it was not Xeiyén in the violet mask, the king will be released."

"We sort of got the idea that this Vreeny guy doesn't like someone called Vong—who is Vong?" Joseph asked.

"The Mighty Vong was the head of the Didee-council while King Tydune reigned during the Golden Age of the Dideetones. Vreeny was only a lesser advisor at that time. Then, came the greatest mystery of Didee-history. King Tydune, the queen, and his court went on a hunting trip from which they never returned. With the new king, Vreeny elevated quickly. The Mighty Vong and Vreeny argued before the Didee-council numerous times, and the new King Windune always sided with Vreeny. Finally, the Mighty Vong washed his hands of the Didee-royal court and moved south. With him went Xeiyén and Xane, two of the three most loved Didee-guards from the king's court."

"The same two Tina mistook masked Zorro and Berna to be?" George asked.

"Yes. Xeiyén, Xane, and Scar Face were called the Triple Didee-delight during happier times. They were loved by all the Didee-folk. When Scar Face disappeared, the Mighty

Vong was alarmed. I think he took Xeiyén and Xane with him to protect them."

"Well, we know what happened to Scar Face, so maybe there's an explanation for King Tydune's disappearance also," Joseph said.

Conversation halted as their cart jerked, before finally settling gently onto what appeared to be the very bottom of the shaft. The red pouch dropped from above onto Big Thunder's head, then bounced off and landed on Michi's palm leaf. She let go of the thick cord the same time Big Thunder began rushing forward.

"George, I hate to be a back seat driver, but I think you'd better look ahead," Michi said.

George spun around just in time to see Big Thunder careen into a group of human-sized troll-like creatures.

"Oh, look at all these Mini-trolls," Michi said.

"Don't talk!" Didee-baker warned before disappearing.

Everyone in the cart froze. Michi saw the largest and most muscled of the creatures grab Big Thunder by the horns and stop the cart. "Hey! Why is this prize cart here?"

"Who knows?" the tallest of them said. "They never tell us anything. However, I've heard that this is the first time humans will be allowed in as challengers. And with so many last minute entries, they're swamped at the Entry Cave."

"Yes, and rumor has it that there's a very special guest from Mowong Castle," the shortest one added.

"What! Mowong Castle?" the strong one that halted Big Thunder asked with excitement.

"Don't get too excited, Zinla. Even if it's true, you'll never get a seat. From what I was told, it's a full house."

"I've got to get in there somehow." Zinla pondered while examining Big Thunder. "This is an outstanding buffalo! I wouldn't mind challenging for it."

"I could use a tree. My kids have been pestering me for one," the tallest said.

"My wife loves honey. From the look of these colossal king and queen bees, I just know they'd produce enough honey to satisfy even her cravings," the shortest chipped in.

The rest of the troll-like creatures laughed. "Are you sure you ought to feed her more—" Zinla began to say, but was interrupted by strange, rumbling growls. A group of armed riders sped toward them on animals resembling rhinoceros. The animals' heads were large, with two thick horns protruding from their snouts, and their bodies were long and armored. The low-pitched rumbles came from the throats of the creatures.

The soldiers reined in their mounts. "What's this?" the leader of the riders asked.

"It's a prize cart," Zinla replied. "With a buffalo for riding, like humans use, instead of our recigs."

The leader frowned while the rider to his left picked up the red pouch on Michi's palm leaf, studying it. "It's Cha's prize cart, Commander Zildow."

"There are enough flowers here for your new garden, Commander," another rider mentioned.

Commander Zildow slowly nodded his head. "I've never seen a more beautiful sunflower. Get the buffalo cart to the Entry Cave, Zinla. The king will arrive shortly. Break it up and get going."

Zinla grabbed Big Thunder's reins and led their cart forward. As they proceeded, they passed many Mini-trolls. Each Mini-troll stopped to admire Big Thunder, the exotic flowers, the palm tree, and the king and queen bees. Then they descended lower into the caves, their surroundings growing more dull, grey, and barren. From the sounds and exclamations around them, Michi suspected Zinla had taken a roundabout route just to show the colorful and flowery cart off, and she was pleased to be on display. Her only regret was that, as soon as they had landed, her fan had shrunk in size and lost its glowing beauty. *I'm pretty sure the Mini-trolls would have been very impressed with it, had it not lost its shine.* She thought of tossing it away, but in the end pocketed it, along with Cha's red pouch.

Zinla finally reached what looked to be a large court-yard with scattered flowers and sickly trees, surrounded by many cave entrances.

Not even a water fountain to soften the harsh look of this garden. No wonder these Mini-trolls called this honeymoon carriage a prize cart.

A Mini-troll was just leading another cart away from the largest cave entrance, and Zinla immediately took the vacated spot. "Zinla, the check-in line is ninety-nine caves long. I don't think you'll make it."

Zinla's beady eyes glinted as he patted Big Thunder. "Commander Zildow fancies these flowers. Especially the beautiful sunflower."

Michi saw the sunflower, or rather Archoy, do a little dance. *She won't be doing any more dancing if that hideous looking commander actually takes her home.*

"Well, that's different. Commander Zildow is the apple of the king's eye right now."

"Is that a fact?"

"Haven't you heard? He captured the highest prize this morning, while herding the beast's food. We're swamped with last minute entries now—everyone's vying for it. The king ordered us to give Commander Zildow royal treat-ment. Mention his name to the guards at the Entry Cave, and they'll whisk you to the front of the line. But hurry, I think they're running out of seats. Hey, you go ahead and check in. I'll get your cart situated as soon as I'm done with this one."

Zinla rushed to the cave entrance. Once he disappeared into the cave, Didee-baker reappeared.

"George, get us out of here as quietly as possible before they find out you're not wildlife," Didee-baker said.

George picked up the reins. "Which way?"

"That way." Didee-baker pointed toward the passage opposite the one Zinla had taken to reach the garden. George started the cart toward it. "Good thing you're all still in your disguises. They certainly look real enough."

"The magic does feel light and comfortable, too. But still…these Mini-trolls…they aren't very smart, are they?" Michi said.

"These Mini-trolls, as you call them, are actually the ancestors of giant trolls," Didee-baker said. "I had no idea there were any still living. However, legend says that these ancestors of trolls are slaves to a foul beast that craves human flesh. Any human unlucky enough to bump into them will be fed to the giant beast."

"I see," Joseph said. "So that's why you told us not to speak as soon as we came upon them."

"Yes, just as a precaution in case the legend was true."

They crossed the vast but deserted garden without raising any alarm, and once they reached the passage, George increased their speed. "Good news. This passage is going up."

"Do you know where we're going, Didee-baker?" Joseph asked.

"No, but at least this passage looked more deserted. And we need to go up to get out."

They came to a fork, and George halted Big Thunder. "Now which way?"

Before Didee-baker could reply, they heard voices coming from the passage to their left. "Vernott you idiot, why did you help him escape?"

"That's Vreeny," Michi whispered.

Joseph nodded, but Didee-baker placed a finger over his mouth to indicate that they should all stay silent. After a moment, they heard Vernott's voice.

"Princess Tianna asked me to help Xeiyén, and I saw no reason not to. Granduncle, I want to be like you, a powerful advisor to the Didee-king. You know Xorro has never liked me. If he becomes king, I won't even be a member of the Didee-council. Xeiyén, on the other hand, is Princess Tianna's choice. He seemed more willing to accept me."

"You fool! If you think you can manipulate Xeiyén, then you're more of a simpleton than I've suspected you to be. If I knew you were foolish enough to help him escape, I'd have dealt with him immediately."

There was a moment of silence, and the pattering of the Dideetone's feet echoed. Vreeny's voice broke the silence.

"No matter. I have another plan to lure Xeiyén. But the subject of this missing buffalo cart puzzles me. It was to be destroyed at the bottom of our trap tunnel. Where did it go? There is so much to deal with."

"I'm sorry, Granduncle."

"Vernott, I have not planned for a thousand years just to see you, my favorite grandnephew, become another Didee-advisor."

"Granduncle, what do you mean?"

They did not hear Vreeny's reply because, at that moment, new footsteps sounded behind them. George jerked instantly on Big Thunder's reins, and their cart rolled quickly toward the right fork. A bend in the passage hid them just as the footsteps reached where they had been a minute before. Then as the footsteps took to the left fork, they breathed a sigh of relief.

"Well, I guess the choice is made for us. We go up," George said. He urged Big Thunder on an upward climb.

"Jo, did I understand Vreeny right? Did Vernott help King Zodune to escape?" Michi asked.

"It seems so. At least we now know he's freed. Although neither Vreeny nor Vernott still seem to realize that it was Zorro behind the purple mask. But from their talk, Vreeny has been trying to locate us, and I suggest we get out of here as soon as possible."

"You're right, young Master Joseph. If that Vreeny doesn't catch us, there's still a human eating monster down here," Archoy reminded.

"Easier said than done," George said as he once again halted the cart. "Now which way?"

"We took the right last time, so let's try the left path this time," Didee-baker suggested.

"Sounds good to me," George agreed, and they headed upward toward the left. As they continued, the air grew heated and thick. After only a few minutes, they came to the end of the passage and found themselves headed toward the extending edge of a cliff. George reined in Big Thunder instantly, and the buffalo stopped just inches before a huge hole in the ground. "Looks like a dead end. We'll have to go back." George hopped down from the driver's seat. "I'm just going to make sure Big Thunder has enough room to turn around." He walked to the hole and looked down. "Strange. I wonder what this is. You've got to come and see."

Descending from the cart, the rest of the group went to join George. A large round hole, cut entirely through a section of the overhanging cliff edge, could be seen. They cautiously peeked down the hole. Hundreds of feet below, a giant valley stretched, surrounded by streams of lava.

Archoy gasped. "Oh my! This hole's big enough for our cart to fall through. George, I'm glad you're a good driver."

"It's most curious," Joseph said. "Why cut a hole here? Just walk another twenty-some feet to the end of this ledge and you get an open view of this valley anyway."

"That down there isn't a valley. It's a coliseum," Didee-baker replied, standing on Joseph's right shoulder.

"It's huge!" Joseph exclaimed. He walked toward the edge of the cliff to get a better view. "Hey! Look, there are other ledges like this one surrounding the coliseum."

"Yes, these are prime seats for the games," Didee-baker said.

"Prime seats?" Archoy asked.

"Kind of like the special balcony seats for the opera, Archoy," Joseph replied.

"Notice how this one we are standing on, and the one opposite us, are the two highest in the coliseum?" Didee-baker said. "This means we're either in the king's balcony or the highest honored guest's. In either case it spells disaster for us, so let's hurry and get out of here."

"Yes," Archoy said eagerly, "let's—" but was interrupted by Michi.

"Jo! I think that's Vreeny and Vernott on the cliff down there."

"Really?" Joseph squinted his eyes and focused on the lower cliffs to their left. "I think you're right. I can't see the riders' faces clearly, but they're wearing the same sort of clothes. And those horses are definitely the Inmee Dungeon's blacks. "

"You've got super eyes, Little Miss. I wonder what Vreeny is doing there? I hope he doesn't look up. Maybe we'd better back off before he sees us. Little Miss! I do think there's a crowd down there."

"Remember the caves surrounding the garden?" Didee-baker said. "I think they're the entrances to the coliseum. We're very lucky. They must have started to allow the spectators to enter soon after we left."

"If there's going to be any games played way down there, I don't see how these balconies up here can be considered prime seats," Archoy said.

Didee-baker laughed. "You are probably the first humans to ever stand here in the highest seats of the coliseum. If I remember right, aside from owning at least one priceless possession for the betting arena, usually the occupants of these prime seats have excellent eyesight, and many are exceptional fighters that have the ability to glide or fly."

"You-you mean like a bird?" Archoy choked out.

"Yes, and the games are not limited to the ground either. Didn't you know wars have been fought in an arena of this sort? Kingships have been decided here and empires overthrown just at a word of challenge."

"Wars? Goodness! I thought this was just an opera house!" Archoy exclaimed.

"I wouldn't mind watching a good fight from up here. Must be a sight to behold," Joseph said.

"Not to mention flying," George added.

"Although I can't make you fly, I can certainly help your eyesight." Didee-baker produced a handful of heart-shaped leaves from his sleeves and passed them to the others. "Just rub them over your eyelids, and you'll be able to see much better—for a while anyway."

Archoy closed her eyes and rubbed the leaves over them. "I can feel moisture seeping into my eyes! What is it?"

"Eye drops to improve your vision. Now test your sight," Didee-baker invited.

"Oh! There's Commander Zildow riding out to the cliff on our right," Archoy said.

"Don't panic," George said, "but I think a purple and a blue monster have just entered the balcony across from us."

"Blue and purple monsters! Where?" Michi eagerly scanned the cliff on the opposing side. She saw two giants, one purple-haired in a suit of armor and one blue-haired in a dark cloak, advancing toward the edge of the cliff just one below the highest cliff across from theirs. *Huh, that big armor looks familiar, and his face . . . .*

"Nice braids," Archoy noted.

"Yes, did you see the glowing jewels, Jo?" Michi asked. No reply came from Joseph, and she looked at her brother. "What's wrong, Jo? You look like you've seen a ghost."

Joseph blinked his eyes and shook his head. "For a moment there I thought I did, but of course it can't be.

He couldn't have grown more than a foot taller in just a few days—not to mention dyeing his hair purple. No, definitely not him."

"The purple monster looks like Cedric Markum, but you know he wouldn't be caught dead looking like that, Jo," Michi assured.

"You're right, Sweet. I don't think Cedric'll be flattered at the resemblance, though."

"All this talk reminds me of Christa. I do miss her and I wish she could be here with us," Michi said with feeling.

"Don't wish too hard, Sweet. This is one place you wouldn't want her to be caught in."

Archoy pointed to the balcony across from Commander Zildow's. "Oh, look! Little Miss, it's Zorro, our little friend in his purple mask. And he's on one of those black horses as well." The housekeeper suddenly waved. "Yoohoo! Zorro!" she shouted.

"Archoy!" Everyone shushed while not just Xorro, but Vreeny, Vernott, Zildow, the giants, and the crowd turned to look in their direction. Joseph and George quickly flapped their bee-like wings and danced around the sunflower while making buzzing noises.

Good thinking! I don't think we fooled Vreeny, but ninety-nine point nine percent isn't bad. Michi almost giggled when she saw Xorro stare at them with a funny expression on his masked face. *I know, Zorro, we shouldn't be drawing attention to ourselves, but you know Archoy.* To her relief, the arrival of Councilman Trumbond and his son Brutan at the balcony to their left claimed the spectators' attention.

"Jo! Didn't Trumbond say he was in a hurry to get to the Firmiana Inn yesterday? What do you suppose he's doing here?" Michi asked.

"He was at the Firmiana Inn at lunch time yesterday," George said. "But he was more interested in the two of you than the lunch menu there."

"Really? Sweet, you don't suppose he's still trying to get your dolly, do you?"

"If he is, he's going to be mighty disappointed, because I left it at Arma's."

"You mean the Councilman was fighting over a doll with you?" George exclaimed. "This is getting very interesting."

"And dangerous. Let's get out of here while the getting is good," Didee-baker, who had disappeared the moment Archoy called out to Xorro, reappeared and suggested.

"We can't do that. Zorro might need our help," Michi said.

"I don't mean leave the coliseum for good. Haven't you noticed? We're on the wrong side." Didee-baker pointed at Xorro across from them. "Let's at least move to King Xodune's cliff."

Before they could make a move, they heard horse hooves coming from their passage. "Too late," George murmured.

Everyone froze, and Michi saw Didee-baker disappear again. *Coward!* Her eyes moved to the newcomers and she gasped. Riding out from the passage toward them was the oddest pair she had ever seen. A wrinkly old man on a grey horse was accompanied by a youth, whose every feature spelled perfection, on a gorgeous white steed. The young man had somehow captured the sun's radiance in his long and flowing golden hair, in contrast to the snowy white hair of the bushy old man.

The pair reined in their steeds in front of Big Thunder. "Magnificent. Are we sharing this cliff, Cha?" the youth asked.

Cha!

"I'm not surprised. I heard it's standing room only down there," the old man replied.

At that moment, the Mini-troll that had offered to move the cart for Zinla appeared at the passage. "Over here! Someone already positioned the cart for you."

A few seconds later, Michi saw Zinla dash out of the passage, pass his friend, and start to run toward Big Thunder and the cart. He halted abruptly on seeing the striking pair of riders.

"Who are you?" the youth asked.

"I-I am Zinla."

"What are you doing here, Zinla?"

"I-I . . ."

Zinla's friend advanced out of the passage and saluted. "You must forgive Zinla, Captain Hua. He's still in shock at his good fortune, being chosen to serve you and your prize cart. I've heard that Commander Zildow fancies your sunflower, Captain Hua. I'd like to see him try to take it from you, though."

"He does, eh?" the captain said as he scanned the interesting merchandise on the cliff. His eyes rested on the sunflower. "Maybe I'll let him keep her." The sunflower shook while the corner of the captain's mouth twitched. He turned his devilish eyes to Michi. "And the palm tree would make the perfect outdoor ladies' room, complete with potted plants. Zinla, make yourself useful. Tie my Nain horse under—er—next to the midget palm."

Perfect outdoor ladies' room? Michi frowned. *Why does that sound familiar to me?*

"Zinla, snap out of it! Hurry up and do Captain Hua's bidding," his friend advised before leaving. Zinla jumped into action.

Captain Hua, eyes glued to Michi's enormous ones, waited. *Didee-troll assured me no one could see through the dense palm leaves to my disguise. But why do I feel this captain is staring straight at me?* She stuck her tongue out at him just as a test.

The captain quirked his brow, then dismounted and passed the reins to Zinla. "Best hurry. It's been more than three hours since the horse's last visit to the ladies' room."

I'm not a fire hydrant! She made a face at Captain Hua, and amusement entered the captain's eyes. *So you can see me.* Michi wrinkled her nose as she saw Zinla guide the white horse to her right side. She slowly inched to the other side. *I've heard horses can pee a whole bucket full...* Michi noticed that she was now shielded by the horse from the captain's gaze. When the Mini-troll tried to tie the reins on her, she grabbed them. *I'm not going to be tied down again if I can help it.* "I'll take that, Zinla." The Mini-troll jumped, and he opened his mouth to speak. "Keep quiet, or I'll spill the beans on you," Michi warned. Zinla sucked in his breath, and studied the palm leaves that could speak with beady eyes.

By now, the old man had ridden his grey horse to the edge of the cliff between Joseph and Michi. He dismounted and passed the reins to Zinla. "Well, what do you know. Hua, the Bond Fire pair are here. Ah, and the barbarian just rode in with Bo-peep."

Barbarian? I've never seen one. Michi whirled around to look, forgetting that she was supposed to be just a palm tree. She saw a jewelry-laden rider approaching the balcony across from Vreeny's. *He's certainly loaded with priceless possessions. So that's the barbarian. Now where's Bo-peep?*

Hua strolled to stand next to the old man. "Do you think he was telling the truth about Black Eye being his, when I brought Bo-peep back to him?"

"Probably. In any case, I'm glad he followed you here. He'll have to put Bo-peep up to challenge you for Black Eye. For once he's going to find it very costly judging his opponent by looks..." The old man ignored the insulted look Hua suddenly shot him, continuing, "...and you'll get the opportunity to own both Nain horses fair and square."

So the white horse here is called Black Eye and the bar-barian's steed is called Bo-peep. What strange names for such beautiful horses. She had no time to wonder further when drums began sounding from the highest cliff opposite them. Michi saw six Mini-troll guards enter the balcony across.

The drums stopped. "The king!" all six guards announced in one voice. A carriage drawn by four recigs, the rhino-like mounts, came out of the passage across from them and advanced to the edge of the cliff. The animals' low, thunderous rumbles resounded throughout the coliseum. Michi saw a Mini-troll who looked exactly like Didee-troll, except for his much smaller frame, riding in the carriage. The Mini-troll king wore a wreath made of fresh flowers for a crown, and in his left hand he held a scepter. He raised his left hand and the crowd cheered. After a while, he low-ered his scepter and the coliseum quieted.

The drums rolled again, and when they stopped, a huge recig came out of the passage leading to the king's cliff. The beast was led by a hunchbacked Mini-troll whose omi-nous features were accented by an eye patch over his left eye. The one-eyed Mini-troll guided the recig to the round hole, and the reason for the hole on each of the overhang-ing cliffs became clear. To Michi's amazement, the beast did not fall through, but instead floated downward out of the king's cliff to circle the arena. Murmurs of approval could be heard from all corners of the coliseum, especially from the spectators down below. When the recig floated in front of their cliff, she realized that a clear and dome-shaped enclosure was what kept the animal from falling. It was obvious that this was the beginning of the contest, and the beast was the first prize. Michi heard Zinla sigh, and she turned to look at him.

"If only I could challenge for it," the Mini-troll grum-bled under his breath.

"What's stopping you?" Michi asked.

Zinla scratched his head as if he couldn't believe he was talking to a tree. "You don't understand. This is the king's prize. The beast is a royal steed, and for sure Commander Zildow'll want to challenge for it."

"So? Couldn't you counter challenge?"

Zinla shrugged. "I don't have any valuable possessions that Commander Zildow'd covet."

"What about the sunflower?"

"Little Miss!" Archoy, who was obviously eavesdropping, protested while a stunned Zinla swung around to look at the talking flower.

"Oh, Archoy, anyone who could stop Big Thunder just by grabbing his horns isn't going to lose so easily in a fight," Michi said.

"Thank you," Zinla said. "Captain Hua's possessions are indeed both priceless and unique. Why, not only can you speak, you even have names for each other. I don't think Captain Hua'll agree to let me risk his valuables, though."

"It's Archoy's neck . . . I mean stem we're risking. Hua can have no objection if you're sure of a victory," Michi insisted.

Encouraged by the palm tree's familiar use of the captain's name, Zinla stole a glance at Hua. "I know I could beat any gladiator Commander Zildow selects. All I need is a chance to enter the arena."

"Well, Archoy, here's your chance to do a good deed," Michi encouraged, not giving Hua an opportunity to put in his two cents worth.

"Are . . . are you sure you'll win, Zinla?" Archoy asked with uncertainty.

"I'm very sure."

"There, you see. It's already in the bag. Come on, Archoy, let's help Zinla out," Michi urged.

"Err . . . what do I do, Little Miss?"

Before Michi could reply, a loud exclamation came from the crowd below when another dome-shaped enclosure, with a pair of jeweled daggers, flowed to hover next to the king's prize.

"What did I tell you?" Zinla said. "Commander Zildow is already upping the bet by offering his family heirlooms. I'm afraid the sunflower alone won't be enough."

"Well, he who hesitates is demoted. Hey, Midget Palm, how about throwing yourself in to make up the difference?" Captain Hua suggested.

Michi's eyes narrowed. *So, using me as a fire hydrant isn't enough and we're resorting to name calling now. I'll show you.* She held out her right hand and exhibited Black Eye's reins to Hua. "If I go, Black Eye goes with me."

Her challenge seemed to surprise not only Hua but also Cha. The old man turned and openly studied her for the first time. "She has a point, Hua. After all, you were the one who ordered Black Eye tethered to her. They're a package deal now."

Hua gave a short laugh. "Now you're making it sound like such a bargain, Cha. Perhaps I should save this bet for later. Zinla, put the buffalo and sunflower into the betting dome."

"Hey, wait a minute! Don't I get to say if we should risk Big Thunder's neck or not?" George protested, while the overjoyed Zinla dashed to do Hua's bidding.

"Oh, George, Zinla's going to win us a royal steed and a couple of treasure swords," Michi said.

"Sweet, this is for real. George could lose Big Thunder— not to mention about Archoy—" Joseph started.

Hua held out his hand to stop the argument. "It's already decided. Don't worry. I'll talk to Zinla before he faces Zildow's champion."

"Talk? That's all you're going to do, Captain Hua? Will it help Zinla?" Archoy asked doubtfully while Zinla unharnessed Big Thunder.

"You don't expect me to go down there and fight for him as well, do you?"

Eyeing the difference between the lean captain and the muscled Zinla, Archoy saw the wisdom of letting the latter do the fighting. Instead of answering, she went to join Big Thunder. It seemed Commander Zildow truly liked the sunflower, because as soon as Archoy stepped into the hole, the clear dome moved downward and floated out to join the other two betting domes. The excitement mounted as the three domes circled the arena. Then Zildow's champion appeared in the coliseum below, riding a fierce looking recig, and the crowd roared with deafening cheers. The three betting domes moved to hover just a foot below the king's cliff.

While the well-armed gladiator paraded in the coliseum, Michi sized up Zinla, who was receiving instruction from Hua. "Zinla, hadn't you better go and get your gear on?"

"Gear?" Zinla asked, dumbfounded.

"Why, yes, you know—helmet, protective armor, sharp swords and such," Michi explained.

"I was born in the labor class, and am forbidden from owning war gear. However, after I beat Commander Zildow's champion, I'll be able to move out of the labor class."

As if that explains anything. "You can't just go down there without any weapon," Michi said.

"You know what, Midget Palm? You're right. How about lending him one of your palm leaves?" Hua suggested.

"Oh, alright, it's better than nothing," Michi said. Zinla reached in to pluck it. "Don't take it from the inside, it's very sticky," she warned. "Grab it by the edge instead—yes, that's it. Just remember, it's a loan." Michi smacked Hua's back with one of her remaining palm leaves. "How about lending him a steed?"

Hua took out a small golden arrow and threw it toward Zinla's feet. "Get on my Mowzui Arrow. Remember, it's also a loan."

The arrow whirled in a circular motion, creating a smooth surface one foot above the ground. As soon as Zinla hopped upon it, it zoomed away from the cliff and made its way down to the floor of the arena. The audience that was cheering for Zildow's champion laughed on seeing Zinla holding the green palm. But it seemed the Mini-troll wasn't without friends, as shouts of encouragement came from the other side of the audience.

The moment Zinla arrived in front of his opponent, the enemy's recig charged. Commander Zildow's champion pointed his trident, ready to confront the ridiculous weapon in Zinla's hand. The confrontation did not occur, as the whirling arrow suddenly brought Zinla up to hover over his assailant. Zildow's champion immediately reined in and turned his steed around. When he lifted his head to search for the whereabouts of Zinla, the latter dropped Michi's palm leaf. Blinded by the palm over his helmet, the attacker stabbed the trident wildly with one hand while trying unsuccessfully to dislodge the sticky palm with the other. The spinning arrow brought Zinla to the left side of the beast. He grabbed the recig's huge horns and brought the beast to its knees. Michi cheered with the crowd.

Commander Zildow's champion threw his weapon in the direction he estimated Zinla might be. While Zinla dodged, Zildow's champion dismounted. He removed his helmet and threw it on the ground, then drew his sword. Zinla hopped off the Mowzui Arrow, helping himself with the spear attached to the side of the beast he had knocked over. Now the two gladiators faced each other on more equal footing, and the spectators quieted for the combat.

The fight between the two Mini-trolls was an eye opener for Michi, as the two combatants hopped from rock to rock like mountain goats. Each fought to gain higher ground while trying to dislodge the other. Armed with a weapon, Zinla's attacks were swift and ferocious. It did not take long before he disarmed and dislodged his opponent, pinning him to the ground. The crowd roared with anticipation as Zinla lifted his head to look at Hua.

"Zinla won!" Michi whooped.

"Not yet," Captain Hua said. "He'll have to kill his opponent—"

"What! Kill? But why?" Michi interrupted.

"That's usually what happens in a fight at the coliseum."

"Why can't it just be a friendly fight?" Michi pursued.

Hua frowned slightly. "A friendly fight in an arena?"

"Yes, you know, like the ones where no one gets killed," Michi explained.

"With single combat challenges like this, there's only one way Zinla could win and still let his opponent live. Most gladiators prefer death with honor over slavery in shame, though," Hua explained, but he gave Zinla the no kill sign anyway. "Zildow isn't going to like this."

Zinla withdrew the spear pointing at his opponent's neck and drove it into the ground instead. The Mowzui Arrow moved to attach itself to the loser's neck, forming a slavery chain. Since the spectators were expecting the coup de grâce, it took them a moment to realize what had happened. Stunned shouts rang through the coliseum. Although sparing the life of the opponent by enslaving him was an option for the victor, it did not occur often. The reaction from the crowd was mixed between anger for shaming the gladiator and approval of condemning him to a worse fate. However, Commander Zildow's reaction to his champion's disgrace was to exercise the Grand Challenge. He signaled to the king his intention, and the drums rolled; the coliseum quieted immediately.

13

THE GRAND CHALLENGE

THE MINI-TROLL KING raised his scepter and the drums stopped. "Commander Zildow has issued the Grand Challenge. I shall leave the decision to Captain Hua," the king announced.

"Now you've done it, Hua," Cha said.

"What? What did you do, Hua? What's happening?" Michi asked.

"I rubbed Commander Zildow the wrong way, Midget Palm. But it would have come down to this in the end, anyway," Hua said. He gave his consent to allow the Grand Challenge to proceed.

"Captain Hua has accepted!" the Mini-troll king declared, and the crowd cheered. The drums rolled once again while the center of the arena opened, a deep rumble shaking the coliseum as a platform raised from below. Michi saw a bundle of rags lying in the middle of the huge dais, and she wrinkled her nose. The drums stopped, but the crowd continued to roar with excitement as betting domes floated freely out of the cliffs.

Michi saw betting domes with war gear, strange looking animals, and even wine barrels circling the arena. "What's going on? Why is there so much betting all at once?"

"Zildow wanted a chance to reclaim his honor," Hua explained. "But he knows I'm not particularly interested in what he's offering on the dais, so he issued the Grand Challenge and got everyone else involved in order to whet my appetite."

"Are you saying all these others are interested in that bundle of rags Commander Zildow's offering on the dais?" Michi asked with disbelief.

"What is one's rag is another's treasure," Hua said.

"You're right, look! The blue and purple giants are offering a bookmark for Commander Zildow's treasure-rag," she said, pointing to the betting dome floating out of the giants' cliff.

"I think it's a necklace," George corrected.

"Necklace ... but it's hideous! That can't be very valuable. Why, I could make prettier ones than that, blindfolded—" Michi began, but at that moment the betting dome that floated from Vreeny's cliff caught her eye. "Jo! It's Berna! What's he doing inside the betting dome?"

"Looks like Vreeny's using him as bait," Joseph said.

"And I'm afraid it's working," George added.

Sure enough, Michi saw a betting dome float out from Xorro's cliff with a silvery jeweled crown in it. "Why does he have to offer a big thing like that? Why couldn't he just offer pencils or erasers," Michi scolded.

"Sweet, it shows he values his friendship above his king-ship," Joseph replied.

"I suppose so. Look! Cha, Councilman Trumbond's offering your empty bottle."

Cha spun around to look at Michi. "How do you know the bottle is empty?"

"I saw Yewza dump the blue liquid from it into the murky stuff in the cave."

"And ... " Cha prompted.

"Like magic, it cleared the poisonous stuff right away," Michi replied.

"The gate, did the gate open?" Cha pursued.

Eyeing the serious looking old man, Michi smiled mischievously. "Actually, the gate control was ripped from the wall, but I rang the butler."

Cha paused in thought for a moment, then his face cleared. "You pulled the cord!"

Not bad. "You might be old, but you certainly aren't dense."

Cha studied Michi with increasing interest. "And you are a little rascal, but a smart one."

"Why thank you," Michi said, curtsying as best a palm tree could, and Cha laughed.

Hua squinted critically at Trumbond's antidote bottle. "It's not the same bottle, though. This one is still filled with the priceless elixir."

"But it looks the same as Cha's! Are you sure? How can you tell?" Michi asked suspiciously.

Hua gave a smug smile, but remained silent.

"Captain Hua, what happens if you don't see anything you like?" George asked.

"Oh, I already see something I like, but I'll wait until the barbarian offers Bo-peep. Let me see ... How does the mortals' saying go? Ah, yes, kill two birds with one stone."

Michi turned to look at this youth who had more good looks than was good for him. "Forgive us mortals, Super Hua, but I don't see the barbarian offering Bo-peep for your benefit."

"Oh, he will," Hua assured.

Hmm ... this Captain Hua is as vain as a peacock. To Michi's astonishment, she saw the betting dome with Bo-peep in it float out of the barbarian's cliff. *Even he wants Commander Zildow's prize catch. There's got to be something special about that bundle of rags.* Curious, Michi focused on the bundle in the middle of the dais and was shocked to realize that it was actually a small sleeping form, wrapped in an old and tattered cloak. The bundle stirred, and Michi was all attention. When the sleepy head lifted, and the rumpled hood dropped back to reveal a cascade of golden hair, Michi gasped. "Christa!"

She dropped the reins and rushed forward, but Joseph grabbed her. "Sweet, you can't help Christa by falling off the cliff."

George lowered the arm he had raised to protect Michi, as well. "Take it easy, Michi. The only way to rescue your friend is to challenge Commander Zildow for her."

"Well, what are we waiting for? Hua, let's challenge Commander Zildow," Michi insisted.

"I take it you've changed your mind and are now also interested in the rag, Midget Palm?"

This is no time to be sarcastic. Michi gritted her teeth. "Stop calling me Midget Palm! The name's Michi, and that down there isn't a rag. She's my best friend. I don't know how Commander Zildow captured her, but you can be sure he's a crook."

"Okay, okay, Midget-I mean Michi, calm yourself. Are you always this hot-headed?"

"Only when my best friend is captured and offered as a prize in a coliseum, while I'm dressed like a useless Midget Palm," Michi retorted.

"Why did you disguise yourself like that, anyway?"

Joseph squeezed the palm tree's trunk to warn Michi not to reveal too much, and she took the hint. "Would Jo, George, and I have been able to enter this coliseum without our disguises?"

"Probably not."

"There you are," Michi said.

Joseph released his hold on Michi and turned to face Hua. "Captain Hua, what must we do to rescue Christa?"

"Right now? Nothing. We wait for all the others to either join forces or fight it out first."

"Join forces?" Joseph pursued.

"Once I accept their betting domes, they can challenge each other. But they can also stop the fight at any time and form alliances ..." Hua paused, signaling to accept Xorro,

Vreeny, Councilman Trumbond, the barbarian, and the giants' betting domes. "My guess is that they'll eventually join forces against Commander Zildow. Rumor has it that Zildow's got himself a fierce beast guarding his prize."

Michi remembered Didee-baker's warnings about the ancestors of the trolls. "You mean the foul beast that craves human flesh," she said.

"Ah, so that's why you're all dressed up like a wild kingdom," Hua said.

At that moment, their betting dome returned with Archoy, Zinla, Big Thunder, the royal steed, and Commander Zildow's daggers. "Little Miss, that was so exciting! Zinla was amazing!" Archoy burst out as soon as she joined them.

Zinla, with a lopsided smile, held Commander Zildow's daggers and the helmet, still with the sticky palm stuck fast upon it, out to Hua. The young captain took the daggers and plucked the palm leaf off the helmet with ease. "Keep the helmet, Zinla."

Yes, Zinla, keep the change.

The Mini-troll surprised Michi by placing the helmet on the ground and kneeling in front of Hua, bowing his head until it also touched the ground.

Although she felt Zinla's gratitude was somewhat misplaced, Michi still felt that the Mini-troll deserved more than just spare change. "Keep the royal steed, Zinla," Michi insisted.

Captain Hua looked at the Mini-troll king on the cliff across from them. "She's right, Zinla. Your king will need your service."

Zinla continued to pay homage to Hua.

"I hope he's not after Big Thunder, George," Michi whispered.

"If he can defeat the foul beast and rescue your friend Christa, I'll consider it," George said.

"You mean it?"

"I've never been more serious in my life," George assured.

"Thank you, George. Zinla, how are you at fighting human-flesh-craving beasts?"

Zinla still stayed where he was.

"Answer her, Zinla," Hua ordered.

Reluctantly, the Mini-troll stood up and faced Michi. "If Commander Zildow has the Inmee Beast guarding the golden-haired child, then no one stands a chance of rescuing her."

Archoy swallowed. "Inmee Beast, what's that?"

"The most ancient and deadliest of the Flexers," Hua said.

Archoy's eyes grew huge like saucers. "What's a Flexer?" she asked.

"A poisonous creature that can change its size."

Archoy fell silent as she tried to digest the information.

"Captain Hua, if all these other challengers fail to take down this Inmee Beast, we'll end up facing it?" Joseph asked.

"That's right."

"We might end up inside the beast's stomach?" Archoy pursued.

"It's possible," Hua replied.

"Little Miss, we're doomed," Archoy moaned.

Michi patted Archoy's sunflower petals. "Oh, Archoy, we're wildlife, remember?"

"I do believe the Inmee Beast likes appetizers before its main meal. I think salad with honey dressing sprinkled with sunflower seeds is its favorite," Hua said, staring absently into the distance.

"Sunflower seeds . . ."

"He's just pulling your leg, Archoy. I bet he'd say the monster loves to drink coconut juice if I hadn't used up all my coconuts in Tina's garden."

"So you have been throwing coconuts around instead of potatoes," Hua muttered.

"Huh?" Michi frowned. "What do potatoes have to do with coconuts?"

"Now that you mention it, Midget Palm, coconut juice has been known to calm beasts. Don't tell me this Tina's got a temper also," Hua said casually.

"And how! She'd arrest you if you don't address her as Princess Tianna," Archoy warned.

Hua quirked a brow. "I bet she would arrest you on sight if you weren't in disguise."

"Of course," Archoy replied. "You think we like to go around like this? Zorro might be good with his sword, but he's clueless when it comes to wooing Tina. We had to—"

"Have you ever seen anything like it?" Joseph interrupted, pointing at the arena.

It seemed while they were occupied with the discussion of the Inmee Beast and Tina, the fight among the challengers with accepted betting domes had begun. Michi saw Brutan, half kneeling on the edge of his cliff, shooting a shower of arrows at the barbarian. The latter stood on a tightrope and blocked the barrage of arrows with swift motions of his hands. He slowly advanced toward Trumbond. The arrows hitting the silver bands on the barbarian's wrists sparked tiny fires before they fell, useless, to the ground below.

Michi noticed that one end of the tightrope, with a blue and a purple jewel joined together, was suspended in midair. *So the giants have teamed up with the barbarian. These glowing jewels remind me of the Magic Helmet inside the Markums' secret room.* Michi moved to get a better look at the giants standing on the edge of the cliff. She realized that the other end of the tightrope was not tied to any post, but was issued straight from the blue giant's hair. "That's not a tightrope the barbarian's standing on!"

"That's right. It's the blue giant's braid," Joseph said.

"Oh, Little Miss, isn't he dreamy?"

"Well, Archoy, if you like the tall, blue, and teenage type, then I suppose he's okay."

"I don't mean that scary giant, Little Miss. I'm talking about the barbarian."

"Oh. Uhh...sure. He's rich, too. But don't get too attached to him yet, Archoy. He might not live through this."

No sooner was this warning issued than they saw Brutan stand and fire the next round of arrows up into the sky instead. The arrows passed over the barbarian's head and flew toward the giants. The purple knight drew his sword and began to deflect the oncoming arrows. But when an arrow slipped through and came straight at the blue giant, he dodged to avoid it. The action caused his braid to shake, and the force tossed the barbarian up like a rag doll. The barbarian grabbed futilely at the rope on his way down. Archoy screamed while Brutan, half kneeling once again, shot another round of arrows aimed at the falling barbarian.

George, ignoring Archoy's outburst, seemed quite impressed with Brutan's unbelievable archery skills. "What does the kid do? Spend all his waking hours playing with bows and arrows?"

"And dollies," Michi added.

Up until now, the spectators had been in awe, watching the acrobatic show. But on seeing the barbarian in trouble, a good portion of the crowd shouted with dismay. The blue giant's braid extended and dipped to rescue him. At the same time, many tiny star-shaped projectiles flew from a hidden slot in the barbarian's headband. The little weapons deflected the arrows as he caught the extended braid.

Michi and Archoy cheered with the crowd. "Little Miss, this is better than the circus!"

"Yes, Archoy, circus clowns can't possibly compete with your barbarian."

There was no time for more conversation, as the action in the coliseum reclaimed their attention. They saw the blue giant's braid swing up in a curve, and when the two jewels on it reached the same height as Councilman Trumbond's cliff, the braid straightened. Taking advantage of the momentum, the barbarian released his hold and sailed toward Councilman Trumbond. Brutan ducked to prevent himself from being knocked over, and the barbarian landed before Trumbond. He grabbed the councilman's shirtfront and lifted him off the ground; Trumbond immediately signaled his willingness to join forces. The barbarian let go of his captive and turned to Brutan. He extended a hand to the youth, and Brutan took it. The muscled man helped Brutan up from the ground, then patted the youth's shoulder before hopping onto the waiting braid. The braid, carrying the barbarian, circled the arena while the crowd cheered.

When it brought the muscled man to face their cliff, Michi whispered to Archoy. "Quick, Archoy, here's your chance to demonstrate your wooing skills."

"Uhh...Hello...Oh, your trousers are torn. Take them off, and I'll—" Archoy started, but was not given an opportunity to finish her offer as the braid carried the startled barbarian away.

As soon as the barbarian returned to his cliff, the betting dome with Trumbond's bottle floated to him. He eagerly snatched the bottle up, waving it at the pair of giants. The blue-haired giant gave the barbarian an enthusiastic thumbs up. The barbarian's smug expression crumpled, however, when the betting dome that housed Bo-peep flew to Hua's cliff. The majestic white horse exited the dome, and Zinla rushed to take care of it.

"What's Bo-peep doing here?" Michi asked.

"She's mine now," Hua replied.

"Yours! But you didn't even lift a finger in the fight."

"That's the beauty of the Grand Challenge, Midget Palm. I get part of the loot from the betting pool in every fight."

"I see. It's a case of heads you win, tails they lose."

"You got it."

"I take it Trumbond saved his own life by joining forces with the barbarian at the last moment," George said.

"Yes, very clever of him," Hua confirmed.

Their conversation quieted when Vreeny challenged the masked Xorro. King Xodune flew out of his cliff to confront his opponent. The two Dideetones met in midair, and their swords clashed.

"Go, Zorro, go!" Michi and Archoy rooted for their Didee-friend.

"Captain Hua," George asked, "which betting dome do you intend to keep this time?"

"Well, I've often wondered what it would be like to be the king of the Dideetones."

"You can't take Zorro's crown. It won't even fit you," Michi protested.

"Then I suppose I'll just have to settle for another slave. It'll be interesting to have a Didee-slave."

"You can't treat Berna like a slave! He's King Zodune's Right Commander," Michi defended hotly.

"But that leaves only the necklace that nobody wants."

"Oh, it's not so bad—"

"I thought you said that you could make prettier ones blindfolded," Hua reminded.

Michi gritted her teeth. *Trust him to remember a detail like that.* "Well, now that I have a better look at it, it really is quite fetching. I mean, it grows on you."

"It does? Tell you what. I'll wait until they all join forces before I decide, and give the necklace a chance to, er, grow on me. Right now let's watch how Xorro's going to defeat Vreeny."

Suddenly realizing that they might have been counting Xorro's chickens before they hatched, Michi returned her attention to the duel below. It was obvious as the fight went on that Xorro was much more skilled with a sword than Vreeny. Knowing Vreeny was treacherous, Michi wasn't surprised when she saw a group of Tina's guards, led by Vernott, bounce out of the cliff.

The guards surrounded the two fighting Dideetones and took out their Didee-hooks. They threw their hooks toward Xorro at the same time Vreeny backed off from the sword fight and dived. Xorro dove after him, a Didee-rope from his cuff popping out. It lassoed Vreeny's right foot, stopping Vreeny's escape. Xorro yanked, and Vreeny shot back up into the air. The moment he passed Xorro, hundreds of Didee-hooks sank into Vreeny. Seeing the hooks meant for Xorro make their mark on Vreeny instead, the spectators gasped. Vernott ordered the guards to withdraw their hooks instantly, but the damage was done.

The severely wounded Dideetone fell helplessly downward. Out of Vreeny's cliff, a badly scarred Didee-guard flew out and caught him. Xorro followed as the Didee-guard brought Vreeny down to the bottom of the arena. Laying Vreeny on the ground, the scarred Didee-guard examined his wounds. The masked Xorro slashed the letter X on a giant rock that he passed on his way down, and the crowd went wild, cheering at the drawing of first blood in the coliseum.

"Oh well, so this Zorro can't spell. He's still awesome," Michi said.

"For your information, this Xorro is one of the most knowledgeable Dideetones I know," Cha said. "And the letter X in Didee-language is pronounced the same as the letter Z in Anguorian."

"You mean...but that means..." Thinking of all her ridiculous comments, and especially the outrageous purple outfit she had insisted on for Xorro, Michi's face slowly turned scarlet. When she realized that both Hua and Cha were watching her closely, she turned away to face the arena. *I wonder why my magic disguise doesn't work on them.* Vernott and Tina's guards claimed her attention once again as she saw them land on the ground. Vernott, with sword in hand, advanced slowly toward Xorro.

King Xodune removed his mask. "Put your sword away, Vernott. You are no match for me. I have no quarrel with you. Take your granduncle and leave."

From the expressions on all the Dideetones' faces, including the scarred Didee-guard's, it was obvious they were surprised to discover who was behind the purple mask. Michi was surprised also at being able to hear Xorro so clearly from the highest cliff.

Vernott hesitated a little before throwing his sword up and turning it back into his cloak. "So you tricked us all, Xorro. I just want you to know, Princess Tianna refused to join her grandfather in the fight against Xeiyén. How does it feel to know that you won because you fooled her?"

"Let me guess. Vreeny's idea of having Tina join the fight was to have her stab me in the back. You do Tina an injustice to think she would have anything to do with such a dishonorable scheme. Be gone before I change my mind and give you what you deserve!"

Vernott took a quick step backward, before suddenly motioning his guards to carry Vreeny away. The scarred Didee-guard, with bowed head, stood up and followed behind the procession.

"Scar Face," Xorro called out.

The scarred guard faltered a little, but continued leaving with the others without a backward glance. Xorro moved to stop Scar Face, but the purple giant, hanging onto the blue braid, landed in front of him. The giant knight yanked at the braid and brought his comrade over as well.

Xorro bounced up and landed on top of the rock with the "X" mark he had made earlier, bringing himself to eye level with the giants. "Since you use the Leaping Frog technique, I assume you are the descendants of Lord Chris and King Nain?"

"We are. I'm Cedric and this is Norlen. The golden-haired child is my sister and I'm here to rescue her. Must we fight?"

Hearing this, Michi turned to look at Joseph. Her brother didn't seem surprised as he nodded, indicating that they should just watch for now. Holding her thoughts back concerning the drastic change of Cedric Markum, Michi faced the arena once again.

"I'm here to rescue my comrade," Xorro said.

"Then let's join forces," Cedric suggested.

"We're going to need more than just the three of us to deal with the Inmee Beast and Commander Zildow's army," Xorro replied.

Yeah, probably a whole lot more, Cedric.

"I've got the valiant Anguo Knights with me," Cedric said.

"The brave Nain Riders are here as well," Norlen added.

At their words, the arena's west gate opened, revealing the mounted armor-clad knights and dark cloaked riders. Michi recognized Cook as the leader of the Anguo Knights immediately. "Jo!" she exclaimed. "Isn't that the Markums' lead chef?"

"Yes, Sweet."

"I know he's good with cooking knives, and he taught you a lot of neat tricks, but what do you suppose he's doing here?"

"Maybe he's broadening his horizons and is here to try his hand at roasting Inmee Beasts," George teased.

Michi giggled. "He'll have to catch the thing first."

She saw the combatants march across a wide stone bridge spanning the lava. When they reached the main valley of the coliseum, where Cedric and Norlen stood, Cook raised his sword. "Lord Cedric! Lord Cedric—!" the knights voiced. The leader of the Nain Riders raised his bow, waving it in the air. "Prince Norlen! Prince Norlen—!" the Nain Riders chorused.

Wow! They do look like they're ready to take on anything.

The arena's east gate opened, and Zildow's troops rode in. They halted just outside the center arena. "Commander Zildow! Commander Zildow—!" the mounted soldiers shouted.

Gee . . . they look tough.

Michi noticed that Commander Zildow's army outnumbered the knights and riders ten to one. Weighing the strength of the two opposing armies, she couldn't help but wonder how Cedric's knights could possibly win.

Suddenly, the north gates opened. Sixty Ghost Chasers, followed by Yewza with his soldiers, entered the coliseum. As the dignified riders marched, they cheered, "Hua! Cha! Cha—! Hua! Cha! Cha—!"

Michi and Archoy burst out laughing.

Cha shook his head. "You know, Hua, without the Inmee Shield, you could die from this. Yet you still have time for jokes."

At the mention of death, Michi and Archoy sobered. But Hua's eyes were lit with laughter. "Come, Cha, be honest. You like it," he said.

"Now that you mention it, it does have a ring to it. But enough of the clowning around."

"If you say so." Hua raised Michi's palm leaf he had taken from Zinla, and the cheering stopped instantly.

Down in the arena, Cedric was looking at Captain Hua's cliff with curiosity. Beside him, Norlen glanced about. "I'm looking forward to meeting this foul beast that so many have been telling me about," Norlen said.

"Look no further. Here it is," Xorro said.

Silence enveloped the entire coliseum as everyone looked to where Xorro was pointing. At first, Michi could make out only a winged form in the distance. But as it came closer, she realized that it was a large white creature.

"What is it?" Joseph asked, and at that instant the beast suddenly quadrupled in size.

"It's an albino dragon!" George cried out as the monstrous creature swooped down.

The pale white dragon issued a high pitched sound that caused everyone to cringe. Then it dove, making straight for the drowsy bundle on the dais.

"Norlen, the Thousand-Anchor!" Cedric urged. He lassoed the dragon's right talon with his detached braid to stop the beast's progress.

Prince Norlen sent his braid to encircle Cedric's armor as the dragon struggled in mid-air, trying to dislodge its bonds. The Flexer shrank in size, but the noose from Cedric's braid changed with it, and the beast failed to free itself. The Inmee Beast flapped its wings and it turned into a gigantic dragon again. Both Cedric and Norlen dug their heels in, trying to fight the strong wind created, as the dragon slowly dragged the giants toward the dais.

While the Anguo Knights galloped their horses to surround the dais, the Nain Riders shot a round of arrows at the dragon. The arrows bounced off the thick scales and fell uselessly to the ground. The archers' actions only seemed to enrage the beast, as it roared angrily and made a succession of loops. Its huge wings knocked most of the Nain Riders from their horses. Seeing the fallen riders' faces turn ashen black, evidence of being poisoned, Cedric and Norlen retracted their braids. Taking advantage of its unbound state, the Inmee Beast made for the dais once again.

The Anguo Knights raised their shields to create a circular protective barrier. They drew their swords, ready to slash at the dragon should it dare to come too close to the dais. Instead of confronting the armed knights head on, the beast brought its long and spiky tail around, swiping the knights with it. The powerful tail flicked most of the knights off their horses and sent them flying in all directions. Xorro let loose his Didee-ropes, catching the knights before they were flung into the bubbling lava, or impaled upon the sharp rocks below. The seven remaining knights, led by Cook, steered their mounts to circle the Inmee Beast. The dragon's head darted forward, its jaws snapping toward the smallest of the knights.

"Light Foot! Watch out!" Cook shouted. Without pause, the young knight flipped to the side of his horse, dodging the oncoming teeth. While the beast's head flew over him, Light Foot fired a projectile at the dragon's eye. The weapon flew, and just as it reached the dragon's face, was knocked off course by one of its large, flowing whiskers. Flinching, the creature gave a screech of rage. It backed away, now cautious of the brave young knight. The others surrounding the dragon cheered for their comrade. "Come on, Magnificent Naked Seven! You can do this!" Cook yelled.

"Naked? Where are the naked men?" Archoy asked, searching wildly, before settling her gaze and staring at Hua.

Hua's eyes widened. "Why are you looking at me?"

At his words, everyone on the cliff turned to look at him, and Hua backed away several steps before waving his hand at the scene below. "Oh! Look over there!"

Regrettably, their attention was not drawn away, and it took a coughing fit from Cha before they finally turned back to the knights.

By now, the brave knights had taken out their grappling hooks. They hurled the sharp hooks to restrain the dragon. This time, the beast flapped its huge wings gently. It rose slowly in a spiral and carried the hooks, ropes, and even the knights with it. None of the knights dared to let go of their ropes, fearing the lightened weight might tip the balance and bring harm to their other comrades. Realizing the knights' plight, Cedric and Norlen caught the dragon's talons with their braids, trying to bring it back down. A tug of war between the Inmee Beast and the giants started, with Cook and the seven knights still spinning wildly around the dragon in a circle.

Taking advantage of the semi-stationary state of the dragon, Xorro drew his sword and charged at the beast. Everyone was so bent on cheering for him, they failed to see two cat-like creatures entering the arena. The white one leapt straight for Xorro while the black one moved toward the dais. The spectators only became aware of the white mousasus as it neared the Dideetone.

The cat-like animal looked just like the wildcat Michi had seen at the Slave Route Junction, save for the difference in coloring. She dismissed it as harmless, but the scarred Didee-guard bounced from Vreeny's cliff to intercept it.

The white mousasus reached behind Xorro and swiped its claws at him. The poisonous claws never made contact with his back, as the scarred Didee-guard took the deadly blow instead. The bloody and limp form of the Didee-guard was thrown backward and crashed into Xorro's back before falling downward. Xorro, who had been so intent on making his mark on the dragon, was finally startled into awareness. He dived to catch the lifeless form. The second blood drawn in the coliseum brought the game to a new climax, and the crowd roared with anticipation. The white mousasus went after Xorro for the second time.

"No!" Michi cried out. She took out the fan-like object and moved it above her head. The fan lifted her up immediately, enlarging as it glowed. She pointed the lighted fan in the direction of the white mousasus at the same time

Joseph and George grabbed her. And off the midget palm tree went, flying out of the cliff while holding a lighted fan, two giant bees clinging desperately to its palm leaves.

"Little Miss! Wait for me!" Michi heard Archoy calling after her, but she ignored the cries. The brave housekeeper jumped toward the just departing palm, attempting to grasp one of its nearby branches. Archoy, however, had overestimated her athletic abilities, and her sunflower leaves brushed just short of the palm leaf, before the housekeeper plunged downward toward the lava below.

Oh, Archoy, don't you know this could be the end of Xorro? Michi turned the fan-like object back toward the cliff and the falling Archoy.

"It's alright, Sweet. Cedric stopped the white cat, and Xorro caught the hurt Didee-guard," Joseph said.

"Thank goodness," Michi said as she saw Archoy fall clumsily onto Black Eye. The horse, sent down by Hua's spinning Mowzui Arrow, had rescued the housekeeper. "Looks like we aren't needed here after all."

"Young Master Joseph, I can't ride," Archoy, sprawled on the horse's back, said nervously.

"Just hang on, Archoy, and Captain Hua's gadget will bring you back up," Joseph soothed while Michi maneuvered the fan-like object to bring them back to the cliff.

As they landed, Hua gave a shake of his head. "Midget Palm, you've got to stop being so hot-headed."

"If Cha was the one the nasty cat was after, you would have rushed out too," Michi argued.

"No, I wouldn't. Cha can take care of himself."

Michi eyed the heartless Captain Hua with annoyance as Cha gave her an amused look. "Not to mention that I wouldn't put myself in the mousasus' path."

"Mousasus! Why, Little Miss, isn't that the creature that almost killed off King Windune and his guards?" Archoy asked, arriving back to the cliff on Black Eye.

"Ah, so King Windune lives...I wonder how Xorro became king, then?" Cha pondered.

"Windune thought he was going to kick the bucket and so he gave the crown to Xorro, but our Little Miss used the mousasus' saliva on him—"

"The deuce! How did she manage to get that?" Cha asked.

"Xorro may not be king for long if he doesn't snap out of it," Hua interrupted, and everyone turned to the scene below.

King Xodune had already placed the scarred Didee-guard's battered form on the ground, and was bending over the lifeless body while holding the fragile hands in his. "...Scar Face...Tina... My Tianna..."

Archoy sniffed, but everyone else was suddenly aware of the black cat advancing toward Christa, as it enlarged into a giant mousasus. They saw Norlen release his braid from the dragon and send it flying toward the black cat. It slammed into the mousasus' body, flinging it away from Christa. The black cat gave an angry hiss and righted itself, readying to spring again. Only the fierce whipping of the braid kept the creature at bay, as Norlen continued his assault.

"That was close," Joseph commented.

"Yeah. But just take a look at those knights. I don't think they'll be able to hold the dragon for much longer—" George began, only to be interrupted by the appearance of another mousasus entering the arena. "Just how many of these cats are there?"

The newly arrived grey cat pounced, attacking Xorro just as the arena's south gate opened. Michi saw Berna, with Xorro's Center Guards, enter the coliseum. They bounced up to pursue the grey mousasus. Puzzled, Michi looked toward Vreeny's betting dome that still had the blue-masked Dideetone in it. "Jo, if that's Berna down there, then who's in the betting dome wearing Berna's mask?"

"An imposter," Joseph said.

George gave a low whistle. "Wow, that was sneaky. Xorro almost fell into Vreeny's trap, trading his crown for an imposter."

"Yes, Vreeny almost got away with it. You know, when I saw Didee-baker disappear earlier, I figured he'd gone off to find help. I guess he found Xorro's Center Guards, but they came a bit late. It's really too bad about Tina," Joseph said with regret.

I guess I misjudged Didee-baker. He's no coward. Although he made himself invisible, he has been helping in his own way.

"Well, at least Xorro's joining his comrades and giving the grey mousasus a hard time now," George said.

At that moment, a thunderous roar from the spectators captured their attention. The dragon had lifted all the knights from their horses and was now spinning them like a carousel as the beast rose higher.

George slowly shook his head. "If that Flexer shrinks suddenly, the hooks will lose their hold and the knights will be in big trouble."

No sooner had those words been uttered than the dragon shrank. The hooks lost their grip upon the beast, and the loosened ropes were thrown out of orbit, flinging across the arena and hitting the sharp rocks and cliffs. Fortunately, Cook and the seven knights had the presence of mind to let go of their ropes in time, preventing themselves from fast, violent deaths. Instead, they were now plummeting downward, toward the ground hundreds of feet below. Once again, Xorro's Didee-ropes snapped out to save the falling knights.

"Where did the dragon go?" George asked uneasily, looking about him.

"Good question. I wish I knew what it's up to right now," Joseph said.

And his wish was granted instantly as, without warning, the albino dragon appeared in front of them.

14

The Taming of Whittigon

ARCHOY SCREAMED, THEN fainted. The smelly beast extended its long neck toward the withered sunflower lying on the cliff and sniffed. *Good thing Archoy's out of it.* Suddenly, sixty metal helmets popped up from the bottom of the cliff, clamping down on the rough bumps upon the Inmee Beast's back. Amazingly enough, the dragon didn't seem to mind, as it continued to check out the wildlife on the ledge. Michi peeped down the cliff and saw that the Ghost Chasers had arrived. Each of them was holding a thread, attached to the spiked helmets on the Inmee Beast. *Well, I hope their grip on the dragon is stronger than the knights'.*

A rumbling sound on the cliff distracted Michi. She spun to find the empty honeymoon carriage moving to the edge of the cliff, without a driver or Big Thunder. The noise also diverted the dragon's attention, and the beast turned to peer at the strange cart.

"Zinla, feed the flowers and plants to the Inmee Beast," Hua ordered.

The Mini-troll seemed to know exactly what to do. He gathered a bunch of purplish-red tulips and threw them into the dragon's partially opened mouth. The beast chewed, then swallowed. Its pale lips and whiskers turned a bright fuchsia, looking so silly that Michi almost laughed. Zinla fed it the roses next, and the dragon acquired two rosy cheeks. Then the lotuses, orchids, and jasmines followed. The dragon seemed to enjoy the exotic treat. It chomped on the flowers, more color appearing on it, and its breath improving with a floral scent. Remembering what Hua had said about the Inmee Beast's eating habits, Michi took note of the fast-diminishing food from the cart. "Jo, what if the dragon wants sunflower seeds and honey after this?" she whispered.

"It's obvious the beast is used to being fed by the Mini-trolls. Let's hope it'll only eat what Zinla chooses to give."

The last bunch of flowers disappeared, and two wisps of smoke escaped the dragon's huge nostrils. It seemed the dragon had shed some of its foul smell, only to replace it with heated breath. *The beast looks like it could use a little cooling off. I wish I hadn't used up all my coconuts.* "Somebody, feed the dragon something cool," Michi said, and a huge snow cone appeared in front of her. "Gee, thanks!" She grabbed it, tossing it toward the dragon's steaming mouth.

"No!" Hua shouted while extending his hand. The sparkling, snowy bunch flew out of the dragon's open mouth to land in his hand instead.

Hua examined the shimmering plant that his pet mousasus had just brought and smiled, finding it to still be in perfect condition. "You did good, my pet."

Michi spotted the newly arrived orange-gold cat hovering between Hua and herself. She realized that the wildcat she befriended at the Slave Route Junction had somehow found its way back to her. Moved by its devotion, she patted the affectionate mousasus. "Where have you been? You silly cat." Then she felt something tugging at her palm leaves, and she froze. When she discovered that the Mini-troll was feeding her palms to the dragon, she hissed. "What do you think you're doing, Zinla?"

"Orders," Zinla replied as he tossed the rest of the palm leaves into the dragon's mouth.

Michi saw streaks of emerald green appear all over the dragon's body, making it look quite magnificent. She studied the much changed Inmee Beast. *His face needs some darker color—brown!* Remembering the palm tree's trunk, she started to remove it.

"Er, you do have something on down there, don't you?" Hua asked.

"Of course!" Michi said indignantly as she peeled off the tree trunk and threw it to the dragon. Then she felt a draft and remembered belatedly that, not knowing how comfortable her disguise would be, she had donned only her nighties in case she became too hot. She considered the last palm leaf in Hua's hand, wondering if it would give her adequate covering, when he tossed it to the dragon.

As it flew over her before plopping into the huge mouth, Michi saw that one of Hua's gold arrows was embedded underneath the palm. The dragon chomped on it, then roared with wrath, nostrils flaring. Sixty Ghost Chasers held their threads tightly to keep the dragon from escaping as the enraged beast bucked, writhed, and shook vigorously. Michi watched the bucking dragon with fascination. The Mowzui Arrow enlarged and attached itself inside the dragon's mouth right underneath the upper jaw.

"Hua, the Defenders can't hold much longer!" Cha urged.

Captain Hua bounced up forty feet, aiming Zildow's daggers at the dragon's head, and threw them. The two weapons split in mid-air, one flying to attach itself to the dragon's right cheek while the other did the same with the left. For a moment, Michi thought she saw something drop from the splitting daggers, but dismissed it when a second look revealed nothing. Commander Zildow's family heirlooms enlarged and formed intricate designs around the dragon's face. As soon as the daggers completed the change, Captain Hua's Mowzui Arrow extended out of the dragon's jaws until both ends connected with Zildow's daggers. The dragon seemed oblivious to the items, however, as it struggled furiously with the Ghost Chasers. By the time Hua landed on the cliff again, the betting dome that housed the necklace had floated to their cliff.

Michi heard Cha chanting in a soft voice, and she moved closer to hear him. "...rugot—noreia—settis—domina—noreia..."

Beautiful! Noreia—now that definitely has a nice ring to it. She was surprised when Cha stopped chanting and the braided chain necklace flew out of the dome, enlarging to look like a piece of rug with an attached braid.

Michi realized that the rug was hovering next to the cliff. "It's a flying carpet!" she exclaimed.

It was then that drums began beating from the king's cliff. When they stopped, Commander Zildow's soldiers drew their weapons. "Commander Zildow! Commander Zildow—!"

Yewza's troops raised their long swords. "Hua! Cha! Cha—! Hua! Cha! Cha—!"

"What's happening?" Archoy asked, awakening from her fainting spell.

That was when Michi realized that the housekeeper was no longer a sunflower. She turned to her brother. "Jo, when did you, George, and Archoy get rid of your disguises?"

"The moment Captain Hua threw your last palm leaf inside the dragon's mouth, our disguises disappeared also."

"I must have been too busy watching the dragon to notice at the time—" Michi started to say, but Cha interrupted.

"The final coliseum battle is about to begin. Hua and I must go, but you'll all be safe if you stay on this cliff."

"We can't. Our friends are down there either fighting or wounded—" Joseph began.

"Alright," Cha cut in, seeing the determined expression on Joseph's face. "So much human death would not sit well with me, either. Get on the horses and go join the barbarian. He's got Trumbond's antidote, so go with him and revive the poisoned Nain Riders and the Anguo Knights."

"With that tiny bottle? Will there be enough to revive all the poisoned riders and knights?" Archoy asked.

Cha stroked his beard. "Judging from its size, it should be just about—"

It was Hua's turn to cut in. "Cha, I've got to go. Wish me luck." He bounced out of the cliff and landed on the hovering carpet at the same moment Michi hopped on it, as well. "What do you think you're doing, Midget Palm?"

"If you think I'm going to miss a chance of riding on a flying carpet, you're crazy."

"Sweet, I don't think that's a flying carpet—"

"Huh?" Michi never heard her brother's reply, as all the Ghost Chasers' spiked helmets popped off the dragon and, with an angry bellow, the Inmee Beast escaped. The flying carpet chased after the dragon instantly.

Michi grabbed a corner of Captain Hua's weather-stained cloak to steady herself, while he took hold of the braided chain and steered the rug in hot pursuit of the escaping beast. The rug flew through the sky, and the cool breeze mingled with the dragon's heated floral breath, caressing her cheeks. Michi tossed her head with exhilaration.

"Enjoying your ride?" Hua asked.

"You bet!" Michi whooped. "Do you have a plan for when we get close to the dragon?"

"Right now, we'll be lucky to catch up before it escapes."

"Oh, that's easy." Michi dipped her free hand into the side pocket of her knee-length camisole top and took out the fan. The moment she pointed it at the dragon, the flying carpet gave a burst of speed, zooming in to arrive right behind the Inmee Beast. "Here we are."

"Right. Hang on, I'm going to saddle the dragon."

"Saddle! Wh-what do you mean?" Michi asked in alarm, grabbing Hua's cloak tighter.

"I've got the harness on the dragon, and now I'm going to saddle it so we can ride it."

Ride on a dragon? Wow! "Okay."

Hua pulled hard on the reins, and the flying carpet slanted upward as it flew past the dragon's tail. "Easy . . ." Hua loosened the reins and the rug leveled. "Here we go."

Michi noticed that they were flying above the dragon's back, as the carpet, or rather the dragon's saddle, slowly descended. She leaned her head out to take a better look, and the slight movement of the fan-like object caused the flying carpet to dip. The rug bumped into the dragon's back, causing the beast to become aware of them. The Inmee Beast dived, and Hua maneuvered the flying carpet to go after it.

So it went on, with the dragon trying to escape being saddled, and Hua persisting. Michi gave moral support by cheering, and every now and again, she would use her fan to help speed up the rug.

Suddenly, the beast changed tactics and turned to face them. As they came straight at the dragon, two trails of heated steam escaped its nostrils. When the dragon opened its mouth, fire jetted out of it. Hua reined in the carpet sharply as Michi, on reflex, waved the fan-like object at the oncoming fire, and the flying carpet shook.

"No!" Hua gritted his teeth while grabbing Michi, bringing them both down on the rug as the dragon's fire burst into full flame. His action caused the flying carpet to dive, and saved them from most of the blast.

"Sorry. I meant to fan the dragon and fire away from us," Michi said as she eyed Hua's singed golden hair and his soot-covered face with trepidation. *Maybe he won't notice.*

Hua, maneuvering the flying carpet's reins to save them from crashing into the cliffs, mumbled something unintelligible. The dragon seemed to have turned the tables around, pursuing them instead. Hua smiled wryly while the retreating carpet dodged another blow from the beast. "It's not as much fun to be pursued by a dragon, is it, Midget Palm?"

"It's definitely more fun to chase after it instead, but beggars can't be choosers—watch out, Hua!"

The sneaky Flexer had shrunk and somehow came up behind them. As soon as the dragon returned to its monstrous size, it breathed fire at them. Hua unclasped his cloak and threw it over them. "Stay down."

His cloak enlarged and turned into a tent-like covering for them both. Michi, still holding her fan steady above her, laid her left cheek on the carpet and looked up. She was mesmerized by the sight within the tent. Hua, lying his right cheek on the carpet and facing her, was holding the shimmering ice plant above him. Between her soft-lighted fan and Hua's snow cone plant, snowflakes formed and swirled all around them. However, the dome-shaped tent above them was burning. "Hua, your cloak's on fire!" He moved the sparkling plant closer to her fan, and more snowflakes formed, putting out some of the flames. Michi moved her fan closer to his plant. "Do you think we can put out the fire if we join these two?"

"We could certainly take care of more than just the dragon's fire if we joined my Belna with your Tensengin Essence, but are you sure that's what you want?"

"I wish you wouldn't speak in riddles. If putting your snow cone with my night light can solve our problems, then let's do it."

Hua roared with laughter. "Wait until I tell my mother about you calling her Belna a snow cone. Not to mention naming one of the most sought-after Tensengin treasures a night light. My father would get a kick out of that one."

Not very pleased with a joke at her expense, Michi's eyes narrowed. "Glad to hear that I'll provide some merriment for your family. This girl scout has done her good deed of the day. It's your turn, boy scout."

Hua sobered. "Girl scout? Boy scout? My turn to do what?"

"Usually boy scouts do useful things like open doors for old ladies, provide a supporting hand, and help them cross the street. Since there're no old ladies here, why don't you just put out the fire and take care of the dragon."

"Okay. Let go of your night light," Hua instructed. And the moment she did, he chanted in a very strange language. "—Tensengin—essen Mowbov—belna—Inmeegon—"

One thing's for sure, both Hua and Cha enjoy singing.

As Hua chanted, the night light moved to join the snow cone, forming a clear ice shield. "With this Inmee Shield, we're going to tame the dragon."

Holding the shield in front of them, Michi and Hua stood. The moment the Inmee Shield touched the burning tent above, the fire disappeared. Then Hua's weather-stained cloak transformed into a shimmering and handsome cape as it came down to fit over his head. Miraculously, Hua's signed golden hair and soot-covered face transformed back, as if he had never been through the fire. *Wow! What Rosalyn would give to get her hands on the secret formula for this transformation.*

Without the tent, Michi was suddenly aware that the fire breathing dragon was right in front of them, still breathing fire. She shivered, and part of Hua's soft new cloak wrapped itself around her body. The flying carpet, with the protection of the Inmee Shield, made straight for the mouth of the dragon. The dragon's fire became weaker as they flew toward it, until only a trace was left. The Inmee Beast opened its mouth wider to try to swallow them, but the Inmee Shield enlarged and attached itself over it like a muzzle. The action immobilized the dragon, and Hua maneuvered the flying carpet over the beast's head, attaching the chain to the harness. Then he positioned the flying carpet over the dragon's back, saddling their ride.

"Why didn't you tell me it was this easy? We could've saved ourselves a lot of trouble."

"And miss all that fun? Besides, I wasn't sure if you would be willing to give up your night light."

Michi shrugged. "You gave up your snow cone."

"Oh, that's right! I've gone and used up my mother's present. Maybe I can surprise her with a pet dragon."

"It won't work. My mother screams and threatens when I surprise her with strays."

"My mother never screams or threatens."

"Lucky you."

"Now you make me feel bad about taking your night light. Hey, how about if I grant you a favor?"

Michi frowned. "Grant me a what?"

"A favor... In my realm—or what you would call the world I live in—money, gold, or gems are of very little value. Instead, we trade favors. That is, what you humans call wishes."

"Oh, you mean like Aladdin's Lamp?"

"Something like that."

Is he a nut case? Michi studied Hua with wary eyes. *Still, he seems to have some special power. Maybe I'd better humor him.* She stuck out her hand. "Okay, Super Hua, where's the lamp?"

"You have Cha's red pouch in your pocket. Keep it safe and, when you find the need, just return the red pouch for a favor, okay?"

"Er, okay. Maybe one of these days when I find Rosalyn too much to handle, I can wish her to the moon."

"This Rosalyn is a tough opponent?"

"You don't know the half of it. Even Jo has a hard time with her. Speaking of my brother, I wonder how he's doing."

"You're right. There's a war going on down below. We'd better go check it out." Hua picked up the braided reins with his right hand. "Are you ready, Girl Scout?" he asked.

"Anytime, Boy Scout."

Hua lifted his left hand, and the Inmee Shield popped off the dragon's mouth, flying to him. Gripping the shield's handle with his left hand, he gave the reins in his right a tug, and they were off. "I know what good deeds boy scouts usually perform, but what about girl scouts?"

"Selling cookies."

"Ah. How about doing another good deed and giving my pet dragon a name, Girl Scout."

"Well, when we first saw the dragon, it was pure white—"

"Pure white dragon...Whittigon it is. I like it, thank you."

"You're welcome." She was about to ask why he kept holding the Inmee Shield in front of them when the flying dragon suddenly breathed a stream of fire. Instantly, fire and extreme heat swirled around them, and she was glad of the protection from the clear shield.

When they arrived to hover directly above the action in the coliseum, the dragon lifted its head, unleashing a piercing cry. The fighting below ceased as everyone, hearing the bone-chilling sound, froze. Then slowly all eyes raised to see the hovering dragon with Hua and Michi riding on its back. Drums rolled from the king's cliff, and all the fighters, save three on the dais, withdrew from the center of the arena. Soon there was enough space for the dragon to descend and land. Hua guided the dragon to stand next to the platform, before he commanded the Inmee Shield to place itself as a muzzle over the dragon's mouth once again. When the drums stopped, the audience broke out into deafening cheers, and the fighters that participated in the battle reassembled themselves.

Michi saw Christa standing between Joseph and George on the dais. All three of them held weapons stained with blood. *They look like they have a tale to tell.* "Christa! Jo! George!"

"Michi, is that you?" Christa asked, squinting.

"Yes, I'm so glad to see you're alright. I'll be right down, and then we can—" She stopped when she saw Cha, riding on Bo-peep, coming up to them. "A flying horse!"

Bo-peep landed on the dragon's saddle, and Cha dismounted. "Hello, you two. I see you tamed the dragon, though you took your time about it."

"How could we impress everyone if we took only a couple of minutes?" Hua asked.

Cha gave a light smile. "How, indeed."

Hua picked up Michi and deposited her on Bo-peep, then bounced up and settled behind her. "Ready?"

"Yup," Michi said, then remembered her manners. "Ciao, Cha, it was nice to meet you."

"The pleasure is mine, Lucky Palm."

As they descended on the majestic steed, she saw Archoy and the barbarian sharing Black Eye and riding toward the dais. The barbarian sat behind the housekeeper and had his arms around her. "Wow! The barbarian sure is a fast worker."

"Fast worker? How do you know?"

"Couldn't you tell? They've only met a short time and he's already sharing a horse with her and holding her so tight."

"I see . . ."

At that moment, Bo-peep landed on the dais. "Christa! Jo! George! Am I glad to see you," Michi exclaimed.

Joseph reached the horse first and helped Michi down. "Sweet, did you thank Captain Hua for taking care of you?"

"Thank you for the ride, Hua."

"You're welcome."

"Michi!" Christa called out, and Michi turned. The two girls rushed to hug each other. "I've got loads of stuff to tell you—" they both said at the same time, then laughed.

Eyeing the laughing and babbling girls, Hua smiled and vaulted down from Bo-peep.

"Christa, come, you must meet Hua." Michi grabbed her friend and brought her to face Captain Hua. "Christa, this is the dragon tamer, Super Hua. Hua, this is my best friend, Christa."

Christa made a clumsy curtsy. "How do you do, Super Hua."

Hua kept a smile in check and saluted. "So you are the face that launched a thousand sheep, Christa of Anguo. News of your valiant effort to free thousands of sheep from Commander Zildow's slaughtering pen reached me from afar."

"Actually, I was just trying to capture one so Cook could make lamb chops out of it," Christa explained, and Michi, Hua, Joseph, and George roared with laughter.

"Is that how you got captured?" George asked.

Christa flushed. "Well . . ."

By this time, Cedric had reached the group and was shaking his head. "Christa disappeared, and can you imagine our shock when we heard she was a prize in this strange coliseum game?"

"Hi there giant Cedric. Goodness, you'd better keep a closer eye on Christa. It sounds like she's becoming a food monster just like my little sister here," Joseph teased, then turned to Hua. "You tamed the dragon just in the nick of time, Captain Hua. We were getting pretty desperate here."

"I'm impressed that you were able to keep Commander Zildow's hunting pack at bay for so long," Hua said.

Joseph grinned. "Not as impressed as we are with your dragon taming skills. The fireworks up there were terrible, yet awesome to behold, Captain Hua."

By now Archoy, the barbarian, Norlen, King Xodune, and Berna had also made their way to the dais. Introductions were made, and everyone seemed to be talking all at once when the drums interrupted their social event. The arena quieted. "I give you the victor," the Mini-troll king announced. "Captain Hua and his allies!"

"Hua! Hua! Hua!" the audience chanted.

"Looks like you'll have to parade around the coliseum to appease this crowd, Captain Hua," George said.

"Would you like to join me, Girl Scout?" Hua invited.

"You go ahead, Hua. Christa and I have a lot to catch up on."

Captain Hua mounted Bo-peep with a swift movement. Then the flying horse took off and circled the arena, to the crowd's delight.

Cedric turned towards Michi. "We were looking for you!"

Joseph slapped Cedric's back. "You could have just written a letter, you know. But yes, we missed you guys too."

"Actually, it's because Michi—" Cedric began.

"Joseph, how well do you know Captain Hua and Yewza?" Prince Norlen interrupted.

"Not too well. Captain Hua seems to be pretty decent, but I don't know much about Yewza. Sweet, what do you know about Yewza?"

Michi remembered their trip down the shaft and her encounter with Yewza and his troops at the cave. "No Butler, that's the tallest Ghost Chaser, didn't like him much," she said. "And I think Yewza might have plotted against Hua's father sometime in the past. I heard Yewza bragging to No Butler about how he was going to deal with Hua the same way or such nonsense."

"Yewza and his troops attacked us at the Slave Route Junction yesterday. Many of the knights and riders were wounded, and Shanui took a poison arrow to save Christa—" Norlen began to explain.

"Shanui! You mean Dei's sister?" Michi asked.

Cedric frowned. "Dei?"

"That's Shanui's brother," Joseph explained. "The two are very close."

"Shanui never said anything about her brother. However, she did mention that you helped gain her freedom, and that you also gave her your new address."

"Well, she must have a reason for not saying anything about her brother. How's she doing? Is she better?"

"That's another thing that bothered me," Cedric said. "Some of the knights and riders were wounded even more severely than Shanui. A couple of them were not expected to live. But by some miracle, they all recovered the next day. Yet Shanui alone has taken a turn for the worse. That's the reason we challenged Councilman Trumbond for his vial—the coliseum prize list said it cures any poison."

BoDak peeped into Trumbond's bottle. "Your Highness, I'm afraid there might not be enough of the potion left."

"How much is left?" Prince Norlen asked.

"Uhh . . ."

Norlen grabbed the bottle from the barbarian and peered in. "Bo, you idiot! It's empty!"

Cedric snatched the bottle from Prince Norlen and shook it. "BoDak, you nincompoop!"

Archoy eyed the helpless barbarian. "King Xodune, would the saliva from the mousasus help Shanui?" she asked anxiously.

"If Shanui's wound is poisoned, then yes. However, I'll have to look at her injury in order to be sure."

"Lord Cedric, Prince Norlen, don't you worry about Shanui," Berna said. "Michi seems to be a very impressive healer, and there's always Didee-doc."

"Michi, the food monster?" Cedric spat. "Excuse me if I'm not thrilled. Let's hope this Didee-doc's much better than that."

Joseph studied Cedric with a frown while Michi's eyes narrowed. "I see you acquired a new personality with your new hairdo, old friend," Joseph commented.

"You'll have to forgive my brother. He's finally fallen in love, and the love of his life is near death on my account," Christa explained.

"Of course we understand," Archoy said with sympathy.

Michi fingered Cha's red pouch in her pocket. "Shanui saved you, Christa, so she won't die. Not if I can help it."

The orange-gold mousasus appeared suddenly, hovering in front of her. There was a second of stunned silence among all those gathered. Michi recovered first and reached out to pat the mousasus. "Why, hello," she said.

"BoDak, quick! Give the empty bottle to Michi," King Xodune urged. The barbarian handed Trumbond's empty bottle to her. "Young one, command the mousasus to refill the bottle," King Xodune instructed.

Michi complied instantly. To everyone's amazement, the mousasus shrank in size until its tongue was able to stick through the small bottle's opening. When the Flexer's saliva filled the bottle, the mousasus withdrew its tongue and turned into a giant cat once again.

"Mousasus very rarely give up their saliva willingly," King Xodune said. "Yet this one came to you for that very purpose. It's obvious that this mousasus has great affection for you. We should count ourselves fortunate. We now have a refill of Trumbond's priceless vial."

"Little Miss, who would have guessed the wildcat you befriended at the Slave Route Junction is priceless," Archoy said with relief.

Michi handed the bottle back to BoDak, then she hugged the mousasus. "Thank you, Wildcat. You know Archoy, all your talk about Wildcat and the Slave Route Junction reminds me of Fifi White Furball. I wonder what happened to that cute puppy." On hearing its true name, the mousasus rubbed its head against Michi's neck affectionately, causing her to giggle. "You're tickling me, but I forgive you because you came all this way looking for me. Now, I wish my puppy could also be here—" Michi paused when a shadow fell above her. Looking up, Michi was surprised to see a pair of the most unusual golden eyes. *I've seen these eyes before.* "Fifi White Furball!"

"You were saying?" Captain Hua asked, quirking his brow and leaning down from Bo-peep.

Michi blinked, realizing that she was actually looking into Captain Hua's sea-blue eyes. She shook her head. *I must be getting tired.* "For a moment there I thought you were..." She trailed off. *I don't think Hua's going to be too thrilled to hear that I mistook him for a puppy.* "Er, it was nothing. So, did you enjoy your victory lap of the coliseum?"

Hua shrugged as he straightened and guided Bo-peep to land next to Michi. "It was okay."

"Captain Hua, there'll be a celebration later on. Will you be joining us?" Archoy asked.

"Thanks for asking me, but I've been away from home for months, and I think it's time I get back."

Archoy made noises of regret, and Hua slanted her an amused expression.

"We wish you a safe journey home, then," Joseph said, then laughed. "It's probably about time our own little party continued its journey to our new home, as well. Who knows what our parents will think happened to us."

Hua smiled, then gave Bo-peep's reins a slight tug. The flying horse sprang into the air and made its way toward the dragon's saddle. The four mousasus flew up to join the departing dragon, as well.

They retreated toward the south exit of the coliseum, and Michi gazed at the backs of the receding figures. The dragon spiraling through the air gave a pause, and Michi was suddenly reminded of that occasion, not so long ago, when she was on the swing under the Markums' old walnut tree. A picture of the endless glorious blooms of white, pink, red, and blue disk-shaped asters stretching to form a winding dragon rising over Aster Meadow arose in her mind. She felt a swift surge of excitement, and suddenly began waving furiously. "Bye, Boy Scout!" she shouted.

Hua turned, looking straight at Michi in the distance, then saluted. "Until next time—my worthy opponent."

Look for

The Inmee Kingdom
Book II of Wosenzard

by C.S.C. Guidarre

Coming soon from Sarus Crane Books

http://www.saruscranebooks.com/

www.ingramcontent.com/pod-product-compliance
Lightning Source LLC
Chambersburg PA
CBHW021310250626
47155CB00002B/461